I took my keys down from the hook on the wall and pulled open the front door, stepping out onto the porch.

Something squished beneath my foot.

It was wet and soft, and made an awful sound—like when my sneakers caught in mud and made a thick *squelch*ing as they pulled free. Or like when Madeline had accidentally killed a rabbit and left it at the bottom of the stairs, so that I'd stepped on it on my way to the kitchen.

I lifted my foot up and away and forced myself to look down.

Bile rose in my throat when I saw the blood pooling on the welcome mat.

a

girl

called

murder.

KENNEDY CANNON

ISBN-13: 978-1983584312

ISBN-10: 1983584312

Printed in the United States of America.

a girl called murder

Heap not on this mound
Roses that she loved so well;
Why bewilder her with roses,
That she cannot see or smell?
She is happy where she lies
With the dust upon her eyes.

- Edna St. Vincent Millay

one

They called us a murder, as in crows.

They had ever since we'd been out in the student parking lot one day and a crow had fallen from the sky and died right at our feet. And Eve—goddamn Eve, with her silver tongue and storm-cloud eyes—had smiled.

They also called us strange. Mysterious. Dangerous.

Strange because when Jack was twelve, he'd been struck by lightning, and had woken up in the hospital with a streak of silvery-white in his dark brown hair. Mysterious because the Shearwater twins had shown up to town two years ago, rich and parent-less and beautiful, and had instantly earned a reputation for themselves. Dangerous because even before the crows, I'd always had a thing for other people's nightmares.

But even if you didn't know us, you knew *of* us.

There were five of us then: Tannyn. Jack. West. Theodore. Evelyn.

Five of us, before Eve—goddamn Eve, with her sunshine hair and poisonous smile—had turned up dead in the branches of an oak tree on her family's property. Heart carved from her chest. Crows perched on her mangled body.

two

The start of that summer, when Eve was murdered and a drought turned the town of Truth or Consequence, Louisiana dry and cracked, I chopped off all of my hair and dyed it lilac.

Eve had been trying to get me to do it for months—I always thought it was because whenever people were trying to differentiate between the two of us, they always said, *the blonde one. No, not that one. The eccentric one.* Or, *no, the quiet one.* I knew she hated it.

At the time of her death, my hair was long enough to donate eleven inches and have it just brush my shoulders. I'd shown up to her funeral feeling weightless and heavy all at the same time. Dressed in black and pale purple, like a fresh bruise.

But even still, there would be no more murmurs of *the blonde one, no, not the one that died. The other one. The angry one.*

I was always the other one. Because when it came to Eve, she was the one that everyone noticed. I did not mind living in her shadow; I was well acquainted with the darkness.

That day, I sat down beside my friends on the worn wooden pew of Truth or Consequence's only church, and Theodore—lovely, wicked, icy Theodore in his crisp black suit—had taken one look at my hair and started laughing. There was no humor in it, but it didn't matter. And it didn't matter that everyone was staring or that his twin sister was lying only a few feet away in a casket lined with white silk.

He laughed and laughed.

8

a girl called murder

A harsh, twisted sound.

A crow's caw.

three

My bare thighs were sticking to the edge of the pool table. Every time I shifted, I had to peel my sweaty skin from the wood. It was an effort to even cross my legs.

I leaned out of the way as a boy with dark skin moved to shoot a solid orange ball. It landed in the pocket with a dull *thunk*.

I brought my plastic cup to my lips, sipping on my rum and Coke. My short, lilac hair was still a disheveled mess from driving in Jack's Jeep with the top down, and my fingers caught in the tangles as I pushed it back from my face.

I caught West's gaze from across the basement where he was sitting next to Jack, and I raised my cup in a silent salute. He tipped his head to the side in answer.

Whenever I looked at West, I was always reminded of the tragic, wistful-eyed love interests in Korean dramas. All he needed was a ridiculously expensive coat and an overbearing mother.

I wasn't sure where Theodore had gone to. Last I'd seen of him, he'd been talking to a pretty girl in a denim skirt in the kitchen. He'd left me with a promise of, "If you still want to go home in a half hour, we're out. No questions asked." Then he'd kissed my forehead and disappeared.

We hadn't been to a party since Eve's death.

There had been invitations, of course. We were the first ones people thought of. Wild, adventurous, always down for a good time—once. It had been Jack that had stripped down to nothing and jumped off Ruby Hammond's roof into her pool; Eve and I that had crowd surfed at one of our school's pep rallies and gotten three days of detention for it. Once upon a time, we'd thought we were untouchable.

"Tannyn!"

I snapped my head towards the sound of my name.

A girl that had been in my history class the previous year was waving me down. When she caught my attention, she pointed to the table beside her, then cupped her hand around her mouth and shouted, "We're playing quarters! You in?"

I gave her what might have passed for an apologetic grin if I didn't have a resting bitch face. "Not tonight!" I told her. "I have work in the morning."

She laughed. "I don't think I've ever heard of the Ten of Crows turning down a challenge!"

"Well, there's a first time for everything."

She turned back to the others at the table, knocking hips with the girl beside her. I watched her bounce her quarter off the tabletop and miss, and everyone cheered as she knocked back a shot of cheap vodka.

I moved to take a sip of my own drink and realized my cup was empty.

I hopped down from my perch on the pool table. There were red, angry splotches on the back of my thighs.

I readjusted the straps on my overalls and forced my way over to where Jack and West were sitting. The air was thick with the scents of smoke and sweat and something heavier, like tar sliding down my throat—*fear.*

Jack gave me a lopsided grin when I stopped before him, reaching up to push that shock of silvery-white hair from his eyes. "Smile, Tannyn," he said. "It's a party."

Then he did what only Jack Harmon could do without getting his

11

fingers bitten off, which was reach out and pinch my cheeks like a plucky Mexican grandmother.

I smacked his hands away, and he chuckled.

I shook my empty cup. "I'm getting a refill," I told him. "You want anything?"

"I'm cut off," he said, stretching his long legs out in front of him. "Designated driver, remember?"

"You're a light weight, that's what you are," I replied. It earned me another grin. I cast him a wave over my shoulder as I headed towards the basement stairs.

The kitchen was packed, body to body, and I had to elbow my way over to the bar. I unscrewed the cap on the bottle of Coke as I scanned the faces for Theodore. He was nowhere to be seen.

I turned from the bar and almost bumped into a boy from the football team.

"Looking good, Tan," he said.

"Bite me," I snapped, shoving past him.

I found a free space against one of the kitchen cabinets to lounge, and I sipped on my drink as I observed the bodies writhing and grinding in time to the music.

I had to shout to be heard over the pounding of the music, leaning in close enough that I could smell the sweat on Eve's skin.

"What time is it?" I yelled. Wisps of blonde hair had come loose from my braid and were plastered to my skin. Eve's hand was intertwined with mine, our palms stuck together, and I didn't know if it was my sweat or hers or both.

Eve tossed her head back, laughing. "Who cares?"

She twirled me in a circle, and the world spun past me in a blur of colors. Laughter bubbled from my lips.

12

Suddenly I was in Eve's arms as she planted a sloppy kiss on my cheek. Then her lips were on mine, tasting of dark, rich berries and damp earth. I wound my arms around her neck and pressed myself against her. When she pulled away, her face was flushed.

"I hope you don't kiss my brother like that," she said, grinning.

Heat rose to my cheeks. *"Otherwise, you'll break his heart, Tannyn Carter."*

My stomach churned.

I pushed off the kitchen counter and elbowed my way to the sliding glass door that led to the backyard.

My Converse sunk into the grass as I moved towards the shadows beneath the tall fence. My drink fell from my hands and splattered against my bare legs. I reached the bushes and dropped to my knees behind them just as everything I'd eaten that day came back up all at once.

I managed to scrape my hair back from my face as I vomited into the grass.

I wiped the back of my hand across my mouth and squeezed my eyes closed. All I could think about was goddamn Eve lying in that casket. It had been closed. I hadn't even gotten to say goodbye properly.

My throat tightened as I tried to take in air.

In through the nose, out through the mouth, I reminded myself. *In, out, in, out.*

I knotted my fingers into my hair and sat there, counting the seconds that passed.

I'm fine, I told myself. And then again with more conviction, *I am fine.*

I heard footsteps approaching, and I scrambled to my feet.

I crossed the yard towards the sliding glass door and slipped back into the kitchen. I snatched a bottle of red wine out of some girl's hand as she passed and took a swig to get rid of the acrid taste at the back of my throat.

She was glaring when I handed it back to her.

I flashed her a grin and moved to the bar to pour myself another drink. I skipped over the rum and coke and filled a cup with whiskey. It burned as it went down.

I drank half of it as I walked towards the basement stairs.

Someone stepped on my foot, and I stumbled backwards. I collided with something soft yet solid—a person? Hands gripped my arms to steady me, and I glanced back over my shoulder to see a boy with a shock of dirty blonde hair looking down at me. He had baby blue eyes and golden skin that wasn't uncommon in Louisiana.

Everyone's fears were different. My mother's had tasted like chardonnay and warm sugar; my father's tasted like too many nights without sleep—like black coffee and Prozac and chewing on the end of a pen until ink stained your teeth.

This boy's fear was the prickling of a thousand tiny feet over my skin.

"Careful," he warned.

"Don't worry," I said. "I'm not as fragile as I look."

He stuffed his hands into the front pockets of his jeans. "So I've heard."

"Well, you can't believe everything you hear," I muttered.

"Such as?"

"Santa Claus isn't real. The Titanic wasn't unsinkable. I didn't stab Reid Wasserman with a pair of scissors."

A smile pulled at the corner of the boy's lip. "I heard it was a pencil."

I shrugged and took a sip of my whiskey. "Like I said."

He cocked his head to the side. "So what is true then?" he asked.

"My hair isn't naturally purple," I told him. He laughed, so I went

14

on. "I'm awful at math, and I have what the school guidance counselor calls a *bad temper* and *issues with authority.*"

"And what about what they say about Jack and Theodore?" he said. His smile made my skin crawl, and when I raised a brow in confusion, he added, "That they take turns fucking you."

I gave him the most frightening smile I could manage. "Only on Tuesdays."

When I turned for the basement stairs, the boy's hand clamped down on my wrist. "Come on," I heard him say. "It was just a joke."

"I must not have a very good sense of humor then," I replied.

His fingers tightened around my wrist, digging into my skin. "Don't be like that—"

I narrowed my eyes.

A spider skittered from the sleeve of my shirt and down my arm. Another emerged from the pocket of my overalls, and three more from my hair.

"Fuck!"

The boy released me and jumped back, swatting at the spiders that were suddenly crawling up the legs of his pants. They fell from the ceiling and squeezed in through the cracks in the hardwood floor.

I watched as the boy stumbled backwards until he collided with the wall. His eyes were wide with fear.

Then the spiders were gone.

Everyone was staring. The boy was breathing heavily, and for a moment, he was frozen where he had pressed himself against the wall.

His eyes flickered to me, and his jaw clenched.

"Maybe I do have a sense of humor, after all," I told him.

I started to turn away, but then he snarled, "Maybe it's also true when they say you and your boyfriends cut out Eve's heart yourselves."

Whiskey splashed onto my hand as I crushed the cup I was holding. Then I spun and slammed my fist into the side of his face.

There was a satisfying crunch as bone met bone. The boy's head whipped to the side.

I shoved my hand into the front pocket of my shorts and ignored the pain in my knuckles. Blood dripped from the boy's split lip and stained his teeth red. He reached up and wiped the back of his hand across his lips.

Then he spat a mouthful of blood at me.

I blinked once, twice, as a furious blush crawled into my cheeks.

There was a sound like white-noise in my ears, and I tried to remember how to breathe. Anger coiled inside me like a venomous snake.

The blood he'd spat at me was hot on my face.

I felt the threads that made up his fears hanging in the air between us. All I had to do was pull, and they would come undone in my hands. That was all it took. Just one . . . tiny . . . pull.

A hand touched my shoulder, and I looked up to see West standing over me. "Tannyn," he said quietly.

"He said—"

"I know what he said."

I swiped at the blood on my face, but only succeeded in smearing it around. I was trembling, and I hoped he didn't notice. My mind was spinning with the thought that I'd almost done it again, after I'd promised myself . . .

I shrugged West's hand from my shoulder. "I'm fine," I told him. It didn't sound convincing.

"Go get some air," he replied. "I'll find the others."

I normally didn't take commands from anyone, but his dark eyes were worried. I nodded and pushed my way towards the front door. A path cleared ahead of me as people moved out of my way, and I wasn't sure if it was because of the expression I wore or the blood. Perhaps it was both.

16

a girl called murder

I stepped outside onto the porch and slammed the front door closed behind me.

A couple making out on a wicker porch swig sprang apart with a startled shout. I stormed past them down the steps.

I sunk down in the grass beneath a willow tree.

The light from a firefly flickered in and out between the branches of the tree as I drew my legs up to my chest and rested my chin on my knees. The blood on my face itched where it had begun to dry, and I wanted to claw it away with my nails.

As I closed my eyes, I hummed "Downtown" by Petula Clark beneath my breath.

I stopped at the sound of footsteps and glanced in their direction.

I held my breath as Theodore crouched down in the grass before me. His pale blonde hair was sticking every which way, and there was a smear of lipstick by the corner of his mouth. I wondered if it was from the girl in the denim skirt.

He was holding a plastic cup, and I snatched it from his hand.

"You won't like it," he told me.

But I was already gulping down the cup's contents. I choked, wiping the heel of my hand across my mouth. "*Water?*" I asked.

The corner of his lip tugged into a smile as I finished the cup. "I told you you wouldn't like it," he said. Then he shifted strands of hair from my face and narrowed his eyes at the dried blood on my cheeks. "Who was it?"

"He didn't say," I replied. "I can go back and ask, if you want."

He wasn't amused. He straightened and offered a hand down to me, and then helped me to my feet.

He held on a moment longer than necessary before dropping my hand and running his fingers through his tousled hair.

17

"Where are the others?" I said.

"Jack was avenging your honor, last I saw of him. West was supervising."

"And what about you?" I crossed my arms over my chest and stared up at him. "You didn't want to avenge my honor?"

He flashed me an icy grin, and it was so much like Eve's that I felt bile rise in my throat. I forced myself to swallow so I wouldn't be sick again.

"What honor?" Theodore asked.

four

They called me the Ten of Crows.

They also called me the quiet one. The angry one. The one with the scar on her cheek. The one who with haunting brown eyes that picked apart your fears.

The one whose mother went crazy and tried to kill her when she was eleven-years-old.

Before Theodore and Evelyn Shearwater came to town, I just existed, moving through the motions and trying to get by without thinking much of anything. I'd heard the rumors on the day they arrived, of course—it was all anyone could talk about—but it was just another thing that didn't concern me. The week before, it had been the class treasurer cheating on her boyfriend.

I glimpsed the twins around school once or twice—blonde and beautiful and mysterious—and that was the most I ever thought of them. If I'd paid more attention, I might have noticed the way the girl watched other people whenever she entered a room. No—not watched. *Appraised.* Evelyn Shearwater collected misfits the way other people collected antique plates or porcelain hand-painted cats: a quiet, angry nightmare of a girl here, a boy who'd been struck by lightning there. She liked strange things and broken things and things that you weren't quite sure what they were but you knew they might be useful some day.

It was raining on the day that she peeled into the parking lot outside the bookstore where I worked and climbed from her black Subaru WRX.

Thunder cracked overhead, and I paused in counting out change for a customer to glance out the front window.

That was the moment Eve walked in from the rain, the bell atop the door chiming as she shook droplets of water from her skin. Her blonde hair was pulled back from her face in an intricate braid, and she was dressed in all black: leather jacket, leggings, platform boots with thick rubber heels. The sunglasses perched on her head were feline and expensive-looking, and her nails shifted color in the light like the sheen on an oil puddle.

Then she turned those smoke-gray eyes to me and grinned a razor-sharp smile that I would come to associate her with.

I finished counting out the change, dumping it into the customer's hand, and they passed Eve on their way out as she sauntered up to the counter.

She leaned against it, gripping it beneath her fingers so that her nails flashed green and purple and pink, and blinked at me.

She was close enough that I could smell her perfume: lavender and verbena.

But the thing that intrigued me most about her wasn't her angry, black car with the tinted windows or the way she stared at me with a predator's gaze. It was that I couldn't get a handle on this girl's fear.

"Tannyn," she said. She had a slight accent, which I'd later found out was from her family living in South Wales for five years when she was little.

I reached up and pushed back the strands of blonde hair that had fallen into my face. "Yes?"

"You're Tannyn Carter." She said it matter-of-factly, as if declaring something we both already knew. Which, clearly, we did.

"Can I help you?"

"I most certainly hope so," she told me. She turned in a circle to face the rest of the store, her long braid swinging behind her, and crossed her arms over her chest as she surveyed the rows of shelves. "I heard that you're the girl to talk when it comes to poetry."

"From *who*?"

She waved her hand dismissively and walked over to a wall of classic books, running her fingers along the spines. "I like good, strong words that mean something . . ." she said, and it was a moment before I realized that she'd pulled out a copy of *Little Women* and was thumbing through the pages. She glanced over at me and tipped her head to the side. "So can you help me?"

I leaned back against the wall behind me. "What kind of poetry are you looking for?"

"I don't know. That's why I need your help," she replied. She glanced at the open book beside me. "What are you reading?"

"*Cat's Cradle*," I told her. "It's not poetry."

"Well, who are some of your favorite poets?" she asked.

I straightened and walked over to the poetry aisle, and the girl followed behind me. She watched with that curious, wolfish gaze as I skimmed the names and selected a thick paperback book of the collected poems of Edna St. Vincent Millay.

I held it out to the girl, and she accepted it, turning it over in her hands and narrowing her eyes as I moved back to the counter and sunk down in my stool behind the register.

She flipped open to a random page and read, "So up I got in anger, / And took a book I had, / And put a ribbon on my hair / To please a passing lad, / And, "One thing there's no getting by— / I've been a wicked girl," said I; / "But if I can't be sorry, why / I might as well be glad!"" She lifted her head and smiled at me. "This will do nicely, I think."

As she slid the book across the counter to me and pulled a wallet from the pocket of her leather jacket, the girl said, "You don't recognize me, do you?"

I did recognize her, of course, but without looking up from the register, I said, "Should I?"

"I'm in your U.S. History class," she told me. "I transferred to TC a few days ago."

"Right."

"It's alright," she said. "I don't pay much attention in that class, either." She held out a hand to me over the register, and this struck me as odd. Several second passed before I realized she was waiting for me to shake it. "I'm Eve."

Her hand was surprisingly cold, like touching ice, and a chill ran down my spine.

With the contact came the sense of her fear: darkness and the sharp smell of iodine and roses. A taste like dirt in my mouth.

I jerked my hand away as if she'd burnt me, but the girl just tossed her head back and laughed. It sounded like glass shattering on the floor, and it was the most beautiful and frightening thing I'd ever heard.

Then she leveled those gray eyes at me. "I also heard you have a thing for nightmares," she said, lowering her voice as if letting me in on a secret. She leaned forward, cocking her head to the side so that her braid fell over her shoulder. "So, tell me, Tannyn, what are *you* afraid of?"

five

I traced my finger over my split knuckles as we walked down the street.

The silence was broken as Theodore said, "I'll take you home. It's on my way."

It took a moment for me to realize he was talking to me. "Okay."

When we reached the black Jeep parked beneath a streetlamp, I paused to give West a quick, one-armed hug. Then I turned to Jack and took his chin in my hand, narrowing my eyes at the fresh bruise on the side of his face.

"I can take care of myself, you know," I told him.

"I know." He dipped his head to kiss my forehead, and then he ruffled my hair. "Take care of her," he said to Theodore. "And try to keep her out of anymore fights."

I flipped him off over my shoulder as I walked to Theodore's car.

The Mustang's dark interior smelled faintly of leather and pine air freshener. As I pulled the seatbelt across my body, Theodore climbed into the driver's seat and slid his key into the ignition.

He twisted in his seat as he backed out of his spot alongside the curb.

"How's your hand?" he asked.

I looked down at my split knuckles. The skin was an angry reddish-purple. "I've had worse."

Theodore shifted from second into third, and we cruised past fields of sugarcane that swayed in the humid air. I rolled down my window and stared out at the green stalks dancing in the darkness.

I draped my arm out the window and weaved my fingers through the cold night air. My voice filled the quiet interior as I sang along to Of Monsters & Men on the radio, swaying in time to the music. I could feel Theodore's eyes on me.

"I'm sorry I ruined your night," I told him.

"You didn't ruin my night, Tannyn."

"Yes, I did. I got in a fight, and I made you all leave early, and now you're driving me home. The only thing that could make this worse is if I threw up on you."

Theodore snorted. "I would hardly call that a fight." He leaned forward to turn down the volume on the radio, and then glanced over at me. "What did he say to you, anyway?" he asked. "That guy?"

"You mean the part about you and Jack taking turns fucking me, or the part about us murdering Eve?"

His nostrils flared. "Fuck," he said.

"Are you reconsidering not avenging my honor?"

He smiled in spite of himself. "I think you can handle yourself."

"I'm glad someone thinks so."

I sighed deeply through my nose and smiled at my reflection in the side mirror though it didn't reach my eyes. I stared at my choppy, disheveled lilac hair. The blood on my face, and the scar on my cheek. The dark circles beneath my light brown eyes.

"I wouldn't have left you alone," Theodore said suddenly. I looked over at him. "At the party. I would have stayed with you, if you'd asked."

"I don't need a babysitter."

He frowned. "You know that's not what I meant."

"A therapy dog, then," I replied. I saw him smile in spite of himself. "Besides, you would have had to miss out on hanging out with—What was her name? Caroline? Catherine?"

24

"Caitlin."

"Caitlin. Right." I leaned my head against the window frame. "Then I would have really ruined your night."

"You're right. Why would anyone willingly want to spend time with you?"

"I know," I said. "Who wants to spend time with a girl who'll give them nightmares?"

"I'm not afraid of you, Tannyn," Theodore said.

And I knew he was telling the truth.

His fear smelled like the air during a thunderstorm, the heavy scent of rain and damp earth and sulfur. It was secrets that caught between my teeth like shards of broken glass and sliced into my gums. My mouth filled with the taste of copper.

I blinked, and my reflection in the car's side mirror did the same.

My nose had begun to bleed, droplets gathering on my upper lip. I reached up and wiped them away with the back of my hand.

Theodore leaned over and popped open the glove compartment, and then he took out a handful of napkins and handed them to me.

I stared down at the logo on them. "You went to Five Guys without me?"

Out of the corner of my eye, I glimpsed Theodore roll his eyes. "Your nose is still bleeding, Tannyn."

I scrunched one in my fist and pressed it to my nose.

"Tell me a secret."

I tipped my head to the side to look at Eve where she was sitting at the other end of the couch. She pulled her legs up to her chest, her fingers curled around the mug of hot chocolate she had balanced on top of her knees. "Like what?"

She looked at the ceiling as she thought. "Like . . . why's your mom

25

in psychiatric care?"

I bit down on my bottom lip as she lowered her head to look at me again. Then I lifted my hand and pulled down the front of my shirt to expose a puckered scar along my collarbone. It was almost identical to the one along my left cheek, but longer and angrier. "She tried to kill me when I was eleven," I told her. "Steak knife. We were in the kitchen, and she just . . . lost it."

"I'm sorry."

I shrugged, taking a sip of my hot chocolate and burning my tongue. "The thing is, after that, she just . . . shut down. She's just not there anymore. I don't know how to explain it."

When I looked up, Eve's face had taken on a strange look that I'd never seen before. Guilt. Or maybe shame. So I said, "My turn."

She smiled at me without showing teeth. "What do you want to know?"

"What are you afraid of, Evelyn Shearwater?"

She went still, and her eyes took on a far away look as she stared down into her hot chocolate. Then she blinked rapidly as if waking from a dream and lifted her gaze to my face. "The dark," she told me. The corner of her lip lifted in a self-loathing smile, and she chuckled sharply. "Ridiculous, right?"

I looked up as Theodore pulled into my driveway and turned off the engine.

I sat in the passenger seat, staring at the plain white farmhouse with its wraparound porch and dark roofing.

To others, it might have seemed cute. Quaint. Homely.

When I looked at it, all I saw was the light that was still on in my father's office. I saw the elm tree outside my window that I'd used to sneak out on nights when he finally went to bed and I didn't want to wake him, and

26

I saw the post in the porch railing that my mother had kicked loose when the paramedics had carried her from the house.

The rest of the windows were dark, including the one to my older brother's room.

Instead of coming home from college that summer, Hollis was backpacking across Europe with friends. Just that morning, he'd emailed me a picture of himself standing before the Cliffs of Moher in Ireland.

I crumpled the bloody tissue in my one hand and reached for the passenger door handle.

"Do you remember June seventh?" Theodore asked suddenly.

I turned my head to glance at him over my shoulder. "What?"

"We stopped at a gas station on the way to Jack's baseball game, and you bought a slushie that turned your lips blue. Eve stole the aux cord, and her entire playlist was some obscure metal band."

"Why—?"

"That was the last time you kissed me before she died."

It was silent except for the sound of Theodore's breathing. He was close enough that if I just shifted an inch in my seat and tilted my head . . .

I swallowed. "Well, a lot of things have changed."

I opened the passenger's side door and climbed out.

As I crossed my arms over my chest and started up the driveway, I heard the driver's door of Theodore's car open. Footsteps crunched over the gravel.

"Is that what you tell Jack?"

I jerked to a stop and my arms dropped to my sides. Heat crawled into my cheeks. "That's different," I said without looking back at him.

"Why?"

I whirled on him. "You know why," I told him. The words came out harsher than I'd meant them to. "Because every time I look at you, I see *her*."

27

He looked as if I'd slapped him. I might as well have.

Finally, he said, "Just tell me what you want. Just say the word, Tannyn, and I'm yours."

I looked away from his face, towards the dark windows of my house. The scar on my collarbone throbbed gently against my skin. What did I want? Eve back. My mother back. My father to stop spending so many nights in his office alone. My brother to come home.

Instead, I said, "I don't know what I want."

"Come over," he said, stuffing his hands into the pockets of his shorts. "Not like that, I just—I want the company.

"Madeline will get lonely," I said. It didn't sound convincing.

"I'm sure she'll survive."

I chewed on my bottom lip, drawing it between my teeth. "Okay."

"Okay?"

I shouldered past him and climbed into the passenger's seat of the Mustang. I propped my feet up on the dashboard.

"Well?" I said out the open window. "Are you coming, or what?"

I stared out the open window as Theodore pulled the car down the long tree-lined road that led to his family's house.

He parked and turned off the engine, sighing through his nose. "Home sweet home," he muttered.

I climbed from the car and followed him towards the front porch of the manor, my Converse crunching over the stones that made up the driveway. The house was three-stories, with large white columns and too many windows—which seemed a little ridiculous, if you asked me. Especially with only one person living there.

The entire sugarcane plantation belonged to Theodore's aunt Ceceli on his father's side, who was off at her apartment in Baton Rouge most weeks and god-knew where else during the others. She was like my older brother, Hollis—always on the move, and never in one place for very long.

Of course, they also kept a live-in housekeeper, but she lived in a separate guest house behind the manor.

Theodore unlocked the front door, and I stepped into the grand front room, shoving my hands into the pockets on my shorts.

"I'll go find something to eat in the kitchen," he told me, starting down a hallway. "Go get cleaned up. You look like Carrie."

I rolled my eyes, but climbed the stairs towards the guest room at the end of the all.

I pushed open the door, breathing in the familiar scent of furniture polish and spiced apple air freshener. My eyes immediately fell on a picture frame perched on the bedside table.

The photo had been taken at junior prom, and the five of us were gathered on the front porch of the plantation house. Eve was front and center, draped against a white column in her strapless black ball gown, her enormous skirts fanned out around her. She'd had to turn sideways just to fit through the doors of the limo we'd rented. She'd reminded me of a fallen angel with her dark red lips and hair slicked back from her face.

I had an arm around Eve's and Theodore's waists as I leaned my head against her shoulder. On Eve's right, West stood holding her hand, and beside him, Jack was grinning at the camera in a maroon tuxedo.

I walked over and turned the frame face-down on top of the bedside table.

I turned on the shower in the bathroom, and while I waited for the water to heat up, I stripped out of my clothes.

Drawing my fingers through my tangled lilac hair, I stood in front of the mirror and stared at myself in my black bra and mismatched gray panties.

I reached down to trace the tattoo along my ribcage, which looked liked a splatter of black paint from far away, but began to take the form of a crow in flight the closer you got. My fingers traveled to the thick scar along my collarbone, and then to the words that had been inked in black cursive overtop it: "And your very flesh shall be a great poem . . ."

I slipped out of the rest of my clothes and climbed into the shower.

The hot water stung as against my split knuckles, but I ignored the pain as I tipped my head back and inhaled a lungful of steam. I pushed my hair back from my face and worked my fingers through the tangles. I scrubbed at my skin, and the water at my feet turned pink as the traces of blood on my cheeks swirled down the drain.

My damp hair dripped onto the mat as I stepped from the shower and slipped into a bathrobe, tying the sash around my waist.

Trying not to glance at the picture frame lying face-down on the bedside table, I padded barefoot from the guest room and into the hall.

Theodore was lounging against the island when I came into the kitchen, arms crossed over his chest. He'd changed into a pair of loose-fitting pajama pants, his chest bare, and I tried to look anywhere but at his stomach as I walked over to stand beside him. I settled for staring at the crow tattoo on his left bicep.

He nodded his head towards a pile of clothes on the counter. "Those are for you." I started to protest, and he added, "They're not hers. They're mine."

"Oh." My voice was slightly surprised. "Thanks." I hopped up onto the counter top, dangling my legs towards the floor as I pulled the pile into my lap. I unfolded the t-shirt and picked at the faded logo. As Theodore took a container of sour cream from the fridge, I glanced towards the oven. "What are you making?" I asked.

"Nachos."

My mouth might have started drooling. "You spoil me."

"It's my only reason for existing," he replied.

I snorted softly and looked back down at the pile of clothes in my lap. "When was the last time we hung out, just the two of us?" I said.

"Is that a rhetorical question or would you like an actual date?"

I lifted my gaze, and suddenly he was right there, hands planted on the countertop on either side of my thighs, bare chest inches from my face. I had to tip my head back to look him in the eye as he stared down at me.

"Tell me what you're thinking," Theodore said.

"I'm wondering how many health code violations you're making by cooking without a shirt on."

He laughed—a startled, genuine laugh. He leaned back and ran his fingers through his pale, unruly hair.

"What are *you* thinking about?" I almost should have known better than to ask.

His eyes flickered to mine, and his mouth twisted into an arrogant smile. "Kissing you."

I hoped he didn't notice the blush that crawled into my cheeks. I pretended to fiddle with the collar of the shirt in my lap. "Well, I hope you have a good imagination," I replied.

"I have a *very* good imagination," he told me, and the way he said it made goosebumps break out across my skin. Then he brought his hand up, brushing a damp strand of hair back from my face. He tucked it behind my ear. "And an even better memory."

A smart retort lingered on my lips, but the oven timer went off before I had the chance to reply. As Theodore picked up a dish towel and opened the oven door, I settled for, "You're an ass."

He glanced over his shoulder at me indifferently. "Does that mean you don't want nachos?"

31

I narrowed my eyes at him and crossed my arms over my chest. "Of course I want the damn nachos. What else are you good for?"

six

I was suspended upside-down in the backseat of a car, the seatbelt digging into my chest. Smoke burned my lungs, and something warm and wet was dripping along the side of my face. Strands of lilac hair hung around me.

Broken glass littered the roof of the car. A drop of blood gathered on the tip of my nose, and I watched as it fell, landing against a jagged shard.

I fumbled with my seatbelt and finally managed to free myself, landing hard on my forearms as I caught myself. Glass sliced into my palms, but I hardly felt the pain.

I crawled towards the window, glass crunching beneath me, and pulled myself onto the pavement. I clung to the side of the car as I pushed myself to my feet. Someone was shouting; sirens wailed in the distance.

I tipped my head back to the dark sky, and droplets of rain water splattered against my skin.

A bit farther down the road, another car was crumpled around a tree. That was where the shouting was coming from.

I turned back to the car behind me, a twisted mass of dark metal and shattered glass. There were two figures in the front seat and one in the back. None of them were moving. All three of them had fair hair the color of dried wheat.

Blood dripped down the arm of the girl in the backseat, gathering in a small pool on the roof of the car. The color matched her glittering red nails.

"Eve." The word left my lips in a choked whisper.

This isn't my dream, I realized suddenly.

I turned my head, and Theodore was beside me. There was a gash

33

on the side of his face, and his pale hair was matted with blood. His eyes were blank.

"Theodore?"

He stared straight ahead, his hand clenching and un-clenching into a fist at his side. I wondered if he'd even heard me. Then he glanced over, and his voice was hoarse as he spoke. "Tannyn?"

Flashing lights caught my attention out of the corner of my eye.

Theodore swallowed. "I have to . . . I have to help them." He dropped to his knees beside the car, reaching for Eve's bloodied hand through the broken window. He grunted in pain as he stretched towards her. "I have to . . ."

"Theodore." I grabbed at his arm, fingernails digging into his skin, as I tried to pull him up. "*Theodore.*" He looked up at my tone. His eyes were rimmed with red, and drops of rain water had collected on the ends of his lashes. "It's over," I murmured. "It's just a dream."

I held a hand down to him, and it was a moment or so before he reached out and curled his fingers around mine. I helped him back to his feet, and he leaned against me for support. I wrapped an arm around his waist as ice cold rain pelted our skin. The sound of it drumming against the contorted metal filled my ears like white noise.

"I'm sorry," I told him quietly.

"I should have helped them."

I knotted my fingers into his shirt. It was damp with rain or blood or maybe both. "It's just a nightmare," I replied. But I knew better than anyone that nightmares weren't always monsters lurking in the shadows. Sometimes they were real. *This* had been real.

Mine had been real once.

"What is it, honey?

A flash of metal.

My fingers coming away stained with red.

The metallic tang of blood filled my mouth as I bit down on my tongue. The song "Tea for Two" by Doris Day drifted through the air, but the sound was warped and horrifying, as if the record were melting beneath the needle.

And then we were in my kitchen.

My mother was standing by the sink, and the knife in her hand was streaked with blood from where she'd already nicked my cheek.

"Mama," I whispered.

Then my mother was coming at me again, swinging the knife in her hand wildly. I ducked out of the way, but she caught a fistful of my hair, and I screamed out in pain. The knife slashed towards my chest, catching my collarbone as I tried to wriggle from her grasp.

I clawed at the hand that still had ahold of my hair.

"Mama, it's me!" I screamed, the way I had when I was little.

Then Theodore was shouting my name and pulling my mother off me. She fell to the ground, knife skittering across the kitchen floor and under the refrigerator. She cowered against the cabinets by the sink, curling in on herself, sobbing.

Theodore said, "Tannyn."

I pressed a hand to the deep gash on my collarbone.

"Tannyn."

"It's alright," I said, my voice quiet. "It's not real." What I didn't add was that it had been once. Real. All of it—the knife, the blood, my mother's screams.

My mother was still crying, and the water began to gather on the kitchen floor, pooling around my feet.

It rose to my ankles, and I thought to myself that it should have been impossible, that it should have leaked out into the hallway, but it was as

35

if a pane of glass covered the doorway. I knew that if I tried to run, I'd crash into it, fingers splaying and clawing, searching for any break in the glass. This wasn't the first time I'd had this nightmare, afterall.

The water was cold—freezing, actually. Nothing like tears at all.

"It's not real," I said again.

I tried to steady my breathing. *In through the nose, out through the mouth.*

The water was at my waist now, and the shorts that Theodore had lent me were clinging to my legs. I reached out to take his hand, lacing my fingers through his.

My mother was underwater; I'd lost sight of her.

In, out.

The water was at my chest, and then my shoulders.

My feet lost touch with the floor as I rose in the water, and Theodore's fingers tightened around mine.

I'm fine, I told myself. *It's not real.*

I squeezed my eyes closed and drew in a breath as the water closed over my head.

My body floated, weightless, in the cold water, and when I opened my eyes, other objects were drifting around me: a dinner plate, magnets from the refrigerator, the daisies from the vase on the kitchen table.

I twisted my head towards Theodore, but he was above the water, paddling lightly to stay afloat.

My lungs began to ache, and my chest swelled from the lack of oxygen. Black spots danced across my vision, and I squeezed my eyes shut. I reminded myself that it was only a dream, but at the back of my mind, I thought, *I'm dying.*

Panic seized me as Theodore's fingers slipped from my own.

I sucked in a breath, but instead of air, cold water rushed into my lungs.

I woke in the Shearwater's guest room, gasping for air and coughing water onto the sheets.

I pushed back the covers and threw my legs over the side of the bed, clutching at my throat. My legs crumpled beneath me, and I fell to my knees, pressing my forehead to the cool wooden floor.

My breathing slowly returned to normal as my brain registered that I wasn't actually drowning.

I climbed to my feet, clinging to the bedside table for support.

My footsteps were silent as I walked to the bathroom and pushed the door open. I turned on the faucet, cupping my hands beneath the stream of water and splashing it against my face. I smoothed my hair back and blinked at my reflection.

I am fine, I thought to myself, and this time it sounded almost believable.

I scraped my hair back into a ponytail and secured it with an elastic.

The rest of the house was quiet as I crept down the stairs and into the kitchen.

I filled a tea pot with water from the sink and set it on the stove. While I waited for the water to boil, I climbed up onto the countertop to reach the shelf where the bags of chamomile tea were kept.

A floorboard creaked as my fingers closed over the box of tea, and I turned my head to see Theodore leaning against the frame of the kitchen door.

Heat crawled through my throat and into my cheeks, and I lowered myself back to the kitchen floor.

"You really can't reach the top shelf on your own?" he asked.

I turned away from him and crossed to where they kept the mugs, taking down one that had belonged to Eve and was shaped like a cat. "Not all of us were born seven feet tall."

He grinned at me. "Hell hath no fury like a five-foot woman scorned."

"Five-one," I snapped. I set the mug down on the island and glanced over my shoulder at him, taking in the dark circles beneath his eyes. "I'm sorry," I said.

He reached up to drag his fingers through his pale hair, shrugging.

"Does it ever stop hurting?" I asked.

He gave me a long, calculating look before he straightened and crossed the kitchen to where I stood. "You tell me," he said. He brushed his thumb over the scar on my cheek. "Your mom did that to you."

"I'm sorry," I said again.

"Stop fucking apologizing, Tannyn."

The teapot began to shriek, and he took a step back as I turned to switch off the burner.

I poured the hot water over the tea bag in my mug and leaned back against the counter, crossing my arms over my chest. "I can sleep outside," I offered quietly.

"What?"

"It's fine," I told him. "I've done it before—"

His eyebrows drew together. "What do you mean, you've done it before?"

"You've met my dad. His insomnia keeps him up most nights, so when he's able to actually fall asleep, I stay outside because it makes it easier for him." I shrugged and avoided his gaze. "It's not that big of a deal."

"Why don't you just come here? Didn't Eve show you where the spare key is?"

"I wouldn't bother you for something like that," I told him. "Like I said, it's not a big deal." I picked up my mug from the counter, curling my fingers around it as I took a sip.

"Promise me," Theodore said, "that next time you'll just come here."

"I told you—"

"Promise me, Tannyn. Please."

"Fine," I said, staring down into my mug. "I promise."

He sighed deeply and knotted his fingers in the hair at the back of his head. "Well," he said. "I'm not going back to sleep anytime soon. Want to watch a movie?"

I followed him into the living room and sunk down on the couch as he moved to a shelf against the far wall that held at least two-hundred DVDs. I curled my mug against my chest, breathing in the steam.

"What do you want to watch?" he asked.

"Something scary," I told him, because that's what Eve would have said.

Theodore pulled a DVD from the shelf and walked over to the theater system beneath the flat screen TV. He slipped the disc in and sat back on his calves, skipping through the previews.

When he sat down on the couch beside me, he draped his arm around my shoulders. I curled against his side and leaned my head against his chest as he drew his fingers through my hair. A smile pulled at the corner of my lip as the opening music to *The Shining* poured from the speakers, but it didn't reach my eyes.

"I miss her," I whispered, staring down into my tea. "So much."

His fingers went still in my hair, and I felt his chest tremble as he let out a breath. Then he said, "Me, too, Tannyn."

I leaned over and kissed him on the cheek, and he stilled beneath me. "That's for the nachos," I told him. "Don't get any ideas."

When I finally fell asleep again, I didn't dream.

seven

When I was little, I was just Tannyn. Quiet and blonde and angry. Not this one, or that one.

I came into the world a roaring, bloody mess just a few minutes before midnight, and my screams caused the other patients at the hospital to have nightmares for five days straight afterward. When I was born, my mother gave me three things: brown eyes, her grandmother's maiden name, and a temperament like a boiling teapot—silent one minute, shrieking the next.

In the memories that I had of my mother before everything that happened, she was beautiful and fierce. She loved books and teaching and the smell of rosemary. She loved summer thunderstorms and honeybees.

There was a picture of us that hung in the living room above the mantle, where I was sitting in her lap on the steps of the front porch. She was reading *Bridge to Terabithia* to me because it was the only way she could put me down for a nap afterward.

You weren't supposed to have a favorite child, but I knew that my mother liked me best.

She didn't mind that with my tantrums came bad dreams and nights without sleep. She once told me that her grandmother, Sophie Tannin-Lawrence, could see other people's secrets—a lipstick stain on the pressed white collar of an unfaithful husband, chocolate frosting beneath the fingernails of a woman on a diet who kept a box of cupcakes hidden at the back of her sock drawer. Things that other people chose not to notice, my great-grandmother was unable to ignore. When my mother was fifteen, she snuck out of the house to meet up with a boy, and even though she cleaned her shoes off with the hose around back and slipped them off before coming in the house, her grandmother still saw the muddy footprints leading from the front door and up the stairs to her bedroom.

I liked to hear stories of my great-grandmother because they made me feel less strange—even if I was reminded afterward by the taste of chardonnay and warm sugar that lingered on my tongue from my mother's fears.

She was afraid of her own mother, who'd beaten her as a child when she'd had too much to drink before my great-grandmother had taken her in. She was afraid of the song "Tea for Two" by Doris Day, which had been playing on the afternoon that she'd found her grandmother dead on the living room floor from a heart attack. But, most of all, she was afraid of being alone.

The air around her thrummed with this fear, like a live wire. It made the hairs on my arms stand up whenever she pulled me into a hug or crawled into bed with me.

It was because of this fear that she married my father when she was only twenty, going on her second year at university with another man's baby growing inside of her. My father offered safety and security, and when he proposed, my mother couldn't think of a reason to say no.

Then came the miscarriage. From the stories I'd heard, she cried so hard that all of the plants in the apartment building where she lived withered from the salt water.

My older brother was born eighteen months later.

Then three summers later, I came along, with tiny golden curls and flailing fists, on a hot and sticky night in June as the stars flickered in and out of existence in the sky.

One of the doctors commented that he'd never seen such an angry-looking child—and I supposed he hadn't. My face had gone so red from shrieking that I could have been mistaken for a tomato.

But my mother just smiled, because I was *hers*. Because I had her eyes, and because I smelled like night air—and would always from that moment on. She didn't realize then that this was the first sign that something wasn't quite right with me. If she had, things might have turned out differently.

On the days when my mother couldn't get out of bed in the morning or I discovered her crying on the laundry room floor, I would curl up beside her and let her hold me until it passed. Sometimes when my father was out of town, she would drag out her grandmother's old record player and listen to "Downtown" on repeat for hours as she sat on the living room floor going through boxes of photos from her childhood.

The day my mother went for the knife drawer in the kitchen, my father was away in Atlanta for the weekend.

He used to travel a lot for work back then—New Orleans, Manhattan, San Francisco. I had a collection of postcards in a shoe box beneath my bed from all the places he'd been. Sometimes he brought things back for my mother; her favorite was a beaded bracelet he'd bought near a Cheyenne reservation in Montana.

My mother had been in her pajamas when I'd come down the stairs that morning, a cup of coffee in her hands as she leaned against the island in the kitchen.

She was singing along to "Downtown" by Petula Clark beneath her breath, the way she always did—it was like a nervous tick. I'd inherited it from her. I could hear my older brother, Hollis, moving around in his room upstairs, and our dog, Madeline, was snoring softly on the couch in the living room.

The memories always came in short bursts of pictures after that:

43

"What is it, honey?"

A flash of metal.

My fingers coming away stained with red.

My mother sobbing.

Then I woke up in the hospital, with stitches in my cheek and collarbone that would later become scars.

They reminded me of a broken porcelain doll that had been poorly glued back together. Until Eve, I'd used to cover them with foundation every morning, even on the days when I was running late to school.

The day Eve had seen them for the first time, she called them lovely. Lovely because I was still here, she explained. Lovely because I was alive, breathing, fighting.

eight

I deposited an armful of SAT books on the counter beside the register and then looked to the girl standing across from me. "Is that all?"

The girl nodded, and I rung her up. The bell atop the front door chimed as she went out.

After she'd left, I slumped in my stool behind the counter and picked up a dogeared copy of Virginia Woolf's *The Voyage Out*.

I popped the cap off my pen and underlined: "They all dreamt of each other that night, as was natural, considering how thin the partitions were between them, and how strangely they had been lifted off the earth to sit next to each other in mid-ocean, and see every detail of each others' faces, and hear whatever they chanced to say."

I tucked the pen back into my ponytail.

The feeling of water rushing into my lungs suddenly flashed into my mind, and I squeezed my eyes closed. I slid my hands along my thighs, and then curled them into fists. When I sputtered a cough, salt water dribbled from my lips.

You're not there, I told myself. *You're in a bookstore. Just breathe—see, no water. It smells like old books and leather bindings.*

I opened my eyes and stared down at the patch of afternoon sunlight that slanted through the front windows of the store and across the pages of the book in front of me. I reached up to wipe away the water on my chin.

My eyes fell on another quote I'd underlined on the same page of the book: ". . . you're always the same, and I'm a creature of moods."

Hands smacked down on the counter, and I looked up to see my boss standing over me.

She was a tall, heavyset woman with glossy black hair and a penchant for noisy bangles, chunky platform sandals, and wailing folk music. She reminded me of that aunt that always intimidated your boyfriend and commented on how short you were.

I raised an eyebrow at her. "Yes?"

"You look like you're turning into a zombie," Ilse said, cocking her head to the side and narrowing her eyes at me. "My insurance doesn't cover that."

I glared at her from behind my glasses.

"Late night?"

"I guess you could say that."

Her eyes fell on the bruised knuckles of my right hand, and she sighed. "Boy or girl?" she asked.

"Boy."

"Did he deserve it?" she asked.

"Yes."

She nodded her head once and crossed her arms over her chest. "Good," she told me. "As long as you're doing it on your own time."

"You know I would never fight in here," I said. I patted the book in front of me affectionately. "Might hurt the books."

She smiled. "Right," she replied. "Well, I just came out to make sure you were alright, so I guess my work here is done. I'll be in my office if you need me."

Ilse turned on her heel and wandered through the shelves, traveling up a flight of stairs and onto the second-floor loft. She disappeared through a door that read *Employees Only*, and I turned back to the pages of my book.

I'd only been reading for several minutes when the bell atop the door chimed again.

46

I looked up to see Jack and West entering the store.

"If you're coming to loiter again," I told them, "Ilse just bought a new broom. She's already beaten Theo with it twice."

Jack threw himself down in an armchair by the window, draping his long legs in front of him and crossing one over the other. He had an open bag of gummy worms in his hand—they were probably his breakfast, because that's how awful his eating habits were. He gave me a boyish grin from beneath his dark sunglasses and popped one into his mouth as West walked over to the front counter.

"Thought you might need this," West said, setting a plastic cup of iced coffee down on the counter in front of me. "No cream, no sugar. Black as your heart, just the way you like it."

I smiled sweetly at him. "Aw, you remembered."

As I accepted the coffee from West, I glanced back at Jack. I noticed for the first time a dark bruise forming along his jaw, and the corners of my lips turned down. He caught me staring and gave me another signature Jack Harmon grin.

"We match," he said. When I quirked an eyebrow, he pointed to my knuckles.

"Oh, lovely." I glanced over at West. "Thanks for the coffee."

"We figured you might need it after your long night," Jack replied, grinning. "Theo told us you slept over."

I tossed him an amused look. "Jealous that he didn't ask you?"

"He'll come around and admit he's in love with me eventually," he replied, stretching his arms behind his head. "Everyone is."

"What's with the sunglasses indoors? Are you going for a vampire look?" I asked.

"Don't worry, *mami*—I don't bite. Much." For emphasis, he tossed another gummy worm into his mouth and flashed me a grin.

I looked down at the bag of gummy worms in his lap. "How are those maggots, Michael?"

Jack raised his eyebrows and followed my gaze. Maggots wriggled inside the bag of gummy worms in his hands. He started and tossed it to the ground with a curse, dozens of maggots splattering across the floor.

I blinked and they were gone.

"*Mierda.* Why do you do that?" Jack asked, wiping his hands off on his pants. He leaned over to pick up the bag, along with the gummy worms that had spilled out. He tossed them all in the trash can beside him. "You know that movie scares the shit out of me."

I snickered. "Just reminding you who you're talking to."

Jack made a *humph* sound and leaned his head back to stare at the ceiling.

West spoke up. "We also came to tell you that we're going to the Boathouse. Theodore texted and called a meeting."

"A meeting? What is this, student council?"

"He said he got some new information."

I set my coffee back down on the counter, afraid that I might drop it. "Did he say what it was?"

"He's being secretive," Jack answered. "Said he wanted to tell us when we were all together."

Glancing at the clock on the wall, I said, "I get off in an hour. I'll meet you guys then."

"Sounds like a plan." Jack hopped up from the armchair and started for the front door. "You coming?" he asked West over his shoulder.

West nodded and caught the door as Jack walked out into the parking lot and climbed into his Jeep. He glanced back over his shoulder, a shock of dark hair falling into his eyes as he stared at me.

He must have glimpsed something in my face because his usually indifferent gaze turned sympathetic.

"We're going to find out what happened to her, Tannyn," he told me.

The door swung shut behind him, and I watched as the Jeep roared to life and peeled from the parking lot.

nine

From the moment they arrived in Truth or Consequence, the twins were beautiful and intense and mysterious. Like a poisonous plant with alluring flowers that could kill you in an instant.

They didn't start calling Eve strange until the incident with the crow. Before that, she was just a little unusual. The blonde one, *no, the one in all black*. Or *no, the one with the storm-cloud eyes*. The one whose laugh was like crackling thunder. The one whose parents had died in a car accident.

The day I met Theodore, Eve and I had gone into the city to Christmas shop and then stopped back at her house to watch a movie.

It was mid-December, almost a month since Eve had walked into the bookstore out of the rain.

By then, I'd gathered enough information about her to know that she was strange, even if the rest of Truth or Consequence didn't.

She liked horror films with lots of blood and suspense, but her all-time favorite movie was *Breakfast at Tiffany's*. She always wore black, except for her nails, which ranged anywhere from silver to mint to bright pink. She was afraid of the dark, but she couldn't sleep if there were any lights on. She owned a collection of first edition *Nancy Drew* books. She had a tattoo of the sun on the back of her neck. Her favorite word was "quicquidlibet."

And she liked to drive twenty miles over the speed limit, which was why we'd taken her car.

She pulled into the garage of her aunt's house, alongside a black

Mustang Boss which had the hood propped up.

One boy was bent over the engine, and another was sitting on a stool, his feet propped up on a toolbox and a book in his hand. There was a streak of silvery-white through his dark brown hair.

I recognized him from school.

The thing about Jack Harmon was that he wasn't a misfit *exactly*; he fit in everywhere, so he fit in nowhere. All I knew about him was that he played shortstop for TC High's baseball team, and that he was always with someone new whenever I saw him. He could have had lots of friends if he wanted to, and he did—but he didn't have anyone *close* to him, at least not in the way that other people around him seemed to have. It was like he was waiting for the Shearwater twins to come along.

In those days, I preferred things that couldn't talk back to me: dogs, books, cars, trees. My best friend was a Great Pyrenees named Madeline— and that was only when she wasn't stealing my socks from the laundry room.

And Jack Harmon was known for his talking.

As the garage door closed, Eve asked, "What's going on?"

"Car won't start," Jack replied. "Something with the engine."

I knew who the other boy was before he even glanced over his shoulder at us. He had the same messy blonde hair and slender frame as Eve. Then his gray eyes locked with mine and narrowed slightly as the corner of his lip tipped up. He was all sharp edges, the sort of person you might accidentally cut yourself on if you weren't careful.

When I looked at Theodore Shearwater for the first time, I thought that he was also the sort of person you might accidentally fall in love with if you weren't careful.

Then he opened his mouth.

"Either say something useful, or close your mouth," he said as he ducked back beneath the hood of the car. He had that same slight accent as

Eve, but his voice was colder. "Staring isn't attractive."

Eve grabbed my arm and began to steer me away, but my feet felt rooted to the cement floor as I stared at the boy who looked just like her. Heat crawled from my throat and into my face, settling in my cheeks.

I hated the way his fear tasted on my tongue; it made my head ache.

The boy lifted his head. "Well?" he asked. "Have you decided which it will be?"

Looking past him at the engine, I suggested, "Have you tried gapping the spark plugs?"

When I slid my gaze back to him, the boy blinked at me once. Twice. I guess he hadn't been expecting me to say anything at all, let alone something actually useful, because he replied, "What?"

"Gapping the spark plugs," I repeated.

"They're brand new," he told me. "They're pre-gapped."

"Doesn't matter," I said, shoving my hands into the pockets of my coat. "Do you have a feeler gauge?"

He looked to his sister. "Who is this?"

"Tannyn Carter," she told him.

"Tannyn? What kind of name is that?"

Eve spoke again before I had the chance to. "She's the one with the thing for nightmares."

"Oh, yeah?" The boy propped his arms on the sides of his car. "What's that like?"

This time, Eve let me answer. "It's just buckets of sunshine," I told him sarcastically. "What do you think?"

Eve snickered, and the boy gave me a long, hard look before he said, "I think my whole life's a fucking nightmare, and I don't need someone like you hanging around."

My face burned, and I felt something furious swell in me. *Someone*

52

like me?

Without having made the decision, I reached out and took hold of his fears.

Thunder cracked overhead, and when he tipped his head back, dark clouds had gathered along the ceiling of the garage. Eve followed his gaze, narrowing her eyes, but I knew all she saw was the stark gray stone. This was Theodore's nightmare.

Which was why I nearly fell on my ass when he leveled his gaze with mine and grinned.

Eve's sharp smile promised adventure and mystery and everything you've ever wanted from the world; this boy's promised danger and hearts shattered on the ground like glass.

My mouth had gone dry, and I swallowed before I said, "Do you want help with your car, or not?"

There was a moment of silence. Then he said, "Alright."

"How do you know all this stuff about cars?" the first boy, Jack, asked.

"Are you asking because I'm a girl?"

He gave me a lopsided grin. "I'm asking because I can barely fill a tank of gas by myself."

"I have an old '65 Mustang," I told him. "It breaks down a lot, so my older brother taught me some stuff."

I pulled off my coat and draped it over the edge of a table. Then I tied my hair back from my face in a messy bun even though I felt an immediate dislike for this icy boy whose fears gave me headaches and who didn't know any manners or how to gap his spark plugs.

Eve leaned back against the wall of the garage, crossing her arms over her chest and trying to hide her grin.

I held a hand out towards her brother, who arched a blonde brow at me. "The feeler gauge," I told him. "And you should probably stop staring; it isn't attractive."

ten

I had the top down on my car as I bumped along the uneven back road that led to the Boathouse.

My tires kicked up dirt as I spun into a small clearing beside the Jeep and parked beneath the trees, and then put on the emergency brake. Her pale blue paint looked out of place between the two black cars, but I reminded myself that I had owned Delilah *long* before Theodore Shearwater had come to town with his loud, angry Boss.

I climbed from the car and shoved my keys into my back pocket.

A mosquito landed on my arm, and I squished it beneath my finger, leaving behind a smear of red.

The air was sticky and thick, and tall grass scratched at my legs as I walked towards the Boathouse. I swatted at a cloud of gnats that swarmed around my head.

West had been the one who'd first found the small wooden building that was perched right on the edge of the water, but it had been Eve's idea to fix it up. The twins had paid in cash for it—*fucking rich people*—and ever since, it had become our point of rendezvous. The outside was still crawling with vines and looked like something that belonged to a swamp witch, but Theodore had installed a new lock on the door, and we each had our own key.

Now, it was propped open as I stepped up onto the wooden dock and walked inside.

Jack looked up from where he was sitting on the couch as I entered, closing the book in his lap. West glanced over his shoulder at me, but then returned to the mural he'd recently begun painting on the main wall of the front room—it was now covered from floor to ceiling with crows and thunderclouds and twisted trees. His clothes were splattered with paint.

"Where is he?" I asked.

Jack nodded to the doorway that led into the backroom, and the floorboards creaked beneath my feet as I crossed to it.

The backroom of the Boathouse had a wall made entirely of glass, and Eve had originally claimed it as a greenhouse. The tables and shelves were overflowing with lavender and dwarf sunflowers and potted ferns. With her death, though, one of the walls had been converted into something from a crime show: pictures of her had been tacked up, alongside post-it notes listing evidence and possible suspects, all connected with lines of string.

Theodore was sitting on a stool before the wall, holding one of Eve's school pictures in his hand.

"Hey," I said, sinking down in the chair across from him and crossing my arms over my chest.

He set the picture down on a coffee table beside a pot of rosemary as he glanced over at me. "Why are you so sweaty? Did you run here?"

I glared at him. "It's almost ninety degrees out."

"Doesn't your air conditioning work?"

"My air conditioning works perfectly fine, thanks for your concern," I replied as I took off my wire-rimmed glasses to wipe the lenses with the edge of my tank top. "Not all of us have a heart of ice to keep us cool." I glanced out the glass wall that overlooked the murky water and twisted the flat silver ring on my thumb in a circle. My voice was almost a whisper as I said, "Jack said you got some new information about Eve."

"Yes," he said just as quietly.

I stood from my chair and looked down at the picture of her he'd set down on the table. She was wearing a black turtleneck and her hair was in a

French twist secured with a pencil. She looked like a goth librarian.

I turned back to Theodore, the floorboards creaking beneath my feet. "Alright," I said. "Come on."

He rose from his stool and followed after me as I walked back out into the main room. Jack was pacing the floor, but he stopped and turned to face us when we entered. West climbed down from his stepladder and wiped black paint off on the legs of his shorts.

We gathered around the coffee table, and then Theodore reached into his back pocket and pulled out a folded envelope. He tossed it down beside Jack's book.

"This was in my mailbox this morning," he said.

For a moment, we all just stared at it.

Then Jack reached over and picked it up, unfolding it with careful fingers. He lifted the flap and dumped the contents out onto the table: a scrap of black fabric, and a silver ring shaped like a coiled snake. There was a dark brown stain on the surface of the ring that I recognized immediately. Blood.

I swallowed the bile that rose in my throat.

West said aloud what we were all thinking. "That's Eve's ring."

"I know," Theodore said.

Jack ran his hands through his hair. "*Mierda.*"

"What was it doing in your mail?" I asked through clenched teeth.

"Someone left it for me to find," he said. "There's no return address, no stamp, no nothing. I doubt there's even any fingerprints."

"Did you take it to the police?" Jack asked, turning the plain white envelope over in his hand

Theodore shook his head. "Not yet. I thought you all should see it first."

I crossed my arms tightly over my chest, staring down at the onyx stones that glinted in the snake's head. "We agreed no more police."

West was silent as Jack turned his narrowed eyes on me. "This is different."

I ran my hand over my face. "I know. I'm sorry. It's just—there hasn't been anything new on their end in a while."

"I know," Theodore said. "But there's no harm in bringing it to them. Maybe they'll find something we missed."

"Like Jack's fingerprints," I muttered. He immediately dropped the envelope in his hands.

"Shit," he said. "That's not incriminating, right?"

A bead of sweat slithered from my hairline, and I reached up to wipe it away with the back of my hand. "Calm down. You have an alibi for that night."

West walked over to the buckets of paint laid out on a tarp before the mural and crouched down, fitting the lids back on them. He straightened, wiping his hands off on his already messy t-shirt. He pushed his dark hair back from his face, smearing a streak of gray paint across his forehead. "I have to get to work."

His gaze flickered to Jack, waiting, as he shoved his hands into the pockets of his shorts. Jack pulled his keys from his pocket.

"Come on," Jack said, walking to the front door of the Boathouse. West ducked his head and followed after him.

The door slammed shut behind them.

Theodore sat down on the couch beside me and leaned forward, putting his head in his hands.

"Have you asked Nettie if she saw anyone?"

He nodded. "And some of the neighbors. The footage from the security cameras didn't pick up anything either. The mail box wasn't in range. I'm going to see about getting one installed closer."

I nodded. "Let me know if the police come up with anything."

"Tannyn."

He said my name a second time, and my fingers clenched into fists on my knees. The front door of the Boathouse hadn't shut properly, and it rattled in a breeze.

"When we find the person who did it," I whispered, "I'm going to tear their fears apart and break them until there's nothing left."

Theodore was silent. Then he said, "Good."

eleven

It happened two days before the start of summer vacation.

I remembered that I'd dreamt about rain that night, before Truth or Consequence was taken over by a drought that turned everything brown and crisp beneath the sun.

I woke in bed covered with a thin sheen of sweat, and my feet stuck to the hardwood floor as I padded down the hall to the bathroom. I took a cold shower, and then tied my long, blonde hair in a knot atop my head. While I slipped into a pair of drawstring shorts and a baggy t-shirt, I could hear my dad moving around in his office downstairs. I didn't think he'd gone to bed at all the night before.

Madeline greeted me at the bottom of the steps, shedding white hair all over my black sneakers.

I filled a water bottle and fetched her leash from the garage, and she eagerly wagged her tail as I fastened the collar around her neck.

On my way to the front door, I poked my head into my dad's office.

He was hunched over his computer screen, his elbows propped up on the desk and his head in his hands. His brown hair was streaked through with more gray than usual for someone in their late-forties, and he was still wearing a button-up shirt from the day before with the tie hanging loosely around his neck.

"Dad?" I asked quietly.

He lifted his head and looked over his shoulder, giving me a weak smile that didn't reach his blue eyes. "Hi, sweetie," he said. His voice was hoarse, and there were dark circles beneath his eyes. "God, what time is it?

Morning already?"

I glanced at my watch. "It's almost ten o' clock," I told him. "Were you up all night?"

He shook his head. "No, no. Of course not." A lie.

Beside me, Madeline nudged at my leg with her wet nose. "I'm taking Madeline for a walk," I said. "Why don't you try and get some sleep?"

He was silent.

"Dad?"

He blinked at me, slowly. "Did you say something?"

I forced a smile. "Never mind," I said.

He noticed Madeline as she thrust her head past my legs and into the office, tongue lolling from her mouth. "Are you taking the dog for a walk?" he asked.

I nodded, stroking the soft fur behind Madeline's ear.

"Alright." He picked up his glasses from where they lay on the desk and slipped them onto his face. He reached for the cup of coffee beside the computer monitor as he said, "Have fun."

I shut the door behind me as I left the office. I led Madeline out through the garage and onto the driveway that glistened in the summer heat. Sweat gathered along my brow, and I reached up to wipe it away with the back of my arm.

I took a long swig from my water bottle.

Then I glanced down at Madeline. "Let's go," I told her.

We walked along the side of the road, past tall Southern oaks that stretched their crooked limbs towards the sky and past fields of sugarcane and cotton where workers were already milling amongst the rows. We walked down a dirt path that had been worn through the woods, beneath tree branches that dripped with Spanish moss.

My t-shirt clung to my back with sweat, and I swatted away clouds

61

of mosquitoes as Madeline panted happily ahead of me.

When we returned home an hour later, the first thing I noticed was the black Mustang parked in the driveway. The second was Theodore sitting on the top step of the front porch.

I pulled my phone out from inside my sports bra as we came up the driveway, and I realized that I had six missed calls from him. Dread began to form knots in my stomach, and I tucked my phone away and jogged the rest of the way to the house.

Theodore's head was in his hands, and he didn't look up when I stopped beside him or when Madeline began sniffing at a dark stain on his button-down. His eyes were squeezed shut, and sweat glistened on the back of his neck as he kept his head bowed towards the ground. His phone sat on the step beside him, and he ignored it as it vibrated with a call.

The air was thick with the taste of his fear; blood began dripping from my nose and onto the front of my t-shirt.

"What happened?" I asked.

His fingers knotted in his hair, but he still didn't look at me. "You wouldn't answer your phone," he said, his voice hoarse.

"*What happened?*"

When he lifted his head, his eyes were rimmed with red. "She's dead."

My heart plunged through my chest and landed on the concrete of the walkway. It spasmed like a fish, droplets of blood splattering onto my sneakers—or maybe that was from my nose. I stared at Theodore, trying to understand what he was saying because somehow as the words were leaving his mouth, they'd come out sounding like *she's dead*. And that couldn't be right.

"What?" I said.

"Someone . . ." He swallowed thickly, looking away. "Someone killed her."

Madeline's leash dropped from my fingers, but she was too preoccupied sniffing at a cluster of dandelions to notice. She sneezed, and the white tufts scattered throughout the air. One of them landed in Theodore's hair.

His phone was vibrating again, and West's name lit up the screen.

I shook my head. "No."

"It was sometime last night," he whispered. "We got in a fight, and she said she was going for a walk. She left the house around eleven, but she never came back. Then this morning, I woke up and went outside and she . . . she was in the tree. And the blood—Christ, it was everywhere."

That's what I realized the stain on the front of his shirt was. Blood.

Eve's blood, I thought.

"They think she'd been dead for at least twelve hours," he muttered. "She was in that tree for *twelve fucking hours.* And they took her heart."

"Eve . . . is dead."

Theodore's eyes moved to my face, but I was staring at the dandelion tuft that was clinging to his blonde hair. He still hadn't noticed it. "Tannyn?" he asked, lowering his hands into his lap.

Spots danced across my vision, and all of the feeling left my body as the ground rushed up to meet me.

I remembered Madeline pushing at the side of my face with her nose, and then nothing at all.

The grass behind Truth or Consequence's only church had turned dry and crisp from lack of rain, crunching beneath my boots as I passed between the gates of the cemetery.

Eve's grave was towards the back, covered with a layer of fresh sod that was still green despite the stifling summer heat.

I clutched a bouquet of white lilies that I'd picked up at a small stand on the side of the road as I passed headstone after headstone, each looking the same as the last. Flat slats of gray rock, indistinguishable except for the names of the dead that lay beneath them.

I reached the plots of cremated flower urns, and stopped before Eve's, which was settled in a corner of nearly-dead hedges and was overflowing with green vines that refused to die despite the dry heat.

"Hey, you," I whispered, crouching down to lay the lilies at the base of the urn. "I brought you flowers. Of course, they'll probably be dead by the end of the day." I sat back on my haunches and shielded my eyes from the sun that beat down against my face. I coaxed several strands of hair back into the bobby pins that held together my messy ponytail.

I sat down in the grass, drawing my legs up to my chest and resting my chin on top of my knees. A trickle of sweat ran between my breasts, and I dabbed it away with the collar of my tank top.

I stared at the flat gray marker embedded in the earth, the poem inscribed beneath her name: "Dirge Without Music" by Edna St. Vincent Millay. One line in particular caught my eye, the same one that was tattooed on the inside of my left elbow: "Into the darkness they go, the wise and the lovely."

My breath caught in my throat as I pressed my hand against where her name was carved into the stone. The bouquet of lilies I'd brought had already begun to grow brown and crisp around the edges.

"I'm so mad at you," I said aloud. "I'm so mad at you, and I can't even tell you because you left me. And I know it's not your fault but I don't know who else to be mad at. They still don't even have any potential suspects. And I just . . . I just wish you were here, so you could tell me what to do. Because I have no fucking clue what I'm doing."

I heard footsteps crunching over the dry grass, and I thought I glimpsed someone standing beneath the skeletons of the trees several yards away. When I turned my head to get a better look, though, all I saw was a flash of blonde hair as someone disappeared behind the trunk of an oak tree.

Another mourner—or maybe my own nightmares coming to haunt me.

I climbed to my feet and brushed off the back of my shorts.

As I slipped between the headstones and passed through the gates of the cemetery, the air tasted like burnt flesh against my tongue.

twelve

eve

It was dark there, in that place where she was resting.

She tried to remember where she was—or *who* she was—but there was only that darkness. It stretched like an ocean around her, pulling at her, forcing its way into her lungs and choking her.

A single memory emerged from the back of her mind.

She was stumbling along a dark road, but she couldn't remember how she'd gotten there.

Her legs hurt, feeling like they might give out at any moment beneath her, but she needed to keep moving. She needed to get . . . Where did she need to get to? She struggled to remember, but the thought kept slipping away before she could grasp hold of it.

She clutched at her side, and when she glanced down, she noticed that her fingers were stained red.

Then suddenly her foot caught on something, and she tumbled to the ground, scraping her palms as she threw her hands out to break her fall. She lay there, staring up at the moon overhead, as she struggled to breathe through the pain.

"Eve?"

Someone was shouting. She squeezed her eyes closed and willed the noise to go away.

"Eve!"

Was that her name? She couldn't remember.

She opened her eyes to see a boy with red hair and dark eyes crouching over her, and he touched his fingers to the wound in her side. *Go away,* she thought, but her mouth couldn't seem to form the words. She closed her eyes again so she wouldn't have to look at his face.

She was bleeding everywhere, and *oh, God,* it hurt. She wished for the darkness again, if it meant that she would stop hurting.

And the darkness willingly obliged, enveloping her in its embrace.

thirteen

Sunlight glittered off the bright blue water in the Shearwater's pool.

I flipped to the next page in my book, balancing a bowl of fruit salad on my thigh. I skewered a strawberry on the end of my plastic fork. My hair was twisted into short twin braids, and my one-piece bathing suit clung to me with sweat.

Jack was dancing around the patio, singing along to Shakira on the radio, as West drifted around the pool on an inflatable chair. His forearm was draped over his eyes, and I thought he might have fallen asleep. He was wearing a thin t-shirt, but the skin on his cheeks had already turned slightly pink.

Jack must've noticed, as well, because he picked up a bottle of sunscreen from the table beside me and tossed it into West's lap.

West lowered his arm and blinked down at the bottle of sunscreen. I glimpsed the dark crow tattooed on the inside of his left forearm as he slowly sat up and flipped open the cap on the bottle.

I picked up a blueberry from the bowl in my lap and popped it into my mouth. "Why's it so goddamn hot out?" I grumbled.

"Global warming," West offered.

"I don't deserve this," I said. "I recycle."

Jack teasingly tugged on the end of my braid. "Come in the pool with me, *mami*."

"I don't want to get my hair wet," I replied, swatting at him with my fork.

The back sliding glass door on the Shearwater's house opened, and I glanced over behind my sunglasses to see Theodore emerge from the kitchen with three bottles of beer. He handed one to me and another to Jack as he shimmied his hips. Then he sat on the edge of the pool and dangled his legs in the water.

"You know," Jack said, twisting the cap off his beer, "I don't think I've ever seen Tannyn touch water before. Are we sure she's not a witch?"

I flipped him off, but I grinned in spite of myself.

"Can you even swim?" he went on. "Should we have a lifeguard on duty?"

I rolled my eyes. "I can swim," I told him. But my dream from the night before was still fresh in my mind. The burning in my chest, the feel of icy water forcing its way into my lungs . . .

I brought my beer to my lips and took a long gulp.

Jack took a swig of his own beer and then set the bottle next to me. He stretched his arms over his head, and the crow tattoo on his chest flexed with the movement. His tanned skin glistened with sweat. He turned towards the pool, exposing the branch-like scars on his tanned back and shoulder from when he'd been struck by lightning as a child. *Lightning flowers,* they were called.

As he dove into the cold water, I shielded my book with my hands.

Jack re-surfaced a moment later, flicking his wet hair back from his face.

"Careful," Theodore warned him. "You almost got her book wet."

Jack offered me a lopsided smile. "Please forgive me, Tannyn."

I ignored him as I used the dry t-shirt beside me—it might have been Theodore's—to wipe the droplets of water from my legs. "You have no respect for Virginia Woolf," I replied. "No wonder Mr. Kestrel hated you."

"He couldn't appreciate my humor. We were bound to clash."

"None of your Shakespeare jokes were funny," West said.

Jack looked offended. "Not even the *villain, I have done thy mother* one?"

"Definitely not that one," I told him. I stabbed a chunk of pineapple on the end of my fork as my phone began ringing on the table beside me. I slid my sunglasses into my hair as I squinted at the screen.

"Who is it?" Theodore asked.

"My brother." I accepted the call and tucked the phone between my shoulder and ear as I closed the book in my lap. I picked up my beer. "Hello?" I said, straightening from the lounge chaise and taking the phone in my hand again.

"Hey, Tan," a voice chirped.

I took a sip of my beer as I padded across the hot concrete of the patio in my bare feet. "Hollis." I pulled my phone away from my ear to check the time, frowning. "Aren't you in Dublin? What time is it there?"

"Almost seven," my brother replied. "We're about to eat dinner. What are you up to?"

"I'm at Theodore's," I told him, I slid the glass back door of the house open and slipped into the kitchen. I could hear the vacuum running upstairs as Nettie cleaned, and I leaned back against the island. "We're out by the pool."

"Let me guess," he said. "You're sitting as far from the water as possible with a book."

"You know me so well." He chuckled into the receiver, and I asked, "So what's up?"

Silence. Then, "Tannyn, do you know what day it is?"

I narrowed my eyes at the calender on the wall across the kitchen, trying to make out the date. "Thursday."

"It's June twenty-third."

I scoffed. "No, it isn't."

70

"Tan."

"I wouldn't forget my own birthday."

He laughed again. "You would, and you did," he said. "I know it's easy to lose track of time in the summer, but this is ridiculous, even for you, Tan."

"If you're going to start singing, I'll hang up."

"Alas, I have decided to spare your eardrums, if only just this once. I'm calling to tell you to look out for a package coming in the mail. It should be in by Tuesday."

"What is it?"

I could hear the hint of a smile in his voice as he said, "Why do you always ask when you know I'm not going to tell you?"

"Because you're horrible at keeping secrets."

"I'm *excellent* at keeping secrets," he said. "Otherwise, I would have told Theodore Shearwater that you're in love with him a long time ago."

I choked on my beer, spilling the rest of it down the front of my bathing suit. "I'm not in love with him," I growled, grabbing a handful of napkins and dabbing at the stain. I picked up my empty bottle and tossed it in the recycling bin by the door.

Hollis laughed, and then I heard someone speaking in the background on the other end of the phone. "Alright," my brother said to me. "Dinner's ready, so I gotta go."

"Okay."

"Call me when your gift comes in, alright?"

"Will do."

"And, Tan? Happy birthday."

"Thanks, Hollis. I love you."

"Love you, too."

There was a click as he hung up, and I dropped my phone onto the

71

island. The front of my bathing suit was sticky and smelled of beer.

I heard the glass door slide open, and I looked up as Theodore stepped into the kitchen. "Hey," I said.

"Hey, yourself."

He stopped in front of me, and I had to tilt my head back to look up at him. Droplets of water clung to his jaw, and his hair was slicked back from his face except for one strand that had fallen into his storm-cloud gray eyes.

He crossed his arms over his chest. "What did Hollis want?" he asked.

"To torment me, as usual."

Theodore tipped his head to the side, grinning. "Doesn't he know that's my job?"

My face heated, but I hoped the sunburn in my cheeks hid it. "You'll have to work that out amongst yourselves."

I was still as he reached out to touch the end of one of my braids. He dropped his hand back to his side. "I have something for you," he said suddenly.

I quirked an eyebrow. "For me?"

He turned and crossed the kitchen to pull open a drawer beneath the liquor bar. He took out a small box wrapped in shiny purple paper and walked back over to me.

I reached for it, and he lifted it above his head. A grin broke out across his face as I went up on my toes to swipe at it, but my fingers were still at least two feet short of reaching it. I scowled and punched his shoulder.

"Give it to me," I said.

"What's the magic word?"

"Now."

There was a mischievous glint in his eyes as he replied, "Wrong answer."

He leaned in close, and I made another grab for the box.

And missed.

I glanced out the kitchen window that overlooked the pool, and then returned my gaze to him. I narrowed my eyes. "Fine. Please."

As he chuckled, I asked, "How did you even know it was my birthday, anyway?"

"You'd be surprised at some of the things I know," he told me. Then he added, "And Nettie told me."

He handed over the box, and I turned it over in my fingers. I picked at the tape on the purple wrapping paper as he leaned back against the fridge.

"You didn't wrap this yourself," I said, looking up at him.

His jaw tightened, and he glanced away, but not before I saw his color rise to his cheeks. "Nettie might have helped."

I laughed and peeled away the wrapping paper, crumbling it onto a ball. When I lifted the lid from the box, I stared down at what was nestled amongst the tissue paper and sucked my bottom lip into my mouth.

"I saw it while I was out and thought of you," Theodore said.

I lifted the pocket knife from the box, and the blade flicked out as I hit a button on the side. It shone a thousand different colors like an oil slick in the kitchen light. I pressed my thumb to the sharp edge.

"I'm going to take that as a compliment."

"Aren't you going to thank me?"

He straightened from the refrigerator. I angled the blade towards him, but he walked until the tip of it was pressed against his bare chest.

He reached down and curled his fingers around mine, prying the knife from my hand and folding the blade closed. His eyes didn't leave my face as he set it on the counter behind me.

"You don't scare me, Tannyn Carter," he said.

He stepped closer, dipping his head to look down at me, and I backed up until the edge of the island counter was digging into my spine. I closed my eyes as he wound his hand behind my head to cup the back of my neck, and my lips parted slightly when I felt his warm breath tickle my skin.

His lips touched lightly to my forehead, and my eyes fluttered open, blinking rapidly as he took a step back. The corner of his mouth lifted in a smile.

When I thought back to this moment later that night, I would blame the beer for what happened next. The beer, and that damned smile.

I narrowed my eyes at him. "Well, I should scare you."

And then I went up onto my toes and kissed him.

His body went rigid with shock, and then a moment later, his arms circled my waist and pulled me against him. My thoughts scattered, and I forgot what I'd been trying to prove as his tongue swept into my mouth.

My bare feet lifted from the floor, and I wound my arms around his neck as his breath mingled with mine. I tangled my fingers in his damp hair, the heat of his bare chest searing me through the thin material of my bathing suit.

He grasped my hips and hauled me onto the countertop, and I wrapped my legs around his waist, pressing him into me. He drew my bottom lip between his teeth and bit down lightly, and I gasped into his mouth.

Fuck, I thought.

I forced myself to plant my hands against his chest and push him back a step, holding him there. I took a moment to catch my breath.

My insides were in complete and utter chaos, but my lips curled into a smile carved from nightmares.

"Better than your imagination?" I asked.

"Not even close," he answered breathlessly.

The sun was sinking behind the trees as I slipped through the front door and stepped into the foyer.

Madeline greeted me, panting happily as her tongue lolled from her mouth, and I reached down to stroke the soft fur on the top of her head.

The smell of something burning reached my nose, and I lifted my head. I set my bag down on the floor and kicked off my flip flops, and Madeline followed at my heels as I crossed to the kitchen.

I grabbed a dish cloth from the drawer by the sink and bent to pull open the oven door.

Christ, I thought, stumbling backwards and covering my face with my arm as smoke poured out into the kitchen. *What the hell?*

I opened the back door, fanning the smoke outside, and a moment later, the fire alarm began to blare throughout the house. Madeline barked anxiously and paced in a circle.

I pulled the charred frozen pizza from the oven and tossed it out into the backyard.

The smoke alarm was still going off as I walked to my father's study and pushed the door open, sticking my head inside.

He was asleep at his desk, his head lying on top of a pile of scattered papers.

I ran my fingers through my hair, tangled from sweat and the braids they'd been in earlier. I thought about waking him, but I didn't know how long it had been since he'd last slept—especially if he was able to sleep through this noise.

I crept across the room and silently flipped off his desk lamp.

By the time I'd gone back to the kitchen, the blaring had stopped and Madeline was curled up on the couch in the living room. I slid the back door closed.

I made myself a peanut butter and jelly sandwich, setting it on a plate on the counter and then fetching a box of candles and a lighter from the drawer by the sink.

I stuck one of the candles in the sandwich, and the light of the flame flickered off the walls of the dark kitchen. I crouched down so I was eye-level with it and drew a sharp breath through my nose. Madeline was snoring softly in the living room and the sun had disappeared behind the trees as I thought, *This is goddamn depressing.*

When I blew out the candle, a trail of smoke curled towards the ceiling.

"Happy birthday to me," I whispered in the darkness.

fourteen

I buried my head beneath my pillow as the doorbell rang for a second time, and then a third.

"Go away!" I shouted, knowing they couldn't hear me.

I heard the sound of the front door opening and then feet pounding along the stairs. My bedroom door opened, and I pulled the covers over my head, snarling, as morning light flooded the room.

I felt weight atop me and I said, "Jack Harmon, I know you did not just lay on me."

He pulled the covers away from my head and gave me a lopsided grin. His elbows were digging into my stomach. "Good morning, Tannyn," he said.

"It *was* good," I replied, glaring up at him, "until you decided to break into my house. How did you get in anyway?" I glanced over at where Theodore and West were lounging in the open doorway.

Theodore braced his hands against the frame of the door. "I stole Eve's key."

"It's eight in the morning."

Jack laid his head on my chest, staring up at me. "I'll buy you an iced coffee."

I peeked out at him from over my covers and narrowed my eyes. "A *large* iced coffee," I said.

"Alright," he replied. "Now get up. Unless you're naked under this blanket." He poked at my side, and I sat up, shoving him off me and knocking him to the floor. He landed on his stomach with a muffled,

77

"*Oomph.*"

I flipped off the covers—revealing that I was, in fact, wearing pajamas—and stepped over Jack as I climbed from my bed.

"You can wait downstairs while I shower," I told them.

Jack rolled over onto his back and smiled up at me, folding his hands behind his head. "You sure you don't want me to come with you?"

I snatched a pillow from my window seat and tossed it at his head. "*You* can wait outside."

"We've all seen your ass before, *mami*," Jack said.

"*Que te den.*" I flipped him off over my shoulder as I stalked from the room.

Sweat glistened along my brow as I finished the last of my beignet, licking powdered sugar from my fingers in the New Orleans heat.

Sunlight streamed down through the clouds as we passed ornate street lamps and colorful buildings with ivy-covered wrought iron balconies and glass storefronts. I paused to drop several crumpled dollar bills into an empty saxophone case in front of a jazz band playing on the side of the street.

Jack took my hand and spun me in a circle, and my feet stumbled beneath me. He jerked me against him, and I shoved him away with a groan.

"You're all sweaty," I said, but the corner of my lip had pulled up into a smile. "Stop it."

He laughed and draped his arm around my shoulders, but this time I didn't push him off me.

Theodore, who had been looking up a map online, shoved his phone into his pocket and looked up. "There's an art gallery in a few blocks."

"Can we go into that antique store?" I asked, indicating a building ahead that was painted midnight blue and had a faded wooden sign hanging over the front door that read *Antiques and Collectibles.*

The three of them followed me inside, and a pretty girl looked up from behind the register, smiling at us from beneath her short black curls. As I began to wander around the store, Jack flashed his trademark lopsided grin and started for the front counter.

West pulled open the door of a grandfather clock, crouching down to peer inside.

Theodore followed me as I wandered the aisles.

I pushed my sunglasses up into my hair and picked up a blue and white teacup with a chip in the rim. "What are we doing here, Theodore?" I asked.

"What do you mean? You're the one who wanted to come in here."

"No—what are we doing in New Orleans?" I set the teacup back down on the matching saucer and turned to look at him.

"You told me once that your mother used to bring you here every year for your birthday," he said. "And she would take you to Faulkner House books, where that Nobel Laureate wrote his first novel, and she'd buy you any book you wanted."

"His name was William Faulkner," I said. "It's not that hard to remember. It's literally in the title."

"Anyway," Theodore said pointedly, "I thought you'd want to continue the tradition. Even if your mom couldn't take you."

"Do Jack and West know this is for my birthday?"

"Only if you want them to."

I bit down on my bottom lip, drawing it between my teeth. "I used to come here with her, you know," I admitted. "There was a woman in the back who would read her tarot cards."

"Let's see if she's still here."

Theodore took my hand, and I stumbled after him as he led me

79

towards the back of the store.

I jerked to a stop when I spotted the beaded curtain swaying lightly in the breeze, and my hand fell from Theodore's. It looked the same as it did in all of my memories.

I took a step forward, lifting a hand to stroke the beautiful turquoise beads.

Theodore followed as I parted the curtain and stepped through.

An older woman was sitting at a table in the corner, but she stood up as we entered.

She wore a long, flowing skirt and silver bracelets that clicked together with her movements. Her hair was wrapped in a silky green head scarf, and her dark brown skin glimmered with sweat from the heat. The shelves behind her were filled with candles and jars of dried herbs.

The statue of a woman in white stared down at me from the wall. Her hands were spread before her, and waves crashed at her feet.

"That's the goddess of the sea, Yemaya," the woman said, following my gaze.

"I'm sorry," I said curtly. "I didn't mean to—"

The woman shook her head. "It's alright."

"I remember you," I said. "My mother used to come here—you read her cards."

She nodded, smiling. "Penny, yes, I remember her. And I remember you, though you've grown quite a bit since I last saw you." The smile fell from her face. "I was sorry to hear about what happened to your mother."

"Thank you," I said softly.

"It's been, what? Five years? But I remember you. Of course, I'd remember you," she told me.

"That last day, when we came to see you . . ." I trailed off. "Did you know? Did you know what was going to happen to her?"

a girl called murder

The woman sighed heavily through her nose. "Reading cards is not like reading a book. I only see what they want to show me. Sometimes I don't see anything." She pursed her lips, and then added, "I'd like to read your bones."

I started. "My what?"

She patted a velvet bag on the table beside her. "*Bones*," she repeated. "It's a sort of divination. Like casting dice, but more complicated. My ancestors speak to me through the bones; where they land, the direction they face, how they fall in relation to the other bones—it all has meaning. The talent has been passed down through my family for generations."

My eyes narrowed skeptically as my gaze slid back to the shelves along the walls. I asked, "How much?"

The woman made a dismissive gesture with her hand. "I won't charge," she replied. "I always liked your mother. Besides, I'm curious what the bones have to say about you."

"Tannyn," Theodore warned from behind me.

"Alright," I told the woman.

She smiled without showing any teeth. "Good."

As Theodore moved to lounge against the wall, the woman dumped the contents of the velvet bag into a wooden bowl on the table. I noticed there were shells and stones and hard nuts, as well as the bones of some small animal.

I frowned and looked up at her. "What sort of bones are those?"

"Possum," she said.

The woman gestured for me to stand before an animal hide laid out on the floor. After I'd reluctantly moved to the spot she'd indicated, she murmured a prayer beneath her breath and leaned down to toss the contents of the wooden bowl at my feet.

She knelt on the floor, her bones creaking with the movement, and lay her hands on her thighs as her dark eyes roamed over the hide.

"Someone close to you has passed away," the woman murmured. "A sister, maybe."

I kept my expression indifferent as she moved her eyes back to the items distributed across the animal hide. Out of the corner of my eye, I saw Theodore shift uncomfortably.

"This is the rib bone," she said, pointing. "I did a reading with the bones for your mother—once, very long ago—and it fell the exact same way. How peculiar." The woman glanced up at me and gave a wry smile. "Then again, it seems that anxiety runs in the family."

I snorted.

Then her eyes flickered back to the hide, and her brows knit together. Her eyes took on a far-away look, staring unseeing at the items before her.

"Excuse me," I said un-surely.

The woman continued to stare blankly at nothing, so I waved a hand in front of her. When she still didn't respond, I glanced over my shoulder at Theodore, who straightened. I could see the discomfort beneath his skin, pulled taut like a rubber band.

Suddenly, the woman blinked as if waking from a dream.

She cleared her throat and began to gather the items spread on the animal hide, scooping them back into the wooden bowl with an oyster shell. But something about her movements were off. "That's all," she said quickly. "I suppose my ancestors don't want to cooperate with me at the moment."

"That can't be all," I said, even as she stood. I clambered to my feet.

"Well, it is," she replied.

"You saw something," I protested. "In the bones. What was it?"

"Tannyn," Theodore warned. "It's not real."

The woman shot him a sharp look, and then turned back to me. "I'm

82

sorry," she said. "I don't know."

"You do," I said. "Tell me what you saw. Please."

She was silent for what seemed like an eternity, and then she sighed through her nose. She gestured for me to give her my hand, so I did, and she turned it over and stared at the lines in my palm. "I'm sorry," she said again.

"What?" My hand dropped back to my side as she released it.

She looked up at me, her eyes dark. "You will die before the next full moon, Tannyn Carter."

At first, I thought I'd heard her wrong.

My whole body tensed up as if I'd been electrocuted, and my mouth went dry.

Theodore started forward from where he'd been leaning against the wall. "What did you just say?"

"I'm sorry," the woman repeated for the third time.

The beaded curtain over the doorway parted suddenly, and the girl from the front of the store stepped through, but she froze when she saw me standing before the animal hide. Her eyes widened as they flickered between the expressions of everyone in the room: shock and confusion, sadness, anger.

"Bibi, what are you doing?" she hissed at the older woman.

Jack poked his head into the room. "What's going on?"

The girl ignored him, speaking to her grandmother. "Mama said that you're not supposed to be scaring off customers with your hoodoo."

The woman waved a hand. "Your mother's just mad I haven't predicted the Powerball for her."

When the girl turned to me, her expression was apologetic. "I hope she didn't charge you for this."

I shook my head; my mouth was still dry, and I wasn't sure if I'd been able to speak.

"I'm sorry," the girl told me. She shot her grandmother another warning look as she held aside the beaded curtain and led us back out into the front of the shop.

West ended up buying a tapestry, and as the girl rang him up, she said, "Again, I'm really sorry about my grandmother. I hope she didn't frighten you."

As West handed across the money, I asked the girl, "That bone reading. Do you believe in it?"

The girl's eyes lifted to my face. "Whatever my grandmother told you," she said, "the bones have different interpretations for everyone." She paused. "Have you ever heard of a self-fulfilling prophecy?"

"We learned about it in English while reading *Oedipus Rex*."

The ancient register stuck, and the girl had to pound on it with her fist to get the drawer to pop open. She handed West his change, and then glanced back to me, her expression softening. "I wouldn't worry about it too much."

From the doorway of the backroom, her grandmother watched the exchange with her arms crossed over her chest.

I felt her gaze on me as we walked to the front of the store, and then the glass door slammed shut behind us. My mouth was set in a thin line as I slid my sunglasses back into place and squinted up at the sky overhead.

"So what did she tell you?" Jack asked.

Theodore reached for my hand again, but I brushed his fingers away and stuffed my hands into the front pockets of my shorts.

Without looking at either of them, I replied, "Nothing."

fifteen

Before they took my mother away, my father didn't stay up all night or forget things like dinner or birthdays.

I remembered that I used to wake up in the morning before school and bound down the stairs to the kitchen where he would have bagels with strawberry cream cheese waiting for me. I remembered that he didn't always look so tired—and sometimes when I began to forget, I looked at the pictures above the mantel where his skin wasn't pale and his eyes weren't surrounded by dark circles.

There was one in particular that I liked, of him and my mother, back when they'd first gotten engaged in college. It was before the miscarriage, and you could make out the small bump of my mother's stomach beneath her rose-colored sweater, as well as the round-cut diamond ring on her third finger.

They were sitting in the grass outside of the library, a blanket spread beneath them and my mother's legs tucked beneath her as she leaned into my father's side. His arm was wrapped around her shoulder, and she had her head buried in the crook of his neck as she smiled at the camera.

Back then, she'd been relatively happy. She still had her bad days, when she couldn't get out of bed or was too tired to go to class, but after the miscarriage, something changed.

She once broke down in the middle of her sociology class, sobbing and swiping at her face with the back of her hand until the pages of her textbooks were soaked with salt water and she had to be excused. Sometimes she cried for hours on end, and all my father could do was rub her back and wait until she'd tired herself out and fallen asleep.

My mother took a semester off from college after my older brother was born, and things seemed to be getting better after that.

One of my first memories was of my family in my backyard, where I was perched on my father's shoulders. I clutched my father's hair between my fingers, shrieking with excitement, as we chased my brother around the yard. My mother watched from the swing beneath the oak tree, and I remembered how her smile had shown in her eyes when I looked at her.

Whenever I thought of that moment, the smell of honeysuckle in the air and the sound of my father's laughter, my chest swelled and I found myself humming "Downtown" the way my mother always had.

She had been listening to the song on the day that she'd come after me, and the record had skipped on the second verse where I'd accidentally scratched it once.

People didn't understand how I could still love my mother after something like that. But in that moment, it hadn't been my mother. It had been something mean and vicious, wearing my mother's skin.

A week before the incident, my mother went to see a psychic in New Orleans, and I sat quietly on the floor and flipped through the pages of the book I'd brought with me as the dark-skinned woman dealt her cards. I didn't remember what I'd had for dinner the night before or what I'd been wearing that morning, but I remembered that the carpet in the woman's back room had smelled like sage and sweet mint on the day we'd gone to visit her.

My mother had gone to see her before—I knew because the woman called my mother Penny, which was something she only did with people she was close with. Everyone else called her Penelope or Mrs. Carter or Professor.

The woman had a curtain of turquoise-colored beads hanging in the frame of her open backdoor, and they swayed in the breeze, clicking together, as she stared down at the spread of cards on the table.

My mother was tapping her fingers against the table, humming beneath her breath. Her eyes slid from the woman's dark purple hair wrap to a clock on the wall to the cards in front of her, and then back again. Her fear clung to my skin, leaving my fingertips sticky with warm sugar as I attempted to turn the pages of my book. The granules stuck to the paper and caught in the spine.

I remembered that I'd been reading a poem about a bluebird and that the woman had remarked that I was a little young to be reading Robert Frost. I pretended not to hear her.

Afterward, my mother took me out for ice cream, and she let me get hot fudge even though she was normally afraid that I was going to spill it on the seats of her car. She turned up the volume on the radio, glancing over at me with a smile—and I smiled back, my teeth stained with fudge.

"Hey, honey," she said suddenly, slipping her sunglasses into her hair. "Let's go to the beach."

So we did, even though it was over an hour drive and even though the water was freezing against my ankles as we splashed around in the ocean.

A week later, as I lay curled up on the kitchen floor with my fingers sticky from the blood, I thought of that moment. I closed my eyes and clenched my hands into fists, trying to hold on to it, clinging to it with everything I had.

As my mother sobbed and sobbed, I went back to that moment, feeling the sand that stuck between my toes and my mother's arms around me, and I pretended that everything would be alright.

sixteen

I set my cup down on the corner of the pool table and picked up my stick from where it rested against the wall.

I shot for a green solid, but missed, knocking one of Jack's stripes into a side pocket. I pushed my hair back from my face. "Fuck," I said.

Theodore smirked, but it was strained at the corners, and I ignored him as I picked up my cup and downed the rest of my rum and Coke. He was leaning back on a chair in the corner, his arms wrapped around the waist of some brunette I'd never seen before. She had a lipstick stain on her teeth, and I'd been debating whether or not I should tell her for the past seven minutes.

As Jack sunk the last stripe into a pocket, I laid my stick down on the table.

"I'm going to the bathroom," I said.

"Game's not over," Jack protested. "I still have to get the eight ball in."

I picked up my empty cup, tossing it into a trash can by the bar. "I've already accepted my loss," I told him over my shoulder.

"*Mal perdedor.*"

"Tannyn—" Theodore said.

"You have lipstick on your teeth," I told the girl as I passed, before I could change my mind. I pointed to my own mouth. "Right there."

Then I hooked my fingers through the belt loops on my jean shorts as I went up the basement stairs, feeling Theodore's gaze on my back. I heard a soft clattering as Jack knocked the eight ball in.

People had crowded around the basement door at the top of the stairs, and I had to shoulder my way through them to get to the bathroom. I tried the handle and cursed when it turned out to be locked. A Metallica song vibrated through my bones as I stood deliberating for half a second before I started up to the bathroom on the second floor.

After I flipped on the switch and locked the door behind me, I braced my hands against the countertop.

In through the nose, out through the mouth.

I squeezed my eyes closed so I wouldn't have to look at my reflection. I already knew what I would see: my cheeks flushed from alcohol and my hair sticking to my face with sweat. The black eyeliner smudged around my light brown eyes, and the worried line between my brows that hadn't gone away since we'd left New Orleans that afternoon.

In, out, in, out.

The flat silver ring on my thumb dug into my skin as I gripped the countertop until my knuckles ached. Tremors ran through my arms, and I clung tighter to the cool marble, but that only made them worse.

I turned on the faucet, splashing cold water against my neck and forehead. My breathing was ragged and uneven as I thought, *In, out,* but there was a stone caught in my throat. I didn't remember swallowing it; perhaps someone had slipped it into my drink.

Someone knocked on the bathroom door.

"Occupied," I shouted, my voice thick.

My eyes flickered to my reflection, and I could feel my heart racing in my chest. Now that I was alone, I could smell the smoke that clung to my shirt, and it made me nauseous.

"You will die before the next full moon, Tannyn Carter."

I dug the heels of my hands against my closed eyelids, trying to think of anything else: how much I sucked at pool, the lipstick stain on that girl's teeth, the shower curtain printed with smiling humpback whales.

I am fine, I thought.

I opened my eyes, meeting the gaze of one of those damned whales in the mirror, and snarled through my teeth.

Flicking off the lights, I yanked open the bathroom door.

My gaze fell on a boy with unruly red hair lounging against the wall opposite the bathroom, and he smiled and straightened when he saw me.

"Well, if it isn't the Ten of Crows herself," he said.

I became aware of how clammy my skin felt as he crossed the hallway to stand in front of me. My mouth turned down at the corners, and I said, "What do you want, Jude? I'm not in the mood."

His dark brown eyes glittered in the dim lighting. "That rhymed. I never knew you were a poet."

"There's a lot of things you don't know about me."

Avenged Sevenfold's "Nightmare" began to play on the stereo downstairs, and I almost laughed out loud at the irony.

Jude moved to lounge against the frame of the bathroom door, stretching out his long legs across the threshold so that I'd have to step over him if I wanted to leave. His eyes flickered to my chest. "I like your shirt."

I glanced down, furrowing my brows. My black shirt was frayed where I'd cut away the sleeves and the hem, and it was printed with the silhouette of a raven that was made up of the lines from Edgar Allen Poe's "The Raven." I'd forgotten I was even wearing it.

Jude said, "Now, remind me, what's the difference between a raven and a crow?"

"Do I look like an ornithologist?" I asked.

"Do you want to know what you look like?" Jude's smile widened. "You look like trouble just waiting to happen." He rested his head against the door frame, staring at me from beneath his lashes. "Tell me something— does Theodore know why your mother tried to kill you all those years ago?"

My body went rigid, and whatever retort I'd been about to snap at him died on my lips. "What do you know about my mother?"

"My mother's friend works at the only psychiatric hospital within a fifty mile radius of TC. Isn't that a damned coincidence?"

"Oh, just the damnedest," I ground out through my teeth.

"And it doesn't seem strange to you that someone would just . . . *snap* like that without warning?"

"You don't know what you're talking about."

The scar on my collarbone began to throb, and I closed my eyes against the images that threatened to surface in my head. My breathing turned shallow again, and I thought I might be sick.

"You will die before the next full moon, Tannyn Carter."

Jude's voice entered my thoughts. "Are you afraid, Tannyn?"

I opened my eyes to meet his gaze, and the taste of his fear filled my mouth. Crisp night air and dark red apples—the kind Eve used to eat because she liked the sense of irony it gave her.

"No," I said suddenly. "But you are." As he narrowed his eyes, I asked, "Why are you afraid of being out by yourself at night, Jude?"

He blinked, and his smirk slipped from his face. "What?"

I cocked my head to the side, like a cat studying an interesting bug, as the hallway lights flickered out one by one. Jude started, losing his footing and clinging to the frame of the door for support.

The music cut off abruptly. The hallway and the bathroom disappeared, and we were standing in the middle of the road, surrounded by forest on either side.

"Stop it," Jude said through his teeth.

He turned to face me, and his eyes seemed to stare right through me. *Where am I?* I thought to him, my voice teasing. *I was standing before you just a second ago. Now you're all alone. And you're frightened—what*

91

are you so afraid of, Jude?

I smiled at him as he searched for me. To him, it seemed as if I'd vanished into thin air.

"Tannyn?" he called.

A girl appeared in the darkness, staggering across the road with one hand clutching her chest, and her dark shirt was wet with something that glimmered in the moonlight. I couldn't make out her face from this distance, but her hair hung in pale blonde waves over her shoulders.

Jude whirled towards her, his eyes going wide. "Not again."

The girl collapsed to the pavement, and her body shattered like glass. Each fractured piece became a dark crow that swirled into the air, and the sounds of their harsh caws blended together until it became deafening.

Jude covered his ears.

A hand clamped down on my shoulder, and I was jerked back into the hallway outside the second-floor bathroom.

I turned my head to see Theodore standing beside me as Jude backed against the wall and blinked in the sudden light. I felt a sharp pain in my palms and realized my nails were digging into my skin, and I slowly unfurled my fingers.

Theodore took my flushed face in his hands. "Tannyn? Look at me. Focus."

I stared at him. "I'm sorry. I didn't—I didn't mean to."

He turned to Jude. "Get out of here. Now." Jude straightened and scrambled towards the stairs as Theodore's eyes flickered back to me, searching my face. "How much have you had to drink?"

"I don't know."

He closed his eyes and muttered, "Christ, Tannyn."

"I'm sorry," I said again.

The tremors in my arms started again, and I held myself rigid, trying to stop them. Theodore noticed, and took my hand, uncurling my fist and pressing his fingers against mine. I closed my eyes, trying to keep my arm still.

"It's just the adrenaline leaving your body," Theodore said. I opened my eyes, staring up at him. "Breathe, Tannyn. Slower. Good."

He held my hand as the tremors ran through my body for another minute.

"You're safe. You're not in danger," he told me. "You can go home, if you want. You don't have to stay."

I nodded my head, swallowing.

"Tell me what you're thinking right now."

"I think I'm going crazy," I whispered.

"You're not going crazy. You're just having a panic attack."

"I know what a panic attack is," I said. I laughed harshly. "Trust me, it's not my first—or my last." My eyes flickered past him, and then a moment later, I met his gaze again. "But what if I do go crazy?"

"You won't, Tannyn. I promise, you won't."

"Okay."

"Okay."

He ran his fingers through his hair, and that was when I glimpsed the bruise just below the collar of his shirt. And just like that, the anger returned.

It felt better than the anxiety—at least I had an outlet for it.

"Why did you come up here?"

"You were gone awhile. I thought I should check on you."

My expression hardened. "Well, thanks for your concern. But I'm fine."

I brushed past him and started down the hallway when he grabbed my wrists and lifted my arms over my head—not roughly, but not gently, either. He pinned me against the wall, his body pressing against mine as he leaned towards me.

I tried not to think about how if I just moved a little closer, my top lip would brush his bottom. His breath tasted like Fireball whiskey on my tongue, and I concentrated on how much I hated cinnamon.

My lips skinned back from my teeth. "What do you think you're doing?"

"Getting your attention," he said, his breath warm against my face. His brows were drawn together, but I couldn't decipher his expression. "And now that I have it, what the hell was that?"

"You said it yourself—a panic attack. I'm sure you've read all about them online or in self-help books or wherever you get your information."

"Not that. With Jude. What the hell did he say to piss you off so badly?"

So he'd seen, known what I'd been doing to Jude.

I swallowed. "None of your business."

"You've been a mess since we left that antique store. You think I didn't notice?"

"I really don't pay enough attention to you to know what you do and don't notice," I told him. But that wasn't true—not in the slightest. I paid attention to every movement, every shift in his expression, every breath that left his lips.

"Talk to me, Tannyn," he said. "I know I'm not Eve . . ."

I shrunk away at the words. He dropped his hands from my wrists, and my arms fell back to my sides.

"It's not that easy," I said.

Without moving his eyes from my face, he tucked a strand of hair behind my ear. I didn't pull away. He moved his other hand to cup my chin, his thumb brushing across my lower lip, and lightning flashed behind his

94

storm-cloud eyes.

I closed my eyes, and I didn't care if he accused me of not looking him in the eyes again.

I thought of when Eve had been alive, how I'd wished so many times that I'd fallen in love with her instead because it would have been easier. The first time she'd kissed me had been a quick peck on the lips, my mouth open in surprise, as she was leaving the bookstore. She collected kisses like lost pennies. She tucked them away in her pockets for safe keeping.

Perhaps that was why I hadn't kissed Theodore in so long—because he was so similar and yet so different from Eve. I didn't know what my kisses meant to him.

I opened my eyes to look up at Theodore.

His hand was still cupping my chin as he whispered, "What are you so afraid of, Tannyn?"

I blinked, and the sense of his fears overwhelmed me so quickly that I almost pulled us back into that nightmare—the crumpled cars, the road sleek with rain water, Theodore crouching on the ground with tears in his eyes.

But I dug my nails into my palm to ground myself.

Theodore hadn't even noticed.

"What are *you* so afraid of, Theodore?" I countered, knocking his hands away. He arched his brows, but took a step back.

Beneath that taste of rain water on my tongue were those glass shards that sliced into my gums, my lips, the insides of my cheeks. *I shall know you, secrets / by the litter you have left / and by your blood foot-prints,* I thought.

"What are you so afraid of?" I repeated. "What secrets are you so afraid of people finding out that you hide behind that false smile and shards of broken glass? Tell me a secret—and I'll tell you what I'm so afraid of."

When he didn't answer, I said softly, "That's what I thought."

I turned my back on him, and he didn't come after me as I walked down the stairs.

seventeen

"Catch."

Eve tossed me an apple, and I caught it reflexively.

I stared down at it in my hands—bright red, so shiny I could nearly see my reflection—and then I tipped my head back to stare up at where Eve was sitting on one of the limbs of the apple tree. She pulled one leg up to her chest and let the other dangle over the edge, and she leaned forward to rest her chin on top of her knee.

Her hair was in a long, intricate braid that wrapped her head like a pale crown, and she was wearing a black dress with a lace train that draped over the branch and towards the ground beneath her. Her lips were coated in dark red lipstick.

Sunlight shone down through the canopy of leaves, so that she seemed to glow as she lounged amongst the tree's branches.

"What are you doing?" I asked.

"Waiting," she told me, swinging her one leg back and forth. She wasn't wearing shoes, and her toenails were painted the same red as her lipstick, the same red as the apple in my hand.

"For what?"

Instead of answering, she said, "You changed your hair. I like it."

With my free hand, I reached up to touch the short purple locks. "Thanks."

"Have you seen my brother?" she asked, glancing over her shoulder and then back at me. "He's supposed to be meeting me."

I shook my head.

Eve let out a breath through her nose. "He's always late."

"I miss you," I blurted.

She cocked her head to the side quizzically, a gentle smile touching her red lips. "Why?" she said. "I'm right here."

I glanced down at the apple I was holding, trying to remember why I'd even said it in the first place. A breeze ruffled my hair, and it smelled like damp earth and freshly mowed grass. Then a cloud passed in front of the sun, casting everything in shadow.

Eve whispered, "I'm afraid of the dark, Tannyn."

I lifted my head, and the apple dropped from my fingers, bouncing harmlessly in the grass and knocking against my bare feet.

Her body was draped through the branches of the tree, looking fragile and mangled like a broken doll's. There was a gaping hole in her chest where her heart should have been, and blood dripped from her fingertips onto the grass below. Crows were gathered on her arms and tangled in the long, black train of her dress.

Her head was tipped to the side, and her smoke-colored eyes stared blankly at me.

A hand touched my shoulder, and I whirled to see Theodore standing beside me.

He met my gaze, and then he bent to pick up the apple that I'd dropped at my feet. He turned it over in his hand before looking up at his sister's body.

He sighed once. "She's so dramatic."

When he bit into the apple, blood dribbled down his chin.

A metallic taste lingered on my lips when I woke in bed, and I realized a moment later that my nose had begun to bleed.

As I swiped the trail away with the back of my hand, I glanced at the clock on my bedside table. Almost three in the morning.

I swung my legs from the bed and crept down the hallway to the bathroom. The water from the faucet turned pink against the porcelain as I wiped the blood from my face and hands. A chill ran down my spine as I remembered the way Eve's empty eyes had stared down at me.

I cupped my hands beneath the stream of water and then splashed it against my face. I smoothed my hair back and leaned in close enough to make out a pimple on my forehead.

I scowled at it and reached out to flick off the bathroom lights.

The floorboards creaked beneath my feet as I walked back to my room and climbed into my bed. I lay my head against the pillow and turned to stare at the climbing ivy that West had painted along my one wall, framing my bay window.

I fumbled in the darkness beneath my covers for my stuffed rabbit, and then drew him close to my chest. His flopping, matted ears tickled my chin. I closed my eyes and sighed deeply through my nose, trying not to think of crows or dead girls with smoke-colored eyes.

When I finally fell asleep again, I didn't dream.

eighteen

him

It was mid-afternoon when he stepped over the curb and onto the sidewalk, stuffing his hands into the pockets of his shorts.

He hadn't meant to come here, but then he'd seen her crossing the street to the bookstore, and his legs had suddenly been moving of their accord.

He wondered when he'd become so . . . He struggled for the right word. Callous? Unfeeling? He supposed it had been the first time he'd killed that girl. Her flesh had been so soft beneath his fingers as he squeezed her throat until she was gasping for air. Even now, he marveled over how simple it had been to take her life.

Sometimes, when he closed his eyes at night, he could still see the bruises that had peppered her skin afterward.

He stopped in front of the bookstore, watching the girl behind the counter take a copy of *The Voyage Out* by Virginia Woolf from beneath it. She wore a pair of wide, wire-rimmed glasses, and she tucked a pen into her lilac hair as she settled onto a stool by the register.

The sun beat down on him, and as he reached up to wipe a bead of sweat from his forehead, he felt a spark of vehemence for the small town of Truth or Consequence, Louisiana.

Why is it so fucking hot? he thought viciously.

A woman passed him on the sidewalk, and he smiled politely at her as she went by. He tried not to think about the way the corners of his mouth itched from the falseness of it.

As another drop of sweat gathered at his hairline and slithered down his face, he reached into the pocket of his shorts and pulled out his wallet. He opened it and slipped out a small photograph that was creased down the middle from all the times when he'd felt his self-control waning.

He ran his thumb over the face of the woman smiling up at him.

The bell atop the front door of the bookstore chimed as someone came out, and he folded the picture of Vivian and tucked it back into his wallet.

He looked through the window again to see the girl behind the counter talking to a plump, beautiful Indian woman whose arms were lined with gold bangles. She nodded, and he watched as the woman trotted up a flight of stairs.

He shoved his wallet back into his pocket.

The bell atop the front door chimed again as he pulled it open and stepped inside into the air-conditioned building.

nineteen

I glanced up as the bell overtop the front door chimed, smiling at a middle-aged woman as she moved towards the adult romance at the back of the store.

There was a thud as someone dropped an armful of books onto the counter, and I frowned as I looked over and saw Jude standing before me. He gave a boyish grin and held up his hands in a gesture of surrender. The silver watch on his wrist caught the light from the window, and I thought that it must've cost more than my entire wardrobe.

"I'm sorry about last night."

I ignored him as I set aside my own book and began to ring up the pile he'd set down. Then I glimpsed the title of one of the thick paperbacks. "Why are you reading about imperial Russia and the Romanovs?" I asked, narrowing my eyes.

"I like learning about history." He tipped his head back to look up at the speakers in the ceiling. "Do you always play this hippie stuff?"

"What?" I replied. "You don't like Icelandic folk music?"

"Of course. Who doesn't?"

I reached over and pressed a button for the intercom system that was hooked up to Ilse's office on the second floor. I said, "Ilse, there's a guy down here who asked if you could turn up the music. Apparently he's a big fan of Hera Hjartardóttir."

"You got it," she chirped back.

A second later, the volume had increased, and Jude's expression turned pained.

a girl called murder

I slipped the thick history books into a plastic bag and pushed it across the counter towards him as he handed me his debit card.

"How many crows does it take to make a murder?" Jude said.

My brows pulled together as I looked up from the register. "What?" I asked, but then I realized he was looking at the knife Theodore had given me where it was sticking out of the front pocket of my shorts. I'd forgotten to put it away after I'd been opening boxes in the back stockroom.

Jude's gaze lifted to meet mine, and he grinned. "Only one, if you give her the right tool."

My eyes darkened. "What are you trying to say?"

"Relax. It was just a joke." Jude lifted his hands, palms facing out, in a gesture of surrender, but his mouth was twisted halfway between a smirk and a sneer. He took his debit card and slipped it back into his wallet.

"I know that you and Eve broke up before she died," I replied.

His skin flushed red, and I noticed that his jaw hardened as he turned his head away. He stuffed his free hand into the pocket of his shorts. "That's none of your business."

"What do you know about what happened to her?"

He glanced back at me, and a smirk played at the corner of his mouth. "More than Theodore's told you."

"What the hell are you talking about?"

His lips pulled back from his teeth as he gave me a wolfish grin. "I guess you'll have to ask him for yourself."

I breathed deeply through my nose, curling my hands into fists at my sides. "Don't push me, Jude."

"That's the last thing I want to do, Tannyn. Trust me," he said. "All I'm saying is that you don't know the Shearwaters as well as you think you do—and if I were you, I'd ask Theodore about that night when I found Eve on the side of the road. I think you'd be interested in hearing the story."

103

"What are you—What night?"

He gave me that same sharp smile, and then made a motion as if zipping his mouth closed. "Like I said, you'll have to ask him yourself."

"I swear to God, if you had anything to do with what happened to her—"

His expression darkened. "You really don't know anything, Tannyn."

I started to reply, but a voice spoke from behind him before I got the chance. "Mr. Kelley. Is everything alright here?"

Jude turned his head to look up at the man standing behind him, and his mouth fell into a frown. "Everything's great," he replied flatly. To me, he added, "Just think about what I said, Tannyn." He reached into the back pocket of his shorts and pulled out several white envelopes. "Before I forget. For your murder."

I ignored the envelopes as he held them out to me, so he set them down on the counter.

"My parents are hosting a masquerade party," he told me. "Invitation only."

When he glanced at me, I met his gaze and narrowed my eyes. There was something almost . . . *sad* in his expression, but it was gone as quickly as it had come, and I blinked as he turned away and stuffed his hands into his pockets.

The taste of night air and dark red apples filled my mouth.

Jude started for the front door, and I scraped the envelopes into a pile from the counter, thinking that I ought to just toss them in the trash. Then I paused, frowning.

"There are five envelopes here," I called after Jude.

He glanced back over his shoulder at me as he pushed open the front door. "Are there?" he asked, arching a brow and grinning. "Oh, well.

Bring a friend."

As the door slammed shut, I quickly stuffed the envelopes into my back pocket. If the invitations got bent, oh well.

I turned back to the man on the other side of the counter. He was in his late thirties, with long blonde hair that was pulled back from his face with an elastic and a white t-shirt that was in desperate need of ironing.

He set a book down on the counter, and I said, "*Game of Thrones*, huh?"

My sophomore year English teacher smiled at me. "What can I say? It's a guilty pleasure."

I grinned back. "No such thing."

His hands shook as he slid several crumpled dollars from his wallet and flattened them against the countertop before handing them to me. His expression turned sympathetic as I passed back his change. "How are you doing, Tannyn?"

"I'm doing better," I told him. "Thanks for asking, Mr. Kestrel."

He slipped the change into the pocket of his shorts. "I'm glad to hear."

"How's your wife?" I asked, hoping it didn't sound like I was prying. All I knew about her was that she'd had some sort of accident before they'd moved to town two years ago and that she'd been in a coma since.

His eyes flickered down to the burn scars on his hands, and he shifted his weight from one foot to another. "She's hanging in there. The doctors are still hopeful."

I opened my mouth to say something else, but then he glanced up and smiled at me. "Have a good summer, Tannyn."

He tucked his book under his arm and walked to the front door, raising a trembling hand to wave at me through the window as he started down the sidewalk.

I sat back on the stool and picked up the book I'd set aside on the counter.

A minute later, the door to Ilse's office opened and she walked over to lean against the loft railing. She twisted her head as she searched the first floor for something. "Is that Hera Hjartardóttir fan still here? I just pulled up a video of her performing a cover of *"Stúlkan Sem Starir á Hafið"* live on my computer."

"He already left," I told her. "Sorry."

I flipped my book open to the page I'd dogeared. Her shoulders slumped, and she stalked back to her office. I could hear her disappointment in the slamming of the door.

I wasn't even sorry.

A line of smoke curled from Eve's mouth as she tipped her head back and parted her lips.

I leaned back against the side of my house, drawing my knees up to my chest and staring up at the dark sky. The roof tiling was scratchy beneath my bare legs, but I didn't mind it as much as I usually did.

I gripped the neck of the wine bottle that sat between us and brought it to my lips, taking a long drink. It tasted like wild blackberries and dark earth against my tongue—or maybe the last part was Eve's fear. I wasn't sure.

I wiped away a stream of it that ran from the corner of my mouth with the back of my hand.

Eve flicked the ashes from the end of the joint, and then held it out to me. Her nails glittered like the ruby slippers from The Wizard of Oz *in the moonlight.*

I accepted it and took a pull, blowing out a breath of white smoke.

As I passed the joint back to Eve, I said, "Why didn't you tell me sooner?"

She shrugged and took a final pull from the joint before stubbing it out against the charcoal roof tiling. "I thought you would laugh at me," she replied. The corner of her lip pulled up. "It is kind of funny."

"Are you in love with him?" I asked. She tossed her head back and laughed, and I smiled. "What?" I said. "I'm serious."

"No, I'm not in love with him."

I frowned. "So why couldn't he pick you up at your house?"

"Because he and Theo hate each other," she grumbled. She picked up the bottle of wine and gulped down several mouthfuls. "You know how my brother gets." She flashed me a wicked, mischievous grin and tickled my side. "And he won't mind me coming home late tomorrow if he thinks I'm sleeping over your *house."*

I smiled, ducking my chin to my knees. I stared down at the fallen leaves scattered throughout the grass below—and then I thought of those same leaves crunching beneath my boots as we walked through the student parking lot. Sometimes Theodore held my hand; sometimes he kissed other girls against the driver's door of his car. Sometimes he didn't come to school at all, and when I went to his house later in the day, he'd be lying in bed with an empty bottle of Jack Daniels.

The smile fell from my face. "Why does it hurt when I think of him?"

Her gaze was soft as she patted my shoulder. "I don't know," she murmured. "That's just how it is sometimes."

I straightened and grabbed the bottle of wine, taking another swig. My body already felt lighter as I sighed and moved my head in time with the music that drifted out my open bedroom window. Fallen leaves skittered across my driveway, and I watched them tumble into the street.

"Why are you afraid of the dark?" I asked suddenly.

*She looked up at the sky, breathing in deeply through her nose.
"Do you see that moon, Tannyn?" She pointed at it, and I followed her
finger and nodded. She shook her head. "This isn't darkness. Not even
close."*

*I started to ask her what she meant, but then I heard the sound of
tires crunching over the pavement.*

*I looked over to see a blue Scion pulling into my driveway, and I
had to squint to make out the driver in the glare of the headlights.*

*Jude put the car in park and climbed out, stuffing his hands in his
pockets as he looked up at us. "What are you doing up there?" he called to
Eve. "You're going to hurt yourself."*

*"Turn off your headlights," I whisper-shouted at him. I pulled my
sneaker off and threw it at his head. It missed by a good ten feet, bouncing
off the bumper of his car, and I covered my mouth with my hand to stifle my
laughter.*

I'll get it tomorrow, *I thought.*

*"I've got to go," Eve said beside me. She leaned over and kissed my
cheek, the scent of her lavender and verbena perfume wrapping around me.
"Thanks, Tan."*

*She slipped back in through my bedroom window, and a few
minutes later, she stumbled out the front door below. She shrieked as she ran
across the grass and flung herself into Jude's arms, and he laughed as he
lifted her and twirled her in a circle. Her pale blonde hair streamed out
behind her.*

*He set her back down on her feet, and she turned to me, grinning
and blowing a kiss.*

*I raised my wine bottle in a silent salute, and as they slipped into
the car, I said, "Take care of her."*

Then they were gone, and I lifted the bottle to my lips as stars

a girl called murder

danced in the sky overhead and on the tip of my tongue.

twenty

Nettie led me through the foyer into the kitchen, a duster hanging from one hand. She used it to gesture towards the door that led to the garage. "He's working on his car. Do you want me to fix you two some snacks?"

"No, thanks," I told her, fanning myself off with the frayed collar of my Stevie Nicks shirt. "We'll be fine."

She nodded and headed towards the stairs. "Holler if you need anything!"

I pulled open the door and descended the steps into the garage.

The first thing I noticed was the car. The front of it was elevated on a jack, and the hood had been propped up. The second was Theodore as he rolled out from the underside, his shirt and jeans splattered with oil stains. His hair was disheveled and sticking to his forehead with sweat, and there was a black smudge along the line of his jaw.

He yelled something, but I couldn't hear him over the music coming from the stereo.

"What?" I shouted back.

He stood up and wiped his hands off on his jeans, and then he turned down the volume on the stereo. "I said, to what do I owe this pleasure?"

I sunk down on a stool beside him, pulling my one leg up to my chest. "Boredom, mostly," I replied. I chewed on my bottom lip. "Do you need help?"

"I know how to change the oil on my car, Tannyn."

I held up my hands in surrender. "It's polite to offer."

The corner of his mouth lifted in a smirk, and he bent to pick up the bottle of oil that rested at his feet. He turned it over in his hands. "Do you remember the day we met?" he asked.

"Yes. You were an ass."

He chuckled. "You were wearing that shirt, you know," he said, pointing at me with the bottle of oil. "Except you didn't have that coffee stain on it then."

I covered the stain by Stevie's head with my hand, spreading my fingers. "You told me you're whole life was a fucking nightmare and that you didn't need someone like me hanging around," I said, changing the subject.

"I meant it," he replied, leaning over the hood of his car to pour the oil. "You've been nothing but trouble since the day you walked in here."

I arched a brow. "Tell me how you really feel."

He replace the fill cap, and then without looking at me, he said, "I thought you were the most beautiful and frightening thing I'd ever seen."

Heat rose to my cheeks, but he didn't give me a chance to respond as he slipped into the driver's seat and started the engine.

I stood and walked over to the stereo on the work bench beside the car, twisting up the volume.

I pushed my hair back from my face and swayed back and forth as I sang along to "What's Up?" by 4 Non Blondes. I lifted my arms over my head and twirled in a circle. I could feel Theodore's eyes on me through the front window.

He slid from the driver's side and leaned against the frame of the car, resting his arms on the hood.

I raised my voice and flung my arms out to my sides. "*What's going on?*"

I danced over to Theodore and tugged on his shirt, pulling him away from the car. I tossed my head back and laughed as he took my hands and joined in with my singing.

As the song came to an end, I leaned against him, my body trembling with laughter.

I lifted my head to find Theodore staring down at me, his gray eyes soft around the edges. A few strands of hair had fallen into his face, and I thought about sweeping them away with my fingers. I swallowed. "The first time I saw you, I thought, *this boy is going to break my heart*," I whispered.

He smiled gently down at me. "You never gave me the chance."

I pulled away from it, crossing my arms over my chest.

"Just say it, Tannyn," Theodore told me.

My head jerked up. "Say what?"

"Whatever it is you've been wanting to say since you walked in here."

Jude's voice echoed through my head. *"You don't know the Shearwaters as well as you think you do—and if I were you, I'd ask Theodore about that night when I found Eve on the side of the road. I think you'd be interested in hearing the story."*

I met his gaze, worry curving my lips into a frown. "We don't keep secrets from each other," I said. "Right?"

There was a second of hesitation. But it was enough.

"Right."

I forced a smile and placed a hand on the hood of his car. "So what do you think? Should we take her for a drive?"

I slipped off my sneakers and socks, and then perched my bare feet on the dashboard of Theodore's car. I propped my elbow on the open window, closing my eyes at the feel of the wind on my face.

I tapped my fingers against the side of the car in time to the music on the radio.

"Did you know that my mom used to take me to New Orleans every year for my birthday?" I told him. "That's why I wanted to go."

I opened my eyes and stared out the window as we cruised past rows of sugarcane.

"If we got bored, we used to play Fortunately/Unfortunately." I smiled at the memory.

"What?"

I twisted in my seat, pulling my legs up beside me. "You know, the car game. Someone starts off by saying something fortunate, and then the next person has to say something unfortunate related to the situation. Like *fortunately, the sun is out.* Then *unfortunately, I forgot to put on sunscreen today.* And you just go back and forth until someone takes too long to reply." I bounced lightly in my seat. "Come on, let's play."

"You can't play a car game with only two people."

"Sure, you can. My mom and I used to do it all the time." I shoved his shoulder. "*Come on.*"

He rolled his eyes. "Fine. You start."

"Hmm." I bit down on my bottom lip, glancing around. "Fortunately, I ate lunch before I came over."

"Unfortunately, your breath smells like egg salad."

"Fortunately, eggs are a good source of protein."

"Unfortunately, brown eggs are more expensive than white."

"Fortunately, you don't do the grocery shopping."

Theodore drummed his fingers against the steering wheel. "Unfortunately, Nettie refuses to buy me crunchy peanut butter."

"Fortunately, neither of us are allergic to peanut butter."

"Unfortunately, I'm allergic to sesame."

I tipped my head to the side. "I didn't know that."

113

"That isn't how the game works," Theodore chastised, glancing over at me. But there was a smile playing at the corner of his lips. "Come on. You're the one who wanted to play."

"Alright, alright." I laughed. "Fortunately, I took a first aid class."

"Unfortunately, I wouldn't trust you to save my life."

I punched his shoulder, and he winced dramatically, clutching his arm. "Fortunately, you're not dying at this moment."

"Unfortunately, that means I have to spend more time with you."

"Fortunately, I know you don't mean that."

"Unfortunately, you're right."

My face flushed. "Fortunately . . ." I pushed my fingers through my hair and frowned. "Damn. I can't think of one."

"Does that mean I win?"

I sighed in defeat. "Yes."

He looked over at me, a mischievous glint in his eyes. "What do I win?"

"What do you want?" I regretted the question as soon as I said it. Heat rose to my cheeks at the thoughts of what he might ask for.

None of them were even close.

"Tell me more about your mother," Theodore said.

My eyes widened. His expression was earnest.

My fingers drifted to the scar along my collarbone, and then I dropped my hand back into my lap. "She was a liberal arts professor. American Literature," I told him. "One of her favorite books was *I Know Why the Caged Bird Sings*. Sometimes I'll read it to her when I visit." I picked at the cuticle of my thumb until it began to bleed. I popped the side of my thumb into my mouth, sucking on the torn skin. The metallic tang of blood hit my tongue. "She used to have these, um, really bad periods of depression, where she couldn't even get out of bed in the morning. I would just lay with her for hours until she finally fell asleep."

I breathed in the dry summer air.

"I think it was all the time to herself. Once she started teaching again and got out of the house, it wasn't as bad," I said. "She used to get me off the bus every day from school, and then we would make pizza bagels or those ants on a log snacks with the celery and peanut butter and raisins. And we'd watch re-runs of the old *Scooby Doo* shows. She loved the one episode where they met Josie and the Pussycats." I stared down at the smear of blood on my thumb. "Anyway, we used to just sit and talk about our day, and then I'd go with her to wait for Hollis at the bus stop."

Theodore smiled. "I remember that episode. I used to love *A Pup Named Scooby Doo*." He began to sing the theme song, drumming his fingers against the steering wheel.

A laugh burst from my lips. I leaned my head back against the seat as I watched him. "Tell me about your parents."

"Madock and Catrin Shearwater," he said, his eyes crinkling around the edges. "They met in college when my dad accidentally spilled coffee all over my mom's notebook. She hated him for an entire year until they were forced to do a project together in civics. They married after graduation and had me and Eve three years later. The rest is history."

The mention of Eve's name formed a lump in my throat. "I'm sorry," I told him.

"For what?"

"For not answering the phone that day. For giving you nightmare. For just being a pain in the ass."

"Fortunately, I've put up with a pain in the ass for seventeen years." His tone was joking, but there was no laughter in his eyes.

"Unfortunately, she's gone now," I said quietly.

He reached across the interior of the car to take my hand, brushing

115

his thumb over my palm. "Fortunately, we're still here."

"Unfortunately, it still hurts."

He squeezed my fingers and brought them to his lips, kissing the back of my hand. "I know," he murmured.

"That's not how the game works," I mocked.

"Fortunately," Theodore said, offering me a dimpled smile and releasing my hand to turn up the volume on the radio, "there's a Taylor Swift song for everything."

twenty-one

eve

The darkness surrounding her was speckled with stars.

She sat in the grass, her feet bare and her skin peppered with goosebumps. There was a girl lying beside her, long blonde hair fanned out around her. There was a scar on her cheek, and her lips were turned down into something like a wistful pout. She watched the pouting girl's chest rise and fall in sync to her own breaths.

She tipped her head back to look up at a constellation overhead.

"That's Ursa Major. It means 'the great bear' in Latin. Do you see how the brightest stars form the Big Dipper?"

She looked back down at the pouting girl, reaching out to trace the scar on her cheek with a feather-light touch. The girl didn't stir, but her lashes fluttered gently.

Shouting reached her ears then, and she turned her head towards the sound. It was just far enough away that she couldn't make out the words. The pouting girl slept on.

She climbed to her feet and moved towards the voice in the darkness.

The grass turned to leaf-strewn earth beneath her feet. Then warm sand. Then pavement sleek with rain water. Wooden floorboards. Cold marble tiles.

She felt fingers brush her hand, but when she looked, there was nothing.

A figure appeared in the darkness ahead of her, standing as if looking down at someone in a bed, arm stretched out and fingers curled around something she couldn't see. She felt the ghost of those fingers against her own hand, and she grasped them tightly.

The figure drew a sharp breath.

"Eve," they whispered.

Theodore.

She threw herself at him.

The darkness around her shattered into a thousand pieces, raining down like shards of glass and slicing at her skin. She screamed, shielding her eyes against the glass, but kept moving towards him. Blood dripped from her skin and dotted the shards at her feet.

She felt pain everywhere—her chest, her eyes, her throat, her arms. Her head ached.

She clung to her brother's hand with all her strength.

A different sort of darkness came for her then. It was a bit like falling asleep.

twenty-two

Sinking down on the steps of the back porch, I balanced a bowl of cereal in my lap and stretched my bare legs out in front of me.

I watched Madeline run around the yard, snapping at honeybees and trampling over dandelions, the white tufts drifting into the air and clinging to her fur. I picked up one of the banana slices from atop my Cheerios and popped it into my mouth.

One of the bees landed on the step beside me, ambling across the white wood.

I lifted a spoonful of Cheerios to my mouth as it crawled along my jean shorts, clinging to the material with its fuzzy legs. I lightly shooed it away, and it flew over to a honeysuckle plant that was climbing along one of the porch support columns.

A bee landed on the sleeve of my t-shirt, and I brushed it off as I climbed from Eve's car.

Madeline barked, running in a circle around a large Southern oak tree and jumping against the trunk.

"Come on," Eve said, stomping through the overgrown grass in her heavy boots, her pale braid swinging behind her.

As I followed after her, Jack said, "Tannyn, watch out for that—"

"I see it," I replied, crushing the bramble thicket beneath my sneakers and stepping over it.

Then the building came into view in a clearing ahead, the small structure sagging slightly to one side and looking dejected amongst the tall grass.

119

"What is that?" I asked.

Eve walked over and pulled open the door, glancing over her shoulder at me. "It's a honey house," she said, grinning. "I was out for a run, and I found it. When Aunt Ceceli extended the property, this was on part of the land she bought."

"You run?" I asked, sounding surprised.

She shot me a dark look, and then thrust the door open wider. When she stalked inside, I followed after her. West propped the door open with a brick as I glanced around the small interior, shoving my hands into the front pockets of my sweatshirt. The shelves were lined with jars of dark honey, and there was a metal cylinder with a hand crank sitting in the corner.

I leaned against one of the walls, scraping at a stain on the wooden floorboards with the toe of my shoe. Theodore sank down onto the stool beside me.

Eve picked up a jar of honey, unscrewing the lid and dipping her finger in.

"Don't," I told her.

She popped the finger in her mouth and blinked at me. "What?" she asked. "It's still good. Honey doesn't go bad." She scooped up another glob on her finger and held it out to me. "Here. Try."

I shook my head, and she bopped me on the nose with her finger, leaving behind a streak of honey. I snarled through my teeth at her, swiping at my face with the back of my hand. "Dammit," I muttered. "I hate honey."

She was still smiling at me, and then slowly, so slowly, it slipped from her face. Her chest rose and fell with heavy breaths.

Then something in her expression shattered.

She snatched up a jar from the shelf beside her and flung it at the farthest wall. Glass rained onto the floor, and honey dripped down the rotted wall. "Shit!" she screamed. "Fuck!" She picked up another jar, and *another, smashing them against the wall. "Goddamn it!"*

Then she sunk to the ground, cradling her head in her hands.

Her body trembled as she crouched on the floor of the honey house, shards of glass glittering at her feet.

When I knelt beside her, I heard the sound of glass crunching underfoot as the boys slowly made their way outside to the cars.

I wrapped an arm around her shoulders, and tears gathered on her chin and dripped onto the floor as she squeezed her eyes closed against them. Her fingers knotted in her hair, and her body shuddered against mine.

"I shouldn't have lived," she whispered. "It's not fair. It's not fair.*"*

She turned her head, burying it against my chest.

"It's alright," I murmured, drawing my fingers through her hair. "I know."

"Tell me . . ." She drew in a shuddering breath. "Tell me that my parents would be proud of me, Tannyn. Tell me that I didn't just survive that crash for nothing."

"Eve." My voice caught in my throat. "The first time I saw you, I thought you were the most frightening girl I'd ever seen. And now . . . I don't know what the fuck I'd do without you. So whatever reason you survived . . . it sure as hell wasn't for nothing."

She choked out a laugh. "Well, that's the best damned confession if I've ever heard one. I love you, too, Tan."

There was a gentle knock at the door of the honey house, and I glanced over to see Theodore easing it open. Eve lifted her head, narrowing her eyes and wiping away the traces of tears on her cheeks with the heels of her hands.

"What?" she said.

Jack stepped around Theodore. "We brought you a present." He held out a metal baseball bat that he'd fetched from his Jeep.

A grin spread slowly across Eve's face. "For me?" she said. "You shouldn't have."

I glanced up as Madeline suddenly thrust her head into my lap, knocking the bowl of Cheerios from my lap and spilling them down the front of my pajama shorts. I jumped up with a startled cry, and she began greedily licking at the mess she'd made on the steps of the back porch.

"Honestly, Madeline," I grumbled as she panted happily up at me.

I picked up the bowl and spoon and took them into the kitchen, and I came back out a moment later with a wet paper towel and cleaned up the spilled milk and Cheerios.

Madeline followed me back inside, and I went upstairs and stripped out of my soaked pajamas.

I climbed into the shower and wiped myself down with a wash cloth, and then I worked my fingers through the tangles that had knotted my hair during the night. When I stepped from the shower, I wrung my damp hair out over the mat and wrapped a towel around myself.

As I changed into a pair of jean shorts and a plain white t-shirt in my room, I glimpsed a picture of the five of us—a murder of crows—sitting on my bedside table. It had been taken out at the Boathouse, and Jack, Theodore, and I were all crowding together on the couch. Eve had stretched out across us, her head in my lap, and West was sitting on the armrest by her feet. I smiled lightly, reaching out to touch the cool glass.

Then I shoved my phone into the back pocket of my shorts and slid my sunglasses onto my face.

Madeline was whining at the steps as I came back down the stairs, and she trotted after me to the front door. I took my keys down from the hook on the wall and ruffled the soft fur between her ears.

"I'll be back later," I told her. "I promise."

Then I slipped out the door and locked it behind me.

twenty-three

west

West Paek liked painting because it brought him a sense of control amongst the chaos that was life.

His back was slick with sweat, and his torso was covered with angry streaks of black and purple paint as he climbed down from his stepladder and admired the lightning that forked from the gray clouds on the wall of the Boathouse.

The world was quiet except for the sounds of the insects in the trees as he picked up a rag and wiped the paint from his hands.

Then he noticed the open book that was lying on the floor at his feet, and he tried to remember if it had been there the last time he'd come to the Boathouse.

He bent and picked it up, staring down at the page it had been left open to.

It read: "Heap not on this mound / Roses that she loved so well; / Why bewilder her with roses, / That she cannot see or smell? / She is happy where she lies / With the dust upon her eyes."

Except someone had crossed out the word *happy* and replaced it with *unhappy*.

The handwriting was Eve's, and as he flipped through the book, he noticed other notes scribbled along the margins and passages underlined in dark ink.

Something stirred in him as he traced his fingers over where she had written her name in the front of the book.

As always, he was struck suddenly by the thought that she was gone. It knocked the wind from his chest and nearly took his legs out from under him. *Gone.* It was such a permanent word.

He squeezed his eyes closed.

Since the moment he'd come into the world, his heart had been trapped in a cage of flesh and bone. When he was little, he'd scratched and clawed and beaten at the bars of it, and all he'd ended up with was bloody knuckles. And sometimes a black eye, if his father had been around.

He learned how to take everything that was thrown at him and stay silent.

Then he'd met Evelyn Shearwater, when he'd been walking down the side of the road in the rain and she'd pulled up alongside him in her car, shoving open the passenger door and telling him to get in. He'd missed the bus that day after two boys cornered him in the library bathroom. He was thankful they'd only left him with a split lip.

It had begun bleeding again when he climbed into the car, and Eve handed him a tissue.

It was there, in the dark interior of her car, his hair plastered to his face with rain water, that he'd broken down for the first time since he'd been seven years old and his father had left.

"I'm going to tell you a secret," Eve had whispered, taking his face in her hands and wiping the tears from his cheeks. "I'm the ugliest crier in the world. So if you think I'm judging you, I promise, I'm not." Then she'd smiled at him.

The next day in school, one of the boys had a broken nose. The other didn't show. When Eve invited West to sit with her at lunch, he'd noticed that she and the other blonde with her—a short, angry nightmare of a girl named Tannyn—both had bruised knuckles.

He'd never properly thanked them for that.

Now whenever he thought of those moments, he felt bile rise in his throat.

Because West had loved her, as all of the crows had.

The crows had loved Eve in the way that people loved music or thunder storms or fairytales with Happily Ever Afters. They loved her in the way that children loved plants with white flowers and pretty red berries because they were too young to know they were poisonous.

When he'd found out Eve was dead, he'd vomited into his mother's favorite vase.

Now, he rubbed at his eyes with the back of his hand. It came away dry. He crossed the front room of the Boathouse and slipped the book back onto the shelf against the one wall.

As he heard the front door creak open he glanced over his shoulder, and Tannyn paused on the threshold. She said, "Oh, sorry. I didn't realize you were here."

He was wearing his chest binder and a pair of cargo shorts, and he shrugged and reached for the t-shirt draped over the back of the couch. As Tannyn walked over to the mural on the wall and traced one of the crows beneath her fingers, he slipped the shirt over his head.

She looked at the mural, admiring it. "I just came to water the plants," she said, turning to face him. She smiled in a way that made her look sad, and she added, "I can give you a ride home, when I'm finished, if you want."

"Sure," he said. "Thanks."

twenty-four

The box was sitting on the front steps of our porch when I pulled into the driveway.

I put my car in park and climbed from the driver's seat, tucking back all of the lilac wisps that had come loose and hung like bits of dandelion fluff around my face. I went up the steps and crouched down in front of the box—which was about the size of a toaster and had my name printed on the front in Hollis's ridiculous chicken-scratch scrawl.

The return address was somewhere in Ireland, and as I tucked it beneath my arm, I pulled out my phone and dialed my older brother's number.

"Tannyn!" he chirped in my ear as he answered.

"Indoor voice," I told him, pulling open the front door and slipping inside. I dropped the box down on the island in the kitchen, and then walked over to the back door and let Madeline outside.

"Sorry," Hollis replied, his voice softening. But I knew he'd be shouting again in another minute. "My friends and I went out to a club. It's kind of loud." The noise in the background quieted to a murmur, and he said, "Alright. I'm in the bathroom. What's up?"

"You told me to call when your package came in." I pulled the pocket knife Theodore had given me from my back pocket and slit the tape along the top.

"Did you open it?"

"I am right now," I told him. I flicked open the flaps and pulled out an envelope that was printed with the word *Mom* in Hollis's handwriting. I frowned. "What's with the envelope?"

"Oh, I forgot about that," he said. "Just some post cards for mom. I figured I'd save on shipping and just send them both at the same time. Will you drop them off for me?"

"You mean, go visit her," I clarified for him.

"Yes, go visit her," he said.

I set the envelope on the counter and reached back into the box, pulling out an object wrapped heavily in bubble wrap. I turned it over in my hands, searching for the tape. "Jesus, Hol," I said. "Do you think you used enough bubble wrap?"

I could hear the grin in his voice as he told me, "I wanted to make sure it wouldn't break."

My fingernails scraped at the piece of tape, and I peeled the bubble wrap away to expose the object inside. The glass was cool in my hands as I held it up to the light, revealing that it wasn't black like I'd originally thought, but a dark purple. The bird was perched on a slender branch, its head tipped back to gaze at the sky.

"It's a crow," I said, startled.

"From Ireland's finest glass blowers," he told me proudly. "I had it custom made, and it was really expensive, so if you break it, I'll have to kick your ass."

"Hollis, you're shouting again."

"Sorry," he whispered. "But you like it, right?"

"Yes. It's beautiful."

I set the glass crow down on the counter and sunk down on a stool, leaning forward until my chin rested on the island as I admired it. Sunlight from the window caught in the smooth lines of the feathers.

"Good. I'm glad you like it."

"Thank you."

"So," he said, drawing out the word. "Will you bring that envelope to mom for me?"

"Only because you asked so nicely."

"Thanks, Tan." Madeline barked at the back door, batting her paws at the glass, and he said, "Is that Maddy? Tell her I miss her."

"I'll be sure to do that," I replied.

"I miss you, too."

I rolled my eyes. "Just not as much as the dog," I said. Then, "Hollis . . . when are you coming home?"

"Soon," he told me. "I promise."

I popped one of the air pockets on the bubble wrap. "Alright."

"How is dad doing?" he asked quietly.

I made to shrug, but then remembered he couldn't see it. As I stood up from my stool and walked over to the back door to let Madeline in, I said, "The same. He forgot my birthday again."

"Shit, Tannyn. I'm sorry."

"It's not your fault."

Madeline bounded into the house, slobbering on my hand as I bent to stroke the fur between her ears. I grimaced and wiped it off on my shorts.

"I wish I was there," Hollis replied.

"No, you don't." I walked back over to the island, popping more of the bubble wrap between my fingers. "It's a million degrees, and there's nothing to do. And I've already got . . ." I twisted my torso to gaze down at the red marks on the backs of my bare legs. "One, two, three . . . Seven mosquito bites."

My brother chuckled. "I really do miss you, Tan. More than the dog, I promise."

"I miss you, too."

"Do you think you can survive a few more weeks without me?"

128

"Maybe," I said, rocking back on my heels. "If you bring me back some chocolates from Belgium."

"Deal," he told me. "Alright, I gotta go. I love you."

"Love you, too."

There was a click, and I shut my phone off and dropped it down onto the counter.

I picked up the bubble wrap and tossed it onto the ground, climbing up onto the stool at the island. Then I jumped. The sound echoed through the house, and Madeline started, smacking her head against the wall.

"Hollis says hi," I told her.

She sneezed in response.

twenty-five

My mother didn't glance up as I sat down beside her, her gaze concentrated on the visiting room TV even though it was too far away to hear.

"Mom?" I said.

She continued to stare straight ahead, her eyes fixated on the people moving across the screen. Her hair was longer than the last time I'd seen her —which I guess was what happened when you didn't visit someone for months. She had the same light brown eyes as me, but her hair was dark and straight, her face skinny and hollow.

"Hi, mama," I whispered.

I reached out to take her hand, her fingers cold in mine, and she finally glanced over at me. I smiled and breathed in her scent of Dove soap and warm sugar.

There was no recognition in her eyes, and a moment later, she turned back to the TV.

Her foot was tap-tap-tapping on the linoleum floor, her plain white shoes making no sound.

"I have something for you," I told her, reaching into the bag at my feet and pulling out an envelope. "Well, it's technically from Hollis."

I flipped open the envelope and pulled out the stack of postcards, shifting in my seat so that she could see them. She looked down, staring at them blankly as I sifted through them—*Greetings from Ireland*, the first one read. The next featured a castle perched on the edge of a cliff. There was another from Scotland, of the Calanais Standing Stones, and two from England.

My heart swelled at how much I missed my brother.

But if I told him that, if I admitted how empty the house felt without him there, he'd fly home without a second thought. And I couldn't do that to him. Not when I heard how excited he was on his phone calls or saw his face in the pictures he sent me weekly.

I looked back up at my mother, forcing a smile that didn't reach my eyes.

"He'll be home soon," I said aloud, though I was speaking mostly to myself. I set the envelope of postcards down on the end table beside her. "Just a few more weeks."

My mother blinked at me—so slowly.

"It's so hard without you both," I whispered.

My mother turned back to the TV, and I watched her foot tapping away on the floor. There was something unsettling about the movement—like a nervous tick, not really intended.

"I went to New Orleans the other day, to that antique store where the woman used to read your cards," I told her. "She read my bones." I stared at a scuff mark on my mother's left shoe. "She said I'm going to die."

A couple on the TV was dancing, and I watched my mother's eyes follow the movements.

"Mama." I squeezed her hand in mine. "I'm sorry."

A commotion at the other end of the room made me lift my head.

I looked over my shoulder to see a patient struggling with two nurses before a third appeared with a needle. There was the sound of tennis shoes scuffling on the linoleum floor, and one of the nurses was shouting instructions. Then the patient went limp in their arms, and someone turned up the volume on the TV.

I watched as the two nurses carried the patient past the main room and down another hallway.

When I turned back to my mother, her hands were balled into fists on her lap.

She began to hum "Downtown" by Petula Clark beneath her breath, so softly that I almost didn't hear her. If I hadn't heard her do it a thousand times before, I would have been sure I was imagining it.

"Mama?" I whispered.

I swung into the kitchen, my sneakers squeaking on the tiled floor. "Mom?"

"What is it, honey?" she asked, turning from where she stood at the island. She had a cup of coffee in her hands, and she was still dressed in her pajamas.

A flash of metal.

My fingers coming away stained with red.

My mother sobbing.

I balled my fingers into the fabric of my t-shirt until my knuckles showed white. I didn't realize that I'd been biting down on my bottom lip until I tasted blood on my tongue.

The tapping of my mother's foot had grown quicker, more urgent, and another patient had begun crying in the corner.

And I hated it.

This wasn't my mother. This was no one. A corpse. An empty shell.

"Alright, settle down everyone," one of the nurses said in a soothing tone. "It's okay."

The scar on my collarbone throbbed beneath my t-shirt, and my throat grew tight. I swallowed, reminding myself to breathe.

In through the nose, out through the mouth.

A hand fell on my shoulder, and a moment later, I realized someone had spoken to me.

In, out.

a girl called murder

I glanced up at the nurse standing over me as she said for a second time, "Are you alright, honey?"

"What is it, honey?"

I un-balled my fists from my shirt and rose to my feet. "I'm sorry," I said, though I wasn't sure if she'd even heard me. I was afraid that my legs were going to give out beneath me. "I need to go."

My mother lifted her head, staring up at me.

I snatched up my bag from the floor, clutching it to my chest as I backed from the room.

"I'm sorry," I said again.

Then I turned and fled down the hallway.

As I walked across the parking lot of the hospital, I pulled my phone from the pocket of my shorts and dialed Theodore.

He picked up on the second ring. "Hello?"

I unlocked my car and slid into the driver's seat, turning up the air conditioning. "Theodore?" I said, my voice trembling. "Where are you?"

The tone of his voice immediately changed. "I'm at home. What's the matter? Are you alright?"

"I'm not—I wasn't—I don't know." I pushed my fingers through my hair, knotting them into the strands. I closed my eyes. "Can I come over?"

"Where are you? Do you need me to pick you up?" I heard the jingling of his car keys before I'd even answered.

"No," I replied. "No, I'm on my way. I just . . . I can't go home right now."

"Alright, babe. I'll be here."

I opened my eyes, tapping my fingers on my thigh. My mouth still tasted like copper from where I'd bitten my tongue. "Theodore?" I asked. "Is it too late to throw together a party?"

"When?"

"Tonight."

I heard the hesitation in his voice as he asked, "Are you sure?"

"I just . . . I need the distraction. Please."

He was silent for a moment. Then he said, "I'll see what I can do."

twenty-six

The wine bottle in my hands was nearly empty, the contents sloshing against the glass as I pounded down the stairs of the hay loft in the Shearwater's barn.

I couldn't remember where I'd gotten the wine—only that I'd finished my rum and coke, and someone had pressed the bottle into my hands, and it had tasted like rich, dark berries.

The music pounded in time to my heartbeat, so that I could no longer tell one from the other. I took a long drink straight from the bottle of wine and danced in a circle, my bare feet kicking up dirt and hay. I couldn't remember where I'd left my shoes, but at that moment, it didn't matter.

"There you are."

I glanced over my shoulder to see Theodore, and he was both angry and concerned and beautiful all at once. I lifted the bottle to my lips and took another swig.

"I've been looking for you everywhere," he said, shouting over the music.

"I doubt you looked *everywhere*," I replied.

He followed me as I walked through the tangle of people that were moving about the barn. Someone bumped into me, and wine spilled from the bottle. I danced out of the way to avoid the dark red stain on the wooden floor.

"Are you having fun?" I asked. My voice was high and giggly.

"I'd be having fun if I wasn't busy worrying about you."

"Why? I'm fine. I'm *fantastic*," I told him. I grabbed his hand and did a small twirl under his arm. I collided with his side and stumbled, and he wrapped an arm around my waist so I didn't go tumbling to the floor. A laugh burst from my lips. "See? Isn't this fun?"

"Tannyn."

I mimicked his scowl and deepened my voice. "Theodore."

"Look at me."

I went up onto my toes and leaned towards him, widening my eyes as far as they would go. "I'm looking."

He took my face in his hands, and his palms were warm and calloused against the bare skin of my cheeks. I blinked at him. "Tell me what's wrong."

His words were like a shock of ice water thrown in my face. I dropped back down to the ground and pulled myself from his grip. I brought the bottle of wine to my lips and finished it off, dark juice dribbling down my chin and onto my shirt. I swiped the back of my hand across my mouth.

"I told you, I'm fine." But my voice was slurred and uncertain.

"We don't keep secrets from each other," Theodore said, throwing my own words back at me. "Right?"

I snorted and rolled my eyes. "Yeah. Right."

"What's that supposed to mean?"

"All you do is keep secrets," I snapped, swatting strands of loose hair from my face. I looked down at my fingers, sticky from wine. Before Theodore could say anything, I told him, "It's my fault, you know. I've never told anyone—but it's my fault."

"What are you talking about?" Theodore asked.

His face blurred in and out of focus, and I had to close my eyes because my temples began to throb. "My mom," I replied, rubbing at my forehead with the heel of my head. "It's my fault."

"That's not—"

"You weren't there," I said, and my voice came out quiet, so quiet. "You don't know."

"But I know you, Tannyn. I know—"

"No," I said. "You don't. You just know what everyone else does. That my mom tried to kill me and I give people nightmares and—"

"And that you're afraid of water," he interrupted.

My eyes went wide. I'd never told him that.

He continued, "You drink black coffee because sugar makes your anxiety worse. You cried reading *Frankenstein* and refuse to watch the movies now because of how they portray the monster. You put Old Bay on your popcorn. You haven't touched bacon since you watched *Okja*. If someone asks your favorite color, you say black, but it's really yellow. Light yellow, like honeysuckle or banana ice cream. Should I go on?"

I shook my head.

"I know you, Tannyn Lourdes Carter."

He reached a hand towards me, and I started, dropping the wine bottle. I jumped back in surprise as it shattered into a thousand pieces on the floor.

I stared down at the jagged shards that sparkled in the lantern light, beaded with droplets of dark red wine like blood.

It was my fault. I was always breaking things.

I squeezed my eyes closed.

"I need another drink," I muttered aloud to no one in particular.

Theodore followed as I stumbled towards the makeshift bar that someone had set up against the far wall. When he realized where I was headed, he stepped in front of me, blocking the way.

I tipped my head back to glare up at him. "Now neither of us is having fun," I told him.

"You're going to make yourself sick."

"So? That's not your problem." When he still didn't move out of the way, I grumbled, "Fine. Whatever you say, mom."

I spotted Jack in the corner of the barn, talking to a pretty boy from the baseball team, but I marched over and took his hand and dragged him away despite his protests.

I reached up to pull the elastic from my hair and ran my hands through the tangled lilac strands as they drifted down around me. My shirt clung to my chest with sweat, and my face was flushed from alcohol and heat and excitement. I let the music take hold of my body.

Jack put his hands on my waist, moving with me, and I grinned at him as the music thrummed through my bones. His skin glistened with sweat in the lantern light, and I thought if only I'd met him before Theodore, if only things had turned out differently . . .

I grabbed Jack by the collar of his shirt and kissed him.

I'd kissed Jack before, but never like this.

I kissed him like I was in love, fingers tangled in his collar, his hands in my hair, our breaths becoming one.

Then Jack's hands were at my hips, and I was sitting on top of a bale of hay, and my legs were wrapped around his waist, and he was laughing breathlessly as he kissed my mouth and neck and collarbone.

I shuddered, dizzy from wine and the feel of his mouth on my skin.

I could feel Theodore watching us, and I hoped it hurt him the way it hurt me to see him kissing other girls.

We were kissing, kissing, kissing, and then I tasted salt water on my lips

It took me a moment to realize I was crying as Jack pulled back to look at me. He cradled my face in his hands, tears dripping silently down my cheeks, and I smiled at him though it didn't reach my eyes.

"I'm sorry," I whispered, choking on the words.

It seemed like I was always apologizing.

"I'm going to go get some air," I told him, ignoring the tears that stained my cheeks.

He said nothing as I pushed past him, didn't follow me as I passed through the large double doors of the barn.

Only when I was outside, out of sight, did I reach up and swipe at my cheeks with the back of my hand. Then I lifted my head to the sky and closed my eyes, feeling the wind in my hair. I breathed through my nose and my shoulders trembled.

I shoved my hands into the pockets on my shorts and walked to the edge of the barn and turned the corner. The air smelled like smoke and dry, cracked earth, and I hated the way it tasted on my lips.

The tall grass brushed my ankles, and I stumbled over fallen branches and discarded plastic cups. The ground beneath my feet hummed in time with the music.

By then I stopped crying, and my eyes were heavy and rimmed with red. I touched a hand to my puffy cheeks, fingers brushing over the scar there.

I saw a flash of blonde hair move between the trees, and I thought, *Eve?* But then I blinked and they were gone. Too much wine—or maybe I was just crazy.

The quiet, angry, crazy one.

I laughed out loud, but there was no humor in it.

A bird in the branches of the trees mimicked the sound, a harsh cawing laugh—I thought it might have been a crow.

I leaned back against the barn, the splintered wood poking me through my shirt.

I was staring up at the stars through the trees when I realized someone was beside me.

Shadows fell across the boy's face, and I had to squint to make out his features in the darkness. He wasn't anyone I recognized, but there were plenty of people there that I didn't know.

"You know," he said. "You really shouldn't be out here by yourself."

"Thanks for the tip," I said. I made to move around him, but his arm shot out and braced itself against the side of the barn, blocking the way. I glared at him. "Can I help you?"

"I know you," he said. "You're one of those damned crows."

I arched a brow. "Am I?"

"The one everyone's afraid of," he added. "But you're not so frightening."

"You know what they say," I replied. "Can't judge a book by its cover."

The corner of his lip turned up in a grin that made my skin crawl. "Maybe, maybe not. So what *are* you doing out here by yourself, little crow?"

"Hosting a cooking show," I snapped. "What does it look like I'm doing? Trying to get some damned peace and quiet." I shot him a look that said, *Or at least I* was.

He chuckled, and before I had time to react, he was closer, his hand brushing the bare skin of my waist where my shirt had bunched up.

I took a step back, and his grin widened.

"What's the matter, little crow? Are you scared?"

I snorted. "Of you? Not likely."

He dipped his head close enough that I smelled the stale beer that lingered on his lips. "That's too bad," he murmured. "Must be a crow thing. Your friend wasn't afraid of me either."

I stopped breathing.

"What did they call her? The Queen of Crows?" He chuckled again to himself. "She was always causing trouble. Never knew when to mind her own damned business."

What the fuck did he just say about Eve?

I meant to say it out loud, but the only word I could form at the moment was, "What?"

"That bitch is always sticking her nose where it doesn't belong." He paused. "Sorry. *Was* always sticking her nose where it didn't belong."

My hands curled into fists at my sides, nails digging into my skin.

He brushed his hand across my cheekbone, and I resisted the urge to shudder at the contact. "Still, it's too bad what happened to her."

My voice was barely a whisper as I demanded, "What do you know about that?"

The boy lifted his head, his brows drawing together in confusion. "Nothing. Just what I heard around town." Then the corner of his mouth lifted in a smirk, and he added, "They say the sick bastard cut out her heart. But do you want to know what I think?"

His hands fell to my hips, fingers digging into my skin as he pulled me towards him.

"I don't think she had a heart to begin with," he whispered.

Something snapped within me.

I brought my knee up between his legs, and he grunted, falling back a step. I grabbed a handful of his hair as he doubled over, and my fist slammed into the side of his face. Blood splattered from his lips onto the side of the barn.

He crumpled to the ground, and I fell on top of him, straddling his torso as my fist met flesh and bone again and again until I could no longer feel the pain in my knuckles.

He threw up his arms, blocking his face, and I felt a sharp pain as

141

his elbow connected with my temple. Something warm trickled down the side of my face from where my skin had broken open along my brow.

The boy took advantage of my shock and bucked me off, but before he had the chance to climb to his feet, I scrambled up and kicked him hard in the ribs. He crumbled around my foot, crying out, and then I was on him again.

"Must be a crow thing. Your friend wasn't afraid of me either."

I smashed my fist into his nose with a satisfying crunch. My knuckles split but I didn't feel it. I didn't feel anything.

"I don't think she had a heart to begin with."

His fear tasted like cold metal and pieces of black peppercorn between my teeth.

Someone shouted my name.

Then an arm looped around my waist, and I was lifted from the ground and away from the crumpled, bloody mess that was once a boy. He let out a gurgled moan, rolling onto his side and clutching at his face.

"Tannyn," Jack said. "*Stop.*"

He set me on my feet, but then he grabbed me again as I lunged for the boy.

"*En serio*? Christ, Tannyn."

The world suddenly went upside-down, and my stomach caved against bone. It took me a second to realize that Jack had thrown me over his shoulder. I spotted two more figures standing over the boy.

"What the hell?" I snarled.

Jack ignored me, clamping his hands down on my legs to keep me from kicking him in the face. "I'm going to take her back to the house," he told Theodore and West.

I pounded my fists against his back. "You're not taking anywhere. Put me *down*."

142

"Tannyn, this is not the time," Jack snapped, and his tone startled me so much that I went still.

I knotted my fingers into the back of his t-shirt as tears pricked in the corners of my eyes. Images of my mother and Eve swirled around in my mind, and I dug my fingernails into my palms, focusing on the pain. "It's not my fault," I said, my voice a whisper.

For the second time that night, I began to cry.

Theodore's eyes slid to me, narrowing to slits, as West crouched beside the bloodied boy in the dirt, poking him in the side with a stick.

Jack sighed beneath me. "I know," he said. "It's alright."

twenty-seven

Jack tossed me down on the bed in the Shearwater's guest room, and I groaned as my head thumped against the pillow.

"I hate you," I growled, clenching the covers in my fists.

"You'd hate me more if I let you do something you'd regret in the morning," he told me.

"I wouldn't have—"

I stopped suddenly as a wave of nausea swept over me, and then I clambered from the bed and stumbled into the bathroom, falling down in front of the toilet. As I emptied the contents of my stomach, I heard footsteps beside me, and then Jack swept my hair back from my face.

"Fuck," I muttered, lines of spit clinging to my lips.

He dug a wash cloth from the cabinets and wet it beneath the faucet, using it to clean my face as I glared miserably at the tiles beneath me.

Then he closed the lid of the toilet and helped me to my feet to sit on top of it. "Stay here," he told me.

He left, and I stared down at the chipped black polish on my toenails.

When he returned, he was holding a bottle of peroxide and a roll of gauze.

I winced, sucking in a breath through my teeth, as he dabbed my split knuckles and the cut on my brow with a cotton ball soaked in peroxide. He bandaged my hand, and my gaze drifted from his long, tan fingers to the freckles along his cheeks while he worked. I tried to remember the last time I'd ever looked at him this closely.

"I don't think you need stitches," he said, almost to himself, brushing my hair back from my face to examine the cut along my brow. "It's not that deep."

Then he helped me to my feet again, and I clung to him as he led me back out into the bedroom. I climbed beneath the covers and laid against the pillows, and my knuckles ached as I curled my hands against my chest.

"Why couldn't I have fallen in love with you instead?" I murmured, staring up at Jack.

A smile touched his lips, and he bent down to press a kiss to my forehead. "*Buenas noches, mami.*"

He walked to the bedroom door and reached for the lights, but his fingers paused above the switch. He glanced back over his shoulder at me, tipping his head to the side and giving me that ridiculous lopsided smile.

"It never would have worked between us, if that's any consolation," he told me.

"Why's that?"

"I'm much too afraid of you." Then he winked and flicked off the lights, closing the door behind him as he left. I smiled lightly to myself as I pulled the covers around me.

The moment I closed my eyes, I was asleep.

In my dream, I wandered through a large ballroom, past men and women with their faces hidden behind intricate masks.

Light danced off the crystal chandelier that hung from the ceiling, and masked servants slipped between the couples, holding trays laden with goblets of red wine over their heads. The music that drifted around me was low and melancholy, the instruments crying out like wounded animals.

A man in a tailored suit stopped in front of me and bowed deeply, extending a gloved hand. "Would you like to dance?" he asked. Dark eyes glittered behind his velvet mask.

The words sent a chill down my spine, and I staggered back a step, tripping over the long, wine-colored skirts of my dress. I collided with something solid, and gentle hands reached out to steady me. I glanced over my shoulder to meet a pair of gray eyes that stared out at me from behind a mask carved from ivory and gold. It consumed the girl's entire face, but I knew what her voice would sound like before she even spoke.

"No," the girl told the man. "She would not."

The man gave another bow and straightened, and then his back was to us as he wove his way through the crowd and disappeared.

The hands slipped from my arm, and I turned to face Eve.

She was dressed in the same black gown she'd worn to prom, but her hair was pulled back from her face and hung over her shoulder in a tangle of pale blonde curls. A crown of gold circled her head, crafted to look like the wings of a great bird and set with pearls and stones of black onyx.

She took me gently by the elbow and steered me towards the glass doors of the room that led out onto the balcony. "You shouldn't be here," she whispered fiercely.

As we stepped out into the cool night air, a breeze drifted through the loose waves of my lilac hair. Eve's own hair looked like white-gold in the moonlight that shone down through the clouds.

She stopped and turned to face me. "Have you seen my brother?" she asked.

I shook my head.

She walked over to a cluster of dark red climbing roses that were clinging to the railing of the balcony. She plucked one free and twirled it between her fingers. She said, "Heap not on this mound / Roses that she loved so well; / Why bewilder her with roses, / That she cannot see or smell? / She is happy where she lies / With the dust upon her eyes."

The rose crumbled and blackened like ashes, and as they drifted from her fingers and landed at her feet, I followed them with my eyes.

"Eve?" I said.

She turned her head to peer out at me from behind her mask. "Yes?"

"What are you doing here?"

She touched a hand to her pale throat, curling her fingers around it. That was when I noticed the dark purple bruises that were scattered across her skin. "I came for the party," she told me.

"What happened to you?"

"*He* killed me," she said, her eyes flickering over my shoulder and through the glass doors.

I followed her gaze inside to the man who'd asked me to dance. He was standing across the dance floor by a table piled high with food, and his features were blurred, as if I were looking through a camera that hadn't quite focused. He smiled at me from beneath his mask and placed his hand against his chest, bowing. Then a servant passed in front of him, and he was gone.

I looked back at Eve. "Who is he?"

"He's killed me before, you know," she said.

"What are you talking about?"

Then her body jerked, as if someone had struck her. She stumbled backwards and clutched the railing behind her as she began gasping for air. Her eyes grew wide with fear, darting to my face.

"Eve?" I said.

Her legs gave out beneath her, and she collapsed to the ground. Her hair fanned out along the stone like a pale halo, her chest shuddering as she struggled to breathe. I dropped to my knees beside her with a startled cry.

"*Eve?*"

She was suddenly still.

Her hand dropped limply to her side, and I grabbed her shoulder in my hand, shaking her. I pressed my fingers against her neck, searching desperately for a pulse that was no longer there.

I reached out and undid the ribbons that held her mask in place.

It fell away, clattering against the stone, and dark, gaunt sockets stared up at me where her eyes should have been.

I screamed and fell backwards, my skirts becoming tangled around my legs. My hands fluttered to my mouth as my own breath caught in my throat, and I thought I might be sick. My chest heaved from the effort to draw in air.

A shadow fell over me, and I looked up into the velvet mask of the man from earlier.

The man who'd killed her.

He extended a hand down to me. "Would you like to dance?" he asked.

I clambered to my feet and ran to the railing, vomiting over the side. The man followed, pulling my hair from my face as my stomach emptied itself into the bushes below. When I'd finished, the man produced a crisp white handkerchief from his pocket and offered it to me. I reluctantly accepted it, crumpling it in my fist as I swallowed thickly.

"What did you do to her?" I whispered, my voice hoarse.

The man glanced over his shoulder at Eve. "Her?" He turned back to me, his teeth reflecting the moonlight as he smiled again. "She was already dead when I got here."

twenty-eight

eve

Bright light blossomed ahead of her. She lifted a hand to shield her eyes.

"Evelyn?" a voice echoed. "Can you hear me?"

The light grew until it was all around her, and when she squeezed her eyes closed, it was there, as well, glowing against the back of her eyelids.

Then she saw nothing.

Felt nothing.

Became

nothing.

She was lying down in a bed, the sheets scratching against her skin.

Her body was heavy; someone had replaced her muscles with cement. She opened her mouth to tell someone, anyone, but her tongue was also cement. It lay against the bottom of her mouth like a dead fish. She swallowed, the movement slow and aching.

Someone was saying her name. She opened her eyes to a white light shining in her face—or at least, her right eye. The left refused to obey, stuck in the darkness.

A scream clawed its way from her throat.

twenty-nine

I crept downstairs to the kitchen, the floorboards creaking beneath my bare feet.

I went up on my toes to take down a glass from the cabinet and filled it with water from the filter on the fridge. I gulped it down, washing away the acrid taste that lingered at the back of my throat, and then fished around for a bottle of aspirin. I swallowed two pills as I leaned against the island.

I started at a noise from the front of the house, and my body tensed.

Glancing over my shoulder, I set the glass down on the counter and straightened up.

I moved silently through the kitchen, trailing my hand along the wall in the dark, and I was already at the end of the hall when the thought of grabbing a knife occurred to me. But I kept moving, crossing through the dining room to the front door.

Someone had left it open, and I stopped breathing as I stepped over the threshold, peering outside onto the porch.

A figure shifted in the darkness, and I nearly screamed.

Then a familiar voice said, "Tannyn?"

I stepped out onto the porch, folding my arms over my chest. I squinted to make out Theodore where he was sitting against one of the support columns. "Christ. You scared the shit out of me."

He smirked lightly, tipping his head back. "That's a first," he said, his words slurred.

That was when I noticed the mason jar of clear liquid beside him.

"Tell me that isn't the Suttons' moonshine," I said. "I'm going to kill those boys."

But I sat down beside him and picked up the mason jar. The moonshine burned all the way down my throat. "Christ," I sputtered, wiping the back of my hand across my mouth. "That's awful. I'm really going to kill them. What are you doing out here?"

He ignored the question—or maybe he hadn't even realized I'd asked one. "That looks bad," he said, wincing and reaching for the cut on my brow, but not quite touching it. He frowned.

"You should've seen the other guy," I muttered.

"I had someone take him to the hospital," he told me. "He won't press charges, don't worry." He waved a hand through the air, in a way that was meant to seem dismissive, but instead resembled a drunk Queen of England.

I snorted a laugh in spite of myself. "I wasn't worried, but thank you."

He picked up the mason jar and brought it to his lips, but I snatched it from his hand. He glanced down, his brows drawing together. "That wasn't nice."

I set the bottle out of his reach and drew my legs up to my chest. "Don't you know? I'm not a nice girl."

"I think you're nice. Sometimes. When you want to be."

"Thanks. I think you're nice sometimes, too," I said.

"And you're so pretty." He tipped his head to the side, and then reached out to run his fingers clumsily through my hair. "Did you know that? I wish you knew how pretty you are."

I smiled softly at him. "You're pretty too, Theodore."

"I mean it."

"I know you do." I leaned my head against his shoulder, and he went still beneath me. I was afraid that he might have stopped breathing. "Theodore?" I whispered after a moment.

"Hmm," he mumbled.

"What are you doing out here?"

"I didn't get to enjoy the party earlier," he replied. "Because I was too busy worrying about *you*." He sighed heavily. "So now I'm making up for it."

"I'm sorry."

"You should be."

I looked down at the bandages on my knuckles, slowly clenching and un-clenching my fist and gritting my teeth at the sharp pain. "Unfortunately, it seems like neither of us had much fun at the party."

"Fortunately, the night is still young."

I laughed. "Unfortunately, it's four in the morning."

"Fortunately . . . *fuck*. I got nothing," he mumbled. He pushed his fingers through his hair. "You win."

"What do I win?"

"Whatever you want," he told me. "The moon. A million red roses. A unicorn."

I sucked my bottom lip into my mouth. "How about a secret?"

Theodore was silent for a moment. Then he said, "I'll tell you a secret if you tell me something you're afraid of."

"Okay."

"I wish it had been me instead of Eve. She's so much better than me. She cared about so many people—people she didn't even know. She didn't deserve to die."

I wrapped my arms around my legs, feeling as if someone had reached into my chest and squeezed my heart between their fingers. "No one deserves to die."

152

He shook his head. "The bastard who killed her deserves to die."

I nestled my head against his shoulder. "I'm afraid of water because I almost drowned when I was little," I told him   softly. "The current was strong. Looking back, I'm grateful because that means there weren't any gators in the water. At the time, though . . . I thought I was going to die. Hollis was the one who jumped in and saved me."

He was silent, and I stared out at the front yard and watched the fireflies blink in and out of existence in the darkness. I listened to the cicadas as they sang in the trees.

Then he said, "Everyone thinks you're so fearless, that you're not afraid of anything." He reached out, taking my hand and running his fingers gently over the bandages on my knuckles. "The Ten of Crows, the one with the thing for nightmares." He dropped his hand back to his side. "But you've got them worse than anyone, don't you? And it scares the hell out of you that someone might figure that out."

He reached down, taking my hand and curling his fingers around mine, and I felt his shoulders rise and fall with his breaths. I closed my eyes, leaning into him.

"What did you mean earlier," he said, "that it was your fault what happened to your mom?"

I stiffened. "Nothing," I replied, and I could hear the lie in my voice. "That was the wine talking."

He hesitated before speaking again. "If Jack asked, would you tell him?"

"No," I said. "I've never told anyone. Not Eve, or Hollis. Not even my dad."

"I'm sorry."

"I know," I whispered. "Me, too."

A firefly landed on the edge of my sleeve, and I watched it light up in the darkness, flickering in and out. I reached a hand towards it, trying to coax it onto my fingers, but it flew off into the night sky.

I curled my hand back towards my chest.

"Theodore," I said. "You can kiss me now, if you want to."

He turned his head towards me, his breath tickling my skin. He kissed my temple lightly and wrapped his other arm around me, tucking me against his side. His head rested against mine, and the scent of whiskey on his lips made tingles spread throughout my body.

"Will you do something for me?" he said, his voice soft.

I nodded.

"That woman said you were going to die before the next full moon," he replied. "Just do me a favor and don't, okay?"

The corners of my lips tilted up, and I tightened my fingers around his. "I'll try my best."

I woke to bright sunlight against the back of my eyelids.

I groaned and rolled over onto my side—and promptly elbowed Theodore in the face.

He shouted a curse and clamped a hand over his nose. There was a loud *thud* as he fell over the side of the couch and landed on his back on the living room floor.

I winced and peered over the edge of the couch. He was staring up at the ceiling, his face contorted in pain.

"Ow," he muttered.

"Sorry," I stage-whispered.

Theodore sat up slowly, rubbing a hand over his face. Strands of his pale blonde hair were sticking straight up into the air. He reminded me of a rumpled baby chick. "What time is it?"

"How should I know?"

154

I slid my legs from the couch and stood up, stretching my arms over my head. A choked sound left Theodore's mouth, and I glanced over at him in alarm. His face had turned slightly pink. It was a moment before I realized I was naked from the waist down save for a lacy black thong.

I dove for the blanket draped over the armrest of the couch and scrambled to wrap it around myself. But not before I also noticed that I was wearing one of Theodore's t-shirts.

"What the hell happened last night?" Theodore asked.

My eyes widened as the memories came rushing back to me. *Theodore in the darkness, sitting against one of the support columns of the porch. "I'll tell you a secret if you tell me something you're afraid of." The fireflies glowing against the night sky. Theodore's breath tickling my skin as he kissed my temple. "Will you do something for me?" Theodore leaning against me as I helped him inside . . .*

I snatched up a pillow from the end of the couch and hurled it at Theodore's head. "You threw up on me, you asshole!"

He threw up his hands to shield himself, and the pillow landed in his lap. "I'm sor—" he began, but was cut off as the second pillow hit him square in the face. "Will you stop that?" he snapped as I picked up a third pillow. "My head is already killing me."

"I'm naked, and I smell like vomit!" I hissed.

He rolled his eyes. "I would hardly call that naked."

I raised the pillow over my head.

"Alright, alright," he said, holding his hands up in surrender. "I'm sorry."

I dropped the pillow to the floor and clutched the blanket around me closed with both hands. "Where are my clothes?"

Jack's voice came from the doorway to the living room.

"I think I saw them in the laundry room. Look's like Nettie found

155

them and washed them for you," he said. I glanced over at him, and he tossed me a grin. "Breakfast is ready, by the way. We ate all the bacon though. *Lo siento*."

"How long have you been standing there?" I demanded.

"If you're asking because you're worried I saw your ass, then I just got here."

I wished I still had the pillow in my hand because I would have chucked it at his head. Instead, I shouldered past him and walked to the laundry room.

My clothes were stacked in a neat pile on top of the dryer. I let the blanket fall from around my shoulders and pulled off Theodore's shirt, tossing it into the basket of dirty laundry. I slipped back into my shorts and shirt from the night before. They smelled like ocean detergent.

I found the others back in the kitchen, gathered around the breakfast nook, which had been piled high with plates of scrambled eggs and toast and bowls of fruit. I made a mental note to tell Nettie how much I loved her.

I poured myself a cup of coffee and sunk down on the chair beside West. I curled my legs up beside me, piling my plate with toast and chunks of honeydew and cantaloupe.

Theodore poured himself a glass of orange juice and took a bottle of aspirin down from the cabinet by the fright, tossing two pills into his mouth.

"How long have you been up?" I asked Jack.

"I got up at ten because I smelled someone cooking, and then West came down about a half hour later. We thought about waking you, but you looked so comfortable."

I kicked him under the table.

"Ow!"

I speared a piece of honeydew on the end of my fork and smiled innocently.

"How's your hand?" West asked, looking down at the bandages on my knuckles. His brows were drawn together with concern.

I gently flexed my fingers, repressing a wince at the pain. "Still working."

"So," Theodore said. "What are the plans for—"

He stopped at the sound of footsteps on the stairs. I glanced over my shoulder towards the doorway of the kitchen.

"Theodore?" a girl's voice called.

I narrowed my eyes and glanced at Theodore. "Who is that?"

A minute later, a girl came down the stairs and walked into the kitchen. She had messy copper-colored hair, and long, willowy legs that went on for miles. There was a dark bruise on her neck, but that wasn't why I couldn't stop staring. She was wearing a pair of Eve's pajamas.

Her eyes widened as they fell on the four of us around the breakfast nook. "Oh."

"Shit," Theodore said.

"I'm sorry," the girl said, sounding genuine. "I didn't realize . . ." She trailed off, her eyes drifting from me to Theodore. "I woke up, and you weren't there, so I thought . . . I'm sorry."

I felt Jack and West staring at me, gauging my reaction.

I calmly set down my fork and climbed to my feet. "I just remembered," I said to no one in particular, "I have somewhere else to be right now."

The girl's stepped to the side as I went past her out of the kitchen and up the stairs. I'd left my wallet and phone in the guest room, and I gathered them now from the bedside table and stuffed them into the back pocket of my shorts.

I was searching for my keys when the door opened and Theodore slipped into the room.

"Tannyn," he said.

I ignored him, clambering down on my hands and knees and pushing aside the skirt of the bed to peer beneath it.

"What are you doing?" he asked.

"I'm looking for my keys," I told him. I stood up, adjusting my shorts, and began checking the drawers on the bedside table.

"Where are you going?"

"Home," I replied. "Does your friend need a ride?"

"She's not my friend."

"Well, that's not very nice."

"I'm sorry," he said. "I don't know what else to say. Last night, after you . . . Jack was taking you back to the house, and I just . . . I don't know what I was thinking."

I whirled on him. "You think that's what I'm upset about?"

"I don't know what else it could be."

My voice caught in my throat. "How could you let her wear Eve's clothes?" I whispered.

He looked as if I'd struck him. "I don't—I didn't. She must have found them and just put them on," he said.

I turned back to the bed, jerking back the covers as I searched for the keys. Tears gathered in the corners of my eyes. "It doesn't matter."

I spotted my keys on the floor of the bathroom, where I must've dropped them the night before when I'd gotten sick. I snatched them up in my hands, and Theodore followed me as I stalked from the room.

"If it didn't matter, you wouldn't be so upset."

I pretended not to hear him.

"Tannyn, I'm sorry about the pajamas. I'll get them back."

I jerked to a stop and turned to face him. Tears spilled over my eyes, and I hated them. "It's not just the pajamas!" I yelled. "It's the jealousy and the lies and the nightmares. I just have enough on my plate without piling on your problems."

"When have I ever lied to you?"

"I don't want to play this game, Theodore. Withholding the truth is still lying."

"What are you talking about?"

"I'm talking about the night when Jude found Eve on the side of the road."

His eyes widened, and his voice dropped. "What did he tell you?"

"Nothing," I snarled. "But I guess you two have that in common."

"Tannyn, I—"

"*Tell me what happened.*"

His mouth opened and closed. He pressed his lips together into a thin line.

"No secrets," I said mockingly. "Right?"

I turned my back on him and stepped into the foyer.

My fingers were trembling as I sorted through my keys for the one to my car, and it took me longer than it should have to find it. I grabbed the handle of the front door and wrenched it open. "Tell Nettie I said thanks for breakfast," I mumbled.

A hand closed around my wrist. "Wait—"

I tore my arm from Theodore's grip and glared up at him through the tears in my eyes. "I'm sorry I've caused you so much trouble," I told him. "That won't be a problem anymore."

I slammed the door shut behind me as I left the house.

thirty

theo

After Theodore had driven Amelia home, he smashed a vase from the living room mantel against the hardwood floor.

He stepped over the bits of jagged blue and white porcelain, fisting his hands in his hair and stalking outside into the heat. He crouched down on the back porch, staring down at a colony of ants that marched along the cement.

He squeezed his eyes closed, but he could still see Tannyn's expression, the tears that had glistened against her light brown eyes.

Through the open windows, he could hear Nettie in the living room, fretting over the shattered vase.

Fuck, he thought. How many things was he going to break in one goddamn day?

He rose to his feet and went back inside. He paused in the doorway to the living room, hands braced on the frame, watching Nettie. He knew that he should say something, apologize, but all he could do was stare dejectedly like a puppy who'd been caught pissing on the carpet.

Strands of gray were woven throughout Nettie's brown hair, and there were deep lines set around her eyes. Sometimes he forgot how old she was becoming. Her own children were grown now, living off in London and New York.

The day he and Eve had come to live with his Aunt Ceceli, she'd passed them off to Nettie as if they were a pair of dirty laundry she'd found at the back of her closet. He ought to hate his aunt for it—but Theodore's heart was already filled with so much hate, he didn't think there was any room left for her. When his aunt had packed her things for Baton Rouge later that day, he'd overheard her tell Nettie that they looked too much like Madock and Catrin. Their parents. *"I can't be here,"* she'd said. *"I can't be around them right now. I'm sorry."*

Looking at Nettie collecting the shattered bits of porcelain, he remembered the rough, calloused feel of her hands against his as she told him that she'd look after them.

He turned sharply from the doorway and took the stairs two at a time as he climbed to his bedroom. He slammed the door shut behind him.

Stripping out of his t-shirt and shorts, he crossed into the adjoined bathroom and turned on the shower. Without waiting for it to warm up, he climbed inside, and droplets of freezing water clung to the ends of his pale blonde hair as he stared at the white tiled wall.

It felt as if he'd been hit by a truck, and his insides were knocked into all the wrong places: his stomach was in his throat, his heart in his fingertips. He wasn't sure where his brain had gone, but it sure as hell wasn't in head.

And all because of a small, sharp-tongued girl with lilac hair and a taste for nightmares.

"Goddamn it, Tannyn," he growled beneath his breath.

His palm smacked flat against the tiled wall, and he leaned forward as water cascaded down his bare back.

"Withholding the truth is still lying."

"What are you talking about?"

"I'm talking about the night when Jude found Eve on the side of the road."

He closed his eyes, his mouth twisting up as if he'd tasted

161

something bad.

Of course Jude would have mentioned that to her. He just couldn't leave it alone, not when he had something to dangle over Theodore's head.

An image surfaced in his mind: Jude laying Eve's body on her bed, a gash torn in her shirt that had become stained with red. God, she'd been so pale. And there had been so much blood. Theodore had never seen so much blood, not since the accident . . .

The muscles in his back tensed.

Tannyn wanted to know his secrets and his fears. She wanted to know what he was so *afraid* of. The problem with that was that Theodore wasn't so sure of the answer himself.

Maybe that scared the hell out of him most of all, because she was the first girl to push him. She was the first girl to try and figure out what was going on beneath those storm-cloud eyes and icy smile.

And he'd let her slip right through his fingers.

He pressed the heels of his hands against his closed eyelids, muttering a curse beneath his breath.

Thirty minutes later, Theodore was behind the wheel of his car, and the stalks of sugarcane on his family's plantation were a blur as he flew past them.

He pulled into the parking lot of the bookstore on Main Street and threw his car in park, and the door crashed shut behind him as he slipped out onto the pavement. His shirt was already clinging to his back with sweat, and he wasn't so sure if it was from the heat.

He shook his hair back from his face and stepped up onto the sidewalk, stuffing his keys into the pocket of his shorts.

He was halfway to the front door when his phone vibrated in his pocket.

He almost ignored it.

Later, he thanked God that he didn't.

He pulled it from his pocket and checked the caller id, shielding his eyes against the sun's reflection.

Dr. Reinhardt.

"Shit," he said.

He took out his key and turned sharply back towards the car. As he did, he accepted the call and brought his phone to his ear.

"Give me good news," he growled into the receiver.

thirty-one

I looked up in time to see Theodore climbing into his car outside the bookstore.

He looked—shocked. Relieved. Happy. I wondered who he was talking to. And then I remembered I didn't care.

But still, I pulled my phone from my pockets and checked my notifications. Nothing.

Not that it was surprising considering I had a total of four friends—five, if I included Madeline, but she couldn't work a phone.

I felt like throwing something. Unfortunately, the only things with in arm's reach were my phone and a stack of books that had never done anything to me. I angrily flicked over the small plastic container of pennies on the counter.

They clattered to the floor, rolling in different directions.

"What was that?" my coworker, Jules, called from the back of the store.

"Just knocked over the pennies!" I shouted back to them.

I got down on my hands and knees and began to collect the pennies in my palm. One of them had rolled under a bookshelf, and I laid on my stomach, wiggling my fingers and willing my arm to grow another inch as I reached for it. The fresh cuts on my knuckles split open, and I growled in pain.

Fuck it, I thought. *It's just a penny.*

I climbed back to my feet, wiping dust bunnies and pieces of lint from the front of my shirt and my shorts.

Jules walked out into the front of the store, the soles of their combat boots squeaking on the laminate floor. They were a few years older than me, a freshman in college, and we'd only talked two or three times before when Ilse had scheduled us to work together.

"I'm running to lunch," they said, sweeping short black curls out of their face. "Do you want anything?"

My stomach was already churning, and the thought of eating anything made bile rise in my throat. I swallowed and forced a smile. "No thanks. I'm fine."

"Alright. I'll be back in thirty."

I watched them leave, and then checked my phone a second time. Still no notifications.

I smacked the penny container to the floor again.

thirty-two

Water dripped from the ends of my wet hair, leaving droplets across my t-shirt.

The trunk of the elm tree was rough at my back, scratching my skin. I pressed my stuffed rabbit tighter against my chest and stared down at the dried grass twenty feet below me.

"Tannyn, come on!"

I quickly unbuckled the straps on my heels as Eve slipped out of her black ball gown and hooked a bare leg over the lowest branch of the tree.

I stumbled and pulled off my other heel, flinging it beside the crumpled pile of midnight blue fabric that already lay in the grass. I picked up the bottle of champagne and tucked it under my arm.

Eve's stifled laughter beckoned me from the higher branches as I climbed after her.

Even one-handed in the darkness, I still scaled the tree as easily as when I'd been a child, fearless and adventurous, so sure that nothing could hurt me.

I pulled myself onto the branch beside her and handed the bottle of champagne to her.

I rested my head back against the trunk of the tree, closing my eyes. Sweat dripped down the back of my neck. The stuffed rabbit suddenly felt so heavy in my arms.

Eve popped the champagne bottle, laughing as bubbles spilled over her hands. She took a long swig and then passed the bottle back to me.

I gulped down several mouthfuls, bubbles dancing across my tongue. I propped the bottle between my legs.

Orange, and then pink, began to tinge the dark horizon. Eve smiled softly, the sunlight turning her hair white-gold. It reflected off her gray eyes as she turned to face me.

Her lipstick was smeared, and I reached over to take her face between my hands, fixing it with the pad of my thumb.

Then I pulled her mouth to mine.

She parted her lips, and her tongue tasted like champagne against my own. I tangled my hands in her hair, stiff with gel and hairspray. My fingers caught in the knots, and I chuckled against her lips.

Her own laughter filled my ears as I worked to untangle them.

I squeezed my eyes closed, losing myself in the warmth of her mouth and the scent of her skin. Strands of hair came loose from my curls and fell into my face. Eve brushed them away, tucking them behind my ears.

Why, *I thought.* Why couldn't it have been you?

"Tannyn," she murmured, pulling back.

"What?"

"I'm sorry. I'm sorry that I'm not him."

My face flushed. "What do you mean?"

"I see the way you look at him. You're both strong and loyal and stubborn as hell," she said. "I wish it had been us—you and me. It would have made things simpler. But I don't love you, and you don't love me—at least not like that."

I opened my eyes, tears dripping down my cheeks. Someone was shouting my name.

I turned my head to see West and Jack standing at the base of the tree, shielding their eyes from the sun as they stared up at me. A plastic grocery bag was hanging by the crook of Jack's elbow.

"What are you doing here?" I asked. My voice cracked.

"Theodore asked us to check on you," West said.

Fuck Theodore, I thought angrily.

It had been two days since the incident with—what had been her name? Had he even mentioned it? I couldn't remember. Two days, and no contact whatsoever. And now he'd sent West and Jack to check in on me.

"We went to the bookstore first, but Ilse said you'd called out sick," Jack told me. "So we brought you soup and ginger ale." He smiled lightly. "From the looks of it though, you exaggerated a bit."

I swiped the back of my hand across my face and forced a smile. "Yeah, well, I always was the best liar of the five of us." *Four of us.*

"Are you and So Big planning to come down any time soon, *mami?*"

"Why don't you come up, *papi?*"

"I'm not even going to bother with an answer since you already know I'm afraid of heights," Jack said.

"What kind of soup did you bring?"

"My mom's chicken posole," he told me. "No radishes, extra hominy—just the way you like it."

I inclined my head towards my bedroom window. "You can come up, if you want. Door's unlocked. I'll meet you inside."

I watched them walk onto the porch, and then I tucked my stuffed rabbit under my arm and scooted along the branch towards the roof of my house. I lowered my bare feet to the rough tiling and slipped from the branch. I ducked back in through my open window.

I cleared a space on my bedroom floor and sat down with my back against my bookshelf. I settled So Big beside me, the way I'd used to when we had tea parties as a child. It brought back a memory of my mother and I, sitting in the grass behind our house on a blanket spread with tiny sandwiches and tea cups. I closed my eyes against the memory.

My bedroom door swung open, and I looked up at West as he sat down beside me.

Jack sat across from me, and Madeline followed him in, sprawling out alongside of him. She favored him because he always snuck her food—which was why she was overweight and needed to be walked so much.

Jack set the plastic bag down in front of him and pulled out a metal soup thermos.

As he unscrewed the lid, steam and warm spices wafted out.

"Since you're not actually contagious," he said, divvying out spoons to West and I, "I guess we can share." He even gave one to So Big.

"Did you steal these from my kitchen?" I asked.

"Yes. It looked like you had dishes to clean anyway." He took out a pile of napkins. "I also got these because I knew you'd yell at me if I didn't."

I dipped my spoon into the soup, cupping my hand below it so I didn't spill of the floor. It burnt my tongue, but I swallowed the entire spoonful. "Tell Mamá Rosa I said thank you," I told Jack.

I watched as West picked pieces of soggy, shredded lettuce from his spoon and set them aside on his napkin.

"They taste sad," he said when he caught me looking.

"I have more in common with lettuce than I thought then," I muttered.

"You taste sad, too?" Jack asked, grinning at me.

"Sad, with too much vinegar," I told him.

"No wonder you make people cry," he said, Then his grin widened. "I'd taste like *mango con chile y limon.* Sweet and spicy."

I glanced at West. "What about you?"

"A sandwich." He didn't elaborate.

"I like sandwiches," Jack said.

I looked back down at the thermos, watching a piece of cilantro that floated on top of the broth. "How was work?" I asked West.

"Full of white women complaining about the prices of avocados."

"That's what you get for working at a farmer's market," I said.

He shrugged halfheartedly. "Could be worse. Remember the diner?"

"Yes. You used to always smell like onion rings. What were they shut down for again?"

"Rats. Not the good kind."

I frowned. "What's the good kind?"

"You know, the one from *Ratatouille*."

Jack rolled his eyes, and I laughed in spite of myself. I glanced down at my warped reflection in the metal spoon, and the smile instantly disappeared from my face.

"Cheer up, Tan," Jack said. I looked up at him, and he bumped my shoulder lightly with his own. "Whoever she was, she's not you. I'm sure Theodore will show up with a bouquet of roses, and you'll kiss and make up."

So they hadn't heard the rest of the argument then. I forced a smile. "Then why did he send you instead of coming himself?"

Jack shook his head. "When he texted, he said he was busy. Said it was important. I texted back and asked if anything was wrong, but he never answered."

I pressed my lips together into a thin line.

I waited another minute, quietly sipping on broth, before I excused myself to the bathroom.

As soon as I shut the bathroom door behind me, I pulled my phone from the pocket of my shorts, released an angry breath through my nose, and dialed Theodore's number.

I waited through the rings, tapping my fingers impatiently against

170

the sink counter.

It went to voicemail.

"Hi, it's Theodore. I can't take your call right now, but—"

I hung up and dropped my phone onto the counter. I dragged my fingers through my damp hair, and they caught in the tangled knots.

"Fuck," I muttered, working to untangle them.

There was a soft knock on the bathroom door.

I pushed my hair back from my face and smoothed it down. When I opened the door, West was standing in the hallway, pinching his shirt between his fingers and frowning.

"What's the matter?" I asked.

"Jack spilled broth on me," he said.

"Oh," I said, pushing the door open wider and stepping out of the way so he could get by. "Well, I'm finished."

As I started back down the hallway towards my room, West said, "Tannyn."

I turned back to face him, hands clenching and un-clenching at my side. A strand of pale purple hair drifted into my face. "Hmm?"

There was worry in West's dark eyes and the set of his mouth. "It's not just that girl, is it? It's something else."

I offered a small, bitter smile. "There's always something else." It was the truth, at least.

The worry didn't leave his face. "Then talk to us, Tannyn. That's what we're here for."

My smile fell. "It's too much," I murmured. "Everyone I care about just ends up getting hurt."

"But that's life," West replied. "You can't help that. Besides, Theodore's tougher than he looks."

"So was Eve."

171

He leaned against the frame of the door. "Well, if you keep pushing Theodore away, you'll lose him, too," he said. "And then you'll both be miserable, and you won't have prevented anyone from getting hurt."

"Thanks, West." I ruffled his hair, and he ducked his head, blushing.

"I'll be here all week," he muttered, smiling softly.

He closed the bathroom door, and I slowly uncurled my fist, relieving the tension in my knuckles. I looked down at the crescent-shaped indents in my palm.

It was late afternoon by the time Jack and West left.

I pulled into the Shearwater's empty driveway and turned off the engine of my car. Theodore's own car was gone, and all the lights in the house were off.

I took out my cell phone, clutching it in my hand.

"Please, pick up," I whispered as I dialed.

"Hi, it's Theodore. I can't—"

I tossed my phone onto the passenger seat and undid my seatbelt. I climbed from the car, squinting in the sunlight as I stalked up onto the porch.

I rang the doorbell once, and then pounded my fist against the door. "Theodore Shearwater, if you're home, you better answer this goddamn door right now!" I shouted. I cupped my hands around my face and peered through the window. I didn't care if it was bad etiquette; he was always coming into my house uninvited anyway.

"Nettie!" I yelled, ringing the doorbell again. "It's Tannyn! I need to talk to Theodore!"

I thought about digging out their spare key, but it seemed pointless.

I waited a moment, and then I went down the porch steps and around the side of the house towards the trail that led to the guesthouse where Nettie stayed. Her car was also gone.

I ran back to my car and slid into the driver's seat, snatching up my phone.

"Hi, it's Theodore. I can't take your call right now, but leave a message and I'll get back to you."

Beep.

"It's Tannyn," I said into the speaker. "What kind of asshole sends his friends to check on a girl instead of going himself? And where are you? I'm at your house, and there's no one here. And now I'm thinking of the end of *The Great Gatsby* when Tom and Daisy disappear and don't answer any of Nick's calls." My fingers tightened around my phone. "You always answer your phone. What's going on?" I asked, my voice cracking. "Call me back. Please."

I hung up, dropping my phone onto the dashboard.

I dragged my fingers through my hair and pressed my forehead against the steering wheel, closing my eyes.

thirty-three

him

He and the crow had been watching each other for a while now.

It sat amongst the tangled branches on the tree as he stood below it, his head tipped back and his hands clasped behind his back.

Where's your murder, little crow? he thought.

It was twilight, the dark sky tinged with orange and pink, as he listened to the sound of cars driving past on the road that wound through the woods. A mosquito landed on the bare skin of his upper arm, and he squished it beneath the pad of his index finger. He stared at the streak of blood along his skin before he wiped it off on the hem of his shirt.

For a moment, he wondered if this was too much—after all, he'd already delivered the heart.

He lifted his head to the branches again, trying to remember how that tale about the crows had gone.

> *"The patient Crows for many a week*
> *No other occupation seek;*
> *But, while one sits and looks around,*
> *The other makes the woods resound*
> *With cawings loud, or frequent brings*
> *Worms, seeds, or such delicious things,*
> *And kindly feeds his brooding mate*
> *From early morn to evening late."*

He bent to pick up a rock from the ground, turning it over in his hand and scraping away the dirt with his thumbnail.

The piece of metal wedged in the waistband of his shorts was cool against his back.

"Bang! Bang! again for every ball
Wounded or dead the young Crows fall;
The old Crows wheeling in the skies
Helpless behold their agonies,
And, piteous cawing up on high,
Answer their young ones dying cry—
Who fall, poor little suffering things,
With broken legs and wounded wings."

The sun sunk below the horizon, bathing the woods in shadow, and the crow let out a harsh caw.

He grinned.

thirty-four

When I woke the next morning, wisps of lilac hair plastered to my forehead, several images were still fresh in my mind.

Black silk and long blonde hair. A garden filled with burning flowers. Pale fingers twisting the neck of a crow.

I sat up, squinting through my tangled hair at the clock on my bedside table, and then pushed aside my covers. As I stood up and stretched my arms over my head, I could hear my father's car backing out of the driveway as he left for work.

I crept down the hall to the bathroom, and as I waited for the shower water to heat up, I hooked my phone up to the speakers on the vanity.

Stripping out of my pajamas, I hummed along to Death Cab for Cutie.

I stepped into the shower and tilted my head back, feeling the scalding water batter my skin as I pushed my fingers through my wet hair. I closed my eyes, and a moment later, a metallic taste hit my tongue.

When I glanced down, the water at my feet had begun to turn pink from the blood dripping from my nose.

I wiped the back of my hand across my lips, and then stared angrily down at the streak of red on my skin. Why was it that my nose was *always fucking bleeding?*

Maybe I had a deviated septum; I remembered that someone in my class had one before and had gotten surgery done to fix it. It would also have explained the headaches—but not the strange nightmares or the feeling in my stomach like something bad was going to happen that never seemed to go away.

I washed my hair and scrubbed off my skin, wincing as my fingers accidentally brushed over the tender bruise along my brow.

I climbed from the shower and dried myself off with a towel, and water dripped from the ends of my hair as I crossed the hall and walked back to my bedroom.

All of my shorts were in the laundry, so I pulled on a black t-shirt that brushed the middle of my thighs and was long enough to pass for a dress, and then slipped on a pair of worn black and white Converse.

When I trotted down the stairs, Madeline was asleep on one of the couches.

I took my keys down from the hook on the wall and pulled open the front door, stepping out onto the porch.

Something squished beneath my foot.

It was wet and soft, and made an awful sound—like when my sneakers caught in mud and made a thick *squelch*ing as they pulled free. Or like when Madeline had accidentally killed a rabbit and left it at the bottom of the stairs, so that I'd stepped on it on my way to the kitchen.

I lifted my foot up and away and forced myself to look down.

Bile rose in my throat when I saw the blood pooling on the welcome mat.

The first time I saw a dead thing, I was four, and a baby bird had fallen from its nest in a tree in our backyard.

I found it a few days later, lying in the grass, its bones protruding at sharp angles. Maggots squirming beneath the soft pink flesh. Dark feathers that had barely begun to form. I'd gotten sick down the front of my new green dress that my mother had bought me for my first day of preschool.

As I stumbled backwards into the house, pulling my cell phone from my back pocket, I was reminded of that broken baby bird and how its eyes had been closed as it rotted in the grass beneath the oak tree.

I called Theodore first. It went to voice mail, so I dialed again and again until he finally picked up, sounding tired and worried and so unlike-Theodore. When I told him what happened, he was silent. Then he said he was on his way. He called the others while I peeled off my Converse and washed the blood from the underside with a hose in the backyard. Then I texted Ilse that I couldn't make it into work—I hinted at nausea and a violent stomach bug—and cleaned the dishes that my father had left in the sink just to give myself something to do.

Now the four of us were gathered around the coffee table in my living room, where the dead crow was laid out on a towel, its black eyes turned towards the exposed beams in the ceiling.

"It looks like it was shot, and then someone broke its neck," Jack said, poking at the dead thing with a pen he'd found between the cushions of the couch.

"Oh, God," I said.

I thought that what I'd texted Ilse hadn't been so far off; I *felt* nauseous, but it certainly wasn't from any stomach bug.

I climbed to my feet and walked out into the kitchen, pouring myself a cup of stale coffee from the pot beside the oven and heating it up in the microwave. When I walked back out into the living room, West had one of the wings pinched between his thumb and forefinger as he extended it.

"Oh, *God.*"

West looked up as I sunk down to the floor, crossing my legs and curling my fingers around the steaming mug in my hands.

"What time did you find it?" Jack asked.

"I was supposed to work at nine-thirty, so it would have been around a quarter after nine."

"Do you think it was left there overnight?"

"I don't know. My dad usually leaves through the garage. He wouldn't have seen it." I tried not to think about the sound the dead crow had made when I'd stepped on it. "How do you tell how long something has been dead?"

West dropped the wing he was holding and said, "Rigor mortis."

The feathers glittered dark blue in the sunlight that streamed down through the living room windows.

Theodore said, "Let's at least dig out the bullet so I can take it to a specialist and see if they can identify the type of gun. Do you have tweezers?"

I realized the last part was directed at me. "Medicine cabinet in the upstairs bathroom," I said.

He pounded up the stairs, and a moment later, he returned with a pair of tweezers, which he used to messily and unskillfully dig the bullet from the crow's body. Nausea rose in my throat at the sound of it.

It looked like I was going to need new tweezers.

"Got it," Theodore said.

Jack handed him something. "Here. I got you a plastic bag."

I stared at the blood leaking from the hole in its side, made larger by Theodore's digging around with the tweezers.

"You will die before the next full moon, Tannyn Carter."

"Will someone please, *please*, just get that fucking thing out of my house?" My fingers tightened around my cup of coffee until the bruised knuckles on my right hand began to scream in pain. "I don't care what you do with it, just *get it the fuck out of here.*"

Three pairs of eyes flickered to my face, and a silence hung in the air like a cloud of smoke. Suffocating. Choking.

179

"Alright," Theodore said finally. "Jack?"

"I'll get the shovel," Jack replied. He glanced at the dark red stains on the throw rug beneath the coffee table. "What about the blood?"

West stood from the couch, tucking his hands into the pockets of his jeans. "Cold water and salt," he said flatly. Then he glanced at me. "Where's your vacuum?"

"In the laundry room," I told him. "Down the hall, second door on the right."

As Theodore and Jack wrapped the crow tightly in the towel and carried it from the room, I stared down into the cup of coffee in my hands. Then I leaned my head back against the couch behind me and closed my eyes, drawing in a heavy breath through my nose.

In, out, in, out.

I heard footsteps and flicked my eyes open as West returned to the living room, rolling the vacuum along ahead of him. I almost told him not to bother; it wasn't as if my father would notice, anyway.

In, out.

"Why do you know how to get blood stains out?" I asked.

He knelt down, blotting at the stains with a wash cloth soaked in cold water. He didn't look over at me, but I saw the muscles in his back tense. "When your dad likes to hit you, you tend to pick up things like that."

"I'm sorry."

"It's not your fault," he said. "Besides, he's gone now."

I watched him as he created a thick paste from the salt and water, rubbing it into the stains with the corner of the wash cloth. Then he sat back, stretching his legs out in front of him.

"It has to sit for fifteen minutes," he said.

He was silent, and I listened to the ticking of the watch on my wrist. A minute went by, then another. I finished my coffee and set the cup down beside me on the hardwood floor.

What the hell is taking them so long? I thought.

West's eyes drifted past me to the kitchen, and I heard the sound of the sliding glass door open and close. A shadow fell over me, and I glanced up to see Theodore standing beside the couch.

Jack said, "It's done."

Theodore offered his hand down to me, pulling me to my feet when I accepted.

I walked out into the kitchen and rinsed out my mug. In the living room, I heard the vacuum whir to life.

As I turned from putting the mug away, I mumbled, "Goddamn it."

I knotted my fingers into my hair and leaned back against the counter behind me for support. I stared down at a spot of blood that I'd missed on the side of my sneaker, blinking—once, twice—as if that might make it disappear.

Theodore crossed the kitchen and wrapped his arms around me, and I buried my face against his chest. He drew his fingers over my hair, resting his chin on the crown of my head.

I closed my eyes, breathing in his scent of cedar wood and the air after a rainstorm. "I know that we said no police, but this . . . This is different. This isn't just a scrap of fabric in the mail," I whispered. "Someone is threatening us."

He went still beneath me, and when I pulled back to look up at him, he was staring out the window over the kitchen sink.

"Why haven't you been answering your phone?"

He didn't answer.

"Goddammit, Theodore. Talk to me."

"I thought you hated me," he said.

"I did. I do. Just tell me what's going on."

181

Silence.

Then, "I have something I need to show you. All of you."

Theodore didn't say anything the entire drive to the Boathouse.

As he pulled to a stop on the dirt path and put the car in park, I braced my hands against the dashboard. "What's going on?" I said. But he still wouldn't look at me—hadn't looked at me from the moment we'd left my house. "Theodore?"

When he climbed from the car and slammed the door behind him, I quickly undid my seatbelt and clambered out after him. Jack's car cruised to a stop behind us, and then he and West joined me as I followed Theodore through the thick undergrowth.

"What are we doing here?" Jack asked.

Theodore slid his key into the lock on the front door, but before he could turn it, I grabbed his wrist and forced him to face me.

"What do you need to show us?" I demanded.

His eyes slid over my shoulder, staring at a big Southern oak several feet away—the same kind that Eve's body had been found in at the beginning of the summer. A bad feeling fluttered in my stomach.

"Theodore, *what the hell is going on?*"

"You wanted to know a secret," he said, his voice barely a whisper. "What I was so afraid of people finding out."

I released my fingers from his wrist, taking a step back.

Theodore glanced over at me, the ice in his pale gray gaze shattering and falling away in pieces to reveal the sadness beneath it.

"This isn't the first time Eve has been killed."

thirty-five

theo

Theodore loved the smell of grass in the springtime.

Because of his mother's allergies, and because his father was almost always busy with work, he and Eve were usually confined to the house—which wasn't so bad, if you didn't mind hide-and-seek with only two people. And Theodore didn't, but Eve was restless. She was the type of child to chop off her hair with scissors or hide all of the silverware from the housekeeper simply out of boredom.

And when Eve had said she wanted to go exploring that morning, he almost told her to go without him. But no one could say no to Eve—certainly and most especially not Theodore.

Now, as he stumbled along behind her as she wove through the trees, ruining her pretty white dress, he wished—just once—that he had the strength to look her in the eye and not let her have her way.

The hem of her dress was muddy, as well as her feet because she'd taken off her sandals and had made him carry them for her—and each time he looked at the dirt beneath her toenails, he wished again that he was better at saying no.

He breathed in the scents of spring that hung in the air as Eve stopped to examine a circle of white mushrooms at the base of a tree. He wasn't sure what sort of tree, as they all looked the same to him, and he didn't understand what his sister found so fascinating about a bunch of fungus.

"It's a fairy ring," Eve said, as if reading his thoughts.

He made to step on one of the pale mushrooms, and she grabbed his arm and jerked him backwards.

"Don't," she hissed.

"What?"

"You shouldn't step inside a fairy ring," she said. "Mair told me that if you do, you'll be whisked away to fairyland, or be driven mad. They're left behind by dancing fairies."

Mair was the Shearwater's housekeeper; Theodore thought she smelled like mothballs and peppermint, and his mother was always calling her eccentric. Eve liked her though because she told stories while preparing dinner or folding laundry, and because she sometimes left candies for the twins beneath their pillows.

"Mom says Mair is crazy," Theodore mumbled, but he took a step back anyway.

"I know," Eve said, grinning. "That's why I like her."

She took his free hand and began leading him through the trees, and she didn't seem to notice when twigs or leaves caught in her blonde hair as she ducked beneath low-hanging branches. He stared at a dark green leaf shaped like a star that had gotten tangled in the ends of her hair.

"Where are we going?" he asked.

"You'll see!" his sister trilled.

The trees began to thin out around them, parting to reveal a clearing of grass and small, white flowers that stretched on and on and on— before ending suddenly about thirty feet away. The rest was all blue sky and clouds.

Theodore dropped his sister's hand as he pulled to a stop, but Eve didn't even glance back in his direction.

As she danced to the edge of the cliff, he called after her, "Eve, *what are you doing?"*

"It's beautiful, Theodore!" she shouted back.

Her hair streamed out behind her, turned gold in the sunlight, and she lifted the hem of her dress as she twirled in a circle. She stopped at the edge of the cliff and tipped her head back to the sky, closing her eyes.

"Eve, be careful," he said, and he hated that he sounded like an adult.

She grinned at him over her shoulder, tucking her hair behind her ear. "You have to come see this!"

"Eve . . ."

Her blonde brows knit together. "Stop saying my name."

"I think we should go home," he replied.

She twisted her mouth up like she'd eaten something sour, and then she sighed through her nose. "Alright," she said. "But only if you come and look first. Then we can go home."

"I don't want to look. It's too high."

Her expression turned sympathetic. "I promise I'll hold your hand if you get scared, okay, Theodore?" she told him.

He almost snapped back that he wasn't scared—but his sister was smarter than him, and she always knew things like that. Like that he hated broccoli, which was why she always ate his whenever Mair or his parents weren't looking. Or that he was afraid of heights.

"Okay," he said.

Then Eve's eyes went wide, and something in the ground shifted beneath her feet.

"Theodore?" she said.

She screamed as the edge of the cliff crumbled around her.

Theodore dropped the sandals in his hand and lurched forward, shouting his sister's name, but she had already disappeared from sight. His shoe caught on something, and he tumbled headfirst into the grass before clambering to his feet again.

He dropped to his knees at the cliff's edge, his fingernails clawing at the dirt as he leaned forward.

"Eve?"

He stared down at his sister where she lay on the rocks below, her neck twisted at an odd angle like a broken doll and her gray eyes staring blankly at the sky overhead.

"Eve!"

A breeze ruffled the star-shaped leaf in his sister's hair, but the rest of her was still.

thirty-six

"This isn't the first time Eve has been killed."

I'd heard him wrong. I had to have heard him wrong.

I swallowed the bile that rose in my throat, forcing myself not to look away. "What are you talking about?"

"She died," he said, meeting my gaze, "in the car crash that killed my parents."

My throat closed up, and it felt as if my heart were trying to escape from my chest as it beat on with the pace of a hummingbird's wings. I closed my eyes, clenching my hands into fists at my sides.

In through the nose, out through the mouth.

"I don't understand," I whispered.

In, out, in, out.

I opened my eyes to see West crouched on the ground, his head in his hands.

"She's died five times before this in her life," Theodore told me. "The first time . . ." He drew a breath through his nose and pushed his fingers through his hair. "She was stillborn. My mom said we were curled together, holding hands, and Eve's skin was so pale it was almost blue. But when the doctors went to take her, she just . . . started breathing. They didn't know how to explain it."

In, out.

"Then, when we were little, we were playing out by the cliffs near our house one day. It was nearly a twenty-foot drop to the rocks below. Eve broke her neck," he continued. "She was *dead*. And I climbed down and pulled her into my lap and just held her. I couldn't stop crying. When I tried to pick her up, her head flopped on her neck like a rag doll." His voice cracked. "So I just sat there with her, until my parents came looking and found us. I remember they kept trying to take her, but I wouldn't let go of her hand. I remember passing out, and I had this dream where I was looking for her—like we were playing hide-and-seek in the dark. And when I woke up, she was fine. I thought I'd dreamt it all. But I could see it in my parents' faces . . . They were so scared that someone would find out that we packed up and moved that day. We ended up in New York for eight years, and then the accident happened.

"After I helped Eve, I tried . . ." he went on, his voice catching in his throat. "I tried to fix them. I tried to *save* them. But it didn't work."

"Christ," I said.

"When we moved here, someone found out," he said. "I don't know how." He whirled, slamming his fist against the wall of the Boathouse, and I started. "We'd only been here about three months when someone broke into our house. Strangled her in her sleep. I didn't find her until the next morning, but I was still able to bring her back. Then a year later, she snuck out to go to party. She was walking down the side of the road when someone stabbed her and—"

He broke off suddenly.

"Each time, it was something different. To see if I could fix her," he said. "And this time . . ." He swallowed. "This time, they took her heart."

Silence.

West opened his eyes, staring up at me, and I noticed that his eyes were red around the edges.

I pressed a hand against my stomach, curling my fingers into my skin. Three sets of eyes were staring at me, and I realized they were waiting for my reaction. Waiting for me to *snap*, because that was what I did. That

188

was what I always did.

"Eve is dead," I said.

Theodore reached for me, but I stepped away from his grasp. "Tannyn—"

And I snapped.

"*Eve is dead.*"

"I couldn't bring her back without a heart," he told me. "And the lists for transplants are so long. There are so many people that need hearts—that are dying. So I had to call in favors, and I had to find a doctor, someone willing to do the operation. And then she didn't wake up immediately after. I didn't know—"

"Shut up," West said.

My head swiveled to look at him, and the look in his eyes was one of the most frightening things I'd ever seen. My heart broke at the sight of it.

"Please. Shut up."

"You wanted to know," Theodore said.

Then he turned the key and pushed open the door.

The first thing I noticed was the suitcase in the corner of the room; the second was that the coffee table had been cleared aside to make room to open the pull-out couch.

"Theodore?" a voice called from the back room. "Is that you?"

If I hadn't felt my heart beating so violently in my chest, I would have been sure that it had stopped at that moment.

Eve, I thought.

Then, *I'm going crazy.*

I started to step over the threshold, but my fingers caught on the frame of the door and I pulled to a stop. *No, no, no.* My heart seemed to pulse in time with my thoughts.

"Theodore?" the voice called again. "Did you get a chance to go to the store yet? I'm already sick of frozen TV dinners."

I swallowed and released my grip on the frame of the door. Then I stepped over the threshold.

West had risen from his crouch and was at my heels as I followed Theodore into the back room. I heard the front door shut, and I didn't need to glance back to know that Jack was right behind us.

I was going to be sick.

We stepped into the back room.

And there she was.

thirty-seven

Eve was sitting before the glass wall, barefoot and eating a cup of strawberry yogurt, when I entered the back room.

She was wearing a black t-shirt and drawstring shorts, her hair swept back from her face in a long braid. Pale blonde flyaways clung to her forehead with sweat. There was a pair of crutches leaning against the wall beside her, and the dark red polish on her nails was chipped at the ends, but it was the crow tattoo on the inside of her left wrist that I found myself staring at.

Then she turned her head, and the left side of her face came into sight.

There was a jagged scar through her left eye—or where her left eye should have been. Instead there was only angry, puckered flesh.

When she spotted us in the doorway, her brows rose slightly. Even the one over her missing eye.

Then a smile touched her lips. "Tannyn. You changed your hair," she said, as if this were the most surprising thing to have happened. "I like it."

As West fell to his knees and was sick onto the wooden floor, I whirled towards Theodore.

"I'm so sorry—" he began.

I slapped him hard across the face.

My palm stung, and his skin flushed red where I had struck him. I gasped in a breath, shoulders trembling, and felt tears gathering in the corners of my eyes.

Then I ran from the room and out the front door of the Boathouse, slipping outside into the heat.

My sneakers pounded against the hard earth as I tore through the trees. Bramble vines and branches scratched at my ankles and caught in my hair.

I didn't know where I was going; I just knew that I needed to get away.

Someone shouted my name.

A cramp formed in my side, but I didn't stop, even as my chest burned with each breath. I clutched a hand against my abdomen, and tears stung at the corners of my eyes.

My foot caught on a tree root, and suddenly I was falling.

I landed hard against the ground, and I cried out as I bit down on my tongue. A copper taste filled my mouth, and strands of red spit dribbled from my lips and onto the ground. I stared miserably at them, chest heaving, my knees screaming in pain from where I'd scraped them. Chunks of dirt caught beneath my fingernails as I curled my hands into fists.

The branches overhead rustled in a breeze, and I squeezed my eyes closed.

My breathing turned shallow, and I felt like I was choking. My chest grew heavy, and I wondered if it was possible for my lungs to have turned to lead. I tried to remind myself to breathe—*in, out*—as I clutched at the ground beneath me.

I began to hum "Downtown" under my breath as I pressed my forehead against the cool earth.

Shudders ran through my body, but no tears would come as I lay there on the ground with aching knees and blood-stained teeth.

I swung into the kitchen, my sneakers squeaking on the tiled floor. "Mom?"

"What is it, honey?" she asked, turning from where she stood at the island. She had a cup of coffee in her hands, and she was still dressed in her pajamas.

A flash of metal.

My fingers coming away stained with red.

My mother sobbing.

Humming to myself and rocking back and forth on the kitchen floor as blue and red lights flashed outside in the driveway.

Eve leaning against the front counter of the bookstore.

"So, tell me, Tannyn, what are you *afraid of?"*

Theodore sitting on the front step of our porch, his head in his hands and his shirt soaked with blood.

"Someone . . . Someone killed her."

A closed casket lined with white silk.

Laughter, like a crow's caw.

I opened my eyes and lifted my head to stare down at the dirt that I'd scraped up beneath my fingernails.

"You will die before the next full moon, Tannyn Carter."

Bile rose in my throat, and I clutched a hand to my stomach just before I vomited onto the ground. When I'd finished, I noticed strands of bright red blood were wound through the mess.

"This isn't the first time Eve has been killed."

I wiped the back of my hand across my mouth.

Footsteps padded gently along the forest floor, and I glimpsed someone moving towards me through the curtain of my hair.

Hands set down a pair of crutches on the ground, and then Eve knelt beside me.

"I would have been here sooner," she said, "but, you know, weak muscles and all."

I turned my head, staring at her with hollow eyes as I took in the scar over her left eye and her hair turned white-gold by the sun streaming down through the trees. When she reached out and brushed back the strands of hair that had fallen into my face, I went still beneath her touch. Her fingers lingered at the bruise along my brow.

Her expression softened. "Oh, Tannyn . . ."

And then suddenly I was crying.

Sobs shook my entire body, and I was gasping for air as she wrapped her arms around me and enveloped me against her. She pulled me into her lap, her fingers moving over my hair as I buried my face against her shoulder.

Tears burned at my eyes, and salt water mixed with the metallic taste on my lips. I clung to Eve, knotting my fingers into her shirt, until my knuckles ached.

I cried for myself and for my mother and for lovely, wicked Eve with her single storm-cloud eye and stolen heart. I cried until there was nothing left, nothing but exhaustion and an emptiness in my chest where all the sorrow had been buried.

Then Eve smoothed my hair back from my face and kissed my forehead.

"I'm sorry," she whispered. "I'm so sorry that I left you alone."

I drew my legs up onto the couch beside me, taking the steaming mug that Eve handed me and curling my fingers around it.

She sunk down next to me, laying her head against West's shoulder and stretching her legs out into my lap. Jack was sitting on the floor at the foot of the couch, and Eve reached out to draw her fingers through the thick waves of his hair.

"I remember . . . walking," she whispered, and the light of the bulb overheard threw strange shadows across her face. "I remember waiting for someone, and . . ." She lifted a hand to her head, touching a light scar along her temple. Her blonde brow furrowed. "Then there was just darkness. I kept seeing memories—you know how they say your life plays out before you in the seconds before you die? It was like that. And then . . . and then Theodore brought me back. And I was just dreaming for a while. Then I woke up in the hospital."

Theodore shifted where he was sitting in an armchair across the room, turning his head towards the boarded front windows, but I knew he was listening from the way his jaw tensed.

The mug in my hand was burning my fingers, but I clung tight to it.

"You should still be in the hospital," I said. "You just woke up from a coma, for Christ's sake."

She smiled like I'd said something amusing. "I've already died five times. I think I can manage taking medicine and doing muscle exercises on my own."

"Six," Theodore muttered.

"What?"

"You've died six times now."

Eve's brows furrowed. "Has it really been six? I'm surprised you haven't wrapped me in bubble wrap and locked me in a padded room."

I lifted the mug to my lips, sipping on the herbal tea that Eve had made for me. It tasted like peppermint, and I grimaced as I set it down on the end table beside me.

Eve took my hand, uncurling it and tracing the lines in my palm with her fingers.

"Do you remember when I told you that I was afraid of the dark?" she asked.

I nodded, but she didn't say anything else.

195

Instead, she dropped my hand and nestled closer to West's shoulder, closing her eye. I watched her chest rise and fall with her steady breaths—and an image of her still and cold, lying against the white silk lining of a casket, flashed into my head.

I squeezed my eyes closed, focusing on the feel of her skin against mine and the soft sounds of her breathing.

She was here.

She was alive.

Tears stung at the corners of my eyes, and I turned my head away as I swiped at them with the heel of my hand.

When I glanced back at Eve, she was staring down at the palms of her hands. Something glistened in her eye, and I thought she might have been crying, but then she blinked quickly and looked away.

"I can't believe you're alive," Jack said.

"It feels like I've been asleep all this time," she replied.

West touched his fingers to the scar where her left eye had been, tracing them with a delicate artist's touch.

"Damn crows," she muttered, laughing. But there was no humor in it.

"Scavengers go for the eyes first," West whispered.

"They couldn't fix it?" I asked.

"There's no such thing as an eye transplant," Eve said, smiling softly under West's touch. "All the money in the world couldn't fix it."

I leaned my head back against the couch and closed my eyes, my heart feeling heavy and light and warm and cold all at once.

We fell asleep like that, crowded around Eve, sharing a single blanket and enduring elbows and legs poking into our sides, none of us wanting to leave her.

A few hours later, I woke in the darkness.

I reached out for Eve, but the spot where she'd been lying was empty. I had a brief moment of panic before I turned my head and spotted her standing before one of the boarded windows.

I slipped my feet down to the floor, careful not to wake the others, and crept across the room to stand beside her.

She wrapped an arm around my shoulders, and I buried my head in the arch of her neck as she pulled me against her. The embrace was so warm and safe and *familiar.*

"Eve?" I whispered. "Who killed you?"

My eyes flickered to her face, but it was shrouded in shadows. Her body had gone still against mine.

Then she said, "I don't know. But I'm going to find out."

thirty-eight

My head was resting against the urn planter, a green leaf tickling my cheek, when I heard footsteps approaching.

"I thought I might find you here," a voice said.

I glanced over as Theodore lowered himself into the grass beside me, stretching out his long legs in front of him and folding his arms over his chest. A bouquet of dried, shriveled lilies sat between us at the base of the urn.

I picked at a scab that had formed on my bruised knuckles. "I was just . . ." I trailed off, drawing in a breath and squinting in the sunlight.

"Are you still mad at me?" he asked quietly.

"Yes. No." I blinked in frustration and looked at the ground, my cheeks heating. "I don't know."

"I'm sorry."

"How long?" I said. "How long has she been alive?"

"I didn't know if I could—" He stopped suddenly, cursing and fisting a hand in his pale blonde hair. "There was so much blood. And she was so *cold*."

"How long?"

"About a week and a half. I brought her back, but she was in a coma for a while. I didn't know if she would wake up."

"We don't keep secrets," I said, scoffing. "Right?"

"I'm sorry, Tannyn. I'm so sorry."

"How could you not tell me?"

"I didn't know . . . I didn't know if she would wake up. I was so scared."

And he had been, I realized. And still was. That's what he was hiding behind his thundercloud eyes and icy smiles. He was scared. Like me.

"You asked me what happened that night Jude found her on the side of the road," he replied. "She was walking home from a party when someone stabbed her. It was deep—they'd punctured her liver, and she was bleeding out. Jude . . . I don't know how he found her. But when he brought her home, she wasn't breathing. He kept saying that we needed to get her to the hospital, and then he tried to take her and I just snapped. I broke his nose and tossed him out onto the front lawn."

"Does he know about her?"

"I don't know." Theodore dropped his hand back to his side. "I honestly don't know."

"And Nettie?"

"She suspects. I haven't told her much, but she pays attention."

I reached up to wipe away a trickle of sweat that ran from my hairline down the side of my face. Then I looked down at the words carved into the gray marker. "Was the casket empty when they burned it?"

He nodded.

"How?"

"You'd be surprised . . . the things people will do for money," he replied.

"You didn't have to buy her a plot. You could have just tossed the ashes in the trash, and no one would have known," I said. "So why?"

"For you. So you could have a place where you felt close to her."

"It's so depressing. When I die, just throw my ashes into the ocean."

His eyes flickered to my face. "You're not going to die."

"Everyone dies," I whispered. "That's the biggest fear of all, isn't

199

it? Death. It smells like ashes and roses. And it's so fucking cold."

"Why are you telling me this?"

"So that you know what a mess I am." I stared down a the blood stain on my sneakers. "Someone might have cut out Eve's heart, but at least she had one to begin with."

Theodore was silent as he reached out and brushed a strand of hair back behind my ear.

Then, carefully, gauging my reaction, he wound his arms around me and grasped my waist in his hands as he pulled me into his lap. I straddled him, my thighs squeezing his hips, and lifted my hands to run them through his hair. My fingers were still tangled there as he lowered his head to rest it against my chest and closed his eyes.

I held my breath, staring down at him.

"There it is," he said.

And then I felt it—that gentle thump-thump-thumping of my heart.

Theodore pulled back to gaze up at me. "You're not a mess, Tannyn," he said.

And then he kissed me, sitting atop an empty grave, surrounded by bouquets of dried, forgotten flowers.

thirty-nine

eve

Eve wasn't supposed to leave the Boathouse.

But Theodore had gone out with the others—someone wasn't repeatedly killing *him*, after all—and she'd already burned through the DVDs that Theodore had brought for her, including all of the *Amityville* films.

So she tucked the small, black pistol that her brother had bought for her into the waistband of her jean shorts and slipped on a baseball cap and sunglasses before letting herself out the front door.

The air was thick and humid as she made her way through the trees, and within minutes, her thin white t-shirt was clinging to her body with sweat. Her crutches caught in bramble bushes and holes in the dirt, and she thought if she was going to go a seventh time, it was going to be because of those damn things.

The Kelleys owned a big plantation house just a few miles north of her Aunt Ceceli's land, surrounded by acres and acres of peach trees. The walk from the Boathouse was much farther by comparison.

Luckily, she'd also thought to bring a water bottle.

Last summer, before she and Jude had their fight, before she'd been killed, before all of this mess—they'd sat beneath the peach trees in the shade and watched the sun set. She'd ruined one of her favorite blouses when they'd been rolling around in the dirt that night, their bodies sticky with peach juice and sweat, but she still kept it in the very back of one of her drawers—even if Jude had torn it to shreds trying to pull it off of her.

She remembered that he'd traced the scar on her stomach with his finger and that his lips had tickled against her skin as he dipped his head to kiss it.

She wondered what he'd think of all the scars she had now.

Now, she stared up at the dark windows of the house from the shadows of a peach tree.

She leaned against her crutches and kicked off her sneakers to dig her toes into the cool earth. When a light flickered on in one of the windows, she lifted her head and glimpsed the silhouette of a figure moving around in one of the upstairs bedrooms.

Jude, she thought.

A memory was trying to surface in her mind, but it slipped through her fingers like droplets of water.

"Hello?"

"I'm sorry. Did I wake you?"

"It's almost midnight. Where are you?"

She blinked as the figure moved to the window, pushing aside the curtain, and she slunk further into the shadows and held her breath as they stood there, staring out at the trees below.

When they finally disappeared, she released a breath through her nose.

She bent and scooped up her sneakers from the ground, and she didn't bother to slip them back on as she started walking.

forty

I set a tray of grilled cheese and tomato soup down on my father's desk, and then took a step back, absentmindedly fiddling with the ring on my thumb.

My father turned from his computer screen to look at me, his glasses pushed up into his gray-streaked brown hair. His tie hung loosely around his neck, and his face was dotted with dark stubble. "Oh," he said, glancing at the tray. "Is it lunch time already?"

I could feel the steady ticking of the watch on my wrist as if the hands were moving in time with my own heartbeat.

"It's one in the afternoon, dad."

He took off his glasses and set them on the desk, and then he pushed his fingers through his hair. "That late, huh?"

I stared at the dark circles beneath his eyes and sucked my bottom lip into my mouth. My fingers worried at a piece of lint at the bottom of my pocket. "Dad . . . when was the last time you actually slept?"

"What do you mean? I slept last night." He picked up one of the triangles of grilled cheese and began to peel off the crust. Crumbs drifted down onto his wrinkled black pants.

"When was the last time you slept longer than three hours?" I corrected.

"Oh, Tannyn . . ."

I frowned and walked over to the light switch on the wall, flipping on the fan. "It's like a furnace in here," I said. Then I crossed my arms over my chest and glanced past him at the document open on his computer screen. "You should go take a nap, at least."

My father set the grilled cheese back on the tray and swept the crumbs from his pant legs onto the floor below. He picked up his glasses and wiped them off on the corner of his shirt tail before slipping them back on. "I'm fine, honey. You don't need to worry about me."

When he turned back to his computer, something snapped within me.

"I went to see mom the other day," I told him.

He looked up, and suddenly, I had his undivided attention. He cleared his throat, but refused to meet my gaze, looking anywhere else—the beads of sweat gathered along my hairline, the scar that was just visible beneath the collar of my tank top. "Oh, well . . . Well, that's good," he said finally. "How is she?"

"Fine," I said. "As fine as she can be." Then I added, "She didn't remember my birthday, either."

"Oh, Tannyn," he said again. "Christ." He closed his eyes and pinched the bridge of his nose, pushing up his glasses. "I'm sorry."

I glanced towards the window that overlooked the front yard, and I tried to remember what he'd looked like before everything had happened. Had his eyes always been so blue, or did they just look that way because of how pale his skin had become? I squeezed my eyes closed, trying to conjure up one of the pictures of him and my mother that sat above the mantel in the living room.

"Do you want to know what you can do to make it up to me?" I asked, and I looked back over at him as he dropped his hands into his lap and stared up at me, waiting. "You can eat your lunch and take a shower, and then go back to bed."

"I have a *deadline*, Tannyn. My boss—"

"It's one in the afternoon on a Saturday," I interrupted. "And you always have a deadline, but—Christ, dad." I pushed my fingers through my

a girl called murder

hair. "Where does it end? What are you trying to accomplish?"

He lowered his head to stare down at where his hands rested in his lap, and his lips pressed together into a thin line.

"I'm going to work," I told him. "Take some of your pills and try to get some sleep before I get back. I'll be home by six, and we can eat dinner together. Alright?"

He nodded solemnly.

"And eat that damned grilled cheese," I added angrily. "I burnt my hand on the stove making it."

I stalked to the door of his office, and it slammed closed behind me as I left.

I was sitting behind the counter when the bell atop the front door of the store chimed, but I didn't bother to glance up.

One of Ilse's folk songs, low and melancholy, poured from the speakers. My forehead and the back of my neck were misted with sweat, and I reached up to tie my hair back from my face as a pair of long, freckled legs stopped at the counter in front of me.

"Stop me if you've heard this one," Jude said. "A crow walks into a bookstore . . ."

I tucked back several wisps of hair and flipped to the next page of the book I was reading. "No, please. Do go on."

Jude smiled. "You know," he said, pointing at the speakers, "this Hera Hjartardóttir is really starting to grow on me."

Sighing through my nose, I shut my book. "Is there something I can help you with, Jude?"

"I was concerned because I hadn't received an RSVP from your little murder of crows yet, so I thought I'd stop by."

"I'm allergic to rich people. I break out in hives."

"But not the Shearwater twins."

"What can I say? Allergy medication is a modern miracle," I told him. "But I forgot to take it this morning, so I'm afraid I have to cut this conversation short."

His grin widened as he leaned against the counter. "I'll put you down as a yes then."

"Well, I hope you enjoy disappointment."

"Have you decided who to bring as your fifth? I did give you an extra invitation, after all."

I frowned. I hadn't even thought about that. Five invitations, five crows—and this was before we'd learned that Eve was alive. I stared at Jude, trying to find anything in his expression that said he knew about her.

"I'm not good at making new friends," I said finally. "You can have it back, if you want."

"Keep it. I'm sure you'll find someone." His expression turned serious. "I know the last time we talked . . . didn't go very well. But I hope you've thought about what I said."

"I did," I replied simply, picking up my book again.

"Have you talked to Theodore?"

"If I did, it's none of your business. And if I didn't, it's also none of your business."

"I wish you would trust me, Tannyn."

I slammed my book down on the counter, harder than I'd meant to. "And why should I?" I hissed at him. "You've given me no reason to."

"Eve trusted me. Isn't that enough?"

I snorted. "Eve trusted a lot of people."

"Like you," he said. "When everyone else was afraid of you, she trusted you. That's how I know that I can."

I bit back whatever retort lingered on the edge of my tongue.

Jude straightened from the counter and shoved his hands into the pockets of his shorts. "Well, that's all, I suppose," he said. "I really do hope to see you at the party, Tannyn. I mean it."

I watched as he walked to the front door and pushed it open. He stopped on the threshold and glanced back over his shoulder at me, his dark eyes pensive.

"You're not the only one who lost her, you know."

Then the door slammed shut behind him.

It was only a moment after he'd climbed in his car and left that my phone began to ring in my back pocket.

I pulled it out and checked the caller ID. West.

I answered and brought it to my ear. "Hello?"

"Tannyn? Where are you?"

"Work. Why? What's wrong? Is Eve okay?"

I could hear the frown in his voice as he said, "She's fine, but there's . . . a problem."

"A problem," I repeated. I plugged my other ear with my finger so I could hear him better over Ilse's folk music. "What does that mean?"

"Someone left a package on my front porch. How quickly can you get to the Boathouse?"

"What kind of package? West, where's Theodore?"

"He's on his way," West said. "And the package was addressed to the Ace of Crows. No return label. Just . . . get here as quick as you can, okay?"

"West—"

But the line went dead before I had the chance to say anything else.

I grumbled an obscenity as I shoved my phone back into my pocket. My coworker Jules was at the back of the store, stacking a new shipment of books on the shelves when I found them.

Jules looked up, strands of curly black hair falling in their face. "Tannyn. What's up?" they asked, and then glanced at the watch on their wrist. "Is it time for your break already?"

"No," I said. "I have a family emergency. Can you cover for me?"

They stood up, brushing off the back of their shorts. "Of course. Is everything alright?"

"Maybe. Yes. I don't know," I said. I pulled my car keys from my pocket, and then my phone, dialing Eve's burner cell. As I started for the front of the store, I added, "Thanks, Jules. I owe you one."

forty-one

The rest of the crows were gathered in the front room of the Boathouse when I arrived.

They were staring at a plain white box tied with a large red bow on the coffee table. When I got close enough, I could make out a small square of paper that read, *To the Ace of Crows,* in bold type print.

I sat down on the couch beside Theodore, and he reached out to take my hand, winding his fingers through my own.

"You said this was left on your porch?" I asked West. "When?"

"About forty-five minutes ago, before I called you."

"You didn't see who left it?"

He shook his head. "They rang the bell, but no one was there when I answered the door. And there were no cars around," he replied. "I asked my neighbors, but they didn't see anything."

"Have you opened it yet?"

"We were waiting for you," Jack said.

"Then what the hell are you waiting for now?" I snapped, and Theodore squeezed my fingers gently in his. I ignored him.

No one moved to open it. The room was silent except for the whir of the air conditioner.

Finally, Eve sat forward and muttered, "Oh, for fuck's sake. I'll open it."

Then before anyone could protest, she'd ripped the ribbon from the box and pulled off the lid. She lifted out a feather, sleek and black, and then set it aside on the table.

We all leaned forward to peer at the rest of the box's contents. Five plain white plastic masks—the kind you could get at any craft store or Walmart—lined up perfectly in a row. A coiled lock of pale blond hair—*Eve's hair,* I thought, nausea rising in my throat—tied with a black ribbon.

There was a single piece of paper, printed with a poem.

Eve took it from the box, and I read it over her shoulder:

Look in the eyes of trouble with a smile,
Extend your hand and do not be afraid.
'Tis but a friend who comes to masquerade,
And test your faith and courage for awhile.

Fly, and he follows fast with threat and jeer.
Shrink, and he deals hard blow on stinging blow,
But bid him welcome as a friend, and lo!

The jest is off — the masque will disappear.

I glanced at Eve's face, gauging her reaction, but it was blank. She handed it across the table to Jack.

"The Kelley's masquerade party is this weekend," I said.

Jack looked at me. "What?"

"Jude dropped off the invitations a few weeks ago—five of them. I didn't think anything of it at the time," I replied. "I wasn't even going to say anything because I figured we wouldn't go."

"Five invitations," Eve repeated. "Do you still have them?"

"I meant to throw them out, but I kept forgetting. They're in my bag at home."

Eve was silent, thoughtful. The expression she wore was

210

frightening; it was one I'd seen plenty of times in the past and that almost always ended in trouble.

"It had to be Jude that left that package then," Jack said.

I looked away from Eve and shook my head. "West said it was delivered right before he called me. Jude was at the bookstore then."

Theodore stiffened beside me. "What was Jude doing at the bookstore?"

"He was concerned that none of us had RSVP'd to the party," I said. I looked over at Eve, who had gone still. "And he was wondering who my plus one was going to be since he gave us an extra invitation."

"He knows," Jack replied. "He has to."

"I don't know," Theodore said. "That night when he brought Eve home after she'd been stabbed, I tossed him out of the house before he could see anything."

"He came over the next day while you were out," Eve said quietly. "He'd called all of the hospitals in the area, and when he heard I hadn't been admitted as a patient to any of them, he wanted to make sure I was okay."

"What *happened* between the two of you?" I asked.

"A few weeks before . . . before someone cut out my heart," she said, the words catching in her throat, "we got into a fight. It was bad. We both said things we shouldn't have, and I . . . I told him that I wished he'd never found me that night." She looked at Theodore. "But you don't think he's the one that killed me."

Theodore was silent, and when her gaze flickered to me, I turned my head away to stare at a paint stain on the wooden floor.

"No," she said, shaking her head. "Jude wouldn't."

"We don't know that," Theodore replied.

"*I* do."

"Eve . . ." I said.

211

"We have to go," Eve announced.

"No," Theodore said.

"You're supposed to be dead," I added. "And don't even say that you can just wear a mask—the fact that it's a masquerade party is too convenient."

"Whoever killed me is going to be there," she said. "I'm not just going to sit around waiting to get killed again." She stared at Theodore, her remaining eye deadly serious. "I'm not asking for your permission. I'm going —with or without you all."

"Christ," I muttered.

"Besides," Eve added, sitting back and crossing her arms over her chest. "I already have a plan."

"Oh?" Theodore replied, raising his brows. "And when were you planning on sharing it with us?"

Eve shot him a look. "Just now, if you'd let me speak."

Theodore spread his hands for her to continue.

"Whoever killed me will be looking for me at the party," she said. "So we lure them away, somewhere secluded. There's a hedge maze behind the Kelley's house—it has only two entrances, and even Jude has gotten lost in it before. It's perfect."

"And how do you suppose we lure them there?"

"Easy. We get them to follow me."

Theodore went rigid. "Absolutely not."

"No," West said.

Eve continued to stare them down with her storm-cloud gray eye. "It's the only way to be sure they'll follow."

"You can barely walk as it is," Jack said. "We're not using you as bait."

As they bickered amongst themselves, I was staring down at my hands in my lap, thinking. I couldn't let Eve do this. I couldn't lose her again; the crows couldn't lose her again.

"You will die before the next full moon, Tannyn Carter."

I looked up at the faces scattered around me. "I'll do it."

Eve broke off in the middle of whatever she'd been saying, turning to face me. "What?"

"I'll do it," I repeated. "It's a masquerade party—all I need is a blonde wig and heels. With a mask, no one will know it's me."

"You think you're more expendable than Eve?" Theodore asked. "No one is doing it, and that's final."

I turned my gaze on him, narrowing my eyes. "You're not my keeper. This isn't for you to decide," I told him. "Besides, you've said it yourself—I can take care of myself."

Theodore spoke between his teeth. "Against drunk high school boys, yes. This is different."

"So, I'll be careful. I'll bring my knife and learn the layout of the maze and have you all there in case something goes wrong." When he opened his mouth again to object, I cut him off. "I'm *not* asking, Theodore."

Theodore pressed his lips together into a thin line, nostrils flared. "Fine," he said finally. "But I have some conditions."

"I would expect nothing less."

"You wear a bullet proof vest. That's non-negotiable. We already know whoever sent the dead crow has a gun," he said. I nodded, and he continued. "We stay in contact *at all times.* I'll pick up some wireless earpieces later."

Eve lips curled into a smile. "I feel like Nancy Drew."

"Nancy Drew lived in the 1930's," I said.

"One of Charlie's Angels then."

"There are five of us," Jack replied.

"You would obviously be Bosley," Eve told him.

Theodore ignored her. "We plan this thing out perfectly. I want it to be foolproof. And lastly—if anything goes wrong, if I say it's too dangerous, you get out of there."

I nodded.

Eve picked up the poem from the box and tore it into pieces. "I can get a map of the maze. And there's a window in one of the offices on the third-floor that overlooks it," she said. "And don't worry about the costumes. Leave that all to me."

"I can't believe I'm agreeing to this," Theodore grumbled, pinching the bridge of his nose.

Jack looked between all of our faces, his mouth set in a worried line. "So, we lure whoever killed you into the maze," he asked Eve. "*Y entonces que pasa*? Then what?"

Eve flashed a grin carved from malevolence and broken glass. "Then we watch the motherfucker burn."

forty-two

I was greeted by the tangy scent of tomato sauce as I walked through the front door, and Madeline pushed at my legs with her nose as I hung my keys up.

"Dad?" I called warily, stepping out of my sneakers and moving towards the kitchen with Madeline at my heels.

I wondered if someone had broken into our house and was making dinner. Somehow that seemed the more likely explanation than my father leaving his office and deciding to try his hand at cooking.

My father was standing at the stove when I walked into the kitchen, his hair still slightly damp from the shower and his button-up exchanged for a plain white t-shirt. Plain, at least, save for the stain of tomato sauce by the collar that he doesn't seem to have noticed.

I blinked once, twice, as he bent over a boiling pot on the stove to make sure I wasn't seeing things.

Then he glanced over his shoulder and spotted me where I was standing in the doorway, and his eyebrows rose to meet his slicked-back, wet hair. "Oh, I, uh . . ." he stammered, looking back at the pot on the stove. His face flushed slightly, like a child who's been caught doing something wrong. "I was trying to make spaghetti."

"Trying?" I asked. I moved to the fridge and took out a water bottle, cracking off the top.

"The pasta isn't cooking," he said.

I set down my water bottle on the island, and he stepped out of the way as I walked over to peer into the pot. "Did you wait for the water to boil

215

before you put it in?"

When he didn't answer, I looked over at him to see his cheeks turn pick again beneath his gray-streaked hair.

"That's alright," I told him, reaching down to adjust the gas burner. I pulled open the drawer beside the stove and took out a wooden spoon, stirring the pasta as I waited for the water to begin boiling. My father stood beside me, watching over my shoulder, and I added, "You can make the salad, if you want."

I continued stirring the pasta as I listened to my father pull open the fridge and take out a bag of lettuce.

"So . . ." he said, shaking the lettuce out into a bowl. "You said your mother was doing good when you went to see her?"

I nodded.

He hesitated before asking, "Did she seem happy?"

The muscles in my shoulders tensed, and I remembered my mother humming "Downtown" beneath her breath as another patient cried in the corner. The gas burner hissed as boiling water spilled over the side of the pot, and I started suddenly, reaching to turn down the heat.

"Tannyn?" my father said.

I swallowed. "You should go see her," I replied without looking at him.

I heard him open the fridge again and glanced over to see him taking out a tomato and cucumber. He bent to take a cutting board from beneath the island, and I involuntarily flinched as I heard the knife drawer slide open.

"It wasn't her fault," I mumbled.

My father shook his head. "If your brother hadn't been there . . ."

"*It wasn't her fault,*" I said again, though I wasn't sure who I was trying to convince: him, or myself.

216

I listened to the sound of the knife against the cutting board, and I stared at the steam that was rising from the pot in front of me. My father's fear lingered on the end of my tongue like black coffee and pen ink, and I pulled out a strand of spaghetti and popped it into my mouth to rid it of the taste.

"I should have been there for her," my father said.

I began to hum "Downtown" beneath my breath, but then stopped when I realized what I was doing a moment later.

"Tannyn, I'm—" my father began.

"Pasta's done," I said.

He was silent as I turned off the burner and moved to the sink to drain the pasta, and then I heated the tomato sauce in a pan on the stove.

My father set the table, and then walked out into the living room to turn on the radio. Madeline sat at my feet and watched as I added the sauce to the pasta. I filled two plates and brought them over to the table, sitting down across from my father.

Madeline laid across my feet beneath the table, resting her head atop her front paws.

As I piled salad onto my plate, a breeze drifted in through the back screen door and brushed my hair back from my face.

When "Tea for Two" by Doris Day started playing on the radio, the scar along my collarbone began to itch. I stood up from the table and walked over to switch off the radio, and my father was staring down at his plate as I slid back into my seat.

"I'm sorry that I forgot your birthday," he said suddenly. "And I'm sorry that I've been so busy I haven't been there for you."

I lifted my head, and there was genuine guilt in his eyes as he met my gaze.

"It's alright," I told him.

"No, Tannyn," he said. "It's not."

My throat grew tight, and I glanced down at my plate, pushing at the spaghetti with my fork. "I needed you," I whispered. "After they took mom away, I needed you, and you weren't there."

"I'm so sorry, Tannyn. You shouldn't have had to go through that alone."

The rest of dinner was silent, save for the scraping of silverware against plates.

I speared the last bits of spaghetti with my fork, and then stood up from my seat, taking my father's empty plate and stacking it on top of my own. "I'll wash, you dry?" I asked, avoiding his eyes as a light flush crept into my cheeks.

When my gaze flickered to his face, the corner of his mouth had tipped up into a smile.

He nodded and pushed back in his chair. "Sounds good."

I turned my back on him, and I heard his footsteps as he followed me across the kitchen to the sink. I dumped the dirty plates into the basin, and then bent to take a wash cloth from one of the drawers.

When I straightened again, my father's brows had drawn together and he was staring at my forearm.

"Tannyn," he said. "Is that a tattoo?"

The alarm clock on my bedside table read 1:14 as I closed the book in my lap and rolled over to flick off the lights.

I lay back against the pillows and folded my arms on top of my chest, staring up at the glow-in-the-dark stars that were plastered across my ceiling. I closed my eyes and listened to the sounds of the cicadas outside my window.

Inside the house, my father's mattress creaked as he rolled over in his sleep.

Outside, an owl hooted.

I felt my father's dreams tugging at the edge of my consciousness— or rather, not his dreams, but his *nightmares*. I pushed at one of my bottom teeth with my tongue, and it wriggled back and forth. I opened my eyes and sat up in bed, spitting out a handful of bloody teeth into my palm.

I dropped them onto the bed and scrambled backwards away from them.

They scattered across the covers, spattering the fabric with blood, and a voice echoed in my mind: *"You will die before the next full moon, Tannyn Carter."*

When I opened my eyes and sat up in bed a second time, there was no blood on the covers and all of my teeth were arranged in my mouth as they should have been and the alarm clock on the bedside table read 1:37.

The cicadas had gone silent, as if they were aware that something had just happened and were waiting to make sure it didn't happen again.

A minute passed. The clock read 1:38.

I ran my tongue along the backs of my teeth as the cicadas began singing again.

A strand of lilac hair came loose from my ponytail and drifted down in front of my face. I stared at it with narrowed eyes.

I slipped from my bed and pulled on a pair of sneakers, and then I snatched Delilah's spare key from where I kept it hidden inside a copy of *Leaves of Grass* on my bookshelf. I tucked the key into the pocket on my pajama shorts.

By the time the numbers on the clock flipped to 1:40, no one was around to see it.

My fingers dug into bark as I scaled the limbs of the elm tree outside of my window, finding the hand and footholds that I'd used time and time again, the movements as natural as breathing.

I dropped to the ground in a shower of leaves, my sneakers making a barely audible *thud* as they hit the grass.

As Delilah rumbled to life, my eyes slid to the front of the house, but the light in my father's room remained off. Even so, I kept the headlights out while I backed from the driveway and didn't turn them on until I was halfway down the street.

I rolled down the windows and stuck my hand out into the cool night air, feeling it slip between my fingers. The trees on either side of the road shivered in the wind.

Staring up at the waxing quarter moon against the dark sky, I reached over and turned on the radio.

"You will die before the next full moon, Tannyn Carter."

forty-three

eve

If it hadn't been for the drops of rain water that clung to the grass on the side of the road, or the fact that she still had two eyes, Eve wouldn't have known she was dreaming.

But Truth or Consequence had been in a drought for almost a month—or so she'd been told—and most of the grass she'd seen since she'd come back had been brown and burnt to a crisp. And as for her eye . . . well, fuck crows.

As she wandered down the middle of the street, she tried to remember what she and Theodore had been fighting about. But they'd been fighting a lot lately, about anything and everything—Jude, their parents, their aunt, Theodore's ridiculous mother-bird complex—and it was hard to keep track.

Eve's feet had begun to bleed because she'd foolishly left the house without shoes and had accidentally stepped in a bramble bush, and now the pavement was sticky with her blood.

She dug her phone from the pocket of her vintage black nightgown and called the only person she could think of at twelve in the morning when she was stuck in the middle of nowhere. The phone rang three times before the person on the other end picked up.

"Hello?" Jude asked sleepily.

Her fingers tightened around the phone, and she closed her eyes. "I'm sorry. Did I wake you?"

She heard the creaking of a mattress, and a second later, he said, "Eve?"

"Yeah. It's me." She chewed on her lower lip, and then said. "Theodore and I had a fight. Can you come get me?"

"It's almost midnight," he replied. "Where are you?"

She wrapped her free arm around herself and squinted at the street sign up ahead. "Goldfield," she told him. It sounded like a question.

"I'll be there in fifteen," he said.

The line went dead.

Eve sunk down into the grass on the side of the road to wait, drawing her legs up to her chest and tucking her chin between her knees. A bead of sweat gathered on her neck and slithered down her back. She reached for a dandelion and plucked it up between her fingers, watching the white tufts sway with her breath.

Twenty minutes later, tires crunched over gravel, and Eve lifted her head to see a car pull to a stop beside her. The headlights were off, and she could just barely make out the form of someone in the driver's seat.

She climbed to her feet and wiped blades of grass from her bare legs.

She and Jude hadn't spoken since their fight, and she knotted her fingers into the skirt of her nightgown. She was trying to think of what to say as the driver's side window rolled down. The smile that she forced didn't reach her eyes.

She could hear the falseness in her voice as she said, "Here's a tip for the future: when a girl calls you in the middle of the night and asks you to come pick her up, you don't make her wait."

A hand reached out from the dark interior and grabbed her by the hair, smashing her head against the side of the car.

She sunk to the pavement and tasted blood on her lips.

She remembered that everything had gone dark after that, but in the dream, she watched as blood dripped from the gash on her forehead. The drops landed on the ground before her, and as she blinked, the pavement turned to glass beneath her fingers.

Her reflection stared back at her, gray eyes wide.

Then the world flipped upside-down, and another pane of glass was against her back. She realized that she was lying in a glass box, and she shoved against the pane over her head until her arms ached. She kicked and struck at it, but it wouldn't budge.

She glimpsed movement out of the corner of her eye, and then someone leaned over the top of the glass box.

"Tannyn?" she whispered, recognizing the girl's wavy lilac hair and brown eyes. She pounded against the glass with her fist. "Tannyn!"

The girl didn't show any sign of having heard her; instead, she reached out and lay a bouquet of white lilies on the pane of glass that hovered over Eve's head. Her eyes were misted with tears.

Theodore came up behind Tannyn, wrapping his arm around her shoulder, and she turned her head to bury it in his chest. Her hands knotted in his black suit jacket as she clung to him, and he stroked his fingers over her hair. He murmured something that Eve couldn't make out from behind the glass.

"Theodore!" Eve threw herself against the side of the glass box, and pain shot through her shoulder. "Tannyn!"

Tears had gathered in her eyes, and she felt as if her throat were closing up. Her breathing became heavy, and she found herself gasping for air. Her chest ached from the effort.

The lid of the glass box opened, but before she could move, hands reached down and wrapped around her throat. The fingers pressed into her skin, and her eyes bulged as she clawed at the person. Didn't they realize

223

they were choking her? Couldn't they see that she was dying?

Dark spots danced across her vision, and her eyes fluttered closed.

Her hands went limp, dropping to her sides.

One moment, there was pain as she felt her heart beating in her throat. Her body give a violent shudder.

The next, nothing.

forty-four

I quietly eased the door of the Boathouse open and pocketed my keys.

The light in the front room was off, but the blankets lay in a crumpled pile at the end of the pull-out couch. A teapot was boiling on a hot plate in the small kitchen, and a mug sat out on the counter.

I closed the door behind me and slid the lock into place.

"Tannyn?"

I jumped, muttering a curse.

I glanced over my shoulder to see Eve standing in the doorway of the back room, her arms wrapped around herself. Strands of hair had come loose from her bun and fell in unruly waves around her face.

"Hey," I said softly. "Did I wake you?"

She shook her head. "Couldn't sleep. Bad dreams."

I smiled gently. "Without me?"

"I know," she replied, grinning. "What kind of friend am I?" She walked past me into the kitchen and went up on her toes to take down a second mug from one of the cabinets. "Theodore sucks at grocery shopping, so I only have tea. No coffee. Is Earl Grey alright?"

"Do you have any bourbon?" I asked, sitting down on the edge of the pull-out couch.

Eve opened another cabinet and produced a half-empty bottle of Jim Bean. "This *is* Louisiana."

She put a tea bag in each of the mugs, and when the teapot began to shriek, she removed it from the hot plate and filled the mugs three-quarters of the way with boiling water. Then she added a splash of bourbon and a spoonful of honey to each.

She walked out into the front room and sat down on the couch beside me, handing me one of the mugs.

I blew on the steam that drifted off the tea, cupping the hot mug with both hands. "Where are your crutches?"

Eve took a sip of hers without waiting for it to cool down—I supposed you weren't afraid of things like burning your tongue when you'd already died more than once. "Around. I've been doing my physical therapy every day so my legs are stronger now."

"I wish you would have stayed at the hospital longer."

"I think Dr. Reinhardt was getting sick of me," she said. "And I hated being secluded like that—all the closed curtains and locked doors. It felt like quarantine."

"Well, you *did* die."

She smiled softly. "Let's not talk about me anymore. What about you? Couldn't sleep?"

"Too worried about you." I elbowed her gentle enough to not spill her tea. "Are you sure you're safe here by yourself? Your aunt's house has better security."

"Someone's already broken in there once. I don't want Nettie or Theodore getting hurt if someone comes after me again," she replied. "And no one knows about the Boathouse but us. Not even Nettie."

I was silent for a moment. Then I asked, "Did it hurt?"

She grinned wickedly. "When I fell from heaven?" Then the smile fell from her face and her brows drew together slightly. She tucked back the strands of hair in her face. "I don't remember."

I picked at a string on the end of my pajama shorts. " I got a tattoo of your date of death. You owe me sixty bucks."

Now her brows rose slightly. "Really? Can I see?"

I lifted the hem of my tank top to show her the Roman numerals beneath the crow along my ribcage, and she chuckled. She traced them lightly with her finger, and I squirmed. "That tickles."

"Do you want to see my scar? It sort of resembles Botswana."

"Don't take this personally, but no."

She snickered. "It's still healing, so it is kind of gross."

"Theodore said he had to find you a new heart." I'd meant it as a question, but I wasn't sure how to phrase it.

Eve made a sound in the back of her throat. "Don't remind me," she said. "God knows where he was keeping me until then. I haven't asked, and I don't plan to." She took another sip of her tea.

"I'm sorry about your eye."

"Don't be. It wasn't your fault."

"I also killed your sunflowers by accident," I told her. My throat began to close up, and I swallowed thickly. "I didn't think you were coming back."

Eve's expression softened. "Tannyn," she said, setting down her mug on the coffee table. I followed suit. "I'm sorry I didn't ask this earlier—How are you doing?"

I shook my head, tears building in the corners of my eyes. "Not good, Eve," I whispered.

She opened her arms to me, and I buried myself against her chest. She enveloped me against her and tucked her chin into the crown of my head. I listened to the rhythmic beating of her new heart as the tears rolled silently down my face and dripped onto her pajamas.

"It's alright," she said softly.

"Don't ever leave me again," I replied, knotting my fingers into her shirt. "Please."

Eve's arms tightened around me. "I promise."

I pulled out of her embrace, swiping at my face with the back of my hand, and a laugh burst from my lips when I saw the redness beneath her gray eye. "Shit, you really are an ugly crier."

She glared at me as she brushed the tears away with her fingers. "Why does no one ever believe me?"

But a moment later, she was laughing, as well. She collapsed into my lap, her body trembling with breathless laughter as she leaned her head against my shoulder. She closed her eye, and her warm breath tickled the base of my throat.

"Were the others nice to you while I was gone?" she asked. "Did they take good care of you?"

"You know me," I said, resting my head against hers. "I can take care of myself."

She reached for my hand, lacing her fingers through mine. "But that's just it, Tannyn. You don't have to."

"I'm just used to it," I replied.

"I know, darling. But I wish you would just let someone else take care of you for once," she said. "What about Theodore?"

A flush crawled into my cheeks. "What about him?"

"I see the way you look at him. You're both strong and loyal and stubborn as hell," she replied. "Do you remember prom night, when we climbed up into the tree to watch the sunrise? You kissed me, and I said that I wished it had been us—you and me. That it would have made things simpler." She smiled. "I'm glad now that it wasn't me."

"It's the new hair, isn't it?"

Her laughter shook my entire body. "No, no. I love the purple."

228

"I do love you," I told her. "You know that, right?"

She kissed my forehead, her lips warm against my skin. "I know." She picked up her mug and finished her tea in a few quick gulps. "Come on," she said. "Let's get to bed. I'll even let you be the little spoon."

forty-five

My first thought as I climbed from my car was, *I shouldn't be here.*

The second was, *Well, I'm going to die anyway.*

I locked my car behind me as I started down the sidewalk, past colorful ivy-covered buildings and street performers with upturned hats and open saxophone cases lying scattered around them. My brow glistened with sweat, and I reached up to wipe away the drops with the back of my hand. The gesture in itself was bitter, but paired with my pursed lips and narrowed eyes, it was mean and spiteful. Like a Mojave rattler shaking its tail in warning before it strikes.

I lifted my sunglasses into my hair to squint at the sign ahead that read *Antiques and Collectibles.* My fingers clenched and unclenched in the pocket of my shorts.

When I pushed open the glass front door, the old woman behind the counter looked up at me. Her head scarf was bright yellow, and I blinked repeatedly at the sight of it—like looking into the sun.

The skin around her eyes crinkled as she said, "You're late."

I looked from her head scarf to a brooch on her shirt shaped like a bumblebee. "You can't be late for an appointment that doesn't exist," I told her.

"I suspected you'd be back." The woman swept out from behind the counter, the bracelets on her wrist clinking together. Without another word, she passed through the beaded curtain into the back room, and I knew that she meant for me to follow.

I lingered in the doorway, the beads brushing my back, as the woman sunk down at the table in the corner. She picked up a deck of cards and began to shuffle through them.

"What happened to your face?" she asked, nodding to the yellowing bruise that was still visible along my brow. The cards expertly slid through her brown fingers.

"There was an incident," I replied.

"I see," the woman said, as if she really did.

I frowned as she flipped over a card and laid it face-up on the table in front of her. The Nine of Swords. Her dark eyes flickered to my face, and I got the strange sense that she wasn't actually looking *at* me.

Then she said, "I can't tell you how you're going to die."

I shoved my hands back into the pockets of my shorts so that she wouldn't see me clench them into fists. "Why not?" I asked.

She shook her head and set the deck of cards back down on the table. "You're angry," she said. "I understand."

"Can't you read my bones again?"

"They're only going to tell me what I already know." She straightened and walked over to one of the shelves on the wall, taking down a jar filled with dried purple flowers. "Heather," she said, holding a sprig out to me. "For luck and protection."

When I made no move to take it from her, she tucked it into the breast pocket on my shirt.

She turned away, starting towards a burner and tea pot at the back of the room. "How about some tea?" she offered. "I have ginseng—"

"So there's nothing you can do?"

The words came out sharper than I'd meant them to, but when the woman glanced back at me, her expression only softened. She pursed her lips, and a line appeared her dark brows as she stared at me.

Finally, she said, "Have you ever heard the phrase, you'll catch your death?

"My mother used to say it when I didn't wear a coat in the winter," I told her.

She sucked her bottom lip between her teeth and looked thoughtful. "If you want to catch your death, you'll find it past the field of stone and empty names."

"I don't have time for riddles."

"That's all I have for you," the woman replied, picking up the tea pot and walking over to fill it at the sink against the far wall. She set the pot back down on the burner and leaned against the table with one hand. "What kind of tea did you say?"

"I didn't."

The woman's lips pulled down at the corners. "Well, in that case, there's nothing more that I can do for you."

"That's it?"

She nodded once and said, "I am sorry. It was nice to see you again, though." An unspoken *before you die* hung in the air at the end of her words.

I didn't know what to say, so I simply turned away from her. The strands of beads in the curtain clicked together as I passed through the doorway. I tried to ignore the feel of the woman's eyes on my back, but it was like trying to ignore her bright yellow head scarf or the pitying way she held her eyebrows, as if I were already dead.

Just as I was about to open the front door, I paused and turned back to face her.

"What do you know about my friend's murder?" I asked.

The woman blinked at me through the beaded curtain and picked up a dainty green tea cup, turning it over in her hands. The ghost of a frown still lingered on her face. "Did you know that crows gather in groups to attack possible predators? There's strength in numbers."

232

I pushed open the front door as the tea pot at the back of the store began to shriek, high and shrill, following me out onto the sidewalk and leaving a taste like burnt flesh on my tongue.

A trickle of sweat ran between my breasts as I cruised down the road past fields of sugar cane and cotton, and I took my hand off the wheel to dab it away with the collar of my tank top.

Strands of hair blew into my face, sticking to my skin, but I hardly noticed them.

My lips pressed into a thin line, and I reached over to turn up the volume on the radio. My fingers drummed against the steering wheel in time to a Sheryl Crow song as I sought to distract myself.

What else was there to think about besides how sticky I felt or the fact that I was going to die?

Staring out at the tall stalks of sugar cane that swayed in the wind, I thought, *You could think about Theodore*, at the same time the small, rational part of me said, *Oh, no you don't.*

But it was too late—an image of him, lying with his fingers tangled through mine, had already entered my thoughts, and a heavy flush was rising to my cheeks. Boys were no good, I'd learned early on. But boys with storm-cloud eyes and lovely cheekbones . . . It was like being hit by a train when I hadn't even known I was standing on the tracks.

My fingers tightened around the steering wheel.

If boys with grins made from broken glass were no good, then what did that say about girls with lilac hair and bruised knuckles with a thing for nightmares?

The thought didn't make me feel any better, and I reached for the radio, scanning through the stations for something loud and distracting and not about paper bags or cement shoes.

"If you want to catch your death, you'll find it past the field of stone and empty names."

What the hell did that even mean? A field of stone and empty names?

While I was trying to not-think about Theodore while not-thinking about dying, a sudden noise like a small explosion came from the front of my car. Delilah shuddered beneath me. An oh-no, this-could-not-possibly-be-good sort of shudder.

I eased the car over onto the dirt shoulder, switching on my hazards.

I knew that my tire had blown out before I climbed from my car, and I splayed my hand across my face as I walked around to the front, peeking out between my fingers at the damage.

"Shit," I said. Then, as I crouched down to get a closer look, "Fuck."

Delilah was tipped slightly to the side, sagging beneath the front right tire that resembled something of a deflated balloon at the moment.

I straightened up and brushed my hands off on the back of my shorts, and then pushed my fingers through my hair. They caught in the tangles as I stared down at the flat tire.

"Fuck," I said again.

I glanced both ways down the empty road, but there were no other cars in sight. I wasn't even sure what road I was *on*.

My footsteps sounded unnaturally heavy as I walked around to the back of the car, and the Sheryl Crow line about cement shoes popped into my thoughts. I opened the trunk, and then reached up to tie my hair back from my face.

The sun beat down on the back of my neck as I hauled the spare tire out from the trunk, grunting beneath the weight, and rolled it around to the front of the car.

Still not-thinking about dying—who wanted to think about dying when their car had broken down in the middle of nowhere?—I wiped the sweat from my brow with the back of my hand and frowned down at the spare.

"Let's get this over with," I mumbled to no one.

I retrieved the tire iron and the jack, and then I knelt down in the dirt. I didn't realize I'd begun to hum beneath my breath until I was interrupted by the sound of tires crunching over gravel.

I lifted my head, squinting behind my sunglasses at the car that had pulled over onto the shoulder behind mine. The engine cut off, and a figure emerged from the driver's side.

"Tannyn? Is that you?" a familiar voice said.

I stood up, wiping the bits of dirt from my knees, and then pushed my sunglasses into my hair. "Mr. Kestrel?" I said, not bothering to hide the surprise in my voice.

"I thought that was you," he replied, walking around my car to stand in front of me. His long, blonde hair was swept back from his face in a ponytail, and his clothes were smudged and wrinkled. He always looked fairly dirty—like he'd just been dug up from the soil. He swiped some loose strands of hair from his face and glanced down at the spare tire that was propped up against the side of my car. "Car troubles? Need any help?"

I arched an eyebrow that might have been disdainful if not for the smile that tugged at the corner of my mouth. "I know how to change a tire," I told him.

He chuckled. "I don't doubt it," he said. "But let me give you a hand."

"Alright," I said, if only because it was hot and my tank top was already damp with sweat and the spare tire was far heavier than it had looked when it had been sitting unused in my trunk.

We worked in silence, and I found myself studying the intricate burn scars on his hands as he placed the spare tire on the hub. The skin was pink and angry and puckered, and his fingers trembled as he fit the lug nuts back on.

When he caught me staring, I flushed.

"Sorry," I muttered. "I should know better not to stare." I gestured to the scars on my cheek and collarbone.

Mr. Kestrel straightened from the ground, wiping his hands off on his pants, and offered a half-smile that was both amused and embarrassed. "Don't worry. I'm used to it."

"What happened? If you don't mind me asking." I stood up, scuffing at the dirt with the toe of my sneaker. I couldn't remember why I'd even brought it up, so I added, "Sorry. It's none of my business."

"No, it's alright." He hesitated a moment, staring out at the fields of sugar cane. "There was . . . an accident. The car had caught fire, and I was trying to get my wife out. She'd hit her head—badly," he added. "That's how she ended up in a coma."

"I'm sorry."

"Well, it's certainly nothing you need to apologize for," he replied.

"The kids at school—"

"Are just being kids," he interrupted. "Don't worry yourself over it."

I chewed on my bottom lip, wanting to say something more, but then he spoke again before I had the chance to.

"We've all got scars," he said, and I noticed his gaze flicker to the thick, puckered line along my collarbone that was just visible beneath my tank top. "It doesn't make us any more or less. It just makes us . . . living," he finished finally. "The natural order."

"Dust to dust," I muttered.

He grinned, blinking in surprise. "Exactly."

"Mr. Kestrel . . . if someone told you that you'd find something past the field of stone and empty names, where would you look?"

His brows rose in surprise, and then knit together as he thought. "Is this for a scavenger hunt?" he asked.

"Yeah," I lied. "I haven't been able to figure it out."

"Sounds like a cemetery, if you ask me."

A cemetery.

A cemetery. Because why the fuck would I die anywhere else?

"Does that sound right?" Mr. Kestrel asked.

"Yes. Thank you."

An awkward silence ensued, the kind that always seemed to happen once a student and teacher had finished a conversation and neither was quite sure how to end it. It was a silence that made me aware of the taste of smoke in my mouth. It was heavy and acrid, and I coughed violently into my forearm.

"Anyway, thanks for your help, Mr. Kestrel," I said, once the coughing fit had subsided.

I bent to pick up the flat tire from where it rested against the side of my car, hefting it into my arms at the same time Mr. Kestrel began to reach for it.

"It's alright," I said. "I've got it."

As I loaded the flat into Delilah's trunk, Mr. Kestrel walked back to his car and climbed into the driver's side.

He started his car and then waved out the window as he cruised past, rolling down the window to call out, "Have a good rest of the day, Tannyn!"

I was sliding into my own car when I glanced into the rear view mirror and noticed that my nose had begun to bleed. I reached across the cab and popped open the glove compartment, pushing aside loose CDs and crumpled receipts for large black iced coffees until I found a half-empty pack of tissues.

I pulled one out and pressed it against my nose, wincing at the tenderness.

A warm breeze ruffled my hair as I stared at my reflection in the mirror, my mouth twisted up like I'd just tasted something bitter.

In through the nose, out through the mouth. In—wince—out.

Maybe that was how I'd go—one giant nose bleed, lying in a puddle of red in the dried grass of the cemetery. It was sort of poetic, in a way. The thought didn't make me feel any better.

As I reached for the keys and the engine sputtered to life, I decided adamantly against that. Red was my least favorite color for a reason.

Too messy.

forty-six

Dried grass crunched beneath my feet as I passed through the open gates of the cemetery.

"If you want to catch your death, you'll find it past the field of stone and empty names."

The cemetery was empty, and afternoon sunlight glittered off the marble headstones. I lifted a hand to shield my eyes as I walked. A crow watched me from the branches of a tall Southern oak.

As I walked along the rows, I glanced at the bouquets of flowers that had turned brown beneath the sun.

I stopped before the planter that I'd once thought had contained Eve's ashes and stared down at the flat gray marker in the earth.

I tipped my head back to the sky, squinting against the sun. "Well?" I yelled as I spread my arms wide. "Come and kill me, then!"

Silence.

"What are you waiting for?" I snapped.

The crow that had been watching me earlier let out a harsh caw and took off in a flurry of feathers and trembling branches.

I curled my arms around my chest and sunk to my knees in the grass. My face was red from shouting. I thought I might start crying, but no tears came to my eyes. They were as dry as the clouds gathered in the sky overhead.

I dipped my head, strands of lilac hair falling into my face.

"So," I whispered to the marker inscribed with Eve's name. "All those times I came to talk to you, and you weren't even listening." My laughter was a choked, guttural sound.

I looked up at the sound of footsteps.

Jude jerked to a stop when he spotted me, looking startled. He was carrying a dozen white carnations, the kind you could buy at any grocery store. "Tannyn?" he said.

My smile was biting. "The one and only."

"What are you doing here?"

"I could ask you the same question."

He took a step forward, and then another. He sat down beside me, stretching his legs out in front of him. "Don't worry," he said as I stiffened. "I wasn't expecting you, so I don't have any fun conversational topics prepared."

"That's a relief," I replied. I nodded at the bouquet in his hand. "What's with the fifty cent flowers?"

He hefted the flowers with a frown, and then set them down beside Eve's marker. "I figured they'd be dead in a day, anyway," he told me. "And it's not like she'll ever know, right?" He leaned back on his hands and sighed through his nose. "Who was it that said funerals are for the living?"

"Are you thinking of John Green?"

"I could have sworn it was Voltaire or Dante or Charles Dickens."

"Nope," I said. "John Green. *The Fault in Our Stars.*"

His brows pinched together, and he ran a hand through his disheveled red hair. "Wow. I really need to brush up on my fiction."

I laughed quietly to myself as I stared down at the words tattooed on the inside of my left elbow that matched the ones etched into Eve's marker. *Into the darkness they go, the wise and the lovely.*

Jude began to hum to himself, a tune that sounded vaguely like a Hera Hjartardóttir song.

"Jude?" I said.

240

"Hmm?" he asked, turning his head to look at me.

I swallowed. "Did you kill Eve?"

He snorted, but there was no humor in it. He glanced towards the trees and picked at a fraying thread on the hem of his shorts. "Do you remember that night at the church carnival, when Eve snuck into the fun house to meet me? And you covered for her with Theodore by telling him that she got sick on the Tilt-A-Whirl and went home early? And then she really did get sick from too much cotton candy?"

"I never understood why she wouldn't just tell Theodore," I said. "Then I realized what a dick you are."

He laughed and stood up, brushing off the back of his shorts. "As always, it's been a pleasure talking to you, Tannyn," he told me. He winked. "I look forward to seeing your murder at the party tomorrow."

The double meaning behind his words didn't escape me.

Jude started to walk away through the headstones, but then he paused and glanced back at me over his shoulder. "And no," he said. "I didn't kill Eve."

He was gone before I had thought of something to say.

forty-seven

Madeline greeted Theodore at the front door, slobber dripping from her muzzle. She'd already coated his shirt with tufts of white fur.

I eased her back inside as I closed the door behind me. "Hey," I said, smiling up at Theodore.

"How was your day?" he asked.

I jumped onto his back, wrapping my legs around his waist, and he held onto my calves as he carried me down the porch steps. I rested my chin against his shoulder. His hair tickled my cheek.

"Bloody nose. Popped tire. Madeline threw up on the living room carpet." *I'm going to die in a cemetery.* "You know, the usual."

I'd decided earlier not to tell him about seeing Jude. I was already worried that he was having second—and third and fourth—thoughts about our plan for the masquerade party. I was afraid that if I told him, he'd decide once and for all that it was too dangerous and call it off. And Jack and West would listen, I knew Eve wouldn't—and I wouldn't put it past her to sneak out on her own.

"Sounds eventful," he said as he carried me down the driveway.

"And your day?"

"Much better now that I've seen your lovely face," he told me.

I slid from his back as he opened the passenger door for me, and I ducked into the car before he could notice the flush that rose to my cheeks. I hoped it just looked like sunburn or a contagious rash.

I pulled my seatbelt across my chest and shouted, "Did you remember to buy groceries for Eve?"

"Yes, ma'am," Theodore said, climbing into the driver's seat. "Dropped them off this morning."

There was a small section of his pale blonde hair that was sticking up, all fluffy and rumpled like a baby chick's feathers. I reached across the interior of the car to smooth it down with my fingers.

A tremor ran down Theodore's back, and he smiled sheepishly. "That tickles."

I laughed. "Sorry."

As he shifted into reverse and backed out of the driveway, my eye traveled to the small crow tattoo on the inside of his bicep.

Theodore glanced over at me. "Why are you making that face?"

I bit down on my bottom lip. "You know that night at the church carnival?" I asked. "When I told you Eve got sick on the Tilt-A-Whirl and went home early? She actually snuck off to hang out with Jude."

A smile tugged at the corner of Theodore's mouth. "I know."

I blinked at him. "What?"

"I said, I know," he replied. "I saw them later, sneaking onto the Ferris wheel. If there's one thing Eve's terrible at, it's subtlety. Is that why you were looking so guilty?"

"Why didn't you say anything?"

He shrugged. "I didn't want to start something with her. Besides, it was funny watching you try to distract me. No one loves ring toss that much."

"They had a giant Piplup!" I snapped.

"Which you still failed to win, even after six attempts."

"I'm sorry. Were we talking about you being a liar, or how terrible I am at ring toss?"

"I can't remember."

I smacked his shoulder. "What else have you lied about? Are you

243

even a natural blonde?"

Theodore chuckled, his eyes crinkling around the edges. I sunk back into my seat, drawing my one leg up to my chest and resting my chin atop my knee. I stared out the window as trees passed in a blur.

"I never thanked you," I said. "For bringing her back."

"I didn't do it for you."

"But you would have," I said. "If you hadn't known her—if I'd asked—you would have."

His hands tightened on the wheel, knuckles turning white. "I can't . . . I don't know if I could."

And I knew what he was thinking of as he said it: that I was going to die before the next full moon. And maybe he didn't believe in hoodoo or palm reading or fortune telling, but I hadn't believed someone could be brought back from the dead either.

"If something happens to me—"

"Nothing's going to happen to you," he said through his teeth, cutting me off. He turned up the volume on the radio, making it nearly impossible to speak.

I looked down at my hands, at the dark blue veins against white skin, the lines in my palm that spoke of my death. I curled them into fists. My knuckles were scarred and covered with yellowing bruises. "*If* something happens to me," I started again, closing my eyes and bracing myself. "I want you to know . . . I think I love you."

At first, I wasn't sure if he'd heard me.

Then he slammed on the brakes.

I was flung forward, knees crashing into my chest, and I gasped as the wind was knocked out of me. I was still recovering my breath as Theodore yanked the wheel and pulled the car over to the side of the road. We were surrounded by sugar cane fields, and the road that stretched out ahead and behind us was empty.

He left the car idling as he flung his door open and climbed out.

I watched as he began to angrily pace through the dirt, kicking at a rock and sending it skittering along the gravel.

"Fuck," I muttered.

I undid my seatbelt and climbed out after him, walking over to where he was still stalking along the side of the road. I shoved my hands into the pocket of my shorts and swallowed, trying for a casual tone as I said, "Is this how you treat all the girls that confess their love for you?"

I meant it to sound suave and devil-may-care, but instead, my voice was small and insecure.

"Get back in the car, Tannyn," he said.

Heat rose in my cheeks, and as he turned his back to me again, I pulled off my left sneaker and threw it at him as hard as I could.

It hit him in the shoulder, and he cursed, whirling towards me, but before he had the chance to say anything, I yelled, "Don't treat me like a child!"

"Then don't act like one."

Whatever I'd been about to say, fell from my lips. I blinked at him, tears forming in my eyes. I tried remembering to tell myself to breathe. "Are you talking about throwing my shoe," I said softly, bitterly, "or about me saying I love you?"

He pushed his fingers through his hair, knotting them into the strands, and closed his eyes. I could tell I wasn't going to get a response.

"Forget it," I said. "I take it back."

I turned back towards the car when he whispered, "Don't. Please."

I glanced over my shoulder at him to see that he was staring at me, pain reflected in this storm-cloud eyes. I blinked against the tears in the corners of my eyes.

245

"Don't take it back," he said. "Please."

I threw my hands out to my sides, smiling against the ache in my chest. "Then I don't know what you want from me, Theodore."

"Don't talk like you've already given up. Don't say you love me just because you're afraid."

"But I do. And I am," I said. "I'm so afraid, Theodore."

He took a step towards me, reaching out as if to touch my cheek, but then he dropped his hand back to his side.

I drew a shuddering breath. "I'm afraid of dying. I'm afraid of losing everything important to me. I'm afraid of water, for Christ's sake." A harsh laugh forced itself from my lips. "But it doesn't matter. Because I love you. I think I've loved you from the first moment I saw you. And I'm not saying it because I'm afraid—I'm saying it because up until now, I *was* afraid."

He was silent, so I continued.

"I'm not this—this strong, fearless person. I'm angry and reckless and insecure and afraid and *I have no idea what the hell I'm doing.* My dad doesn't remember my birthday and my best friend has been killed more than once and my mom—" I broke off, the words catching in my throat. "My mom is broken, and it's my fault."

Theodore took my face in his hands, and it was only then that I realized I was crying.

He brushed a tear away with his thumb, and then drew me against him. I clung to him and buried my face into his chest and I didn't care if I ruined his shirt because he deserved it for making me cry.

He drew his fingers through my hair and pressed a kiss to the crown of my head.

"I think I love you, too," he said softly.

"You better," I grumbled.

His laughed shook my body, and I smiled into his chest.

I pulled back, wiping at my eyes with the back of my hand. I knew I looked a mess—I *felt* a mess.

"Let's skip the Boathouse," I said. "There's somewhere I want to take you."

He nodded and bent his head to kiss me. This kiss was less urgent than all the others, slow and burning, and I closed my eyes as his tongue brushed my bottom lip. I breathed in the scent of cedar wood and the air after a rainstorm that clung to his skin.

Our lips broke apart as he leaned his forehead against mine.

"You might want to put your shoe back on first," he told me.

The nurses had sat my mother before an open window.

Her hair was pulled back into an impeccable knot at the nape of her neck, and the gray strands that were threaded through looked silver in the sunlight. She was wearing a cream-colored knit cardigan over her clothes despite the heat.

Theodore stood a few feet away as I sat down in the chair beside her.

"Mama?" I reached out and took her hand, curling my fingers around her own. "There's someone I want you to meet." I glanced back over my shoulder at Theodore, forcing a smile. "This is Theodore Shearwater."

Theodore cleared his throat. "It's nice to meet you, Mrs. Carter."

My mother's gaze flickered to his face and remained there a moment before she looked back out the window.

There was a nurse pushing a man in a wheelchair, and I watched my mother's eyes follow them as they walked around a pathway woven through the trees. My mother's foot tapped against the floor, bouncing softly off the linoleum.

I glanced to the seat beside me. "You can sit down, if you want," I told Theodore.

He sat down, scooting his chair closer to me, and a breeze ruffled his pale blonde hair. He looked at my mother, the dark circles beneath her eyes and the hollowness of her cheeks. "What happened to her?" he asked.

I took a breath, squeezing my mother's fingers. She didn't notice.

"What is it, honey?"

A flash of metal.

My fingers coming away stained with red.

My mother sobbing.

It was my fault. But I'd never told anyone.

I stared down at the flat silver ring on my thumb as I said, "My grandmother was an alcoholic. Growing up, she used to abuse my mom—like West's dad, I guess, before he left. But worse. She broke her arm in three different places once." I breathed in my mother's scent of Dove soap and chardonnay and warm sugar. "This was before my great-grandmother got involved and took her in."

Theodore was quiet as he listened.

I felt heavy—even the weight of my skin was too much. I wanted to claw it from my bones. But I forced myself to breathe and continue.

I needed him to know. If I was going to die, I needed someone to know.

"The day that she came after me . . ." I paused. "Back then, I wasn't good at controlling the nightmares." I swallowed. "That day, I wanted to go to the park. The sun was out and it wasn't too hot and it was one of her good days, you know? I got dressed and made my bed and fed Madeline, and then I went into the kitchen to ask her if we could go. She was standing by the sink—we used to keep the knives out on the counter there, but now they're in a drawer."

I looked up at my mother, who turned her head to stare blankly at me. I smiled at her despite the feeling as if my chest were being crushed.

"I asked if we could go to the park, but she said she had errands to run all day. And I was a kid," I whispered. "I didn't understand why she just couldn't put them off. It was only one day. We got in an argument—a stupid, *stupid* argument. And I just . . . snapped. The way I always do."

The scar on my collarbone began to throb.

"Her worst nightmare was of my grandmother—not a particular incident, just my grandmother trying to hurt her," I told him. "Except I was there, too." I squeezed my mother's fingers until my knuckles turned white. "She was just trying to protect me. But she got confused. And then she cut me. And I panicked, and I just latched tighter onto the nightmare, and she thought I was her mother, and she came after me again, and I kept screaming *Mama, it's me, it's me.*"

Theodore reached for my other hand, and it was then that I realized a tear had escaped from the corner of my eye. I brushed it away with my shoulder, not releasing either of their hands.

"If Hollis hadn't been there that day, she would have killed me," I said. "When the paramedics took her, she wouldn't stop screaming. They had to sedate her. When she woke up in the hospital, she was like this."

I looked over at Theodore for the first time, and I hated the pity in his eyes. Nausea rose in my throat at the sight of it. He should have hated me. I hated me.

"I'm sorry," he said. "I'm so sorry."

"It's my fault," I said. "I lost control."

"You couldn't have known. You were just a kid."

I pulled my hand from his grasp. "What about at that party? When Jack had to pull me off that boy? Or with Jude? I almost did it again. After I *promised* myself . . . I almost did it again."

"Why didn't you tell us?"

"No one knows. Not even Hollis," I told him. "I'm afraid he'll hate me if he finds out. He *should* hate me."

When Theodore reached for my hand again, I let him take out.

"No one could hate you, Tannyn."

"That's not true. That girl in my history class last year hated me."

He tried to suppress a smile. "No one could *really* hate you," he said. Then his tone turned serious again. "Especially not Hollis. He knows how much you love your mom. He knows that you would never have done something like this on purpose." He ran his thumb in circles over the palm of my hand. "I don't blame the person that crashed into my parent's car—and I know that Eve doesn't either."

"That's different. That was an accident."

"*This* was an accident, Tannyn. You said it yourself—things got out of control," he replied. "I never met your mom, but I'm sure she wouldn't want you to blame yourself."

"But what if it happens again?" I whispered.

"It won't. Because I know you, Tannyn Lourdes Carter, and you're one of the strongest people I know—despite what you think."

I closed my eyes and leaned to press my forehead against his.

"Thank you, Theodore."

The air that drifted in through the window was hot and dry. Not for the first time that summer, I wished for rain.

forty-eight

Theodore flicked on the lights to the kitchen, and I followed after him.

The world outside the windows was dark, and the rest of the house was quiet.

"Thanks for letting me stay over," I said.

He walked over to the sink, filling a kettle with water and then setting it down on the stove to boil. As he reached up into one of the cabinets, he said, "It's chamomile, right? To help you sleep?"

I nodded and dropped my bag of overnight clothes onto the floor at my feet, and he took down a tin of tea bags and a mug.

I lifted myself to sit on the edge of the island counter, staring down at my dangling legs.

"Tell me what you're thinking," I said.

He opened another cabinet over top of the stove. "That I don't know where Nettie put the honey."

"Cabinet to your left, second shelf."

He pulled open the cabinet I'd indicated, scanning the shelf. Then he snatched up the bottle of honey.

"Now tell me what you're thinking."

"Honestly," he replied, "I'm trying very hard *not* to."

"I doubt you have to try that hard."

Theodore turned towards me, raising his brows. "And here I thought you liked me."

"I don't know where you got that idea."

251

He took a step closer, easing between my legs, and placed his hands flat on the counter on either side of my thighs. "Perhaps it was that last time you were on this counter, when your hands were in my hair and you were kissing me like you'd forgotten how to breathe."

He took my hand, tracing the veins on the inside of the wrist with his thumb, gently stroking his fingers across my skin. The touch was soothing, but it also sent goosebumps scattering across my flesh. I felt heat rise to my cheeks, but I ignored it.

"Funny," I said, grabbing the hem of his shirt and pulling him closer to me. "I was going to say the same thing about you."

A smirk pulled at the corner of his lip, and he leaned in close enough that I could smell the scent of sweat and thunderstorms that clung to his skin. He skirted his nose along my throat and across my jaw.

"Theodore," I murmured, knotting my fingers tighter in his shirt.

"I told you I would make you beg," he said.

Then he took my face in his hands and kissed me.

It was soft at first, his lips molding to mine. He held me in his hands like he was afraid I might shatter. Then I parted my lips and tangled my fingers in his hair, dragging him flush against me.

His tongue entwined with mine, and a moan escaped from my lips.

Theodore's fingers found the hem of my shirt, and he tugged on it lightly, a question in the gesture. I lifted my arms for him to pull it over my head, and he tossed it to the floor.

Thank God I'd worn one of my good bras, I thought.

And then he claimed my mouth again.

I whimpered as his tongue swept into my mouth, and I hooked my legs around his waist, pressing my heels into his back. I untangled my fingers from his hair to run my hands beneath his shirt, reveling over the smooth planes of his stomach.

Then his lips left mine to leave a trail of scorching kisses along my jaw and throat and collarbone. I tipped my head back and held him against me.

The kettle on the stove began to whistle.

I screamed and clamped my hand over my mouth, biting down on my lip. Then a giggle burst from behind my hand.

"Fuck," I whispered, snickering.

Theodore groaned, dropping his head against my shoulder. Then he straightened and walked over to remove the kettle from the stove top.

As he prepared my tea, I slipped down from the countertop and picked up my shirt from the kitchen floor. I turned it right-side-out again and began to pull it over my head.

"Oh no, you don't."

Theodore's arm encircled my waist, and he swept me over his shoulder. I gasped as my bare stomach caved around his shoulder, and the shirt dropped from my fingers. I clung to his t-shirt, praying that he didn't drop me.

While I was worrying about that, he picked up the steaming mug of tea in his other hand and carried me out into the living room.

"Theodore," I whisper-hissed, although there was no one else in the house to hear us.

He set the tea down on the coffee table first, and then dumped me down on the sofa cushions. He grabbed my ankle and pulled me towards him, grinning in a way that made my entire body break out in goosebumps.

He crawled on top of me, nudging his knee between my legs.

His nose skimmed my ear, and he nibbled lightly on the skin below my lobe. "Tell me what you want."

I shoved him off of me, and he rolled onto the floor, landing on his back with a hard *oomph*. A moment later, I was on top of him.

253

He grasped my hips in his hands, as I leaned down, skimming my tongue along his jaw.

He groaned, his fingers digging into my skin.

"I told you, you should be scared of me," I whispered.

He smiled up at me. Then it slipped from his face. "Please," he said, his grip softening. "Be safe tomorrow."

I touched the side of his face, trying to smooth the worry away with my fingertips. "I will. I promise."

He wrapped his arms around my waist and pulled me against him, covering my lips with his own until we'd both forgotten how to breathe.

I stared at my reflection in the living room window, the moon glowing overhead.

My leg was bouncing quietly against the hardwood floor, and I clasped my hands together in my lap to keep them from trembling. It only made it worse. I squeezed my eyes closed.

"You will die before the next full moon, Tannyn Carter."

My throat was closing up. I remembered reading somewhere that there were no cases of anyone ever dying from a panic attack, but at that moment, it seemed entirely possible. *Never say never,* I thought, and then choked on a breathless laugh.

I began to feel lightheaded, and I reminded myself to breathe.

In through the nose, out through the mouth.

It was always easier said than done, but I managed to draw a breath through my nose and hold it for several seconds before releasing it through my nose. I did it again. And again.

Tremors ran through my body. I was shaking as if I were caught in the arctic without any clothes.

I remembered what Theodore had said about them being the

adrenaline leaving my body, so I got up and began to pace back and forth across the living room, clenching and un-clenching my fists, careful not to wake him where he was sleeping on the couch.

I went into the kitchen and filled a glass of water, gulping it down. Then I filled it a second time and sipped on it as I walked back out into the living room.

The water was tasteless in my mouth. The cold seeped into my bones.

Don't think about tomorrow, I thought. But the more I tried not to think about it, the larger it grew in my mind.

"Tannyn?"

I jerked my head around to see Theodore sit up on the couch, rubbing at his eyes.

"I'm sorry," I said, my voice catching in my throat. "Did I wake you?"

"No. What's the matter? What's wrong?"

He stood up and came over to me, and I shook my head until he cupped my face in his hands and forced me to look at him. "I can't breathe," I said.

"In through the nose, out through the mouth," he told me. "Like this." He breathed slowly with me, and I matched my breaths to his, feeling my chest expand and deflate like a balloon. When my breathing returned to normal, he led me over to the couch and pulled a blanket around my shoulders as he helped me sit. "Drink your water," he instructed. "Did you bring So Big with you?"

I shook my head.

"Alright," he murmured, thinking. Then he kissed my forehead. "I'll be right back."

I watched as he dashed from the room, and then stared down at the hardwood floor, counting the seconds he was gone in my head.

. . . twelve, thirteen, fourteen . . .

I heard footsteps overhead as he ran into his room.

. . . nineteen, twenty, twenty-one . . .

It sounded like he was rummaging around for something. Then I heard his door slam shut and footsteps on the stairs. He stopped in the kitchen. Cabinets opened and closed.

. . . thirty-three, thirty-four . . .

A second later he appeared in the living room doorway.

Thirty-five.

He came over and knelt down in front of me, dumping two sleeping pills into my hand. I swallowed them obediently.

Then he settled a small stuffed bear in my lap. It was brown, with a small blue bow around its neck and dark eyes. There was a hole in his armpit where stuffing had begun to poke out.

"This is Blue," he said.

"Hello, Blue."

Theodore smiled softly. "I've had him since I was little, but I figure you need him more than I do right now. He's very good at keeping you company when you're upset."

I picked up the worn bear and brought him to my chest, pressing my cheek against his fur. "He smells like you," I whispered.

"Sorry. I haven't washed him in a while."

I bit down on my lip to hide my smile. "No. It's nice," I told him. "Thank you."

I ran my fingers over his soft fur and began to hum "Downtown." Theodore sat down beside me on the couch, and I rested my head against his shoulder. A moment later, his hands were playing with my hair and he was singing along to my humming beneath his breath.

I closed my eyes, clutching the bear to my chest.

I didn't remember falling asleep, but sometime later, I woke to the feeling of Theodore's arms around me as he carried me up the stairs. The bear was still tucked against my chest.

He laid me down gently on the bed in the guest room, and I clung sleepily to his hands over top of the covers when he tried to leave.

He didn't protest as I pulled him towards me, and he climbed into bed beside me and wrapped his arms around me. I held his hand against me and buried my face in the stuffed bear, breathing in the scent of Theodore on his fur.

"Thank you," I murmured.

Theodore kissed my shoulder. "For what?"

"Just for being you."

"That's not much."

"It's everything," I told him.

I heard the smile in his voice as he said, "Go to bed, Tannyn."

forty-nine

Three cars sat parked outside the Boathouse: Theodore's Mustang, Jack's Jeep, and a shiny silver rental BMW from three towns over.

I'd cringed when I'd entered the front room to see five identical garment bags draped over the couch. Eve had yet to let me see the costumes she'd picked out for me, and I was both looking forward to and dreading it.

She pounced on me as soon as I stepped over the threshold. She herded me towards the bathroom, snatching up two of the garment bags.

"Get dressed," she hissed at the boys. "And no peaking until we're finished."

I stepped into the bathroom, eyes widening at the spread Eve had laid out on the small counter.

When it came to subtlety, Eve was a stranger.

Her hair was pulled tight into a bun at the back of her head, the pale blonde wisps slicked back with gel. Her makeup was gold, her cheekbones accentuated with flakes of glitter, even though we'd agreed that a full face mask was best for her.

She closed the bathroom door and turned to me, grinning. "Alright. Strip."

Theodore was standing by the passenger side door of his car when Eve and I emerged from the Boathouse.

He wore plain black pants and a necklace of silver, and the top four buttons on his white shirt were open to show off the whorls of black paint that decorated his chest. His mask was two swans intertwining, carved from

258

glistening black metal.

I nearly tripped at the sight of him, but quickly found my footing again, reminding myself that this was serious—life or death, actually.

Focus, bitch.

Beside me, Eve snorted a laugh.

She wore a mask of intertwining golden leaves that covered her entire face, including her bad eye, and her green dress was loose and flowing. The v-neck dipped low in the back and front, and it was sleeveless, leaving her arms exposed to show off the whorls of golden paint that covered them. Oak leaves and twigs were woven amongst the tangled knots in her dark brown wig.

She looked beautiful, but I knew beneath it, there was a pistol strapped to the holster on her thigh.

Theodore turned to face us, and his eyes widened when they landed on me. I saw his Adam's apple bob as he swallowed.

Well, at least it wasn't just me.

My mask was identical to his, except silver. My floor-length dress was white, with a lace-up corset bodice and long, pointed sleeves that draped towards the ground, and the loose waves of my lilac hair were crowned with a circlet of yew branches. A gold and silver chain hung around my neck.

My phone and knife were tucked into my bra. Damn pocket-less dresses.

"Let me guess," Theodore said, his eyes traveling along my body. "You're the Irish goddess of dreams."

I tilted my head to the side. "How did you know?"

"I'm your husband, the god of love." He bowed deeply and took my hand, pressing a kiss to the back of it. "My lady," he said, grinning up at me as I felt my cheeks warm. He opened the passenger door and made a sweeping gesture towards it.

259

I turned to Eve, pulling her into a tight hug and pressing a kiss to the cheek of her cold metal mask. "I love you," I told her. "Please be safe."

I heard the smile in her voice as she said, "I love you, too. See you there."

As she started for the rental BMW, I climbed into the passenger side of Theodore's car, settling my leather satchel in my lap. I'd already checked it three times to make sure I had everything I needed, but my fingers were itching to check it a fourth.

I glimpsed Jack and West in the Jeep behind us, but I had yet to see their costumes.

Theodore walked around the front of the car to the driver's side, and I reached over to turn up the volume on the radio, drowning out my thoughts.

As he shifted the car into gear, he glanced over at me.

"You look beautiful, by the way," he said. But there was a restlessness behind his eyes that had been there since I'd seen him earlier that morning.

"Don't worry," I told him. "Everything's going to be alright."

But I wasn't so sure myself.

fifty

him

He stared at his reflection in the mirror, and then lifted the mask to fit it over his face.

He retrieved his pistol from the drawer on his nightstand and slipped it into the concealed pocket inside his suit jacket.

Tonight.

Tonight he would finish what he started.

fifty-one

I reached out to snatch a glass of peach champagne from a server as they went past with a tray.

I downed it in several quick gulps, and Theodore put a gentle hand on my elbow.

"Easy, Tannyn," he said.

I twirled the champagne flute between my fingers. "Where are they?" I whispered, glancing around the main room. "They were supposed to be here ten minutes ago."

"Relax, *mamí*," Jack's voice chimed from the speaker in my earpiece. "We're coming in now."

I turned towards the front door, breathing a sigh of relief as I saw two figures in black making their way towards us.

West was dressed in a slim velvet suit, and his dark eyes stared out from behind an intricately carved wolf mask.

Jack also wore a black suit, save for the jacket, and the sleeves of his black button-up were bunched to his elbows. He wore a top hat, and an extension of black feathers hung from where he'd clipped them into his hair. The mask that hung around his neck was metal and had a long, curved beak.

He caught me staring at it and gave me a smile that sent chills down my spine. "I'm the Black Death," he told me. "It was my idea."

"You smell like potpourri," I said.

He tapped the end of the metal beak. "Herbs."

"Where did you even find that?" I asked.

"Ebay," he replied, still grinning.

262

From my ear, Eve asked, "Has everyone forgotten about me?"

"No one could forget about you," I replied, taking Theodore's hand and leading him over to a table laden with appetizers. West and Jack followed. I speared a cube of fancy-looking cheese on the end of a toothpick and nibbled on it as I asked, "Where are you?"

"About fifteen minutes away," she told me.

In through the nose, out through the mouth.

"Alright," I said. "See you soon."

Jack plucked a glass of champagne from a server's tray as they offered it to us. I stopped myself from taking another.

"Have you seen Jude yet?" West asked.

"No, but his parents are over there." I nodded to a couple in the corner dressed like Marie Antoinette and Louis XVI, chatting away with a group of people. "I'm sure he'll make himself known eventually."

"In the meantime," Theodore said, offering his hand to me, "would you like to dance?"

"You can't be serious," I hissed at him.

"I've never been more serious in my life," he told me. To Jack and West he said, "Keep an eye out for anyone *particularly* interested in us."

I took Theodore's hand and followed him as he moved through the crowd towards the dance floor.

A woman in the corner was playing the harp, her fingers plucking deftly at the strings as she sang on in Gaelic or Welsh or some other beautiful, melancholy language. I lost myself in the music as Theodore placed a hand on my waist.

Then he was leading me around the dance floor, and I stared up into his face as our movements fell into synch with one another. I smiled at him, feeling the knots in my stomach begin to untangle.

I winced as I stepped on his foot. "Sorry," I muttered.

"It's alright," he said, grinning down at me. "Not all of us can afford formal dance lessons."

"You're a piece of shit, you know that?"

"Yes, but I'm *your* piece of shit."

I snorted a laugh and leaned my head against his chest. "That you are."

Light from the chandelier overhead glittered off the marble floor as he whisked me around the room.

"By the parlor room door," Jack's voice said in my ear.

I started in Theodore's arms, accidentally stepping on his foot again. "What?"

I turned my head, searching from him and West, but I'd lost them in the crowd. I squeezed Theodore's fingers as he continued to dance as if nothing had happened. I reminded myself to do the same.

In through the nose, out through the mouth.

Theodore inclined his head slightly to the left and whispered, "There."

I followed his gaze to a man across the room.

The man was dressed in a plain black suit, though the jacket had a hood that was pulled over his head, casting shadows across his silver mask, which had been carved to look like a skull.

"I see him," I murmured.

I caught his eye, and the corner of his mouth tilted up in a smirk.

The air tasted like smoke and burnt flesh. I swallowed the bile that rose in my throat and pressed myself closer to Theodore, breathing in his scent.

In, out.

"How can we be sure it's him?" West said.

I could hear the smile in Eve's voice as she said, "Would you like me to go and ask?"

"No," I said hoarsely, the taste of his fear still fresh against my tongue. I was struck with the realization that I recognized it—but I couldn't pinpoint where from. "It's him."

"Can you tell who it is?" Theodore asked.

"No. Too hard to tell," West replied. "His face is completely covered."

Eve said, "I'm coming in now."

As Theodore swept me in a circle, I glanced around the room and spotted Eve walking through the front door. If I hadn't seen her earlier, I wouldn't have even known it was her. She moved gracefully towards the bar, ordering a drink, and then my back was to her.

The song ended, and Theodore bowed deeply like a Victorian gentleman.

"If you'll excuse me," I said, loud enough for anyone who might have been eavesdropping, "I have to use the ladies' room."

I turned to leave, but Theodore took my hand and pulled me back to him, covering my lips with his own. Then he pressed his forehead against mine.

"I love you," he whispered, low enough for only me to hear.

I kissed him quickly in response.

I made my way through the crowd of people towards the stairs, and then gathered the skirts of my dress as I went up to the second-floor. I glanced over the railing of the balcony at the people moving about below and spotted Theodore walking back to West and Jack.

I ducked into the first bathroom I saw, locking the door behind me.

I moved quickly, setting my satchel down on the counter and stripping out of my dress. Beneath it, I wore a bulletproof vest and compression shorts. I took off my mask and yew branch crown.

Then I opened the satchel and pulled out a second dress and a pair of heels.

I slipped into the dress, smoothing it down over the vest so it lay flat.

The dress had a tight black bodice and long sleeves, with dark feathers along the shoulders and collar that glittered red and green and purple in the light. The skirt was loose and flowing, allowing me to move freely—which I would need to. The heels I wore were several inches tall to give me Eve's height.

The wig was the hardest piece of the costume to maneuver, and it took some time before I got in properly into place. The pale blonde locks fell in loose curls around my face.

I stuffed the rest of my belongings into my satchel and hid it in the linen closet behind a stack of towels where Jack would retrieve it later.

I stared at my reflection in the mirror, and a small laugh escaped my lips at the sight of myself with long, blonde hair again.

The other one. The quiet, angry one. The Ten of Crows.

"Tannyn? Everything alright?" Theodore asked.

I smoothed a hand over my abdomen one last time and released a breath through my nose. "Yes," I told him. "I'm coming to meet you now."

Then I pulled the crow mask over my face, obscuring my features.

I slipped from the bathroom and walked down the hall, towards the servants staircase that Eve had told me was behind a door at the end of the second-floor.

The sound of my heels on the wooden stairs echoed through the small space

I ended up in the kitchen, much to the surprise of the cooks, and babbled something about being lost and too many glasses of champagne. They pointed me towards the party, and I thanked them before hurrying off.

a girl called murder

I stopped in the entrance to the main room, quickly scanning for Theodore.

He was lounging against the wall by the dance floor, the man with the skull mask lingering nearby, pretending to occupy himself with a plate of appetizers. He speared a cherry tomato on the end of his toothpick and popped it in his mouth.

I wanted to jam the toothpick in his throat and watch him choke on the blood.

"Eve, where are you?" I whispered, pretending to cover my mouth to cough.

"To your left," she said.

I turned my head.

She was sitting on a loveseat in the corner, close enough to another group of women that, to any onlooker, it seemed as if she were with them. She lifted a glass of wine to her lips, and her eye flickered to me.

"I have to say," she told me through the earpiece, "you look damn good as me."

I smiled behind my mask and started across the room to Theodore.

"And action," Jack murmured in my ear.

Theodore straightened when he saw me, his hands clenching into fists at his sides. The man in the skull mask noticed immediately and followed his gaze, and he went still when he saw me.

I was halfway across the room when Theodore marched over to me, grasping my arm and pulling me aside in one swift, not-so-gentle movement.

"*Ow*," I hissed through my teeth.

"Sorry," he murmured. Then louder, "You shouldn't be here."

He pulled me from the room, and I pretended to stumble after him —except I was really stumbling, trying to keep up with him those damned high heels. I clawed at the hand on my arm, but he didn't release me.

267

"He's taking the bait," Eve said. "West, I'm coming to meet you."

I followed Theodore down a hall and outside onto the back porch of the house, where the air was hot and dry and crisp despite the setting sun. It was nearly dark, the sun painting the sky with vivid pinks and oranges and yellows.

We went down the stairs into the backyard, following a stone pathway that led towards a towering hedge maze set amongst the peach trees.

Theodore yanked me to a stop before the entrance and said, "Stay *here*. I'm getting the car, and we're leaving."

I nodded my head.

Then he whispered, "I'll see you on the other side."

As he walked off, I stared after him and nervously twisted the ring on my thumb in a circle. The heels of my shoes were sinking into the rough earth, and I paced in a slow path at the entrance to prevent them from getting stuck. I wished that I'd swiped that third glass of champagne.

I looked towards the windows on the third-floor. "Jack? Can you see me?"

"I'm right here, Tan. All eyes on you."

A light in one of the windows flashed on and off, and I breathed a sigh of relief.

"Alright," Eve said. "It looks like he waited for Theodore to leave. He's coming out. Move. *Now*."

I glanced over my shoulder to see the man in the skull mask starting down the stairs of the back porch, and then I ducked into the hedge maze.

As soon as I rounded the first corner, I peeled off my heels and mask, chucking them into the bushes.

"He's coming," Jack said. "*Ve*."

I ran.

fifty-two

The ground was rough under my bare feet.

I pounded along down the pathways, counting out the turns in my head. *Two lefts. A right. Another left. Keep straight for the next turn. Left.*

My heart was thundering in my chest.

"Evelyn!" a voice called through the hedge maze.

It startled me enough that I tripped, landing hard in the dirt and biting down on my tongue. I ignored the taste of copper that filled my mouth as I scrambled to my feet and gathered the skirts of my dress and kept running. I spat a mouthful of blood onto the ground.

"It *is* you, isn't it, Evelyn?" the voice called.

I knew I recognized it. I dug my nails into my palms, trying to remember.

He killed Eve, I thought, tears gathering at the corners of my eyes. *And he'll kill me if he catches me.* I couldn't say for sure how I knew. But I did.

A cramp began to form in my side. I kept running. Spat more blood onto the ground.

In my ear, West said, "Eve and I are lighting the first fire at the entrance."

Left. Two rights. Left. Straight for the next three turns. Left.

There was an explosion in the hedge wall to my left and then I felt a sharp sting on my ear as something whizzed past me and crashed into the bushes ahead.

I nearly tripped a second time as I cried out, clasping a hand over

269

my ear, but forced myself to keep going.

"Stop running, Evelyn," the voice shouted from the other side of the wall.

"What is it?" Theodore demanded. "Are you alright?"

My fingers came away sticky and wet; blood dripped onto my shoulder and ran down the front of my dress. "You were right," I said, choking on the words. "He has a gun."

"*Are you alright?*"

"I'm fine." I winced at the pain. "Stay where you are."

It was then that I noticed the smell of smoke.

I lifted my head to see a dark cloud of it forming overhead, but I didn't glance back to see if the fire was spreading.

Fuck.

I took a wrong turn and pulled to a stop in front of a dead end. The smoke was thicker now, clouding the air, and I accidentally breathed in a lungful, choking on it.

"Go back and take a right," Jack said.

"Alright."

I did as he said, trying to remember the last few turns as blood ran down my neck and arm and chest. The feathers on my dress were matted and sticky. Strands of blonde hair from the wig clung to my skin.

"Almost there, Tannyn," Jack told me.

From somewhere else, Eve said, "Starting the fire on the east side. West?"

"Good over here."

I rounded another corner and spotted the maze exit several feet away. I sprinted for it, feeling as if my legs were going to give out beneath me.

They buckled as soon as my feet touched grass, and then Theodore's arms were around me as he caught me. I fell to my knees, vomiting a mixture of blood and champagne and God knew what else onto the ground.

"Christ, Tannyn. You're bleeding," Theodore said.

"I'm . . . fine," I muttered, spitting into the grass. "Set the last fire."

I pulled the wig from my head and dropped it to the ground as Theodore reluctantly stood and took a lighter from his pocket.

A moment later, the smell of smoke became overwhelming.

I vomited a second time and wiped my mouth off on the skirt of my already-ruined dress. Tears stung at my eyes, and I couldn't tell if it was from the smoke or everything I'd been through.

Then Theodore gathered me under the arms and helped me back to my feet.

"Come on," he said. "Let's get out of here."

I heard sirens wailing in the distance. Someone must have already called the fire department.

We stumbled off through the trees, Theodore half-carrying, half-dragging me. Then suddenly, he picked me up around the waist and swept my legs out from under me. My head fell against his shoulder as he carried me bridal-style towards the side of the house.

I could hear people shouting towards the back of the house.

"Alright," Theodore said. "Let's meet up and—"

"*No, no, no!*" Jack cried suddenly in my ear, and I flinched at the sound.

"What is it?" Eve demanded.

"He just left through the front entrance! *Mierda*! I don't know—He must have turned back! I don't know how he got through! Shit!"

Eve roared in my ear, and the sound was like a wounded animal.

"Eve?" West shouted. "Where are you going?"

"What's going on?" I said. "What's happening?"

West sounded out of breath as he replied, "Eve just ran after him! He went through a side door on the west side of the house!"

"Stay with her!" Theodore yelled. "Jack, get down there *now*!"

No, I thought.

No, no, no, nononononononono.

Tears blurred my vision, running down my cheeks. "Eve?" I screamed. "Eve, answer me! *Eve*!"

fifty-three

eve

Eve had stopped thinking.

She was just moving—moving, moving, moving—pushing through the crowd after that scorched figure in black, shoving people out of her way, dodging furniture that had been knocked over in her path. Her breathing was heavy.

She'd lost West at some point, but she didn't care.

The others were shouting at her her. She reached up and pulled out the earpiece, tossing it to the ground.

The scorched figure ducked down a hallway, and she followed after him.

She clambered for the gun in its holster on her thigh, and she pulled it free, her thumb moving to the safety and staying there, waiting.

Suddenly, someone from the crowd collided with her, grabbing her by the wrists and forcing her towards one of the rooms off the hall. The gun dropped from her hand, skittering across the floor and swept away beneath panicked feet.

She opened her mouth to scream, and another hand clamped over her mouth.

Eve found herself thrust into a dark room, and she heard the click of a lock as the door closed.

She blinked against the darkness, making out a figure before her.

Her hands curled into fists at her sides, and she planted her feet, readying to fight and claw and kick her way out if she had to.

Then a light flickered on, and she started at who was standing before her.

Her arms went limp at her sides.

"Jude?" she whispered.

fifty-four

I grabbed West by the collar, and I didn't care that he flinched or that I was covered in blood or that it was the first time I'd ever seen him cry.

"Where is she?" I screamed at him. "How could you lose her?"

My blood was rushing, fast, fast, fast, in my ears. I could hardly think over the sound of it. The air was thick with the fears of everyone around me: smoke, dark apples, salt water, black pepper, thunderstorms, vinegar, blood, *blood, blood, blood* . . .

Eve wasn't answering over the earpiece. She could have been dead already. She—

Oh, god, I thought. *She could be dead already.*

"I'm sorry," West stammered. "There were so many people—"

Theodore looped an arm around my waist and pulled me away from West. He set me down on my feet and took my face in his hands, forcing me to look at him. "Tannyn, you need to breathe," he told me. "We all want to find her."

I stared up into his eyes—Eve's eyes—through the tears that clouded my vision.

I weakly nodded my head.

fifty-five

eve

Eve stared at Jude from behind her mask.

He was dressed in an all-black suit, but his mask was silver and carved to look like intertwining snakes. His cuff links and the clip on his black tie were also snakes. There was a crown of small, white flowers nestled amongst his messy red hair, but now it was askew.

And they weren't just any flowers, she realized suddenly. They were apple blossoms.

"Eve," he said. "It's you . . . isn't it?"

She forgot about everything, forgot that someone was trying to kill her, forgot that she'd been angry the last time she'd seen him, forgot that she was meant to be dead.

She crossed her arms over her chest and tipped her chin up. "And just what are you supposed to be?" she asked. Her voice came out steadier than she'd thought it would.

Jude smiled at her. "Isn't it obvious?" he asked, moving closer. "I'm Temptation."

Eve snorted.

"What are you doing here?"

"I got your invitation."

Jude was close enough now that she could smell the smoke that clung to him. He reached a hand towards her, and when she nodded softly, he reached out and pulled the wig from her hair. Then he undid the ribbons

276

that held her mask to her face.

It clattered to the ground at their feet.

He cupped the left side of her face gently in his hand, and she leaned into his touch as he brushed his thumb over the scar where her left eye had been. She couldn't read his expression. Eve bit down on her bottom lip. It had been painted gold, and it glistened in the dim lighting as Jude stared down at her.

"What happened?"

"Damn crows," she muttered. "I've been told they always go for the eyes first."

He delicately ran his thumb across her lashes, and then traced the lines of the scar with his fingers. Then he pulled the elastic from her hair, and the blonde waves tumbled across her shoulders.

When he bent to kiss her, she placed her palms flat against his chest and pushed him back a step. The look in his eyes made her insides flutter—but not with butterflies. No, there was a murder of crows in her stomach and her chest and even in the tips of her fingers.

Jude kept moving towards her until her back was pressed against the wall.

He took her face in his hands.

When he dipped his head, she closed her eyes. But instead of kissing her, he pressed his forehead against hers, and Eve was still as she felt the gentle rise and fall of his chest beneath her hands.

She opened her eyes to find him staring down her.

"I thought you'd left me," he whispered.

She curled her fingers into the fabric of his jacket and felt tears gather in her eye. "I'm sorry."

"I came looking for you that night," he told her. "I looked everywhere for you."

"I'm sorry," she said again.

Then she was crying, and he put his arms around her and tucked her against his chest. And she clung to him with all the strength in her.

"I was so scared, Jude. I still am."

He kissed her hair and her scarred eye and her tear-stained cheeks. He brought her hands to his lips and kissed those, too. "It's alright," he murmured.

"No," she sobbed. "He's here. He's here."

"Who's here?"

She dug her fingers tighter into his jacket. "The man who killed me."

Jude stiffened. She'd never seen him look frightened before, and it turned her heart to lead.

"We're leaving," Jude said. "I'm going to take you home. I'm not going to let him hurt you again."

He bent his head, and she went up on her toes, meeting his lips with her own. The kiss tasted of salt water and white wine and smoke, and she never, ever wanted it to stop. It was the most familiar thing in the world to her.

Then Jude pulled back and released her.

He motioned for her to stay there while he opened the door and peaked out into the hallway.

When he held out a hand towards her, she took it and followed him out, staying hidden behind him as he led her down the hall towards the kitchen. She could still hear sirens and people shouting from the back of the house. She stepped around the jagged pieces of a vase that had shattered against the marble floor.

Suddenly, a dark shape emerged from around the corner.

The man struck Jude against the side of the head with the heel of his

278

gun, and Eve screamed as he crumpled to the ground.

Then the man grabbed her by the arm and pressed a cloth against her mouth.

She struggled to keep her eye open as her body swayed beneath her. Strong arms swept her from the floor, and her head lolled to the side.

Jude? she thought, her lips soundlessly forming the word.

She didn't remember ever having closed her eye, but suddenly the world had gone black.

fifty-six

theo

The smell of smoke was making Theodore nauseous.

It reminded him of the night when his parents died, and he couldn't help but think that he was about to lose Eve again.

West had found Jude lying on the floor by the kitchen, the back of his head sticky with blood. At first, they'd thought he was dead, but realized a moment later that he was breathing. They carried him to a loveseat in the parlor room and threw a glass of cold water in his face like they did in the movies.

When he'd woken up, he'd begun yelling—nonsense at first, but then Theodore realized what he meant. The man dressed like Death—the man in the skull mask—had taken Eve.

Now, Tannyn was crying again, and West had broken several wine glasses, and the sleeves of Theodore's white button-down were smeared with blood. He clenched his hands into fists at his sides.

Eve, where are you?

When his phone vibrated in his back pocket, he almost didn't check it.

He pulled it out and saw it was a text from Eve's burner phone, and his fingers shook as he opened it.

Come alone, it read.

A second later, another text came in.

It was an address.

a girl called murder

Theodore pulled out his earpiece and set it down on the table beside him. No one noticed as he slipped from the house.

fifty-seven

My knuckles were split, and there was a cracked, blood-stained dent in the wall of the Kelley's parlor room.

By then, almost everyone had left the party, and the housekeepers had begun to clean up the mess left behind. Furniture lay on its side. There were stains on the expensive oriental carpets, and champagne flutes lay shattered across the marble floor.

Not that any of us cared.

I sat with my head between my knees, hands knotted into my hair.

I kept telling myself to breathe—*in through the nose, out through the mouth*—but it felt like someone was crushing my lungs. I closed my eyes until I saw spots against my lids in the darkness.

I began to frantically hum "Downtown." I didn't care who heard me.

"Tannyn," Jack said softly. "Calm down."

I lifted my head. "Calm down," I repeated. "*Calm down?* Did you know that on the list of things *not* to say to someone having a panic attack, *calm down* is number one? Eve has been kidnapped, Jude is bleeding and probably needs stitches, and we just burned down nearly half of the Kelley's backyard!"

"I'm fine," Jude said. He was standing by the window, holding a damp washcloth to the back of his head.

West's voice was hoarse from crying as he spoke, "We'll find her. We have to."

I climbed to my feet, pacing from one end of the room to the other. My dress was a torn, tangled mess of blood and vomit and soot. At least my ear had stopped bleeding where the bullet had ripped through the cartilage.

"I'll try calling her again," Jack said.

"There's no point," I snapped.

But he'd already taken out his phone. I turned away as he brought it to his ear.

Then I froze.

"Where's Theodore?" I whispered.

West turned towards me. "What?"

"Theodore. Where is he?"

I felt like I was speaking ancient Greek. It was several seconds before they seemed to understand, and by then, it was clear that Theodore was not in the parlor room. I pulled out my phone and dialed his number, but it went straight to voice mail.

"Fuck!"

I slammed my fist into the wall again, my knuckles screaming in pain.

"Tannyn, stop. You'll break your hand," Jack told me.

"Who the fuck cares?" I shouted. "We have to—we have to find them. We have to, or else . . . or else . . ." I didn't think I had any tears left, but there I was crying again.

"We have no idea where they are," West choked.

I walked to the window and pressed my forehead to the cool glass, closing my eyes. "I can't lose her again," I pleaded softly to anyone who might have been listening. "I can't lose either of them."

When I opened my eyes, I noticed the moon hanging above the trees.

"You will die before the next full moon, Tannyn Carter."

"We need to go to the police," Jack said. "Even if they find out about Eve . . ."

"If you want to catch your death, you'll find it past the field of stone and empty names."

As I stared up at the waxing moon in the sky, I said, "I think I know where they are."

I clung to the handle on the roof of Jack's Jeep as it sped over the uneven terrain.

"You're *sure* this is where the are?" Jack growled at me from the driver's seat.

"I told you, *I don't know!*"

"God dammit," Jack said. But he pressed his foot down harder on the accelerator.

I stared out at the trees as they passed by in a blur. In the backseat, Jude vomited for the second time.

Truth or Consequence's only church loomed in the distance, its high-tipped spire stretching towards the dark clouds. Jack swerved to a stop in front of the arched gateway to the cemetery, its entrance secured with a heavy padlock.

The marble and granite headstones glowed eerily in the moonlight.

He shut off the engine and glanced over at me. "There's no use in me asking you to stay with the car, is there?"

In response, I kicked open the passenger door and climbed out. I folded my arms around myself as I walked to the fence, staring up at a sign that read, *No trespassing after dark.*

Fuck you, I thought. *And fuck your stupid fence.*

The others joined me a moment later.

Jack said, "Alright. Ladies first."

284

I climbed into his interlocked hands, and he boosted me over the fence. I grabbed the top of the fence, metal digging into my palms, and threw my leg over. The hem of my dress caught on one of the exposed pieces of metal along the top, and I heard the sound of fabric tearing as I dropped to the ground on the other side. My legs buckled beneath me, and I threw my hands out to break my fall.

When I glanced back up, a strip of black was fluttering from the fence in the breeze. My dress had ripped all the way to the tops of my knees.

Jack and West boosted Jude over next, and he landed less gracefully beside me on the ground with a string of obscenities. I helped him to his feet as Jack and West climbed over.

"Are you sure you're okay?" I asked Jude as he leaned against me for support.

"No," he replied. "But it doesn't matter. We have to find Eve."

I couldn't argue with that.

Jack used the flashlight on his phone to guide us as we wandered between the headstones—and that was what it was. Wandering. Up and down the rows, scanning the darkness, breathing heavily in the silence.

"*Pues aquí estamos,* " Jack muttered. "This is so fucking creepy."

Something shrieked in the branches overhead, and I nearly screamed. I jumped, knocking into Jack, who caught me in his arms and steadied me.

"What was that?" I hissed.

"Sounded like a barn owl," West said.

"Fuck," I muttered. As if my heart hadn't been beating fast enough already. I pressed a hand against my chest and tried to steady my breathing.

Then West said, "What's that?"

I glanced over at him and followed his gaze to where I could make out a soft light glowing between the trees.

"It looks like the old groundskeeper's cabin," Jude grunted. He was leaning against West for support and his face was paler than usual. "They have to be there."

My nose began to bleed. I wiped it off on the sleeve of my dress.

And then I started towards the place where I was going to die.

fifty-eight

eve

Eve couldn't remember where she'd parked her car.

It wasn't that she was drunk—she'd only had one beer, about three hours ago, because she knew she'd be driving home. It was that it was dark out and her car was black, of course—as if she'd ever get it any other color —and she couldn't hear the sound of the alarm over the music coming from the house behind her.

Where had she parked the damn thing?

A figure emerged from the shadows between two cars, and she started, stumbling back several steps.

"Christ," she said, chuckling lightly. "You scared the shit out of me."

The figure just stood there, staring at her, their face cast in shadow. All she could make out was long blonde hair beneath the hood of their sweatshirt.

She began to cross to the other end of the street, and then she heard footsteps. She turned her head.

A moment later, she felt a sharp pain at her side.

Her body jerked involuntarily, and she screamed. She looked down at the knife protruding from just below her rib cage and fumbled to pull it free. She dropped it to the ground, the blade clattering against the pavement and spattering blood across her shoes.

She pressed a hand to the wound, and her fingers came away sticky and red.

Eve lifted her head, looking for the figure, but they had disappeared.

She staggered forward a step, and her legs nearly gave out beneath her.

Help. She needed help.

If she went back to the party, they'd take her to the hospital. And she was dying. She knew she was dying. She knew how it felt because it wouldn't be the first time she'd died. She could feel her life dripping away between her fingers and staining her shirt. She needed to . . . she needed to get to her brother. Theodore would know what to do. Theodore would help her.

She forced her legs to move beneath her.

She forgot about her car and began stumbling in the direction of their aunt's house. She didn't think of how far it was or that she could barely walk or that it was so dark she couldn't see where she was going.

Where was her phone? Has she set it down at the party? She fumbled in her pockets, trying to find it, but her fingers were clumsy and numb and blood-stained. She winced at the pain of the movement.

"Theodore," she whispered.

Her legs were dead weights beneath her, but somehow she kept moving.

She clutched at her side, pressing her hand into the wound with all her strength.

Then suddenly her foot caught on something, and she tumbled to the ground, scraping her palms as she threw her hands out to break her fall. She lay there, staring up at the moon overhead, as she struggled to breathe through the pain.

"Eve?"

Someone was shouting. She squeezed her eyes closed and willed the noise to go away.

"Eve!"

She opened her eyes to see a boy with red hair and dark eyes crouching over her—Jude Kelley? *she thought, and she might have laughed if she weren't dying. Theodore hated him. Of all the people to find her.*

Jude touched his fingers to the wound in her side.

Go away, *she thought, but her mouth couldn't seem to form the words. She closed her eyes again so she wouldn't have to look at his face.*

"We have to get you to the hospital," he said.

She opened her eyes and grabbed his hand, nails digging into his skin hard enough that she drew blood. He didn't flinch. "No," she choked. "No hospital. Take me home—take me to Theodore."

"Eve—"

"Please."

"You need a hospital."

She could hardly keep her eyes open. "Home," she said, the words catching in her throat. "Promise me."

"I can't—"

"Promise me. "

Her eyes drifted closed, and her hand dropped from his. She remembered the feeling of strong arms around her as they lifted her from the ground.

"Promise," she whispered.

Before she lost consciousness, she heard Jude say, "Alright, Eve. I'll take you home. I promise."

Eve woke up to the feeling of ropes digging into her wrists and ankles.

She sat up slowly, wincing at the pain where the ropes dug into the raw skin of her wrists. There was cold metal against her back—a radiator, the ropes tied through the exposed pipes. She blinked as she took in her surroundings, trying to make sense of where she was. A smell like rotted meat made her head ache. She didn't recognize any of it. Not the worn wooden floors or the peeling floral wallpaper or the medical equipment or—

The woman.

There was a woman lying on a bed across the room, propped up slightly against the pillows. Her eyes were closed.

"Hello?" Eve whispered.

The woman didn't respond.

"Please," she said, louder. "Where am I?"

Then Eve noticed the unnatural blue-tinge to her skin, the way she lay stiff and unmoving on the bed. There was a gash on her forehead, but the wound looked old and unhealed, yellowed around the edges. Bruises scattered her skin.

"Oh, my God."

Her stomach churned. She turned her head and vomited against the wall. Spit dribbled from her lips.

She forgot about the woman or her vomit at the sound of footsteps outside the bedroom door, and she frantically pressed herself against the radiator behind her. She curled in on herself, trying to make herself as small as possible.

The footsteps stopped. The door opened.

A man entered the room, carrying a tray with a glass bowl of water and two wash cloths.

He was wearing the same suit from the masquerade party, but he'd removed the jacket and rolled up the sleeves of his button-down shirt. His clothes were scorched, and his face was coated with soot. Bits of ash lingered in his long blonde hair.

Eve knew she recognized him from somewhere, but she couldn't place it.

The man set down the tray at the desk against the adjacent wall and pulled out a chair to sit. He said nothing as he picked up the cloth and dipped it into the bowl of water.

Eve watched warily as he set to wiping away the soot on his face. Then she swallowed and clenched her hands into fists behind her. "What did you do to Jude?"

Without looking at her, he said, "Nothing—although he might have a bit of a headache when he wakes up. But other than that, he's fine."

Eve flinched at the sound of his voice, which had haunted her dreams for months now. It was both familiar and foreign to her. She hated it. She wanted to rip out his throat with her bare hands.

But Jude was alright.

She closed her eye for a moment, and then she asked, "Who are you?"

The man paused, and that was when Eve glimpsed the burn scars on his hands. They were healed, and he used his hands with such ease that they couldn't have been from that night.

The man set aside the wash cloth and picked up another. He dripped it in the water and rose from his chair, walking over to crouch in front of her. Eve was still as he wiped the trails of spit and vomit from her lips.

"I'm sorry about your eye," he said. "That wasn't part of the plan, but—well, you know crows."

"How did you know where I was all those nights?"

"This is the age of technology. Do you know how easy it is to hack someone's phone nowadays?" He sounded proud of himself.

Eve lunged at his hand, her teeth sinking into the soft flesh of the side of his thumb. She bit down until the tang of blood filled her mouth and tears pricked in her eyes from the taste of it.

Then his fist connected with the side of her face with a sharp crack.

She released him with a gasp and fell back against the radiator. Her temple throbbed where he'd struck her. She spat a mouthful of blood onto the floor and glared up at him through her lashes.

The man stood and looked down at the wound on his hand, sighing deeply through his nose. "Now that was uncalled for."

"Why do you keep killing me?" Eve asked.

"I had to be sure."

"Sure of what?"

The men met her gaze with such intensity that Eve was nearly sick again. "That it wasn't a matter of circumstance for him to bring you back. The last was a test to see if it had to be immediate, or if it could be some time after. It took longer than I'd thought it would, actually."

"What?"

"Did you know that a body that's been frozen has to be defrosted slowly, at thirty-eight degrees exactly? Otherwise, the outside of the body will start to decompose. Isn't that fascinating?" Then he frowned. "Of course, the defrosting period can take up to a week."

Eve's gaze flickered to the dead woman on the bed. "What happened to her?"

He laughed sharply and said, "I know what you're thinking, but no I didn't kill her." He inclined his head slightly to the side. "You don't remember, do you? The night of the crash, the other car? Of course not. You were dead."

He walked over to the desk and picked up his used washcloth, and then he used it to clean off the blood on his hand. The water in the bowl turned pink as Eve stared at him.

It was a moment before she realized he meant the crash that had killed her parents.

"Who are you?" she whispered.

The man turned from the desk and crossed the room to where the woman lay. He stopped at the edge of the bed, looking down at her. His expression was all wounded longing, but Eve felt no pity for him.

He reached out a scarred hand and brushed it against the woman's cheek.

"My name is William Kestrel," he said finally. "And your brother is going to bring back my wife."

fifty-nine

I crouched in the bushes, staring at the cabin through the darkness.

It was a plain, two-story wooden building surrounded by towering trees. The flowers in the window boxes had shriveled and turned brown in the summer heat. It was surrounded by a waist-high, wrought iron fence, and the gate was swinging gently in the night breeze. The air whistled through the gaps in the hinges.

"You will die before the next full moon, Tannyn Carter."

I pushed the thought as far away as possible and focused on the cabin.

The light we'd seen was coming from the first-floor through a window that looked in on the living room. From what I could tell from where we hid, it was empty. There was another light on around the back, in a room on the second-floor.

"We need to get closer," I hissed.

"We need a plan," Jack said.

"We don't have *time* for a plan."

"He has a *gun*, Tannyn. We can't just break in and hope that he'll only have time to shoot one of us."

"Eve is in there. I know she is. I can't just stand here—"

Suddenly, Jude collapsed.

"Fuck," I said.

He lay crumpled in the dirt, his face ghostly white and covered with a sheen of sweat.

West crouched down beside him, lifting him in a sitting position

294

and propping him against a tree. "He might be concussed," he said. He patted Jude's face, once, twice, and then a third time, more forcefully.

Jude blinked slowly, squinting at West in the darkness.

"You need to stay awake," West told him.

I glanced over my shoulder towards the cabin, clenching and un-clenching my hands into fists.

"I'm fine," Jude muttered. He tried to stand, but winced and slumped back down to the ground.

West touched a hand to the back of Jude's head, and his fingers came away bloody.

My gaze flickered from the blood to the cabin and back again. I bit down on my lip until I tasted blood. I pulled my knife from where it was wedged in my bra and clutched it tightly at my side.

I'm sorry, I thought. *Please don't kill me for this, Jack.*

While Jack and West were crowding around Jude, I slipped away through the darkness towards the cabin.

As I grew closer, I could hear voices coming from the second-floor.

I hid myself behind the trunk of a tree and peered around it, searching for the best way in.

An ash tree was growing by the edge of the cabin, its branches just brushing the first-floor roof over the porch. The lit second-floor window cast a small square of light on the dark wood shingles.

I tucked my knife back into my bra and raced across the grass towards the tree.

I scaled it easily, my nails digging into the bark and my bare feet gripping the branches. The knuckles on my right hand screamed at the movement, and the cuts along them split open again and began to bleed. I ignored the pain. I hoisted myself onto a branch that hung over the roof and inched across it on my stomach, praying that I didn't fall.

This isn't how I die, I thought, gritting my teeth.

I lowered myself onto the roof and let go of the branch when my feet touched the shingles. I dropped to my knees and waited, holding my breath, hoping that no one had heard.

Then I scrambled across the roof and pressed myself against the side of the house.

Now, I could hear three voices from inside the room.

One of them was Theodore's.

"I can't," he was saying. "I've never done it before."

"Yes, you have. I've seen you do it," another man's voice growled. The man dressed as Death from the maze. It was still so familiar. I closed my eyes, trying to remember where I'd heard it before that night.

"With her. Never with anyone else."

"Well, there's a first time for everything," the second voice said, bitter-sweet. Silence. And then gunfire and the sound of something shattering. "Move. *Now.*"

Someone screamed. It sounded like Eve. I clamped my hands over my own mouth to keep me from crying out. A sob shook my chest, but I swallowed it and held myself as still as possible.

"Alright," Theodore said, his voice cracked and desperate. "Just don't hurt her."

I released the breath I was holding, pressing a hand against my chest. She was alright. He hadn't shot her.

I moved closer to the window, the shingles rough beneath my bare feet.

I was trying to decide what to do next when my phone began to vibrate where I had it stashed in my bra. I pulled it out and slid my finger across the screen to answer the call, pressing it against my ear.

"What?" I hissed at Jack, cupping my hand around my mouth and the receiver.

"Where the hell are you, Tannyn?"

I flinched at the anger in his voice and shrunk farther into the darkness. "On the roof. I need you to cause a distraction so I can get to Eve and Theodore."

"What the *fuck*, Tannyn?"

"Please, Jack. Just trust me."

And then I hung up and turned my phone off, praying that once, just once, he would listen to me.

I stuffed my phone back into my bra and waited. Blood from my split knuckles dripped down my fingers, and I watched the droplets gather on the roof below my feet. I counted the seconds that ticked by in my head.

Please, Jack, I thought.

When I reached forty seconds, a crash came from one of the rooms downstairs. It sounded like a window shattering.

Thank you.

"What the hell was that?" the man said.

Footsteps. The sound of a door opening.

"*Stay here.* If you try anything, she dies."

More footsteps.

I waited until they'd faded before I crouched down in front of the window and peered over the ledge.

I spotted Eve first, where she was tied to a radiator against the wall adjacent to me. A bruise had begun to flower along her temple, and there was blood on her lips. Her eye was red from crying.

Then I glanced across the room to where Theodore was standing beside a bed. There was a woman in it, propped up against the pillows, an IV connected to her arm. I couldn't tell if she were merely sleeping or unconscious.

Theodore's hands were tied in front of him, and his eyes were closed. And he was doing—something. Touching her forehead and then her chest, almost as if he were feeling for something.

A lamp from the bedside table lay broken in pieces on the floor.

I fumbled for the edge of the window, trying to pry it open. I grunted and braced myself, pushing.

Theodore opened his eyes at the sound. A moment later, he was at the window, flipping the locks, and it gave way beneath my fingers. I forced it open.

The smell that hit me nearly made me double over. I breathed through my mouth, but somehow, that didn't help.

"What the hell are you doing here?" Theodore hissed through his teeth. "You need to leave."

"Theodore, I love you, but shut the fuck up." I pushed past him and ran over to Eve, who wearily lifted her head as I dropped down beside her. I pulled my knife out and flicked it open. I grit my teeth as I worked at the ropes binding her to the radiator.

"You shouldn't have come," Eve whispered. She leaned her head against my shoulder, and I wanted so desperately to take her in my arms and comfort her. But I kept cutting away at the ropes.

I'll kill him for this, I thought. *I swear I will.*

"How did you know where we were?" Theodore demanded.

I was silent. The first rope gave way beneath my hands, and I started on a second.

"Tannyn. *How did you know where we were?*"

"Keep your goddamn voice down," I snarled.

Then I froze at the sound of footsteps pounding up the stairs.

"*Tannyn.*"

I pressed the knife into Eve's hands behind her back. Theodore pushed me towards the window.

I didn't argue.

I heard the door open as I tumbled out the window. My elbow knocked hard against the shingles, and I cried out without thinking. I rolled, rolled, rolled towards the edge of the roof, and I threw my hands out, trying to grab something, anything, to keep myself from falling.

My left hand caught on a branch, and I held on tight enough that I thought I might have dislocated something as I jerked to a stop. I ignored the scratches covering my body and the pain in my arm as I clambered to my feet and dove for the closest branch that looked like it could support me. I clung to it so hard that my nails bent back as I pulled myself up and swung my leg over.

I scrambled towards the trunk in the dark and began climbing down as quickly as I could.

Eve was screaming, sobbing, begging, her pleas echoing in my ears. Not for herself, I realized a moment too late.

A gunshot.

Something struck me in the chest. The force knocked me backwards, and I lost my grip. I crashed down through the branches, which cracked and fractured beneath my weight. I hit the ground, and all the air was forced from my lungs. A sharp pain pierced my side. My head smacked against the hard earth.

I stared up at the moon through the branches of the tree as leaves fluttered down around me.

Spots danced across my vision.

Then nothing.

sixty

kestrel

Fuck.

Kestrel dropped the gun on the table beside him and pressed his hands against the sides of his head, squeezing his eyes closed.

He'd shot her. He'd shot Tannyn Carter.

This hadn't been part of the plan.

He dug his nails into his scalp until he thought they might break skin.

The girl, Eve, was still screaming, yanking against the ropes that held her. The boy, Theodore, was staring out the window, his hands gripping the sill so hard his knuckles had turned white.

"Shut up!" he snapped at the girl. "*Shut up!*" When she kept on screaming, he picked up the gun and whirled on her. "I said *shut up!*"

He forgot about the boy in that moment, until something connected with the side of his face. Hard. Bone crunched. His teeth knocked together. He tasted blood as he stumbled back a step, but then the boy was on him again.

He was swinging his bound hands wildly, but they connected with Kestrel's nose, and there was the sickening sound of bone and cartilage shattering.

The gun was still in Kestrel's hand. Through the pain and the spots that flickered across his vision, he somehow managed to aim it.

A shot rang out.

There was more screaming. It dug at Kestrel's skull like needles.

The boy staggered a step back, clutching the wound on his thigh. The dark blood was hardly visible against the black of his pants.

Kestrel turned to the girl again and pressed the barrel of the gun against her forehead.

"You're going to bring back my wife," Kestrel told him. "Or your sister dies, too."

sixty-one

jack

Jack was helping Jude into the passenger side of the Jeep when he heard the gunshot.

He whipped his head towards the sound, his blood going cold. "Fuck!" he exclaimed.

Jude had also turned in the direction of the sound, but now he reached across and unbuckled the seatbelt strapped across him. "Go," he rasped.

Jack looked back at him, the color drained from his face, the blood dripping down the back of his neck. "I can't leave you," Jack said. "You could die."

"So could they!" Jude snapped. He lowered his feet to the ground and clung to the side of the car as he climbed out. "Just give me the goddamn keys. I'll drive myself to the hospital if I have to."

Jack glanced back over his shoulder in the direction of the cabin. Then he took out his car keys and pressed them into Jude's hand. "Try not to crash," he muttered.

And then he climbed the fence of the cemetery in one swift, fluid movement, dropping to the ground on the other side.

He heard the Jeep roar to life, and then he was out of earshot as he raced towards the cabin.

sixty-two

I opened my eyes, gasping in air.

Everywhere hurt. A dull ache at the back of my head, a throbbing in my elbow, a sharp sensation in my side. Scratches all over my body from where twigs had clawed at my skin as I fell.

My breathing was still coming too quickly, and my fingers fumbled at the neckline of my dress, tearing at it, as if somehow this might allow me to breath. I loosened the straps of the vest beneath my dress. Moonlight reflected off the bit of metal that was embedded in heavy material.

Then I hissed in a breath at the pain in my side.

I glanced down at where a branch had pierced my side, entering at an upward angle below the vest. I curled my fingers around the end of it and pulled it out, slowly, slowly, slowly, my breathing heavy.

I dropped the branch to the ground, spattering blood across the grass.

The remaining limbs of the tree overhead swayed softly in the breeze, and I stared at the splintered fragments where branches had broken beneath me.

Someone was shouting my name.

It took some time for me to register West in front of me, crouched on the ground, his hands on the side of my face.

"West," I muttered.

"You're bleeding."

"I'm fine." I waved his hands away from my face and braced my own against his shoulders, pushing myself to stand. He rose with me.

"Jack . . . Where's Jack?"

"He took Jude back to the car. He could hardly stay awake. He needs a hospital bad. Jack tried to make me go, but—" He broke off. *But he wouldn't leave without Eve,* I thought. He looked at the branches that littered the ground, and the scratches on my face. "What happened? I heard a gunshot and found you here."

"Fucking asshole shot me," I hissed. I pressed a hand to my throbbing head. My body ached all over. "I fell out of a tree."

I started towards the front of the cabin, and West grabbed my arm. Not roughly, but I winced at the contact.

"Where are you going?"

"Eve and Theodore are still in there," I said. "I have to get them out."

"I'm going with you."

"It's too dangerous. I still have a bulletproof vest," I told him. I didn't know if it would hold up for another blow, but I didn't care. "If I'm not out with them in fifteen minutes, you need to call the police.

"You can't go by yourself."

The air around West smelled like the harsh scent of hospitals and whiskey. I pulled my arm from his grip. "Then stop me," I said.

He didn't.

I followed the voices on the second-floor to the bedroom at the end of the hall.

The door was propped slightly open, light flooding out onto the wooden floors.

I moved silently towards it, trying to make out the conversation inside.

"You think I'm not trying?" Theodore was yelling, his voice

304

desperate. I'd never heard him sound like that before. "I couldn't even bring back my own goddamn parents!"

I reached the room, my view partially blocked by the ajar door.

I saw Eve staring across the room in the direction of the voices, her head resting against the radiator. But I glimpsed her hands working behind her as she cut away at the ropes on her wrists.

"You're not *trying hard enough*," the man snarled. "I've already lost patience with you. You've got another minute before I put a bullet in your other leg—or maybe your sister would be a better motivator."

The man stepped into view, crossing the room to Eve.

Her hands froze behind her, and she lifted her chin to look at him, eye wide as he leveled the gun at her face.

I braced my hands on the frame of the door as the shock of it hit me.

The blonde hair. The scarred hands. The scent of smoke and charred flesh. The voice. He'd been right there. *He'd been right there the whole fucking time.*

"Perhaps your sister could do without her other eye," Mr. Kestrel said.

"Please," Eve whispered.

I stepped into the room, knocking the door open with a crash. "Don't you fucking touch her," I said.

Three pairs of eyes whipped towards me. Kestrel's mouth twisted into something between shock and anger and confusion, and he raised the gun at me.

Then I grabbed his fears in my hands and pulled as hard as I could.

The world slid away. Eve, Theodore, the woman in the bed. The broken lamp. The windows. The door behind me. Until it was just the man who had murdered Eve and a small, purple-haired girl with a thing for nightmares in a dark room. Then I was gone, too.

Kestrel's eyes went wide, and he spun frantically in a circle with the gun held out ahead of him. His hands trembled. "You bitch! What did you do?"

The flames started in the corner, flickering and bursting to life, their fingers clawing at the floral wallpaper, eating it away.

Kestrel dropped the gun in his hand as if it had burnt him.

"No," he said, shaking his head. "No, no, *no, nonononono . . .*"

He turned to where the window had been a moment ago, feeling along the wall, tearing at the wallpaper with his fingers. He pulled off his button-down shirt, beating at the flames, but they were spreading too quickly.

Smoke curled towards the ceiling. The wallpaper peeled away in blackened strips.

You promised. The thought flitted through my mind as I wrapped his fears around me, the smoke stinging at my nostrils. *You promised you wouldn't do it again. You promised, you promised, you promised—*

"What is it, honey?"

A flash of metal.

My fingers coming away stained with red.

My mother sobbing.

I grasped the threads of his fears until my knuckles turned white and my skin split open. The weight of them was heavy, heavy, **heavy** in my hands. I squeezed my eyes closed.

In through the nose, out through the mouth.

Smoke filled my lungs. I choked on it, gasping—*not real, not real,* I reminded myself. *You promised, you promised, you promised . . .*

I opened my eyes.

The entire room was engulfed in flames.

Kestrel was on his knees, clawing at the floorboards, and there were bloody prints on the wood from where his nails had split. He was begging for someone, anyone, to save him and screaming a woman's name—Vivian. The words were hoarse and choked.

"Tannyn! Tannyn, please!" he cried. "I didn't mean to hurt you—I just wanted my wife back!"

Theodore sitting on the front step of our porch, his head in his hands and his shirt soaked with blood.

"Someone . . . Someone killed her."

A closed casket lined with white silk.

Laughter, like a crow's caw.

The roaring of the flames and Kestrel's screams swirled together into a symphony of white noise in my ears.

My mother staring blankly out the window of the visiting room.

Blood began to drip from my nose. It was on my lips, tasting of copper and rain water and coffee and warm sugar all at once. Warm sugar— like on the morning my mother had come after me.

You promised, you promised, you promised . . .

A sob worked its way from my chest, lost amongst the smoke and flames.

"If you want to catch your death, you'll find it past the field of stone and empty names."

I took a step closer to Kestrel. The flames moved with me.

He was raking at his chest with his fingernails, as if he meant to tear himself open to get rid of the smoke in his lungs. Blood flowed from the deep gashes in his skin.

The scar on my collarbone throbbed as if the wound were fresh.

"You promised," Kestrel rasped.

His lips didn't move as he spoke. I couldn't tell if I'd imagined it.

Then his clothes caught fire.

The screams were the worst thing I'd heard in my entire life. I closed my eyes and hummed "Downtown" beneath my breath to drown them out, but they were inside my head, echoing through my skull, thrumming through my bones.

Tears spilled over, the salt water stinging the scratches on my cheeks.

You promised . . .

His fears were so heavy, and the smoke turned to lead in my lungs, pulling my chest towards the floor. Pain tore at my insides, dug into my skull like needles until spots flecked my vision.

I screamed, pressing my hands against the sides of my head.

Then silence.

Like a candle snuffed out.

I opened my eyes to four beads of blood on the floor at my feet.

The bedroom was silent except for the whir of medical equipment at the bed in the corner. I lifted my head, blinking back the tears on my lashes.

Everything about the room was the same—except for William Kestrel. He lay on the floor, his eyes wide and unseeing, and his fingers curled towards his chest. A single stream of blood ran from his nose.

Theodore and Eve were staring at me, their expressions frozen with horror and shock.

I forced a smile, my lips stained with blood.

And then I collapsed.

sixty-three

theo

Tannyn hit the ground before Theodore had time to react.

Then he was on his knees beside her, pulling her into his lap despite the ropes which dug into his wrists.

Her black dress was slick with blood, clinging to her side, and it soaked into the legs of his pants. Her lashes fluttered softly against her pale cheeks. She was so cold—the way Eve had been when Jude had brought her home that night, the way she'd been when he'd found her in the tree.

"Tannyn? Tannyn!" He brushed her hair back from her face and shook her—gently at first, and then harder when she didn't respond. He was crying—sobbing, really—his shoulders trembling with the movement. He didn't have the energy to try and hold back the tears. "Answer me, dammit! Don't do this!"

Eve was screaming, struggling against the remaining rope that held her to the radiator. She broke free with a strangled cry, her wrists raw and bleeding, and clambered across the floor on her knees with her ankles still bound.

She touched her hand to Tannyn's cheek. "Tannyn, please."

"Wake up!" Theodore yelled, choking on his tears. "Don't you fucking die on me, Tannyn Lourdes Carter!"

He shook her again. Kissed her forehead, cheeks, lips that had turned blue.

She stirred in his arms, opening her eyes weakly and staring up at him through her dark lashes. There were tears in her eyes. "Theodore?" she whispered.

"You will die before the next full moon, Tannyn Carter."

He wanted to break something, hit something, but instead he cradled her in his arms. "I'm here."

"I'm sorry." Her breathing was heavy, and the blood on his hands was growing cold. "Tell Hollis I love him—and my mom and dad." She choked on a laugh and winced at the movement. "They're gonna be so mad at me."

"Tell them yourself, dammit!" Theodore snapped.

"I'm sorry," she said again.

"Stop! Stop, please." His shouts turned to begging, barely above a whisper. "You're not going anywhere. Tannyn, please."

"I love you," she told him. Her eyes flickered weakly to Eve. "Both of you. I wouldn't die for just anyone, you know."

A laugh bubbled from Eve's lips and quickly turned to sobbing. "I know. I know. I love you, too." She reached out and clasped one of Tannyn's hands in her own. She looked down at the split knuckles, gently brushing her thumb across them. "You're the most fearless person I've ever known."

"That's not true," Tannyn said softly. The tears in her eyes brimmed over. "I'm so scared, Eve."

"Please don't die."

"You're one to talk." Theodore saw Tannyn's fingers tighten around Eve's. She closed her eyes. "Promise you won't leave me?"

Eve swallowed thickly and nodded. "I promise."

Tannyn's breathing hitched.

Theodore pressed a hand to the side of her face. "Tannyn? Please. Stay with me." His voice broke on the last word, shattering into a thousand pieces on the floor beside his heart. *Good,* he thought. He didn't want it

310

anyway. Not without her.

"*Please.*"

A moment later, the girl he loved was still.

sixty-four

eve

No, Eve thought.

She stared down at Tannyn through the tears in her eye. The hand that she clasped in her own had gone limp.

Eve looked up at Theodore. "Do something."

"I can't," he said, his voice broken, cracked, hollow.

"Yes, you can. Bring her back. You have to try."

"*I can't.*" Theodore stood suddenly. He crossed the room took the desk and picked up the wooden chair, smashing it to pieces against the wall.

Eve winced at the sound, still clutching Tannyn's hand in her own.

He grabbed one of the splintered legs in his bound hands and put his whole body into throwing it across the room. He struggled against the ropes around his wrists, cursing and shouting, until they'd turned red from the blood. Then he dropped to his knees, his head in his hands. He squeezed his eyes closed.

Eve placed Tannyn's hand gently on her chest and got to her feet.

She walked over to where the knife lay discarded on the floor, moonlight reflecting off the rainbow blade.

She picked it up and walked over to Theodore, crouching before him. He didn't resist as she reached out and cut away the ropes. They fell away from his wrists but he didn't move or even open his eyes.

Eve closed the blade and pressed the knife into his hands.

Theodore opened his eyes and lifted his head to look at her.

a girl called murder

"You have to try."

sixty-five

A light flickered to life in the darkness.

It shone like the sun at the end of the tunnel, and as I walked towards it, the sounds of my footsteps echoed in my ears. I reached a hand out into the darkness, curling my fingers through it like a heavy fog.

The darkness gave way to a small kitchen.

My bare feet stuck to the linoleum floor.

I looked up, lifting a hand to shield my eyes from the sunlight streaming through the window across the room.

There was a woman standing by the sink in her pajamas, a steaming mug of coffee in her hands. Brown hair fell in soft waves around her face. "Hey, sleepy head. You're certainly up early."

The woman turned towards me, a smile spreading across her face.

I staggered back a step in surprise. *I know you.*

"What is it, honey?"

There was something so familiar about her—the gentle eyes, the curve of her smile, the scent that lingered around her of chardonnay and warm sugar. Even her blue pajamas, patterned with small stars and crescent moons.

I tilted my head to the side, my eyes flickering over her features as I tried to remember where I'd seen her before. "I know you," I muttered out loud.

The woman's brows pinched together, and her lips turned down at the corners. "Honey?"

The record player in the corner skipped—once, twice. A song I

314

recognized began to play. The name of it lingered at the back of my mind. A moment later, I had it. "Tea for Two" by Doris Day.

The woman's head turned at the sound.

A crash broke through the rich, lovely voice on the track as the coffee mug in the woman's hand hit the floor, shattering to pieces.

She looked back at me. "You," she said, her voice barely a whisper. "What are you doing here? What did you do with Tannyn?"

My eyes widened, and my voice caught in my throat. "Mama?"

My mother reached behind her, fingers fumbling, spreading across the counter top, searching for something. She knocked over the knife stand, and her fingers closed around the handle of a steak knife.

"Where's my daughter?"

"Mom . . ."

The hand holding the knife trembled. "Get out of my house."

I held out my hand towards my mother. "Mama, please. It's me."

A sharp pain slashed across my cheek. I cried out, stumbling backwards, and pressed a hand to the cut. My fingers came away stained with red.

Then my mother was coming at me again, swinging the knife in her hand wildly. I ducked out of the way, but she caught a fistful of my hair, and I screamed out in pain. The knife slashed towards my chest, catching my collarbone as I tried to wriggle from her grasp.

I clawed at the hand that still had ahold of my hair.

"Mama, it's me!" I screamed.

Then footsteps pounded down the stairs and someone was shouting my name and pulling my mother off me. She fell to the ground, knife skittering across the kitchen floor and under the refrigerator. She cowered against the cabinets by the sink, curling in on herself, sobbing.

"Mama!" I lunged for her, not caring that my chest felt as if it were on fire or that it was her fault or that she might hurt me again.

The arms that had pried my mother from me now wrapped around me and pulled me against them, turning me away so I couldn't see her. *Hollis,* I thought in surprise. *Oh, Hollis.* I dug my fingers into his arms and buried my face in his chest.

Then the body I was holding tightly against mine vanished. I grasped at empty air.

"Hollis?" I yelled, whirling in a circle. "*Hollis!*"

Tears streamed down my face, stinging the cut on my face.

I crumpled to my knees, pressing my hands against the floor. My chest contracted, folding in on itself, crushing my lungs. "Please," I whispered, choking. "Don't leave me. I'm so scared."

The darkness swept in around me.

I closed my eyes and let it take me, and with it, the pain.

sixty-six

west

West had planned to wait only ten minutes before following Tannyn into the cabin.

The screaming had started after four.

Or perhaps howling was a better word. It was inhuman, the sort of noise a wounded animal made. It made bile rise in his throat.

That was when Jack burst through the trees and spotted him next to the splintered branches that littered the ground. Jack glanced once at the blood staining the grass and then grabbed West by the collar of the shirt.

"Where the fuck is Tannyn?" he shouted.

West managed a nod towards the cabin. Bile rose in his throat, and he thought he might be sick.

Jack set him down on his feet, and West forced himself to follow him as he ran through the front door. He dragged himself up the stairs after Jack, fingers biting into the railing.

A light came from the end of the hall, slanting across the wooden floor where the door to a room had been left half-open. He could make out Eve's voice—soft, desperate. It sounded like she was crying.

Then Theodore's voice.

"Tannyn! Please, Tannyn, come back to me!"

Jack and West rushed into the room, but they both froze in the doorway when they saw Tannyn lying on the ground. Theodore was on his knees beside her, his hands on her chest. Her eyes were closed, and blood had pooled onto the floor around her from a wound in her side.

Eve held Tannyn's head in her lap, brushing her fingers through the tangled locks as tears dripped from her chin.

Jack's legs gave out beneath him, and he fell to his knees. Eve looked up at the sound, her eye flickering from Jack on the floor to West in the doorway.

"She's gone."

Jack looked to Theodore, who was staring down at Tannyn. And the pain in his eyes . . . "You can bring her back," he said.

At first, Theodore didn't respond.

Then, without looking up, he whispered, "I can't."

"But Eve—"

"Is my sister," Theodore said, cutting him off. "It's different. It's like—a connection. I don't have that with Tannyn. I need to be able to find her to reach her. With Eve, it's like . . . searching for myself. I can't find Tannyn if I don't know what to look for."

West said, "You can."

"I can't."

Jack started to speak, when someone else interrupted him.

"No."

They all looked to Eve, who straightened suddenly. She picked up a knife from the floor and flicked the blade open. It reflected like an oil spill in the light, all greens and purples and pinks.

"She doesn't get to do that," Eve said, almost to herself. "She doesn't get to die for me."

West watched as Eve pressed the blade against her open palm and drew a line of blood in one single motion. She hissed out a breath through her teeth. Then she lifted Tannyn's hand and did the same.

She clasped Tannyn's hand in her own, blood dripping between their fingers.

Then she took Theodore's hand.

"Bring her back," she said. "Or I'll go over there and drag her back myself."

sixty-seven

Trees rose up from the darkness like small islands.

They towered out of the ground, tendrils of shadow creeping along the trunks. Droplets of rain water glistened on their branches.

I splashed through a puddle, and the drops of water hung suspended in the air around me. My hair was wet, strands clinging to my skin. The torn hem of my dress dragged through the water and snagged on branches.

"Sixteen . . . Seventeen . . . Eighteen . . ."

I spotted a tree with a hollow worn into its side, large enough for a small girl to fit herself into it. I tucked myself into it, pressing against the damp bark.

I smiled and bit down on my lip.

"Nineteen . . . Twenty! Ready or not, here I come!"

I held my breath as I heard footsteps splashing past me in the darkness. I counted the seconds that passed in my head.

"Ah-ha!"

I shrieked as hands reached out from around the trunk of the tree and grabbed me, pulling me into a hug. I looked up into the face of a woman with soft brown hair and lines that crinkled in the corner of her eyes.

Mama, I thought.

I wound my arms tightly around her, breathing her in.

"Tannyn . . ."

I lifted my head, looking over her shoulder, squinting to see through the darkness.

My mother looked down at me, concern in her dark eyes. "What is it, honey?"

"What is it, honey?"

A flash of metal.

I stumbled back from my mother's arms, colliding with the tree behind me.

I cried out at a stinging sensation on my right palm. I looked down to see beads of blood forming along an open cut.

"Tannyn . . ."

The tree disappeared from behind me, and I fell backwards, throwing out my hands to catch myself. Pain shot through my arm as I landed on the cut on my palm.

I clambered back to my feet.

"Mama?" I yelled. "Where are you?"

"Tannyn . . ."

Two figures appeared in the shadows, kneeling on the ground and clasping hands. Tangled blonde hair hung around the girl's face. The sleeves of the boy's shirt were stained with blood.

They seemed to be looking down at something I couldn't see.

A memory came back, hitting me so suddenly that it knocked the wind from my chest.

"I love you. Both of you . . . Promise you won't leave me?"

"I promise."

I took a step towards them, uncertain.

The boy leaned forward, reaching for something, and I felt the feather-like touch of fingers gently cupping my chin. I tipped my head up and closed my eyes at the brush of the boy's mouth against mine.

My lips parted, and I breathed in his scent of rainstorms.

Then the feeling was gone, as suddenly as it had come.

My eyes flashed open.

Theodore. Eve.

I threw myself at them.

The darkness shattered around me like shards of glass, raining down and slicing into my skin. My reflection danced around me on their blood-stained surfaces.

I screamed.

My body stung all over, as if someone were rubbing salt into the wounds. My head throbbed and pounded. There was a pain in my side like I'd never felt.

I doubled over and vomited onto the shards of glass at my feet.

Someone was grasping my hand—it was just the whisper of a feeling, like the kiss, but it was there. I squeezed the fingers in mine, clinging to them, even though the pain of it was nearly unbearable.

"That's it. Hold on, Tannyn," someone whispered in the darkness. "Hold on."

So I did.

sixty-eight

eve

"Tannyn?" The word was hardly there on Eve's lips. "Oh, God. Tannyn."

Theodore was unconscious on the ground beside her, his eyes moving quickly beneath his pale eyelids. Tears had gathered on the ends of his lashes.

Suddenly he sat up, gasping in a breath of air. His head whirled towards Tannyn, and he stared down at her, unblinking. Eve wasn't even sure if he was breathing.

The fingers in her own twitched, and then tightened, squeezing her hand back.

"That's it. Hold on, Tannyn," she whispered. "Hold on."

a girl called murder

sixty-nine

The smell of hospitals stung at my nose.

Light shone against my eyelids, and I groaned. Something poked at the inside of my right elbow. I moved to reach for it, but my left arm remained firmly tucked against my chest. It took me a moment to recognize the rough feel of bandages and a sling against my skin.

"Sweetheart?" an unfamiliar woman's voice said. "Can you hear me?"

"Turn off the lights," I muttered, the words garbled.

I forced my eyes open, though my lids were heavy and it took a few tries before I could fully see. I glanced around at the crisp white sheets, the pale blue walls, the IV dripping fluids into my arm. Several vases of flowers were scattered around the room.

My tongue was heavy in my mouth, and I swallowed, looking over at the nurse.

"Where am I?" I asked, though I already knew the answer.

She had cool brown skin and a braid of black hair that fell over her shoulder. Her scrubs were wine-colored and smelled like fabric softener. She was smiling gently at me from behind her glasses.

"You're at the hospital. Do you remember what happened?"

"What is it, honey?

A flash of metal.

My fingers coming away stained with red.

My right hand fluttered to my collarbone despite how much it hurt to move my arm. I was searching for bandages, but the skin was smooth save for a long, puckered scar. Then I looked down at my bandaged knuckles and turned my hand over to stare at the pink line of healing tissue on my palm.

I remembered the darkness, my mother, Theodore, Eve, holding on even though it hurt . . .

"I died," I said without looking at the nurse.

The nurse chuckled softly. "Almost, but not quite," she replied. She began to fiddle with some of the equipment beside me. "You fell out of a tree, hun. It must have been quite a drop."

I frowned, struggling to keep my eyes open. "No, I . . . That doesn't sound right."

She picked up the clipboard hanging by the end of my bed and flipped through it. "You've got quite a list of injuries, Miss Carter. Aside from the bruising and scratches, it looks like you have ripped cartilage in your left ear from a gunshot wound, a torn muscle in your shoulder, and a fairly minor head injury. Not to mention, you lost a significant amount of blood due to a puncture wound on your abdomen. Luckily, no major organs were ruptured," she told me. "You're going to be feeling sore for quite a while, though."

I turned my head, and that was when I noticed someone in the corner of the room.

My fingers clenched into the stiff hospital sheets, and my knuckles ached at the movement.

The nurse followed my gaze, and she said softly, "He was the one who brought you in. I don't think he's left your side since. Caused me a bit of trouble, actually."

Theodore was asleep in one of the chairs, long legs stretched out in front of him, his cheek resting lightly against his shoulder. He'd changed out of his clothes from that night into plain sweatpants and a t-shirt. There were bandages on his wrists and dark circles beneath his eyes. His hair shone like white-gold in the sunlight streaming through the window.

"Theodore," I whispered.

"He's very handsome," the nurse said, the hint of a smile in her voice.

I might have snorted if it weren't for the pain. "Don't let him hear you," I muttered. "He's already conceited enough."

Another nurse entered with a drip of some sort, but I ignored her as I stared at Theodore. I watched the gentle flutter of his lashes against his cheeks.

"I'll let your doctor know you're awake," the first nurse told me. "Why don't you get some rest? He'll still be here when you wake up, I promise."

Promise you won't leave me?"

"I promise."

The nurse turned to leave, and I started to reach for her, but my body felt so heavy and the movement pulled at the stitches in my side. I grunted in pain.

"Don't move around too much," the nurse said. I leaned back against the pillows and allowed her to tuck the sheets back around me. "If you need something, just ask."

"Eve," I murmured as my eyelids began to drop. "Is she alright?"

"Eve?" the nurse asked. "Is that one of your friends?"

I turned my head to press my cheek against the soft pillow and let my eyes fall closed. It was too much of an effort to keep them open. "She died, too," I told the nurse. "More than once." Then I opened my eyes. "I wasn't supposed to tell anyone. It's a secret."

The nurse took my hand, her fingers warm and calloused against my own. "It's alright. I won't tell."

I nodded into my pillow and closed my eyes. "You're a good

person. What's your name?"

"Lorena."

"Like the poem by Lucille Clifton . . ." I started to drift off, then I remembered that I hadn't told her my name. "I'm Tannyn." My voice was hardly a whisper, and I wasn't sure if she'd even heard me.

I felt her hand slip from mine.

I recalled the last line of the poem and said, "*She thought it could fly . . .*"

Then I was asleep.

It was darker when I woke for the second time.

The sun outside the window had begun to set, casting a soft pink-orange glow over the room. As I opened my eyes, I heard footsteps moving to the side of my bed and someone took my hand.

"Hey, Tannyn."

I turned my head, blinking slowly at the familiar blue eyes. "Hollis," I croaked, smiling at the sight of my brother. "What are you doing here?"

I started to sit up, but he put his hands on my shoulders and gently pushed me back against the pillows. "Whoa, there. Tannyn. You're not supposed to be moving around. The nurses'll kill me."

I stared at my brother, taking in the tanned skin, the easy smile, the waves of dirty blonde hair that had gotten longer since I'd last saw him. He wore cargo shorts and a black t-shirt, along with a flat silver Claddagh ring on his third finger. "You're supposed to be in Denmark."

"You thought you could almost die without me here?"

I laughed despite the pain in my side. "Sorry. Next time I'll call first."

"You really look like shit, Tan," he told me.

"You're one to talk. When's the last time you got a haircut?"

Hollis touched the back of his neck, and his face flushed lightly. "Cian likes it long."

"Cian?" I raised a brow. "And why is this the first time I'm hearing about Cian?"

He cleared his throat, an embarrassed smile pulling at the corner of his mouth. "Well, I was waiting until I came home to introduce you. We met when I was staying at a hostel in Ireland, and he decided to join our group. He was going to come stay with us once I came home," he told me. "But when we got the call that you were in the hospital . . . He's actually back at the house right now."

"Good. I don't want to meet your boyfriend for the first time wearing a paper gown."

"Speaking of boyfriends . . ." Hollis's gaze moved to the corner of the room, and I followed his gaze to the chair where Theodore had been sleeping the last time I'd woken up. Now, it was empty. "I heard Theodore was the one who brought you in."

"Where is he?"

Hollis smiled. "Don't worry. He hasn't left you. He and dad just went to get something to eat from the cafeteria."

"Dad's here?"

"Don't look so shocked. You *are* his only daughter."

I might have punched his shoulder if even the idea of it hadn't made me wince. "He's been doing better, Hollis," I said. "He even cooked dinner and managed not to set the house on fire." I didn't mention the time I'd come home to the smoke alarms going off and a charred pizza in the oven.

"I'm glad. I was worried that no one was taking care of you while I was away." His gaze flickered to the chair in the corner again. "He's a good one, Tannyn," he said, and I knew he wasn't talking about our father anymore.

"I guess I'll keep him around then."

Hollis chuckled. "I still haven't thanked him." He looked down at the bandages on my knuckles of the hand he was holding, and the smile fell from his face. "What happened, Tannyn? They said you were attacked by some teacher . . ." He shook his head. "That you fell out of a tree trying to escape him. And your friend Eve . . . she's alive."

"What?" I whispered.

Hollis reached for a newspaper on the bedside table and handed it to me. "Honestly. Didn't they tell you anything?"

I took the paper from him, staring down at the picture of Eve on the front page. It was the same one they'd used on her memorial cards. I touched my fingers to her smiling face, and tears pricked in the corners of my eyes. I quickly read over the article, muttering the words under my breath.

Evelyn Sheartwater, a seventeen year old girl from Truth or Conssequence, was recently discovered alive after two months of being presumed dead.

A body thought to be Evelyn's was found at the beginning of summer on the Shearwater property with the heart carved from the chest cavity. At that time, Evelyn had been missing for approximately twelve hours. Officials are now saying that the body was too damaged for proper identification. Further investigation is underway, though no other girls in the area have been reported missing and the body, thought to be Evelyn's at the time, was cremated.

As for Evelyn herself, she was found on the side of the road last Monday morning after escaping from the home of local forty-three year-old William Kestrel, where officials say she was being kept against her will for the past two months. Kestrel was a teacher at TC High School, and his motives are still unknown at this time. Officials suspect that he was also responsible for the death of the girl found on the Shearwater's property.

The details of Evelyn Shearwater's escape are still murky, but sources state that the opportunity for it arose while her captor attended a party Saturday night. The party ended in disaster when Kestrel set fire to a hedge maze in the host's backyard and attacked two of Evelyn's friends that were also in attendance. One was brought to the hospital in critical condition after falling twenty-feet from a tree while fleeing Kestrel; the other received a mild concussion following a blow to the head. Both teens are expected to make full recoveries.

William Kestrel was found dead in his car around two a.m. Sunday morning on Morrow Road, where it is suspected that he crashed into a tree after suffering from a stroke brought on by smoke inhalation.

When Kestrel did not return home Sunday, Evelyn Shearwater managed to shatter a vase in the room where she was being held and use a shard of glass to cut through the ropes that Kestrel was keeping her tied up with.

Upon later raiding the home, police discovered the body of Kestrel's late wife, Vivian Lincoln-Kestrel. It is presumed that she has been dead for at least two years following a car crash, and that her body was being kept in a freezer in Kestrel's basement until this time. It had begun to decompose by the time police arrived.

Evelyn Shearwater had this to say about why he might have chosen to defrost the body after keeping it frozen for two years: "Perhaps he was into some Norman Bates-type s***. I don't know."

She is currently in the care of St. Agnes Hospital, where she is expected to be released by the end of the week. Her family has declined to make any statements at this time.

"Eve," I said. "She's okay."

"She's actually right down the hall," Hollis told me, and my head snapped up. "Apparently they found her Monday morning, wandering around on the road by that old cemetery. The bastard that attacked you was keeping her tied up in his house for the past two months."

"She's here?" I demanded.

"Yes, but don't go getting all excited. The nurses said I'm supposed to keep your blood pressure down."

"And Kestrel. He's dead."

Hollis nodded gravely, but there was hatred in his eyes. "I only wish I could have killed him myself."

I bit down on my bottom lip and slipped my hand from his grasp.

My brother's eyes softened. "Tan? What's the matter?"

I shook my head.

"You can tell me anything. Please." Hollis took my face in his hands. "Did he hurt you?"

My fingers went to the scar on my collarbone, touching it lightly with my fingers. "I killed him, Hollis," I whispered.

"What?"

"I killed him."

"He had a stroke and crashed his car, Tannyn. You didn't do that."

"Yes, I did. The stroke, at least," I said quietly. "Theodore must have staged the car accident. But I killed him."

"You couldn't have. You didn't."

"I did," I told him, "because I almost did it to mom six years ago."

Hollis went still. "What did you just say?"

I drew a breath, and then I told him everything.

About the day my mother came after me. About Eve's death. About the woman who'd read my bones. About the masquerade party and William Kestrel and the caretaker's cabin in the cemetery where I'd died.

". . . and I felt Eve's hand in the darkness," I told him. "And she told me to hold on, and I did. But it hurt." Tears brimmed in the corners of my eyes. "It hurt so much, Hollis. But I kept thinking about you and mom and dad and Theodore and Eve and who would feed Madeline if I was gone. I didn't want to die. So I held on. And then I woke up here."

Hollis's head was in his hands, his fingers knotted in his hair. He might have been holding his breath; I couldn't tell. His eyes were trained on the tiled floor.

"Hollis?" I asked.

He lifted his head. His eyes looked far away. "You died," he said.

My voice was small. "The nurse said none of my internal organs were ruptured, but I felt it. I felt it when the stick pierced it. Here." I touched my fingers to my abdomen, a few inches from the bandages. "I felt it when I died."

"Fucking hell, Tannyn." And then he was crying. "Why didn't you *tell* me any of this? I could have helped you."

"You were in Europe," I said. "You looked so happy in the pictures you sent me. I didn't . . . I couldn't make you come home for me."

He leaned over and pulled me against him, and I grit my teeth at the pain and hugged him back with one arm. I buried my face in his shoulder. His scent had changed, but it wasn't the new soap or the hint of cologne that threw me. It was the sense of a new fear—the smell and taste and heat of airline coffee in a styrofoam cup at four in the morning, clenched tightly in fingers that couldn't stop shaking.

"Don't be an idiot, Tannyn," he mumbled. "You wouldn't have made me do anything. I would have come because you're my sister and I love you."

"Even though what happened to mom was my fault?"

He stiffened in my arms, and then he pulled back to look at me. "Tannyn, I . . ."

There was something in his eyes that made me forget to breathe. "You knew," I said. "You knew this whole time."

His mouth opened and closed. Then he told me, "I suspected, but . . . no, I didn't know. Not for sure. Until now."

"You knew," I said again.

"I'm sorry, Tannyn."

"How can you not hate me?"

"Is that what you've thought this whole time? That I would hate you if I knew?" There was a deep sadness in his eyes. *That's exactly what I thought,* I wanted to say. "You were just a kid, Tannyn. I saw how scared you were. I saw what it did to you. You couldn't have known what would happen."

The words lifted a weight from my chest. I nearly gasped at the sensation; it had been there for so long, I'd gotten used to it. I grasped the rail of the bed, afraid I might start to float away without it.

Thank you, I thought. *Thank you so much, Hollis.*

I looked up at the sound of footsteps in the doorway.

My father and Theodore paused when they saw me awake. Theodore's eyes widened, his lips parting as if he wanted to say something, but didn't know what. He was carrying two steaming cups of coffee, and he'd changed into a fresh set of clothes.

Theodore handed one of the cups to Hollis. "I have to warn you, it tastes like swamp water."

Hollis made a face, but accepted.

Theodore looked at me. "Hey, babe. How are you feeling?"

"Like shit, actually. Don't they have any morphine in this place?"

The corner of his lip jerked in a smile. "It's nice to see you, too."

"I'll be happy to see you when you bring me coffee," I told him.

"The nurses said no fluids right now. And I'm already on thin ice with your nurse," he added. "At least she doesn't have a broom like Ilse."

My eyes widened. "Shit. Ilse. I had work on Monday. What day is it?"

"Don't worry about that," Hollis said. "I talked to her. She said take as much time as you need and something about not wanting you to get blood on the books."

I laughed. Then my eyes drifted to my father where he still stood in the doorway. He was holding his own cup of coffee, and his shirt was slightly wrinkled, the sleeves rolled up to his elbows.

"Hi, daddy," I said.

He smiled at me in a way he hadn't in a long time. The skin around his eyes crinkled with it. It reminded me of the memory where I was on his shoulders in the backyard, the air heavy with the sound of his laughter and the scent of honeysuckle as my mother watched from the swing beneath the oak tree.

"Hi, Tantrum."

I mock-frowned at the childhood nickname. "I thought I told you not to call me that."

"Old habits die hard," he said. He scratched the back of his hand and looked around as if he wanted to say more. Then he told me, "I'm glad you're alright."

"Thanks."

"Come on, dad," Hollis said. "Let's go take a walk and leave the lovebirds to their crooning. Tannyn's not going anywhere any time soon. I'm sure she'll still be here when we get back."

I stuck my tongue out at him.

Theodore waited until they'd left the room before he walked over to sit in the chair beside my bed. Or rather, he limped over, keeping pressure off his right leg.

"Your leg," I said.

"I'm fine." He set his cup of coffee down on the bedside table—far out of my reach, the bastard. Then he brushed several strands of hair out of my face and sighed through his nose. "You really kill me, Tannyn."

"I'm the one who died."

"I know," he said. "And you scared the shit out of me."

"Sorry. I promise not to do it again."

"You also promised not to do die at all, so that doesn't mean anything."

"Sorry," I said again. "Hollis said Eve is here. I saw the article in the paper, about how they found her on the side of the road after she escaped Kestrel's house."

Theodore rubbed a hand over his face. "Right. That," he said. "Eve had a bit too much fun staging the evidence and playing damsel-in-distress. I think she's watched *Gone Girl* too many times."

"But she's alright."

"She's got some bruising and her wrists are pretty scraped up from the ropes, but she's loving the attention. And I know one of the doctors here, and he's making sure no one asks too many questions."

"And Jude? Kestrel hit him pretty hard."

"He was released from here yesterday, actually, but he's been hanging around Eve's room since. It's kind of annoying, actually."

Kestrel, I thought. *Kestrel killed Eve. All along . . . He'd been right there all along.* "What did he want? Kestrel?"

"The crash that killed my parents. He was in the other car," Theodore told me. "His wife hit her head hard. She didn't wake up. He

337

wanted me to bring her back."

His wife, I thought. *The woman in the bed.*

"He told everyone she was in a coma. I remember the other teachers talking about it . . ."

"Wishful thinking," Theodore said.

I stared at a lock of blonde hair that had fallen into Theodore's face so I wouldn't have to look him in the eye. "I killed him, didn't I?"

Theodore nodded.

"Good."

"I'm taking care of everything. The police found his car a few miles from the cemetery." He pressed his lips into a thin line. "You didn't know if I could bring you back. But you still went into that house."

"I didn't care," I told him. "He had you and Eve."

"You think your life means less than mine or hers?" he snapped. "There are people who love you, who would miss you if you were gone. What about your mom and dad? What about Hollis?" The anger in his expression shattered. His voice broke as he whispered, "What about me?"

My throat tightened at the pain in his eyes. "I'm sorry," I said, and this time I meant it.

"I could feel you. I could feel you, but I couldn't reach you."

"I heard you. In the darkness. Calling my name. I heard you and Eve."

He pressed his forehead against mine and tangled his fingers in the hair at the nape of my neck. "I thought I lost you."

I tipped my chin and met my lips with his own. The kiss was feather-light, as if he were afraid I might break beneath him. I tasted salt water on my tongue, though I didn't know whose tears they were—mine or his.

His mouth left mine to trail along my jaw. He kissed the scar on my

338

cheek and my closed eyelids and the bandages over my knuckles.

"I love you," he said, and then moved his mouth back to mine.

This kiss was hard, desperate. I cupped the side of his face in my aching hand and held him against me. He claimed my bottom lip between his teeth and kissed me like we weren't in a hospital bed, separated only by sheets and a thin paper gown, surrounded by frantically beeping monitors as my heart rate spiked.

Theodore pulled back and dropped his head into my lap, closing his eyes. He knotted his fists into the sheets. I drew my fingers gently through his hair.

"I love you, too," I told him.

I could hear the smile in his voice as he said, "I know."

seventy

Hospital food was absolute shit—though who was surprised—so when Jack arrived with a pizza in hand that afternoon, I nearly launched myself at him.

Now, I was on my third slice.

"Slow down, Tannyn," Jack said from where he sat on the floor by my bed. "You're gonna make yourself sick."

I shot him a look.

Theodore said, "I once watched her eat an entire bag of brown sugar in two hours. Another slice of pizza won't kill her."

West twirled the metal tab from his soda can in his fingers. He was leaning against Jack, his legs stretched out in front of him. "Why did you eat an entire bag of brown sugar?" he asked.

"It was a bad time."

"I heard the police came in to speak to you earlier," Jack said. "What did you tell them?"

"The same thing that Theodore told them: I was upstairs when the fire started, and that's when Kestrel came after me. He shot at me, but the bullet only grazed my ear. I climbed out one of the windows and into a tree, but the branch wasn't strong enough to support me. So I fell," I told them. "I hit my head pretty hard, so they're not too concerned with all the details."

I looked over at Jude where he was sitting in a chair across the room, his body angled slightly towards us. His chin was propped in his hand. "What about you? How's your head?"

"They said I'll live."

340

"That's a relief. I was beginning to worry." I waved my slice of pizza at him. "Are you sure you don't want a piece?"

"No, thanks. I don't eat cheese."

"Lactose-intolerant?"

"Vegan, actually."

I raised my eyebrows. "Really?"

He grinned teasingly. "There's a lot you don't know about me, Tannyn. I'm not a complete piece of shit."

"Imagine that," I said around another mouthful of pizza.

There was a knock at the hospital room door.

I looked over as Jude rose from his seat and walked over to open it. The others were smiling as if they were in on a secret.

Then Eve stepped into the room.

"*Eve!*" I started to rise out of my bed, but grunted from the pain and fell back against the pillows. "Eve!" I reached for her with my good hand as she rushed over to me. I pulled her against me, her hospital gown crinkling with the movement. I buried my face in her shoulder.

"They wouldn't let me out of bed to see you," I sobbed into her hair.

"I bribed my nurse with tickets to *Hamilton*." She pulled back, brushing the hair from my face and cupping my cheeks in her hands. There were tears in her eye, and the bruise along her cheek had yellowed. There were bandages on her wrists where the ropes had rubbed them raw. "You look like hell, Tannyn."

"I feel like it."

"Serves you right, charging in there like some sort of knight in shining armor. What the hell were you thinking?"

I forced a smile. "I was thinking it was someone else's turn to die. You're always the center of attention."

"You bitch," she said. "I love you."

I moved over to make room as she crawled up onto the bed with me, curling up against my side. She laid her head on my chest and knotted her fingers through mine.

"You have pizza breath," she muttered.

"Shut up."

"Don't you ever do anything like that again, do you hear me?" she asked.

"Next time, don't get kidnapped."

"Alright," Theodore said. "Don't get her too worked up. We don't want the nurses to come in wondering why her heart rate is spiking."

I looked back down at Eve. "I saw the article in the paper," I said. "How is Nettie taking it?"

"Surprisingly well," Eve replied, grinning. "She came to visit me right after they found me. Theodore and I told her everything. Afterward, she went home and locked herself in the guest house for two days, so Theodore scattered dirty laundry around the yard until she couldn't stand it anymore and came out to wash it. Then she came back to the hospital and cried for an hour. She called me a brat."

"That's 'surprisingly well?'"

"At least she didn't hit Theodore."

"I have problems expressing my emotions," I said, frowning. "It seemed justified under the circumstances."

Eve snickered. "Anyway, I'll just be glad to be back in a house with a decent shower and hot water once they release me."

"What about your aunt? Have you spoken to her?"

"She's actually been back in town for a few days," Eve said. "She thought about suing the coroner who identified my body, but Theodore talked her out of it. The whole thing has her fairly stressed. I'm sure her therapist is thrilled."

I squeezed Eve's fingers in mine. "But you're okay," I said. "It's over."

"Not yet," she replied. "Not until you're all healed. Then we can relax and drink shitty beer and do other normal teenager things. But right now you're only job is to stay here and get better."

"But the coffee here is terrible," I moaned.

"Tannyn Lourdes Carter, that is an order," Eve said.

I sunk back against my pillow with an exaggerated groan.

Jack clapped his hands together. "Enough serious talk," he said, unzipping the backpack at his feet. "Who's up for a game of Monopoly?"

I was woken several hours later to the sound of a soft knock at the door to my room.

I sat up slowly, blinking in the dim evening light through my window as the hospital room door opened and my brother peeked his head in.

"Hey, Tan," he whispered. "You up for visitors? I've got someone I'd like you to meet."

"If you hired another singing telegram, tell them I died."

My brother smiled and opened the door wider, stepping into the room. My father followed him, along with another boy I didn't recognize.

The boy stepped close to Hollis, standing behind him and smiling shyly without showing teeth, a faint flush spreading over his cheeks. He had chestnut hair that fell in soft curls around his face and deep-set green eyes. Hollis took his hand, and I noticed they wore matching Claddagh rings.

"You must be Cian," I said. "Hollis is horrible at introductions."

The boy's grin widened. "So I've noticed," he replied, his words heavy with an Irish accent. "It's nice to meet you. Hollis talks about you all

343

the time."

"He neglected to mention you for quite some time." I shot a sharp look at Hollis, narrowing my eyes. "Probably because he knows how nosey I am."

Color rose to Hollis's cheeks, but he chuckled. "Told you I could keep a secret."

Cian rolled his eyes. "Hardly."

"Well, I'm glad to see Europe hasn't changed him," I said.

"I wouldn't say that," Hollis replied. He patted his stomach. "I think I ate my weight in Belgian chocolate."

Cian kissed my brother's cheek. "Stop telling everyone that. You can't even tell."

I looked at my father, who was standing by the door holding a worn stuffed rabbit with flopping ears. "Hi, dad."

"Hi, honey." He walked over and handed the rabbit to me, an embarrassed flush in his cheeks. "I thought you might like the company."

I smiled as I took the stuffed rabbit with my good arm and pulled him into my lap. I breathed in the familiar scent of lavender on his soft, matted fur.

"We'll see you later, alright, Tannyn?" Hollis said, leading Cian towards the door.

I nodded. "It was nice meeting you, Cian."

"You, too."

They shut the door behind them.

My father sat down on the edge of my bed, the sheets crinkling beneath him. He smiled without showing teeth and ran a hand through his graying hair.

"Cian seems nice," I said.

"He is. And he certainly helps out around the house more than your brother." He looked at the fresh vase of carnations and the stack of books on my bedside table. "Hollis said your friends stopped by earlier."

I picked at a piece of lint that had gotten tangled into my rabbit's fur and nodded.

"So that boy who's been here," my father said. "Is he your boyfriend?"

"You know his name."

An embarrassed smile pulled at the corner of my father's mouth. "Fine. Theodore. Is he your boyfriend?"

"I don't know what else you'd call him."

"He seems to like you quite a lot."

"What can I say." I tried to sit up straighter, but grunted at the pain. I smiled weakly. "He has good taste."

My father reached for my good hand, and I let him take it. He rubbed his thumb soothingly against my palm. "And what about you?" he asked.

"I tolerate him."

"I heard he's the one who brought you in," my father said. "I didn't even know you were out that night, Tannyn. And I almost lost you."

"I'm fine, dad. I'm tough--like a cockroach. It takes more than a tree to kill me."

My father frowned. After a moment, he said, "I guess I need to thank him for taking care of you when I didn't."

"I'm sure enough people have called him a hero. His ego can only take so much."

"I'm not just talking about bringing you to the hospital. I'm talking about being there for you, watching out for you."

"That's what friends are for."

"And what about fathers?"

345

I pressed my lips together. "I thought we were past this, dad."

"You might be, Tannyn. But I've got a ways to go before I've made it up to you," he said.

"Good thing my heart's still beating then," I said, smiling softly.

"Good thing," my father repeated, mirroring my smile. "You're tough—just like your mother."

The smile fell slowly from my face, and I looked away at the vertical shades covering the window. I slipped my hand from my father's and pulled my stuffed rabbit closer to me, trying to figure out how to phrase what I'd decided to tell him earlier that afternoon.

"Tannyn, what's the matter?"

I took a breath. "I want to bring mom home."

seventy-one

I rolled down my window as we cruised past fields of sugar cane and wheat swaying in the wind.

I closed my eyes and breathed in the dry summer air. Locks of hair whipped against my face, and I reached up to tuck them back with my good arm. The left was still sore, so I couldn't lift it higher than my shoulder.

A Stevie Nicks' song was playing lightly over the radio, the volume turned down low enough that I only recognized the words because I knew them by heart. I hummed along under my breath.

I glanced back over my shoulder into the backseat, and my father reached across the cabin of the car to take my hand in his. I smiled at him, squeezing his fingers.

My phone buzzed in my lap, and I looked down to see a text from Hollis.

Where are you? it read.

So damn impatient, I thought. I shot back a quick text letting him know that we were five minutes away.

I rested my arm on the open car window, moving my fingers against the wind.

My father turned down the street that led to our driveway.

Our house came into view, and I could make out Hollis and his boyfriend, Cian, sitting on the front steps of the porch. Hollis stood up and brushed off the back of his pants when he saw us.

"Your brother remembered to put Madeline outside?" my father asked.

I nodded. "I reminded him before we left."

My father parked in the driveway next to a small Nissan and turned off the engine, and I unbuckled my seatbelt and climbed from the car before Hollis and Cian even reached us. I walked to the back passenger door and pulled it open as my father unloaded a suitcase from the trunk.

My mother turned her head to look at me.

I smiled at her. "Welcome home, mama."

My mother's arm was linked through mine as we went up the porch steps. Her new caretaker, a young woman with soft eyes and an orange hijab, followed close behind us with my father as he juggled a suitcase in each hand.

"Your room is on the second-floor and shares an adjoined bathroom with Penelope's," my father was telling her. "There are spare blankets in the closet—though you probably won't be needing them this time of year. The one window tends to stick, so you just have to push hard if you want to open it. The bathroom's fairly modern so you shouldn't have any problems there."

The woman, Sana, nodded along to my father's ramblings.

I pushed open the front door and led my mother into the kitchen.

"Tannyn and Hollis are home most days, so if you need anything, you can just ask them," my father continued. "Let's see, what else . . . I already told you that we have a dog. The hospital's gone over her medication with you."

I helped my mother sit down at the kitchen table, and then I got her a glass of water from the fridge.

She stared at it for several seconds. Then she lifted her head and glanced around the kitchen, taking in the cabinets and lighting and linoleum floor. She looked at me and Sana and my father.

She looked back down at the water.

My father said to Sana, "Can I get you something to drink?"

"I'll have water as well, please."

Hollis and Cian entered a moment later, each carrying a load of luggage. Hollis dropped his to the floor with a heavy *thud*.

"Christ, Hollis," Cian said.

My mother turned her head towards the sound, blinking at Hollis and Cian. Then she looked around the kitchen again, her eyes stopping on the china hutch against the wall and the record player sitting out.

"Wow," Sana said, following her gaze. "I haven't seen one of those in years."

"It was my great-grandmother's," I told her.

I walked over and crouched down to open the cabinet doors beneath it, sifting through the records until I found the one I was looking for. I straightened up and pulled the record from its sleeve. I slipped it onto the record player and lowered the needle.

My mother's foot had been tapping against the floor, but it stopped as the music started.

A moment later, "Downtown" by Petula Clark began drifting through the kitchen.

I looked over my shoulder at Sana. "This is my mom's favorite song."

My mother began to hum along softly beneath her breath, the sound nearly lost amongst the music.

I pulled out the kitchen chair next to my mother and sat down, taking her hand in mine. I watched as the record spun in slow circles beneath the needle.

"Why don't I show you the rest of the house?" my father said to Sana.

I saw her nod out of the corner of my eye and follow him from the

349

kitchen.

"Should we take these bags upstairs?" Cian asked Hollis.

Hollis nodded, and then looked to me. "You okay by yourself for a few minutes, Tan?"

I smiled and hoped that it didn't look forced. "Of course."

They picked up the bags off the kitchen floor, and I watched them walk off down the hallway—stumbling into one another and bumping shoulders and laughing.

Then I looked back at my mother.

The last time I had been alone in this kitchen with her, I had been eleven-years-old.

I looked across the room to the sink where my mother had been standing that morning. I touched my fingers to the scar on my collarbone through my shirt, though I could hardly feel it beneath the fabric. But I knew it was there.

"What is it, honey?"

I closed my eyes for a moment, breathing softly and focusing on the music.

In through the nose, out through the mouth.

My lungs filled with the scent of Dove soap and warm sugar on my mother's skin.

I started to stand, but my mother's fingers tightened around my own, holding me there. I froze, holding my breath, afraid that I'd imagined it. I looked down at her, but her expression was blank, staring at the record player against the wall.

I felt the tension in her fingers release, and her gaze flickered over to me, to the scar on my cheek.

So I sat back down, and I stayed with my mother through the rest of the song.

seventy-two

The basket of flowers was heavy in my good arm as I nudged open the door of the antique shop with my shoe.

It hadn't changed since the last time I'd been there, though I hadn't expected it to. I was the one who'd changed after all.

Sweat beaded along the back of my neck, and strands of hair clung to my forehead. My good arm ached from carrying the basket of flowers from the car. I wasn't supposed to be carrying anything heavy with my arm and the stitches on my side still healing, but the bouquet had looked light when I'd first picked it out.

The woman behind the counter looked up as the bell overtop the door chimed.

And promptly dropped the tea cup in her hand.

It shattered harshly against the floor, and I winced. The woman muttered a prayer in another language.

"I brought you these," I said, walking across the shop and setting the white lilies down on the counter as the woman continued to stare at me. "Just in case you were in mourning."

She was dressed in all white, a contrast to her dark skin. The tea had drenched the bottom of her long skirt, but she hadn't seemed to notice yet. I hoped it wouldn't stain, but I wasn't an expert on things like that.

"You," the woman said. "I felt you die. How."

It wasn't a question, but rather, a demand. I pressed my lips together into something not quite a smile. "I did die," I said. "And it hurt like hell, actually." I lifted up the hem of my tank top to show her the edge of my

351

bandage. "But I came back. That's all I can tell you."

She touched her hand to her chest and closed her eyes. "Thank God," she murmured. "Thank God."

"No, thank you. For telling me where I was going to die. I can't tell you how, but it helped."

She nodded solemnly. "I'm glad."

"I brought my mother home," I said suddenly.

The woman inclined her head to the side. "Oh?"

"I don't know if it will help, but I couldn't leave her in that place."

The woman looked thoughtful. Then she said, "One moment."

She walked into the back room, the beaded curtain swaying after she'd gone through it. A moment later, she returned and handed me a small bottle of oil and a bag of tea leaves. She pressed them both into my hands. "Lavender oil for the scarring," she told me. "And an herbal blend for your mother. It might not help, but it certainly can't hurt. Have her drink one cup of tea each night before bed."

"Thank you."

The woman nodded. "Next time you come, bring your mother. I'll give you a reading on the house—as long as you don't tell my granddaughter." She chuckled lightly.

I started for the door, but turned back just as I reached it. The glass was cool beneath my fingers. "I just realized," I said," I never asked your name."

The woman smiled again—an amused, secretive smile. "Isabis," she told me.

"Isabis," I repeated. "Thank you."

"And don't worry about the stain," she told me. "A little white vinegar will get it right out."

"Bye, Isabis. I'll be back. I promise."

"Goodbye, Tannyn."

The bell atop the door chimed as I stepped outside into sun.

I parked my car behind Eve's Subaru, my tires crunching over the gravel.

I turned off the engine and unbuckled my seatbelt, and then picked up the takeout bag from the passenger seat. I walked up the drive and onto the front porch, wiping the sweat from my forehead with the back of my hand.

The front door was unlocked, so I pushed it open and stepped into the foyer.

The sound of the door closing behind me echoed through the house.

"Hello?" I shouted. "Anyone home? I brought nachos!"

A moment later, an unfamiliar voice called, "In here."

I followed it to the kitchen, stopping in the doorway when I spotted a woman sitting at the island counter. She was tall and reed-thin with stork-like legs and strawberry blonde hair. She was wearing a black sundress and holding a glass of wine.

She turned to face me, a smile lightly pulling at her red lips. "You must be Tannyn," she said, setting down the glass of wine and straightening. "I'm Ceceli Shearwater, Theodore and Eve's aunt."

I stared at her: the high, sharp cheekbones, the daunting blue-gray eyes, the curious tilt of her head. That goddamned smile like we were long lost friends. The scent of her fears like ashes and white wine and and dozens of roses.

I swallowed harshly. "We've met before," I said. "Twice. The last time was at Eve's funeral. Before you disappeared again." I narrowed my eyes, and my lips skinned back from my teeth. "Where were you?"

The thin strawberry-blonde brows rose in surprise. "Pardon?"

"Where were you the last two months? Or the last year?" I snapped.

"Where were you when Eve was—" I stopped myself. "When she was rotting away in that place."

Ceceli Shearwater was silent. Then she smiled again, though it didn't reach her eyes. "Right. Tannyn. The first time we met, your hair was blonde."

"Yes. I'm Tannyn," I said, although we'd already established this.

"Theodore and Eve have told me a lot about you. That you're strong, determined." She looked down at her wine glass. "I'm glad they have someone like you."

"You—"

I stopped at the sound of footsteps pounding down the stairs. I turned my head as Eve appeared in the kitchen doorway.

"I heard someone say nachos!" The grin slipped from her face, and her good eye flickered from me to her aunt. "Oh. Aunt Ceceli, this is Tannyn. Tannyn, Aunt Ceceli."

"We've been introduced," her aunt said.

"I can tell by the awkward tension," Eve replied. "You'd think someone died." She winked at me.

I ignored her. "Your aunt was just telling me where she's been all this time."

Her aunt picked up the glass of wine, swirling it delicately in her hands. "Oh, here and there. Baton Rouge, Atlanta, Dallas." She smiled softly at me without showing teeth. "Theodore's out back, if you're looking for him."

"Come on," Eve said.

"I'm going to grab a bottle of water," I told Eve. I handed her the takeout bag. "I'll meet you out there."

She flitted to the back door, and I felt her aunt's eyes on me as I watched it slide closed behind her.

"She looks so much like her mother, you know. The pictures don't do it justice."

I turned my back on her as I pulled open the fridge door and took out a bottle of water. "So I've heard."

Ceceli nodded her head lightly. Her slate blue eyes were sad—I recognized the look. I'd seen it so many times in the mirror. "I should have been here. I know."

"I don't care about your excuses," I said.

"I don't have any."

"My dad was like you. He still is in some ways," I told her. "He's not an alcoholic, but he's addicted to other things." Her eyes widened, and I knew I'd guessed right. I'd smelled similar fears on alcoholics before. "He abandoned me when I needed him, just like you did with Theodore and Eve."

I walked over to the back door and pulled it open. Before I stepped outside, I glanced back over my shoulder. "She deserves better," I said. "They both do."

Their aunt gave me a bitter, self-loathing smile. "Why do you think I left?"

seventy-three

I sat down next to Eve on the living room couch, cupping the steaming mug of coffee in my hands.

I passed the second mug to her and curled my legs up on the couch beside me, resting my head against Theodore's shoulder. Light from the TV flickered on the floor of the dark living room.

Eve took a sip from her coffee and narrowed her eyes. "Is there whiskey in this?"

"Oh, sorry. That's mine." I moved to trade mugs, but she held hers out of my reach.

She settled back against the couch and took another sip. "It's mine now."

I stuck my tongue out at her, and then drank from my own cup, wincing at the cream and sugar in it. Eve snickered like a child.

I picked up my book from the coffee table and flipped open to the page I'd dogeared.

Eve said, "What are you reading?"

"*One Hundred Years of Solitude*," I said.

"Will you read aloud?"

"I'm in the middle of chapter three," I told her. "You're not going to know what's going on."

"I'll use my imagination."

I rolled my eyes, but as always, Eve got her way.

"One night about the time that Rebeca was cured of the vice of eating earth and was brought to sleep in the other children's room, the Indian woman, who slept with them awoke by chance and heard a strange, intermittent sound in the counter."

Eve set the mug of coffee down on the table beside her, and then she leaned her head back against the pillows behind her and closed her eye.

I kept reading. "She got up in alarm, thinking that an animal had come into the room, and then she saw Rebeca in the rocker, sucking her finger and with her eyes lighted up in the darkness like those of a cat . . ."

Theodore ran his fingers through my hair, his eyes lingering on my mouth as I read aloud.

Out of the corner of my eye, I watched Eve's chest rise and fall with her breaths.

I heard the floorboards creak in the darkness as someone stepped into the living room, and I turned my head to see their aunt Ceceli leaning against the door in her night robe, her arms wrapped around herself. Her hair was piled in a loose knot atop her head, and their were tired circles beneath her eyes.

I looked back down at the book and continued.

". . . Úrsula, who had learned from her mother the medicinal value of plants, prepared and made them all drink a brew of monkshood, but they could not get to sleep and spent the whole day dreaming on their feet . . ."

I read like that until the end of the chapter, and by then, Eve had fallen asleep and the clock read 12:46.

I closed the book and glanced over my shoulder, but Ceceli was gone.

As I set the book down on the table, Theodore stood from his spot beside me and stretched.

"I'll bring her upstairs," he told me. "She'll kill me in the morning if I let her sleep on the couch."

I nodded, stifling a yawn.

Theodore lifted Eve in his arms, and she mumbled something incoherent. Strands of blonde hair fell into her face, and she swatted sleepily at Theodore's face with her hand.

I picked up Eve's cup of coffee from the end table and downed it in one gulp, wincing at the bite of whiskey as it went down. Theodore snorted.

"What?" I said. "It was mine."

I followed him as he carried her up the stairs and nudged open her bedroom door with his foot. Theodore dropped her down on the bed, albeit rather un-gently, and I pulled the covers around her. Eve rolled over and nestled further into the pillow.

"Night, Eve."

I started to back away, but she reached for me in the darkness, her fingers fumbling for mine.

Her eye cracked open, and she smiled softly at me. "Goodnight, Tannyn."

I squeezed her fingers gently in mine. "Now get some sleep."

My fingers were sticky with blood.

I stared down at the shards of broken mirror on the floor at my feet. My reflection stared back at me in pieces: one light brown eye, strands of lilac hair, the twisted corner of my mouth. One of the shards had a smear of blood on the jagged edge.

There was a sharp pain in my right hand.

I glanced down and realized that I was clenching one of the shards in my fist. Blood dripped between my fingers.

I dropped the shard with a start. It cracked in half on the tiled floor.

There was a gash on my palms and the insides of my fingers. There was so much blood I couldn't tell where it was coming from.

I lifted my head at the sound of footsteps.

Jack was holding a bottle of peroxide and a roll of bandages. "You know, it never would have worked between us," he said as he set them down on the bathroom counter. "I'm much too afraid of you."

When he turned back to me, there were maggots wriggling in his hair and between his teeth. A clump of them fell and landed with a sickening *splat* against the floor. They squirmed from holes in his skin, their bodies pale in the fluorescent light.

Bile rose in my throat.

I shoved past him out into the hallway, slamming the bathroom door shut behind me. I leaned my back against it as I steadied my breathing.

The smell of smoke reached my nose. It was coming from the kitchen.

I straightened and forced myself to take a step forward. My legs wobbled beneath me. I clung to the railing as I descended the stairs.

Smoke gathered along the ceiling like a dark cloud. It stung at my eyes, and tears gathered in the corners. I lifted the collar of my shirt to cover my nose and mouth.

My mother was standing by the kitchen sink, holding a mug of coffee in her hands. The curtains over the window and the cabinets were on fire. The wallpaper was curling away in blackened strips. Flames licked at the bottoms of my mother's pajama pants.

"Hey, sleepy head. You're certainly up early."

My mother turned to face me as I pressed the collar of my shirt tighter over my face.

Her loose hair caught fire, forming a blazing orange halo around her head, but she didn't seem to notice as she smiled at me. Her skin bubbled from the heat.

I staggered backward.

"What is it, honey?"

My mother dropped the mug in her hands, and it shattered as it hit the ground. Coffee and bits of ceramic scattered across the kitchen floor.

"You promised," she said as her flesh melted away. Her voice was harsh and gravely from the smoke. "You promised you wouldn't do it again."

"Mama," I whispered, choking on the word.

She fell to her knees, flaming hair falling into her face.

When she lifted her head, it was William Kestrel staring back at me.

His mouth was gaping, wider than humanly possible. The sounds of his screams pierced my skull like rusted nails, scraping against bone. Dark blood oozed from his lips.

He stretched a hand towards me, his fingers red and blistering.

I ran to the back door of the kitchen and flung it open, stumbling out into the backyard. I collapsed into the grass.

Smoke poured from the open door and into the sky.

A hand entered my field of vision, and I looked up to see Eve standing over me.

Firelight glinted off her eye as she stared down at me. The hem of her white dress was blackened and curled from the flames, and the tips of her fingers were coated with soot. Theodore was standing beside her, his hands tucked into the front pockets of his dress pants. His mouth was curved into a cruel smile.

I took Eve's hand, and she helped me to my feet.

"So what do you think?" Eve said, turning her head to look at her brother.

He removed a hand from his pocket, and his fingers were wet with blood. He ran them through his hair, and the pale strands turned red and sticky. "The whole world's a fucking nightmare," he told her. "She only makes things worse."

"That's too bad," Eve replied.

Theodore glanced at me out of the corner of his eye. "There's plenty of other girls," he said to his sister.

"You're right. No one will miss her, anyway." Eve giggled as if she were a child with a secret. When she turned to me, her mouth had twisted into a frightening grin.

"What are you—?" I began.

She shoved me backwards.

Suddenly I was falling, crashing through the branches of a tree, the ground rushing towards me in a blur of earth tones.

I landed hard on my back at the bottom of a deep hole, and all the air rushed from my lungs. The back of my head smacked against the ground.

Dark spots danced across my vision as I stared up at the sky.

A small group of people huddled around the edges of the hole, hunched over as they leaned forward to peer down at me. Their faces blurred together. They were whispering, but I couldn't make out their words.

Someone crouched down to get a better look at me.

"Is she dead?" I recognized West's voice.

Eve's face swam into focus above me. "It doesn't matter," she told him.

My body was so heavy. It felt as if someone had replaced my insides with cement. I managed to part my lips, and a choked sound left my throat.

Eve smiled as she leaned towards me. "What's that?" she taunted. "I can have your car? Well, if you insist."

She stood and dusted off her hands on her skirt. She accepted a shovel that someone handed to her, and she pierced it into the ground, using the heel of her foot to drive it in deeper. She smiled as she held the shovel over the edge of the hole—no, not a hole. A grave. Bits of dirt fell and scattered across my skin.

Other shovels filled with dirt appeared.

"It *was* nice knowing you, Tannyn," Eve said.

She upended the shovel, and dirt rained down onto my head, blocking out the sky. I opened my mouth to scream, and dirt poured down my throat, choking me. My fingers curled into fists at my sides, but that was all I could manage.

Dirt piled up around me, clogging my senses.

The last thing I remembered was the sound of laughter, and then that, too, faded away.

I woke in the Shearwater's guest room to hands clutching my shoulders.

Eve's face was contorted with fear as she stared down at me in the darkness.

Strands of hair were plastered to my forehead with sweat, and my cheeks were wet with tears. I swallowed thickly. "Eve?" I whispered.

"It's alright," she said, pulling me against her. I realized I was trembling. I wound my arms around her back and knotted my fingers into her shirt. She rocked me gently in her arms as she ran her fingers over my tangled hair. "It's just a bad dream."

"Eve," I said again.

"I'm here." She kissed the crown of my head. "I'm right here."

I buried my face in her chest, breathing in her scent. Like Hollis', it had changed. Her fears now smelled of peach champagne and the tang of blood. They left the tips of my fingers numb and as cold as death.

"I'm not going anywhere," Eve told me.

I released a breath through my nose. Life returned to my fingertips.

She crawled into bed beside me, and I curled up against her. She took my hand, fitting her fingers between mine as she slung her arm over my chest.

I nestled our intertwined hands beneath my chin and closed my eyes.

"I love you," Eve said.

"I love you, too," I murmured into the darkness.

Neither of us dreamt for the rest of the night.

seventy-four

Sunlight glittered off the water in the bayou as I sat in the grass behind the Boathouse.

My back was propped against a tree, and Theodore lay with his head in my lap as I read beneath the shade. I absentmindedly played with his hair while he listened to music.

Eve was in the garden, wearing overalls and a sunhat and carting a huge metal watering can like a grandmother in a children's movie. Jude was helping her, hacking away at the dried earth with a trowel, his clothes already dirty and clinging to him with sweat. West was on his knees beside him, coaxing several plants from their plastic containers.

The front door of the Boathouse slammed opened, and I glanced over to see Jack walking out with a six-pack of beer.

He handed one to me.

"Here you go, *mami*," he said, and then handed one to Theodore with a wink. "*Papi*."

I popped the cap off mine and took a long swig. Jack walked over to hand two more to Eve and Jude, and then he sat down beside West in the dirt. I pressed the cold glass bottle against my forehead.

"What are you listening to?" I asked Theodore.

He pulled out one of his headphone and offered it to me.

I slipped it into my ear, and then raised an eyebrow. "Stevie Nicks?"

He grinned. "What can I say, you've corrupted me."

I closed my book and tossed it into the bag at my feet. I took another sip of my beer and leaned my head back against the tree behind me, humming along to the music beneath my breath.

When I felt Theodore's gaze on me, I looked down to find him watching me.

He smiled when he caught my eye.

"Tell me a secret," I said.

He reached up to touch the end of my hair, pinching a strand between his fingers. "I like the purple hair," he replied.

A faint flush rose to my cheeks, but I rolled my eyes. "That's a horrible secret."

"I know." He chuckled lightly. Then the smile slipped from his face, and he swallowed. "I would have done anything to bring you back."

"I'm sorry," I murmured.

"You should be. You promised me you wouldn't die."

"Next time you should make me swear on something important," I told him. "Like my car, or coffee."

His fingers grazed across the scar on my cheek. "There won't be a next time."

"How do you know?"

"Because I won't let anyone hurt you," he said.

"I can take care of myself," I reminded him.

I curled my hand into a fist and punched him lightly in the shoulder, but he caught my wrist and smoothed my fingers out. Then he pressed a kiss to my palm.

He lifted his head to give me a wicked grin. "I'm not afraid of you, Tannyn Carter."

"Well, you should be," I whispered.

I felt something hit my arm, cool and wet.

I tipped my head back to look at the clouds overhead and another drop of rain splattered against my cheek. I blinked in surprise, and a laugh burst from my chest.

"What's so funny?" West asked, and then a drop hit him in the eye.

Perhaps it was the beer. Perhaps it was West's expression. Perhaps it was being there, with all of them. But suddenly, I was laughing. The type of laughter that left you squinting and out of breath and grasping your stomach because you just couldn't stop.

I grabbed Theodore's other hand and pulled him to his feet, and the bottle in his hand fell and splashed beer against our ankles but neither of us cared.

Eve shrieked and ran for the front door of the Boathouse, but a moment later, Jude caught her around the waist and threw her over his shoulder.

"Put me down!" she yelled, but she laughed as she clung to him.

My clothes clung to my body, and water dripped from the ends of my hair. Theodore's skin was slick with rain water as I took his face between my hands and kissed him, his mouth warm and soft and lovely.

I took his hands again and spun him in a circle, our feet slipping in the dirt that had been turned to mud by the rain. I held out a hand for the others to join us. Eve came first, pulling Jude with her. Then West, and Jack.

I clasped Theodore and Eve's hands tightly in mine as we danced in a circle beneath the trees. She grinned at me, her storm-cloud eye glittering beneath her wet lashes.

There were six of us: Tannyn. Jack. West. Theodore. Evelyn. Jude.

And for once, the world was not made up of anyone's fears, but of the smell of rain on our skin and the sound of my heart pounding in my ears.

I threw my head back and laughed at the sky.

A harsh, twisted sound.

A crow's caw.

a girl called murder

acknowledgments

As always, I have so many people to thank for their support and love.

First and foremost, my friends on Twitter. Karli, Sierra, Jess, Ellen, Eden, Alana, Bayy, Finn, Bree, Aspen, Loren, Nicole, Mariah, Zen, Michaela, Jamie, Freddy, Sofia, Britt, Zahra, Moe, Rhys, Rae, Angelica, Marley, Shauna, Jodi, Abby, Natasha, Rachel, Jamie, Mackenzie, Ash. It is impossible to name all of you, but I always try my best. I don't know what I would do without y'all cheering me on every single day and sending hilarious gifs to keep me motivated.

For Michele Prichard and Heather Donahue, for being my first dedicated fans and spreading the word to everyone you know.

For Anelis & Kelsea, because I will never not be grateful for them.

For Ellen Lewis, for encouraging an eighth grader with horrible grammar and ridiculous ideas to pursue her dreams—and for somehow enduring her non-stop talking and pre-teen energy.

For Kayla, because you deserve your very own acknowledgment. Your words of encouragement are always appreciated and I'm so happy to be a source of inspiration for you. I know you'll do amazing things.

For everyone who read *How to Kiss a Flower Girl (and Live)* and loved my characters as much as I did.

For my mom and dad, who have somehow put up with me for twenty-one years. Congrats—both of the parents are alive in this book.

And lastly, for everyone who saw themselves in one of these characters. It is the reason we continue to push for diversity and own voices in books. You are loved. You are valid. You are not alone.

Tannyn's Top 20 Most Played Songs

"Downtown" – Petula Clark

"Rhiannon" – Stevie Nicks

"Rooms on Fire" – Stevie Nicks

"Edge of Seventeen" – Stevie Nicks

"The Chain" – Fleetwood Mac

"Landslide" – Fleetwood Mac

"Home" – Edward Sharpe and the Magnetic Zeros

"Dirty Paws" – Of Monsters and Men

"Come on, Eileen" – Dexys Midnight Runners

"Set Fire to the Third Bar" – Snow Patrol

"Control" – Halsey

"Sober" – Lorde

"Sweet Dreams (Are Made of This)" – Eurythmics

"What's Up?" – 4 Non Blondes

"Bad Reputation" – Joan Jett

"Demons" – Imagine Dragons

"Bedroom Hymns" – Florence + The Machine

"Heavy In Your Arms" – Florence + The Machine

"I Will Follow You Into the Dark" – Death Cab for Cutie

"Such Great Heights" – Iron and Wine

Made in the USA
Lexington, KY
29 July 2019